Praise for the *New York Times* bestselling series

GWENDY'S BUTTON BOX

"A different sort of coming-of-age story about a mysterious stranger and his odd little gift. . . . Cowritten with Richard Chizmar, King's zippy work returns to the small-town Maine locale of *The Dead Zone*, *Cujo*, and other early novels . . . Extremely well-paced . . . a fun read that never loses momentum. . . . *Gwendy's Button Box* feels like it belongs in this locale that's always been a pit stop for scary Americana and the normal turned deadly . . . Nicely captures that same winning dichotomy between the innocent and the sinister."

—*USA Today*

"Man, I love this story! The whole thing just races and feels so right-sized and scarily and sadly relevant. Loved the characters . . . and the sense of one little girl's connection to the whole world through this weird device. It all just sang."

—J. J. Abrams

GWENDY'S MAGIC FEATHER

"Chizmar carries the tale forward into Gwendy's future with sympathy and grace. The result is at once an independent creation and a particularly intimate form of collaboration. . . . Chizmar's voice and sensibility dovetail neatly with [Stephen] King's own distinctive style, and the book ultimately reads like a newly discovered chapter in King's constantly evolving fictional universe."

—*The Washington Post*

"[An] appealing chiller. . . . Short, punchy chapters keep the pages turning. . . . The charming protagonist and thrill of temptation will enthrall fans and new readers alike."

—*Publishers Weekly*

GWENDY'S FINAL TASK

"Stephen King and Richard Chizmar's Gwendy saga comes to a satisfying conclusion. . . . Unexpectedly moving. Like its predecessors, *Gwendy's Final Task* is both a seamless act of collaboration and a deeply felt reflection on the perilous state of our fractured modern world."

—*The Washington Post*

THE GWENDY TRILOGY

GWENDY'S BUTTON BOX

Stephen King and Richard Chizmar

GWENDY'S MAGIC FEATHER

Richard Chizmar

GWENDY'S FINAL TASK

Stephen King and Richard Chizmar

GALLERY BOOKS

New York   Amsterdam/Antwerp   London
Toronto   Sydney   New Delhi

G

Gallery Books
An Imprint of Simon & Schuster, LLC
1230 Avenue of the Americas
New York, NY 10020

Gwendy's Button Box copyright © 2017 by Stephen King and Richard Chizmar

Gwendy's Magic Feather copyright © 2019 by Richard Chizmar

Gwendy's Final Task copyright © 2022 by Stephen King and Richard Chizmar

First Gallery Books trade paperback edition February 2025

GALLERY BOOKS and colophon are registered trademarks of Simon & Schuster, LLC

For information about special discounts for bulk purchases, please contact Simon & Schuster Special Sales at 1-866-506-1949 or business@simonandschuster.com.

The Simon & Schuster Speakers Bureau can bring authors to your live event. For more information or to book an event, contact the Simon & Schuster Speakers Bureau at 1-866-248-3049 or visit our website at www.simonspeakers.com.

Manufactured in the United States of America

10   9   8   7   6   5   4   3

Library of Congress Cataloging-in-Publication Data is available.

ISBN 978-1-6680-8362-8
ISBN 978-1-6680-8386-4 (ebook)

TABLE OF CONTENTS

INTRODUCTION

Butch and Sundance

Stephen King

Gwendy Peterson should never have seen the light of day. Should have, so to speak, died *in utero*.

I sometimes have a good idea for a story and start in with no idea of where it will go. When it works, it's great. When it doesn't, it's idiocy—like driving into a bridge abutment at 100 miles an hour.

My ideas almost always start with *what if*s. In the case of *Gwendy's Button Box*, it was "What if some magical being gave a child a box that could cause unlimited destruction?" I was thinking about this because of the real-world implications. After all, huge nuclear arsenals are controlled by men who often behave childishly, for macho or religious reasons. Or, of course, for personal gain.

The story went well at first, but it kept trying to expand. I plugged along for a bit, then lost the thread when that expansion grew to include Gwendy's family. I struggled with it for awhile, then gave up and moved along to something else (probably *End of Watch*, the last book in the Bill Hodges trilogy). I never sent Gwendy away to the trash can on the lower right-hand side of my computer screen, however; every day when I went to work, a Word document on the upper left-hand corner of my desktop continued to read GWENDY BUTTONS.

So things stood until Rich Chizmar asked me if I would consider taking part in a round robin type of story, where a number of horror writers would each write a section, sort of like the funny (not to say notorious) *Naked Came the Manatee*, a mystery novel written by a number of primarily Florida writers. (It was the brainchild of humorist/guitarist Dave Barry.) I told Rich I had no interest, wished him luck, and then, pretty much as an afterthought, asked if he would like to take a shot at finishing a story I'd hit a roadblock on. He expressed guarded interest, I sent him the GWENDY BUTTONS document, and everything else followed.

Rich is good at scares, he's comfortable with fantasy, and there's something else he doesn't get enough credit for: Rich Chizmar really understands family dynamics, and that—strictly IMHO, you understand—is what made *Gwendy's Button Box* work. Not to mention his standalone follow-up, *Gwendy's Magic Feather*, and our final Gwendy collaboration, *Gwendy's Final Task*—which is one of my very favorite duets, right up there with *Sleeping Beauties*.

I wrote; Richard wrote; we rewrote each other; the result was something new. I'm so glad Gwendy didn't die before she could be born . . . and go to Washington . . . and then on into the cosmos.

Richard Chizmar

Collaborating on a story is a lot like riding on the back of a motorcycle piloted by a daredevil with a hunger for speed. There's an awful lot of trust involved. It's also slightly terrifying and, when it works, about as much fun as a writer can have without breaking the law.

Instead of a solitary traveler sitting behind a desk, tapping his foot and staring at the blank computer screen, now there are two of you. Partners in crime. In our cases, hundreds of miles apart. The journey ahead may remain uncertain, but hey, at least you're not lonely.

At times, the path is wide and clear, your passage as enjoyable and refreshing as traversing the roller-coaster streets of San Francisco in a trolley on a cloudless spring afternoon. And yet at other times, that same path grows dark and narrow and twisting, and you find yourself entirely at the story's mercy, forced to hang on as tight as you can, knuckles whitening, hair whipping, lips peeling back in the wind as winged insects hurtle into your gaping mouth and nest between your teeth.

But still you hang on.

And keep going.

Following the story wherever it takes you.

I wholeheartedly believe *that* is the key to any successful collaboration: everything you and your partner do should be in service to the story.

The *story* is boss.

Or at least that's how Steve and I approached it.

There were no outlines. No rules. No drawn-out discussions regarding character or plot or locales. There were no egos and no "Hey, look at how smart and fancy I can write" blocks of extended narrative.

Instead, we pretty much linked hands and jumped feetfirst—not unlike Butch Cassidy and the Sundance Kid grabbing hold of each other as they leapt off that cliff into the raging river below (*"Who are those guys?"*)—into the world of Gwendy Peterson and Richard Farris with a grand sense of fun and adventure and freedom.

And, oh yeah, *trust*—don't forget about trust.

I still have a text, sent to me by Steve on the eve of our beginning to work on *Gwendy's Final Task*, saved somewhere on my phone. It reads: *Hang on tight.*

So that's exactly what I did.

I hung on tight and followed the story wherever it took us, and when it was my turn at the wheel—every fifty pages, if memory serves—I tried my absolute best to stay on the path and carry my weight.

Even now, when I think about those words—*Hang on tight*—I can almost hear the giggle in Steve's voice and picture his eyes sparkling with wonder.

I mentioned *fun* a couple of times up above. Whenever readers ask me what it was like to collaborate with my good friend and literary hero Stephen King, that's inevitably the first word that comes to mind: it was *fun*.

I hope all you Constant Readers enjoy Gwendy's journey as much as Steve and I did. I hope you have fun with the story, and maybe a sleepless night or two. I'll tell you a secret: the two of us pretty much fell in love with her along the way.

GWENDY'S BUTTON BOX

STEPHEN KING AND RICHARD CHIZMAR

1

THERE ARE THREE WAYS up to Castle View from the town of Castle Rock: Route 117, Pleasant Road, and the Suicide Stairs. Every day this summer—yes, even on Sundays—twelve-year-old Gwendy Peterson has taken the stairs, which are held by strong (if time-rusted) iron bolts and zig-zag up the cliffside. She walks the first hundred, jogs the second hundred, and forces herself to run up the last hundred and five, pelting—as her father would say—hellbent for election. At the top she bends over, red-faced, clutching her knees, hair in sweaty clumps against her cheeks (it always escapes her ponytail on that last sprint, no matter how tight she ties it), and puffing like an old carthorse. Yet there has been some improvement. When she straightens up and looks down the length of her body, she can see the tips of her sneakers. She couldn't do that in June, on the last day of school, which also happened to be her last day in Castle Rock Elementary.

Her shirt is sweat-pasted to her body, but on the whole, she feels pretty good. In June, she felt ready to die of a heart attack every time she reached the top. Nearby, she can hear the shouts of the kids on the playground. From a bit farther away comes the chink of an aluminum bat hitting a baseball as the Senior League kids practice for the Labor Day charity game.

She's wiping her glasses on the handkerchief she keeps

in the pocket of her shorts for just that purpose when she is addressed. "Hey, girl. Come on over here for a bit. We ought to palaver, you and me."

Gwendy puts her specs on and the blurred world comes back into focus. On a bench in the shade, close to the gravel path leading from the stairs into the Castle View Recreational Park, sits a man in black jeans, a black coat like for a suit, and a white shirt unbuttoned at the top. On his head is a small neat black hat. The time will come when Gwendy has nightmares about that hat.

The man has been on this same bench every day this week, always reading the same book (*Gravity's Rainbow*, it's thick and looks mighty arduous), but has never said anything to her until today. Gwendy regards him warily.

"I'm not supposed to talk to strangers."

"That's good advice." He looks about her father's age, which would make him thirty-eight or so, and not bad looking, but wearing a black suit coat on a hot August morning makes him a potential weirdo in Gwendy's book. "Probably got it from your mother, right?"

"Father," Gwendy says. She'll have to go past him to get to the playground, and if he really is a weirdo he might try to grab her, but she's not too worried. It's broad daylight, after all, the playground is close and well-populated, and she's got her wind back.

"In that case," says the man in the black coat, "let me introduce myself. I'm Richard Farris. And you are—?"

She debates, then thinks, what harm? "Gwendy Peterson."

"So there. We know each other."

Gwendy shakes her head. "Names aren't knowing."

He throws back his head and laughs. It's totally

charming in its honest good humor, and Gwendy can't help smiling. She still keeps her distance, though.

He points a finger-gun at her: pow. "That's a good one. *You're* a good one, Gwendy. And while we're at it, what kind of name is that, anyway?"

"A combination. My father wanted a Gwendolyn— that was his granny's name—and my mom wanted a Wendy, like in *Peter Pan*. So they compromised. Are you on vacation, Mr. Farris?" This seems likely; they are in Maine, after all, and Maine proclaims itself Vacationland. It's even on the license plates.

"You might say so. I travel here and there. Michigan one week, Florida the next, then maybe a hop to Coney Island for a Redhot and a ride on the Cyclone. I am what you might call a rambling man, and America is my beat. I keep an eye on certain people, and check back on them every once and again."

Chink goes the bat on the field past the playground, and there are cheers.

"Well, it's been nice talking to you, Mr. Farris, but I really ought to—"

"Stay a bit longer. You see, you're one of the people I've been keeping an eye on just recently."

This should sound sinister (and does, a little), but he's still smiling in the aftermath of his laughter, his eyes are lively, and if he's Chester the Molester, he's keeping it well hidden. Which, she supposes, the best ones would do. Step into my parlor, said the spider to the fly.

"I've got a theory about you, Miss Gwendy Peterson. Formed, as all the best theories are, by close observation. Want to hear it?"

"Sure, I guess."

"I notice you are a bit on the plump side."

Maybe he sees her tighten up at that, because he raises a hand and shakes his head, as if to say *not so fast*.

"You might even think of yourself as fat, because girls and women in this country of ours have strange ideas about how they look. The media . . . do you know what I mean by the media?"

"Sure. Newspapers, TV, *Time* and *Newsweek*."

"Nailed it. So okay. The media says, 'Girls, women, you can be anything you want to be in this brave new world of equality, as long as you can still see your toes when you stand up straight.'"

He *has* been watching me, Gwendy thinks, because I do that every day when I get to the top. She blushes. She can't help it, but the blush is a surface thing. Below it is a kind of so-what defiance. It's what got her going on the stairs in the first place. That and Frankie Stone.

"My theory is that somebody tweaked you about your weight, or how you look, or both, and you decided to take the matter in hand. Am I close? Maybe not a bullseye, but at least somewhere on the target?"

Perhaps because he's a stranger, she finds herself able to tell him what she hasn't confided to either of her parents. Or maybe it's his blue eyes, which are curious and interested but with no meanness in them—at least not that she can see. "This kid at school, Frankie Stone, started calling me Goodyear. You know, like—"

"Like the blimp, yes, I know the Goodyear Blimp."

"Uh-huh. Frankie's a puke." She thinks of telling the man how Frankie goes strutting around the playground, chanting *I'm Frankie Stoner! Got a two-foot boner!* and decides not to.

"Some of the other boys started calling me that, and then a few of the girls picked it up. Not my friends, other girls. That was sixth grade. Middle school starts next month, and . . . well . . . "

"You've decided that particular nickname isn't going to follow you there," says Mr. Richard Farris. "I see. You'll also grow taller, you know." He eyes her up and down, but not in a way she finds creepy. It's more scientific. "I'm thinking you might top out around five-ten or -eleven before you're done. Tall, for a girl."

"Started already," Gwendy says, "but I'm not going to wait."

"All pretty much as I thought," Farris says. "Don't wait, don't piss and moan, just attack the issue. Go head-on. Admirable. Which is why I wanted to make your acquaintance."

"It's been nice talking to you, Mr. Farris, but I have to go now."

"No. You need to stay right here." He's not smiling anymore. His face is stern, and the blue eyes seem to have gone gray. The hat lays a thin line of shadow over his brow, like a tattoo. "I have something for you. A gift. Because you are the one."

"I don't take things from strangers," Gwendy says. Now she's feeling a little scared. Maybe more than a little.

"Names aren't knowing, I agree with you there, but we're not strangers, you and I. I know you, and I know this thing I have was made for someone like you. Someone who is young and set solidly on her feet. I felt you, Gwendy, long before I saw you. And here you are." He moves to the end of the bench and pats the seat. "Come sit beside me."

9

Gwendy walks to the bench, feeling like a girl in a dream. "Are you . . . Mr. Farris, do you want to hurt me?"

He smiles. "Grab you? Pull you into the bushes and perhaps have my wicked way with you?" He points across the path and forty feet or so up it. There, two or three dozen kids wearing Castle Rock Day Camp t-shirts are playing on the slides and swings and monkey bars while four camp counselors watch over them. "I don't think I'd get away with that, do you? And besides, young girls don't interest me sexually. They don't interest me at all, as a rule, but as I've already said—or at least implied—you are different. Now sit down."

She sits. The sweat coating her body has turned cold. She has an idea that, despite all his fine talk, he will now try to kiss her, and never mind the playground kids and their teenage minders just up the way. But he doesn't. He reaches under the bench and brings out a canvas bag with a drawstring top. He pulls it open and removes a beautiful mahogany box, the wood glowing a brown so rich that she can glimpse tiny red glints deep in its finish. It's about fifteen inches long, maybe a foot wide, and half that deep. She wants it at once, and not just because it's a beautiful thing. She wants it because it's *hers*. Like something really valuable, really loved, that was lost so long ago it was almost forgotten but is now found again. Like she owned it in another life where she was a princess, or something.

"What is it?" Gwendy asks in a small voice.

"A button box," he says. "Your button box. Look."

He tilts it so she can see small buttons on top of the box, six in rows of two, and a single at each end. Eight in all. The pairs are light green and dark green, yellow and orange, blue and violet. One of the end-buttons is red.

The other is black. There's also a small lever at each end of the box, and what looks like a slot in the middle.

"The buttons are very hard to push," says Farris. "You have to use your thumb, and put some real muscle into it. Which is a good thing, believe me. Wouldn't want to make any mistakes with those, oh no. Especially not with the black one."

Gwendy has forgotten to feel afraid of the man. She's fascinated by the box, and when he hands it to her, she takes it. She was expecting it to be heavy—mahogany is a heavy wood, after all, plus who knows what might be inside—but it's not. She could bounce it up and down on her tented fingers. Gwendy runs a finger over the glassy, slightly convex surface of the buttons, seeming to almost feel the colors lighting up her skin.

"Why? What do they do?"

"We'll discuss them later. For now, direct your attention to the little levers. They're much easier to pull than the buttons are to push; your little finger is enough. When you pull the one on the left end—next to the red button—it will dispense a chocolate treat in the shape of an animal."

"I don't—" Gwendy begins.

"You don't take candy from strangers, I know," Farris says, and rolls his eyes in a way that makes her giggle. "Aren't we past that, Gwendy?"

"It's not what I was going to say. I don't eat *chocolate*, is what I was going to say. Not this summer. How will I ever lose any weight if I eat candy? Believe me, once I start, I can't stop. And chocolate is the worst. I'm like a chocoholic."

"Ah, but that's the beauty of the chocolates the button box dispenses," says Richard Farris. "They are small, not much bigger than jelly beans, and very sweet . . . but after you eat one, you won't want another. You'll want your meals, but not seconds on anything. And you won't want any other treats, either. Especially those late-night waist-line killers."

Gwendy, until this summer prone to making herself Fluffernutters an hour or so before bedtime, knows exactly what he's talking about. Also, she's always starving after her morning runs.

"It sounds like some weird diet product," she says. "The kind that stuffs you up and then makes you pee like crazy. My granny tried some of that stuff, and it made her sick after a week or so."

"Nope. Just chocolate. But *pure*. Not like a candybar from the store. Try it."

She debates the idea, but not for long. She curls her pinky around the lever—it's too small to operate easily with any of the others—and pulls. The slot opens. A narrow wooden shelf slides out. On it is a chocolate rabbit, no bigger than a jellybean, just as Mr. Farris said.

She picks it up and looks at it with amazed wonder. "Wow. Look at the *fur*. The *ears*! And the cute little *eyes*."

"Yes," he agrees. "A beautiful thing, isn't it? Now pop it in! Quick!"

Gwendy does so without even thinking about it, and sweetness floods her mouth. He's right, she never tasted a Hershey bar this good. She can't remember ever having tasted *anything* this good. That gorgeous flavor isn't just in her mouth; it's in her whole head. As it melts on her tongue, the little shelf slides back in, and the slot closes.

"Good?" he asks.

"Mmm." It's all she can manage. If this were ordinary candy, she'd be like a rat in a science experiment, working that little lever until it broke off or until the dispenser stopped dispensing. But she doesn't want another. And she doesn't think she'll be stopping for a Slushee at the snack bar on the far side of the playground, either. She's not hungry at all. She's . . .

"Are you satisfied?" Farris asks.

"Yes!" That's the word, all right. She has never been so satisfied with anything, not even the two-wheeler she got for her ninth birthday.

"Good. Tomorrow you'll probably want another one, and you can *have* another one if you do, because you'll have the button box. It's your box, at least for now."

"How many chocolate animals are inside?"

Instead of answering her question, he invites her to pull the lever at the other end of the box.

"Does it give a different kind of candy?"

"Try it and see."

She curls her pinky around the small lever and pulls it. This time when the shelf slides out of the slot, there's a silver coin on it, so large and shiny she has to squint against the morning light that bounces off it. She picks it up and the shelf slides back in. The coin is heavy in her hand. On it is a woman in profile. She's wearing what looks like a tiara. Below her is a semicircle of stars, interrupted by the date: 1891. Above her are the words *E Pluribis Unum*.

"That is a Morgan silver dollar," Farris tells her in a lecturely voice. "Almost half an ounce of pure silver. Created by Mr. George Morgan, who was just thirty years old when he engraved the likeness of Anna Willess

Williams, a Philadelphia matron, to go on what you'd call the 'heads' side of the coin. The American Eagle is on the tails side."

"It's beautiful," she breathes, and then—with huge reluctance—she holds it out to him.

Farris crosses his hands on his chest and shakes his head. "It's not mine, Gwendy. It's yours. Everything that comes out of the box is yours—the candy and the coins—because the *box* is yours. The current numismatic value of that Morgan dollar is just shy of six hundred dollars, by the way."

"I . . . I can't take it," she says. Her voice is distant in her own ears. She feels (as she did when she first started her runs up the Suicide Stairs two months ago) that she may faint. "I didn't do anything to earn it."

"But you will." From the pocket of his black jacket he takes an old-fashioned pocket watch. It shoots more arrows of sun into Gwendy's eyes, only these are gold instead of silver. He pops up the cover and consults the face within. Then he drops it back into his pocket. "My time is short now, so look at the buttons and listen closely. Will you do that?"

"Y-yes."

"First, put the silver dollar in your pocket. It's distracting you."

She does as he says. She can feel it against her thigh, a heavy circle.

"How many continents in the world, Gwendy? Do you know?"

"Seven," she says. They learned that in third or fourth grade.

"Exactly. But since Antarctica is for all practical purposes deserted, it isn't represented here . . . except, of course, by the black button, and we'll get to that." One after another, he begins to lightly tap the convex surfaces of the buttons that are in pairs. "Light green: Asia. Dark green: Africa. Orange: Europe. Yellow: Australia. Blue: North America. Violet: South America. Are you with me? Can you remember?"

"Yes." She says it with no hesitation. Her memory has always been good, and she has a crazy idea that the wonderful piece of candy she ate is further aiding her concentration. She doesn't know what all this means, but can she remember which color represents which continent? Absolutely. "What's the red one?"

"Whatever you want," he says, "and you *will* want it, the owner of the box always does. It's normal. Wanting to know things and do things is what the human race is all about. Exploration, Gwendy! Both the disease and the cure!"

I'm no longer in Castle Rock, Gwendy thinks. *I've entered one of those places I like to read about. Oz or Narnia or Hobbiton. This can't be happening.*

"Just remember," he continues, "the red button is the only button you can use more than once."

"What about the black one?"

"It's everything," Farris says, and stands up. "The whole shebang. The big kahuna, as your father would say."

She looks at him, saucer-eyed. Her father *does* say that. "How do you know my fath—"

"Sorry to interrupt, very impolite, but I really have to go. Take care of the box. It gives gifts, but they're small recompense for the responsibility. And be careful. If your parents found it, there would be questions."

"Oh my God, would there ever," Gwendy says, and

utters a breathless whisper of a laugh. She feels punched in the stomach. "Mr. Farris, why did you give this to me? *Why me?*"

"Stashed away in this world of ours," Farris says, looking down at her, "are great arsenals of weapons that could destroy all life on this planet for a million years. The men and women in charge of them ask themselves that same question every day. It is you because you were the best choice of those in this place at this time. Take care of the box. I advise you not to let *anyone* find it, not just your parents, because people are curious. When they see a lever, they want to pull it. And when they see a button, they want to push it."

"But what happens if they do? What happens if *I* do?"

Richard Farris only smiles, shakes his head, and starts toward the cliff, where a sign reads: BE CAREFUL! CHILDREN UNDER 10 UNACCOMPANIED BY ADULT *NOT ALLOWED!* Then he turns back. "Say! Why do they call them the Suicide Stairs, Gwendy?"

"Because a man jumped from them in 1934, or something like that," she says. She's holding the button box on her lap. "Then a woman jumped off four or five years ago. My dad says the city council talked about taking them down, but everyone on the council is Republican, and Republicans hate change. That's what my dad says, anyway. One of them said the stairs are a tourist attraction, which they sort of are, and that one suicide every thirty-five years or so wasn't really so terrible. He said if it became a fad, they'd take another vote."

Mr. Farris smiles. "Small towns! Gotta love them!"

"I answered your question, now you answer mine! What happens if I push one of these buttons? What

16

happens if I push the one for Africa, for instance?" And as soon as her thumb touches the dark green button, she feels an urge—not strong, but appreciable—to push it and find out for herself.

His smile becomes a grin. Not a terribly nice one, in Gwendy Peterson's opinion. "Why ask what you already know?"

Before she can say another word, he's started down the stairs. She sits on the bench for a moment, then gets up, runs to the rusty iron landing, and peers down. Although Mr. Farris hasn't had time enough to get all the way to the bottom—nowhere near—he's gone. Or almost. Halfway down, about a hundred and fifty iron steps, his small neat black hat lies either abandoned or blown off.

She goes back to the bench and puts the button box—*her* button box—in the canvas drawstring bag, then descends the stairs, holding the railing the whole way. When she reaches the little round hat, she considers picking it up, then kicks it over the side instead, watching it fall, flipping over all the way to the bottom to land in the weeds. When she comes back later that day, it's gone.

This is August 22nd, 1974.

2

HER MOM AND DAD both work, so when Gwendy gets back to the little Cape Cod on Carbine Street, she has it to herself. She puts the button box under her bed and leaves it there for all of ten minutes before realizing that's no good. She keeps her room reasonably neat, but her mom is the one who vacuums once in a while and changes the bed linen every Saturday morning (a chore she insists will be Gwendy's when she turns thirteen—some birthday present that will be). Mom mustn't find the box because moms want to know everything.

She next considers the attic, but what if her parents finally decide to clean it out and have a yard sale instead of just talking about it? The same is true of the storage space over the garage. Gwendy has a thought (novel now in its adult implications, later to become a tiresome truth): secrets are a problem, maybe the biggest problem of all. They weigh on the mind and take up space in the world.

Then she remembers the oak tree in the back yard, with the tire swing she hardly ever uses anymore—twelve is too old for such baby amusements. There's a shallow cavern beneath the tree's gnarl of roots. She used to curl up in there sometimes during games of hide-and-seek with her friends. She's too big for it now (*I'm thinking you might top out around five-ten or -eleven before you're done*, Mr. Farris told her), but it's a natural for the box, and the canvas bag will keep it dry if it rains. If it really *pours*, she'll have to come out and rescue it.

She tucks it away there, starts back to the house, then remembers the silver dollar. She returns to the tree and slips it into the bag with the box.

Gwendy thinks that her parents will see something strange has happened to her when they come home, that she's different, but they don't. They are wrapped up in their own affairs, as usual—Dad at the insurance office, Mom at Castle Rock Ford, where she's a secretary—and of course they have a few drinks. They always do. Gwendy has one helping of everything at dinner, and cleans her plate, but refuses a slice of the chocolate cake Dad brought home from the Castle Rock Bake Shop, next door to where he works.

"Oh my God, are you sick?" Dad asks.

Gwendy smiles. "Probably."

She's sure she'll lie awake until late, thinking about her encounter with Mr. Farris and the button box hidden under the backyard oak, but she doesn't. She thinks, *Light green for Asia, dark green for Africa, yellow for Australia . . .* and that's where she falls asleep until the next morning, when it's time to eat a big bowl of cereal with fruit, and then charge up the Suicide Stairs once more.

When she comes back, muscles glowing and stomach growling, she retrieves the canvas bag from under the tree, takes out the box, and uses her pinky to pull the lever on the left, near the red button (*whatever you want*, Mr. Farris said when she asked about that one). The slot opens and the shelf slides out. On it is a chocolate turtle, small but perfect, the shell a marvel of engraved plating. She tosses the turtle into her mouth. The sweetness blooms. Her hunger disappears, although when lunchtime comes, she will eat all of the bologna-and-cheese sandwich her mother has left her, plus some salad with French dressing, and a big glass of milk. She glances at the leftover cake in its plastic container. It looks good, but that's just an intellectual appreciation. She would feel the same way about a cool two-page spread in a *Dr. Strange* comic book, but she wouldn't want to eat it, and she doesn't want to eat any cake, either.

That afternoon she goes bike-riding with her friend Olive, and then they spend the rest of the afternoon in Olive's bedroom, listening to records and talking about the upcoming school year. The prospect of going to Castle Rock Middle fills them with dread and excitement.

Back home, before her parents arrive, Gwendy takes the button box out of its hiding place again and pulls what she'll come to think of as the Money Lever. Nothing happens; the slot doesn't even open. Well, that's all right. Perhaps because she is an only child with no competition, Gwendy isn't greedy. When the little chocolates run out, she'll miss them more than any silver dollars. She hopes that won't happen for a while, but when it does, okay. *C'est la vie*, as her dad likes to say. Or *merde se*, which means shit happens.

Before returning the box, she looks at the buttons and names the continents they stand for. She touches them one by one. They draw her; she likes the way each touch seems to fill her with a different color, but she steers clear of the black one. That one is scary. Well . . . they're all a little scary, but the black one is like a large dark mole, disfiguring and perhaps cancerous.

On Saturday, the Petersons pile into the Subaru station wagon and go to visit Dad's sister in Yarmouth. Gwendy usually enjoys these visits, because Aunt Dottie and Uncle Jim's twin girls are almost exactly her age, and the three of them always have fun together. There's usually a movie-show on Saturday night (this time a double feature at the Pride's Corner Drive-In, *Thunderbolt and Lightfoot*, plus *Gone in 60 Seconds*), and the girls lie out on the ground in sleeping bags, chattering away when the movie gets boring.

Gwendy has fun this time, too, but her thoughts keep turning to the button box. What if someone should find it and steal it? She knows that's unlikely—a burglar would just stick to the house, and not go searching under backyard trees—but the thought preys on her mind. Part of this is possessiveness; it's *hers*. Part of it is wishing for the little chocolate treats. Most of it, however, has to do with the buttons. A thief would see them, wonder what they were for, and push them. What would happen then? Especially if he pushed the black one? She's already starting to think of it as the Cancer Button.

When her mother says she wants to leave early on Sunday (there's going to be a Ladies Aid meeting, and Mrs. Peterson is treasurer this year), Gwendy is relieved. When they get home, she changes into her old jeans and goes out back. She swings in the tire for a little while, then pretends to drop something and goes to one knee, as if to look for it. What she's really looking for is the canvas bag. It's right where it belongs . . . but that is not enough. Furtively, she reaches between two of the gnarled roots and feels the box inside. One of the buttons is right under her first two fingers—she can feel its convex shape—and she withdraws her hand fast, as if she had touched a hot stove burner. Still, she is relieved. At least until a shadow falls over her.

"Want me to give you a swing, sweetie?" her dad asks.

"No," she says, getting up and brushing her knees. "I'm really too big for it now. Guess I'll go inside and watch TV."

He gives her a hug, pushes her glasses up on her nose, then strokes his fingers through her blonde hair, loosening a few tangles. "You're getting so tall," he says. "But you'll always be my little girl. Right, Gwennie?"

"You got it, Daddy-O," she says, and heads back inside. Before turning on the TV, she looks out into the yard from the window over the sink (no longer having to stand on tip-toe to do it). She watches her father give the tire swing a push. She waits to see if he will drop to his knees, perhaps curious about what she was looking for. Or at. When he turns and heads for the garage instead, Gwendy goes into the living room, turns on *Soul Train*, and dances along with Marvin Gaye.

3

WHEN SHE COMES BACK from her run up the Suicide Stairs on Monday, the lever by the red button dispenses a small chocolate kitty. She tries the other lever, not really expecting anything, but the slot opens, the shelf comes out, and on it is another 1891 silver dollar with nary a mark or a scratch on either side, the kind of coin she will come to know as uncirculated. Gwendy huffs on it, misting the features of Anna Willess Williams, then rubs the long-gone Philadelphia matron bright again on her shirt. Now she has two silver dollars, and if Mr. Farris was right about their worth, it's almost enough money for a year's tuition at the University of Maine. Good thing college is years away, because how could a twelve-year-old kid sell such valuable coins? Think of the questions they would raise!

Think of the questions the box *would raise!*

She touches the buttons again, one by one, avoiding the horrid black one but this time lingering on the red one, the tip of her finger circling around and around, feeling the oddest combination of distress and sensuous pleasure. At last she slides the button box back into its bag, stashes it, and bikes to Olive's house. They make strawberry turnovers under the watchful eye of Olive's mom, then go upstairs and put on Olive's records again. The door opens and Olive's mom comes in, but not to tell them they must lower the volume, as both girls expected. No, she wants to dance, too. It's fun. The three of them dance around and laugh like crazy, and when Gwendy goes home, she eats a big meal.

No seconds, though.

4

CASTLE ROCK MIDDLE TURNS out to be okay. Gwendy reconnects with her old friends and makes some new ones. She notices some of the boys eyeing her, which is okay because none of them is Frankie Stone and none of them call her Goodyear. Thanks to the Suicide Stairs, that nickname has been laid to rest. For her birthday in October, she gets a poster of Robby Benson, a little TV for her room (oh God, the joy) and lessons on how to change her own bed (not joyful but not bad). She makes the soccer team and the girls' track team, where she quickly becomes a standout.

The chocolate treats continue to come, no two ever the same, the detail always amazing. Every week or two there's also a silver dollar, always dated 1891. Her fingers linger longer and longer on the red button, and sometimes she hears herself whispering, "Whatever you want, whatever you want."

Miss Chiles, Gwendy's seventh grade history teacher, is young and pretty and dedicated to making her classes as interesting as possible. Sometimes her efforts are lame, but every once in a while they succeed splendidly. Just before the Christmas vacation, she announces that their first class in the new year will be Curiosity Day. Each pupil is to think of one historical thing they wonder about, and Miss Chiles will try to satisfy their curiosity. If she cannot, she'll throw the question to the class, for discussion and speculation.

"Just no questions about the sex lives of the presidents," she says, which makes the boys roar with laughter and the girls giggle hysterically.

When the day comes, the questions cover a wide range. Frankie Stone wants to know if the Aztecs really ate human hearts, and Billy Day wants to know who made the statues on Easter Island, but most of the questions on Curiosity Day in January of 1975 are what-ifs. What if the South had won the Civil War? What if George Washington had died of, like, starvation or frostbite at Valley Forge? What if Hitler had drowned in the bathtub when he was a baby?

When Gwendy's turn comes, she is prepared, but still a tiny bit nervous. "I don't know if this actually fits the assignment or not," she says, "but I think it might at least have historical . . . um . . . "

"Historical implications?" Miss Chiles asks.

"Yes! That!"

"Fine. Lay it on us."

"What if you had a button, a special magic button, and if you pushed it, you could kill somebody, or maybe just make them disappear, or blow up any place you were thinking of? What person would you make disappear, or what place would you blow up?"

A respectful silence falls as the class considers this wonderfully bloodthirsty concept, but Miss Chiles is frowning. "As a rule," she says, "erasing people from the world, either by murder or disappearance, is a very bad idea. So is blowing up *any* place."

Nancy Riordan says, "What about Hiroshima and Nagasaki? Are you saying blowing them up was bad?"

27

Miss Chiles looks taken aback. "No, not exactly," she says, "but think of all the innocent civilians that were killed when we bombed those cities. The women and children. The babies. And the radiation afterward! That killed even more."

"I get that," Joey Lawrence says, "but my grampa fought the Japs in the war, he was on Guadalcanal and Tarawa, and he said lots of the guys he fought with died. He said it was a miracle *he* didn't die. Grampy says dropping those bombs kept us from having to invade Japan, and we might have lost a million men if we had to do that."

The idea of killing someone (or making them disappear) has kind of gotten lost, but that's okay with Gwendy. She's listening, rapt.

"That's a very good point," Miss Chiles says. "Class, what do you think? Would you destroy a place if you could, in spite of the loss of civilian life? And if so, which place, and why?"

They talk about it for the rest of the class. Hanoi, says Henry Dussault. Knock out that guy Ho Chi Minh and end the stupid Vietnam War once and for all. Many agree with this. Ginny Brooks thinks it would be just grand if Russia could be obliterated. Mindy Ellerton is for eradicating China, because her dad says the Chinese are willing to start a nuclear war because they have so many people. Frankie Stone suggests getting rid of the American ghettos, where "those black people are making dope and killing cops."

After school, while Gwendy is getting her Huffy out of the bike rack, Miss Chiles comes over to her, smiling. "I just wanted to thank you for your question," she says. "I was a little shocked by it to begin with, but that turned out to be one of the best classes we've had this year. I believe everybody participated but you, which is strange, since you posed the question in the first place. Is there a place you would blow up, if you had that power? Or someone you'd . . . er . . . get rid of?"

Gwendy smiles back. "I don't know," she says. "That's why I asked the question."

"Good thing there isn't really a button like that," Miss Chiles says.

"But there is," Gwendy says. "Nixon has one. So does Brezhnev. Some other people, too."

Having given Miss Chiles this lesson—not in history, but in current events—Gwendy rides away on a bike that is rapidly becoming too small for her.

5

In June of 1975, Gwendy stops wearing her glasses.

Mrs. Peterson remonstrates with her. "I know that girls your age start thinking about boys, I haven't forgotten everything about being thirteen, but that saying about how boys don't make passes at girls who wear glasses is just—don't tell your father I said this—full of shit. The truth, Gwennie, is that boys will make passes at anything in a skirt, and you're far too young for that business, anyway."

"Mom, how old were you when you first made out with a boy?"

"Sixteen," says Mrs. Peterson without hesitation. She was actually eleven, kissing with Georgie McClelland, up in the loft of the McClelland barn. Oh, they smacked up a storm. "And listen, Gwennie, you're a very pretty girl, with or without glasses."

"It's nice of you to say so," Gwendy tells her, "but I really see better without them. They hurt my eyes now."

Mrs. Peterson doesn't believe it, so she takes her daughter to Dr. Emerson, the Rock's resident optician. He doesn't believe it, either . . . at least until Gwendy hands him her glasses and then reads the eye chart all the way to the bottom.

"Well I'll be darned," he says. "I've heard of this, but

it's extremely rare. You must have been eating a lot of carrots, Gwendy."

"I guess that must be it," she smiles, thinking, *It's chocolates I've been eating. Magic chocolate animals, and they never run out.*

6

GWENDY'S WORRIES ABOUT THE box being discovered or stolen are like a constant background hum in her head, but those worries never come close to ruling her life. It occurs to her that might have been one of the reasons why Mr. Farris gave it to her. Why he said *you are the one.*

She does well in her classes, she has a big role in the eighth grade play (and never forgets a single line), she continues to run track. Track is the best; when that runner's high kicks in, even the background hum of worry disappears. Sometimes she resents Mr. Farris for saddling her with the responsibility of the box, but mostly she doesn't. As he told her, it gives gifts. *Small recompense,* he said, but the gifts don't seem so small to Gwendy; her memory is better, she no longer wants to eat everything in the fridge, her vision is twenty-twenty, she can run like the wind, and there's something else, too. Her mother called her very pretty, but her friend Olive is willing to go farther.

"Jesus, you're gorgeous," she says to Gwendy one day, not sounding pleased about it. They are in Olive's room again, this time discussing the mysteries of high school, which they will soon begin to unravel. "No more glasses, and not even one frickin' pimple. It's not fair. You'll have to beat the guys off with a stick."

Gwendy laughs it off, but she knows that Olive is onto something. She really *is* good-looking, and gorgeosity isn't out of the realm of possibility at some point in the future. Perhaps by the time she gets to college. Only when she goes away to school, what will she do with the button box? She can't simply leave it under the tree in the backyard, can she?

Henry Dussault asks her to the freshman mixer dance on their first Friday night of high school, holds her hand on the walk home, and kisses her when they get to the Peterson house. It's not bad, being kissed, except Henry's breath is sort of yuck. She hopes the next boy with whom she lip-locks will be a regular Listerine user.

She wakes up at two o'clock on the morning after the dance, with her hands pressed over her mouth to hold in a scream, still in the grip of the most vivid nightmare she's ever had. In it, she looked out the window over the kitchen sink and saw Henry sitting in the tire swing (which Gwendy's dad actually took down a year ago). He had the button box in his lap. Gwendy rushed out, shouting at him, telling him not to press any of the buttons, especially not the black one.

Oh, you mean this one? Henry asked, grinning, and jammed his thumb down on the Cancer Button.

Above them, the sky went dark. The ground began to rumble like a live thing. Gwendy knew that all over the world, famous landmarks were falling and seas were rising. In moments—*mere moments*—the planet was going to explode like an apple with a firecracker stuffed in it, and between Mars and Venus there would be nothing but a second asteroid belt.

"A dream," Gwendy says, going to her bedroom window. "A dream, a dream, nothing but a dream."

Yes. The tree is there, now minus the tire swing, and

there's no Henry Dussault in sight. But if he had the box, and knew what each button stood for, what would he do? Push the red one and blow up Hanoi? Or say the hell with it and push the light green one?

"And blow up all of Asia," she whispers. Because yes, that's what the buttons do. She knew from the first, just as Mr. Farris said. The violet one blows up South America, the orange one blows up Europe, the red one does whatever you want, whatever you're thinking of. And the black one?

The black one blows up everything.

"That can't be," she whispers to herself as she goes back to bed. "It's insane."

Only the world is insane. You only have to watch the news to know it.

When she comes home from school the next day, Gwendy goes down to the basement with a hammer and a chisel. The walls are stone, and she is able to pry one out in the farthest corner. She uses the chisel to deepen this hidey-hole until it's big enough for the button box. She checks her watch constantly as she works, knowing her father will be home at five, her mother by five-thirty at the latest.

She runs to the tree, gets the canvas bag with the button box and her silver dollars inside (the silver dollars are now much heavier than the box, although they *came* from the box), and runs back to the house. The hole is just big enough. And the stone fits into place like the last piece of a puzzle. For good measure, she drags an old bureau in front of it, and at last feels at peace. Henry won't be able to find it now. *Nobody* will be able to find it.

"I ought to throw the goddamned thing in Castle

Lake," she whispers as she climbs the cellar stairs. "Be done with it." Only she knows she could never do that. It's hers, at least unless Mr. Farris comes back to claim it. Sometimes she hopes he will. Sometimes she hopes he never will.

When Mr. Peterson comes home, he looks at Gwendy with some concern. "You're all sweaty," he says. "Do you feel all right?"

She smiles. "Been running, that's all. I'm fine."

And mostly, she is.

7

BY THE SUMMER AFTER her freshman year, Gwendy is feeling *very* fine, indeed.

For starters, she's grown another inch since school let out and, even though it's not yet the Fourth of July, she's sporting a killer suntan. Unlike most of her classmates, Gwendy has never had much of a suntan before. In fact, the previous summer was the first summer of her life that she'd dared to wear a swimsuit in public, and even then, she'd settled on a modest one-piece. A granny suit, her best friend Olive had teased one afternoon at the community swimming pool.

But that was then and this is now; no more granny suits this summer. In early June, Mrs. Peterson and Gwendy drive to the mall in downtown Castle Rock and come home with matching flip-flops and a pair of colorful bikinis. Bright yellow and even brighter red with little white polka dots. The yellow bathing suit quickly becomes Gwendy's favorite. She will never admit it to anyone else, but when Gwendy studies herself in the full-length mirror in the privacy of her bedroom, she secretly believes she resembles the girl from the Coppertone ad. This never fails to please her.

But it's more than just bronzed legs and teeny-weenie polka dot bikinis. Other things are better, too. Take her parents, for instance. She would've never gone so far as to label mom and dad as alcoholics—not quite, and never out loud to anyone—but she knows they used to drink too much, and she thinks she knows the reason for this: somewhere along the way, say about the time Gwendy was finishing up the third grade, her parents had fallen out of love with each other. Just like in the movies. Nightly martinis and the business section of the newspaper (for Mr. Peterson) and sloe gin fizzes and romance novels (for Mrs. Peterson) had gradually replaced after-dinner family walks around the neighborhood and jigsaw puzzles at the dining room table.

For the better part of her elementary school years, Gwendy suffered this familial deterioration with a sense of silent worry. No one said a word to her about what was going on, and she didn't say a word to anyone else either, especially not her mother or father. She wouldn't even have known how to begin such a conversation.

Then, not long after the arrival of the button box, everything began to change.

Mr. Peterson showed up early from work one evening with a bouquet of daisies (Mrs. Peterson's favorites) and news of an unexpected promotion at the insurance office. They celebrated this good fortune with a pizza dinner and ice cream sundaes and—surprise—a long walk around the neighborhood.

Then, sometime early last winter, Gwendy noticed that the drinking had stopped. Not slowed down, but completely stopped. One day after school, before her parents got home from work, she searched the house from top to bottom, and didn't find a single bottle of booze anywhere. Even the old fridge out in the garage was empty of Mr. Peterson's favorite beer, Black Label. It had been replaced by a case of Dad's Root Beer.

That night, while her father was getting spaghetti from Gino's, Gwendy asked her mother if they had really quit drinking. Mrs. Peterson laughed. "If you mean did we join AA or stand in front of Father O'Malley and take the pledge, we didn't."

"Well . . . whose idea was it? Yours or his?"

Gwendy's mother looked vague. "I don't think we even discussed it."

Gwendy left it there. Another of her father's sayings seemed applicable: *Don't look a gift horse in the mouth.*

And just a week later, the cherry on top of this minor miracle: Gwendy walked out into the back yard to ask her father for a ride to the library and was startled to find Mr. and Mrs. Peterson holding hands and smiling at each other. Just standing there in their winter coats with their breath frosting the air, looking into each other's eyes like reunited lovers of *Days of Our Lives.* Gwendy, mouth gaping open, stopped in her tracks and took in this tableau. Tears prickled her eyes. She hadn't seen them looking at each other that way in she couldn't remember how long. Maybe never. Stopped dead in her tracks at the foot of the kitchen stoop, her earmuffs dangling from one mittened hand, she thought of Mr. Farris and his magic box.

It did this. I don't know how or why, but it did this. It's not just me. It's like a kind of . . . I don't know . . .

"An umbrella," she whispered, and that was just right. An umbrella that could shade her family from too much sun and also keep the rain off. Everything was okay, and as long as a strong wind didn't come up and blow the umbrella inside out, things would stay okay. And why would that happen? *It won't. It can't. Not as long as I take care of the box. I have to. It's my button box now.*

8

ON A THURSDAY NIGHT in early August, Gwendy is hauling a garbage can to the bottom of the driveway when Frankie Stone swings to the curb in front of her in his blue El Camino. The Rolling Stones are blaring from the car stereo and Gwendy catches a whiff of marijuana wafting from the open window. He turns down the music. "Wanna go for a ride, sexy?"

Frankie Stone has grown up, but not in a good way. He sports greasy brown hair, a shotgun pattern of acne scattered across his face, and a homemade AC/DC tattoo on one arm. He also suffers from the worst case of body odor Gwendy has ever come across. There are whispers that he fed a hippie girl roofies at a concert and then raped her. Probably not true, she knows about the vicious rumors kids start, but he sure *looks* like someone who'd slip roofies into a girl's wine cooler.

"I can't," Gwendy says, wishing she were wearing more than just cut-off jean shorts and a tank top. "I have to do my homework."

"Homework?" Frankie scowls. "C'mon, who the fuck does homework in the summer?"

"It's . . . I'm taking a summer class at the community college."

Frankie leans out the window, and even though he's still a good ten feet away from her, Gwendy can smell his breath. "You wouldn't be lying to me now, would you, pretty girl?" He grins.

"I'm not lying. Have a good night, Frankie. I better get inside and hit the books."

Gwendy turns and starts walking up the driveway, feeling good about the way she handled him. She hasn't taken but four or five steps when something hard plunks her in the back of her neck. She cries out, not hurt but surprised, and turns back to the street. A beer can spins lazily at her feet, spitting foam onto the pavement.

"Just like the rest of the stuck up bitches," Frankie says. "I thought you were different, but you're not. Think you're too good for everyone."

Gwendy reaches up and rubs the back of her neck. A nasty bump has already risen there, and she flinches when her fingers touch it. "You need to go, Frankie. Before I get my father."

"Fuck your father, and fuck you, too. I knew you when you were nothin but an ugly fuckin chubber." Frankie points a finger-gun at her and smiles. "It'll come back, too. Fat girls turn into fat women. It never fails. See you around, Goodyear."

Then he's gone, middle finger jutting out the window, tires burning rubber. Only now does Gwendy allow the tears to come as she runs inside the house.

That night she dreams about Frankie Stone. In the dream, she doesn't stand there helpless in the driveway with her heart in her throat. In the dream, she rushes at Frankie, and before he can peel out, she lunges through the open driver's window and grabs his left arm. She twists until she hears—and feels—the bones snapping beneath her hands. And as he screams, she says, *How's that boner now, Frankie Stoner? More like two inches than two feet, I bet. You never should have fucked with the Queen of the Button Box.*

She wakes up in the morning and remembers the dream with a sleepy smile, but as with most dreams, it vanishes with the rising sun. She doesn't think of it again until two weeks later, during a breakfast conversation with her father on a lazy Saturday morning. Mr. Peterson finishes his coffee and puts down the newspaper. "Your pal Frankie Stone made the news."

Gwendy stops in mid-chew. "He's no pal of mine, I hate the guy. Why's he in the paper?"

"Car accident last night out on Hanson Road. Probably drunk, although it doesn't say so. Hit a tree. He's okay, but pretty banged up."

"How banged up?"

"Bunch of stitches in his head and shoulder. Cuts all over his face. Broken arm. Multiple breaks, according to the story. Going to take a long time to heal. Want to see for yourself?"

He pushes the paper across the table. Gwendy pushes it back, then carefully puts down her fork. She knows she won't be able to eat another bite, just as she knows without asking that the broken arm Frankie Stone suffered is his left one.

That night, in bed, trying to sweep away the troubled thoughts swirling inside her head, Gwendy counts how many days of summer vacation remain before she has to return to school.

This is August 22nd, 1977. Exactly three years to the day from when Mr. Farris and the button box came into her life.

9

A WEEK BEFORE GWENDY starts the tenth grade at Castle Rock High, she runs the Suicide Stairs for the first time in almost a year. The day is mild and breezy, and she reaches the top without breaking much of a sweat. She stretches for a brief moment and glances down the length of her body: she can see her entire damn sneakers.

She walks to the railing and takes in the view. It's the kind of morning that makes you wish death didn't exist. She scans Dark Score Lake, then turns to the playground, empty now except for a young mother pushing a toddler on the baby swing. Her eyes finally settle on the bench where she met Mr. Farris. She walks over to it and sits down.

More and more often lately, a little voice inside her head is asking questions she doesn't have answers for. *Why you, Gwendy Peterson? Out of all the people in this round world, why did he choose you?*

And there are other, scarier, questions, too: *Where did he come from? Why was he keeping an eye on me?* (His exact words!) *What the hell is that box . . . and what is it doing to me?*

Gwendy sits on the bench for a long time, thinking and watching the clouds drift past. After a while, she gets up and jogs down the Suicide Stairs and home again. The questions remain: *How much of her life is her own doing, and how much the doing of the box with its treats and buttons?*

10

Sophomore year opens with a bang. Within a month of the first day of classes, Gwendy is elected Class President, named captain of the junior varsity soccer team, and asked to the homecoming dance by Harold Perkins, a handsome senior on the football squad (alas, the homecoming date never happens, as Gwendy dumps poor Harold after he repeatedly tries to feel her up at a drive-in showing of *Damnation Alley* on their first date). Plenty of time for touchie-feelie later, as her mother likes to say.

For her sixteenth birthday in October, she gets a poster of the Eagles standing in front of Hotel California (*"You can check out any time you like, but you can never leave"*), a new stereo with both eight track and cassette decks, and a promise from her father to teach her how to drive now that she's of legal age.

The chocolate treats continue to come, no two ever the same, the detail always amazing. The tiny slice of heaven Gwendy devoured just this morning before school was a giraffe, and she purposely skipped brushing her teeth afterward. She wanted to savor the remarkable taste for as long as she could.

Gwendy doesn't pull the other small lever nearly as often as she once did, for no other reason than she's finally run out of space to hide the silver coins. For now, the chocolate is enough.

She still thinks about Mr. Farris, not quite as often and usually in the long, empty hours of the night when she tries to remember exactly what he looked like or how his voice sounded. She's almost sure she once saw him in the crowd at the Castle Rock Halloween Fair, but she was high atop the Ferris wheel at that moment, and by the time the ride ended, he was gone, swallowed by the hordes of people flocking down the midway. Another time she went into a Portland coin shop with one of the silver dollars. The worth had gone up; the man offered her $750 for one of her 1891 Morgans, saying he'd never seen a better one. Gwendy refused, telling him (on the spur of the moment) that it was a gift from her grandfather and she only wanted to know what it was worth. Leaving, she saw a man looking at her from across the street, a man wearing a neat little black hat. Farris—if it *was* Farris—gave her a fleeting smile, and disappeared around the corner.

Watching her? Keeping track? Is it possible? She thinks it is.

And she still thinks about the buttons, of course, especially the red one. She sometimes finds herself sitting cross-legged on the cold basement floor, holding the button box in her lap, staring at that red button in a kind of daze and caressing it with the tip of her finger. She wonders what would happen if she pushed the red button without a clear choice of a place to blow up. What then? Who would decide what was destroyed? God? The box?

A few weeks after her trip to the coin shop, Gwendy decides it's time to find out about the red button once and for all.

Instead of spending her fifth period study hall in the library, she heads for Mr. Anderson's empty World History classroom. There's a reason for this: the pair of pull-down maps that are attached to Mr. Anderson's chalkboard.

Gwendy has considered a number of possible targets for the red button. She hates that word—*target*—but it fits, and she can't think of anything better. Among her initial options: the Castle Rock dump, a stretch of trashy, pulped-over woods beyond the railroad tracks, and the old abandoned Phillips 66 gas station where kids hang out and smoke dope.

In the end, she decides to not only target someplace outside of Castle Rock, but also the entire country. Better safe than sorry.

She walks behind Mr. Anderson's desk and carefully studies the map, focusing first on Australia (where, she recently learned, over one-third of the country is desert) before moving on to Africa (those poor folks have enough problems) and finally settling on South America.

From her history notes, Gwendy remembers two important facts that aid this decision: South America harbors thirty-five of the fifty least-developed countries in the world, and a similar percentage of the least-populated countries in the world.

Now that the choice has been made, Gwendy doesn't waste any time. She scribbles down the names of three small countries in her spiral notebook, one from the north, one from the middle of the continent, and one from the south. Then, she hurries to the library to do more research. She looks at pictures and makes a list of the most godforsaken ones.

Later that afternoon, Gwendy sits down in front of her bedroom closet and balances the button box on her lap.

She places a shaky finger on top of the red button.

She closes her eyes and pictures one tiny part of a far-away country. Dense, tangled vegetation. An expanse of wild jungle where no people live. As many details as she can manage.

She holds the image in her head and pushes the red button.

Nothing happens. It doesn't go down.

Gwendy stabs at the red button a second and third time. It doesn't budge under her finger. The part about the buttons was a practical joke, it seems. And gullible Gwendy Peterson believed it.

Almost relieved, she starts to return the button box to the closet when Mr. Farris's words suddenly come back to her: *The buttons are very hard to push. You have to use your thumb, and put some real muscle into it. Which is a good thing, believe me.*

She lowers the box to her lap again—and uses her thumb to press the red button. She puts all her weight on it. This time, there's a barely audible *click,* and Gwendy feels the button depress.

She stares at the box for a moment, thinking *Some trees and maybe a few animals. A small earthquake or maybe a fire. Surely no more than that.* Then she returns it to its hiding place in the wall of the basement. Her face feels warm and her stomach hurts. Does that mean it's working?

11

GWENDY WAKES UP THE next morning running a fever. She stays home from school and spends most of the day sleeping. She emerges from her bedroom later that evening, feeling as good as new, and discovers her parents watching the news in silence. She can tell from the expressions on their faces that something is wrong. She eases down on the sofa next to her mother and watches in horror as Charles Gibson takes them to Guyana—a faraway country of which she recently learned a few salient details. There a cult leader by the name of Jim Jones has committed suicide and ordered over nine hundred of his followers to do the same.

Grainy photographs flash on the television screen. Bodies laid out in rows, thick jungle looming in the background. Couples in a lovers' embrace. Mothers clutching babies to still chests. So many children. Faces distorted in agony. Flies crawling all over everything. According to Charles Gibson, nurses squirted the poison down the kiddies' throats before taking their own doses.

Gwendy returns to her bedroom without comment and slips on tennis shoes and a sweatshirt. She thinks about running Suicide Stairs but decides against it, vaguely afraid of an impulse to throw herself off. Instead, she travels a three-mile loop around the neighborhood, her footsteps slapping a staccato rhythm on the cold pavement, crisp autumn air blushing her cheeks. *I did that*, she thinks, picturing flies swarming over dead babies. *I didn't mean to, but I did.*

12

"You looked right at me," Olive says. Her voice is calm, but her eyes are burning. "I don't know how you can say you didn't see me standing there."

"I didn't. I swear."

They are sitting in Gwendy's bedroom after school, listening to the new Billy Joel album and supposedly studying for an English mid-term. Now it's obvious Olive came over with what she likes to call ISSUES. Olive often has ISSUES these days.

"I find that hard to believe."

Gwendy's eyes go wide. "You're calling me a liar? Why in the world would I walk right by you without saying hello?"

Olive shrugs, her lips pressed tight. "Maybe you didn't want all your cool friends to know you used to hang out with other lowly sophomores."

"That's stupid. You're my best friend, Olive. Everyone knows that."

Olive barks out a laugh. "Best friend? Do you know the last time we've done something on a weekend? Forget Friday and Saturday nights with all your dates and parties and bonfires. I'm talking the entire weekend, any time at all."

"I've been really busy," Gwendy says, looking away.

She knows her friend is right, but why does she have to be so sensitive? "I'm sorry."

"And you don't even like half those guys. Bobby Crawford asks you out and you giggle and twirl your hair and say 'Sure, why not?' even though you barely know his name and could care less about him."

And, just like that, Gwendy understands. *How could I be so stupid?* she wonders. "I didn't know you liked Bobby." She scoots across the bedroom floor and puts her hand on her friend's knee. "I swear I didn't. I'm sorry."

Olive doesn't say anything. Apparently the ISSUE remains.

"That was months ago. Bobby's a really nice guy, but that's the only time I went out with him. If you want, I can call him and tell him about you—"

Olive pushes Gwendy's hand away and gets to her feet. "I don't need your goddamn charity." She bends down and gathers her books and folders into her arms.

"It's not charity. I just thought—"

"That's your problem," Olive says, pulling away again. "You only think about yourself. You're selfish." She stomps out of the bedroom and slams the door behind her.

Gwendy stands there in disbelief, her body trembling with hurt. Then the hurt blooms into anger. "Go to hell!" she screams at the closed door. "If you want to address an issue, try your *jealous bone!*"

She flings herself back on the bed, tears streaming down her face, the hurtful words echoing: *You only think about yourself. You're selfish.*

"That's not true," Gwendy whispers to the empty room. "I think about others. I try to be a good person. I

53

made a mistake about Guyana, but I was . . . I was tricked into it, and I wasn't the one who poisoned them. *It wasn't me.*" Except it sort of was.

Gwendy cries herself to sleep and dreams of nurses bearing syringes of Kool-Aid death to small children.

13

SHE TRIES TO SMOOTH things over the next day at school, but Olive refuses to talk to her. The following day, Friday, is more of the same. Just before the final bell rings, Gwendy slips a handwritten apology note inside Olive's locker and hopes for the best.

On Saturday night, Gwendy and her date, a junior named Walter Dean, stop by the arcade on their way to an early movie. During the car ride over, Walter pulls out a bottle of wine he lifted from his mother's stash, and although Gwendy usually passes on such offers, tonight she helps herself. She's sad and confused and hopes the buzz will help.

It doesn't. It only gives her a mild headache.

Gwendy nods hello to several classmates as they enter the arcade and is surprised to see Olive standing in line at the snack bar. Hopeful, she flips her a tentative wave, but once again Olive ignores her. A moment later, Olive walks right past her, large soda cradled in her arms, nose in the air, giggling with a pack of girls Gwendy recognizes from a neighboring high school.

"What's her problem?" Walter asks, before sliding a quarter into a Space Invaders machine.

"Long story." Gwendy stares after her friend and her anger returns. She feels her face flush with annoyance. *She knows what it was like for me. Hey, Goodyear, where's the football game? Hey, Goodyear, how's the view up there? She should be happy for me. She should be—*

Twenty feet away from her, Olive screams as someone bumps her arm, sending a cascade of ice-cold soda all over her face and down the front of her brand new sweater. Kids point and start to laugh. Olive looks around in embarrassment, her eyes finally settling on Gwendy, and then she storms away and disappears into the public restroom.

Gwendy, remembering her dream about Frankie Stone, suddenly wants to go home and shut the door of her room and crawl under the covers.

14

THE DAY BEFORE SHE'S scheduled to attend junior prom with Walter Dean, Gwendy rolls out of bed late to discover that the basement has flooded overnight after a particularly heavy spring thunderstorm.

"It's wetter than a taco fart down there and just as smelly," Mr. Peterson tells her. "You sure you want to go down?"

Gwendy nods, trying to hide her rising panic. "I need to check on some old books and a pile of clothes I left for the laundry."

Mr. Peterson shrugs his shoulders and returns his gaze to the small television on the kitchen counter. "Make sure you take off your shoes before you go. And hey, might want to wear a life preserver."

Gwendy hurries down the basement stairs before he can change his mind and wades into a pool of ankle-high scummy gray water. Earlier this morning Mr. Peterson managed to unclog the sump pump, and Gwendy can hear it chugging away over in the far corner, but it's going to have a long day. She can tell by the water line that marks the basement's stone walls that the floodwater has dropped maybe two inches at the most.

She wades to the opposite side of the basement where the button box is hidden and pushes aside the old bureau. She drops to a knee in the corner and reaches down into the cloudy water, unable to see her hands, and works the stone free.

Her fingers touch wet canvas. She pulls the water-logged bag out of its hidey-hole, puts it aside, then picks up the loose stone and places it back into the wall so her father won't notice it once the water has finished receding.

She reaches to the side again for the canvas bag containing the box and coins—and it isn't there.

She flails her hands under the water, trying desperately to locate the bag, but it's nowhere to be found. Black dots swim in her vision and she suddenly feels light-headed. She realizes she's forgotten to breathe, so she opens her mouth and takes in a big gulp of foul, moldy basement air. Her eyes and brain immediately begin to clear.

Gwendy takes one more calming breath and once again reaches down into the dirty water, this time trying her other side. Right away, her fingers brush the canvas bag. She gets to her feet and like a weightlifter performing a deadlift squat, she raises the heavy bag to her waist and waddles her way across the basement to the shelves next to the washer and dryer. She grabs a couple of dry towels from an upper shelf and does the best she can to wrap the canvas bag.

"You okay down there?" her father hollers from upstairs. She hears footsteps on the ceiling above her. "Need any help? Scuba tank and fins, maybe?"

"No, no," Gwendy says, hurrying to make sure the bag is fully concealed. Her heart is a triphammer in her chest. "I'll be up in a few."

"If you say so." She listens to her father's muffled footsteps again, but going away. Thank God.

She grabs the bag again and shuffles across the flooded

basement as fast as her tired legs will carry her, grunting with the weight of the box and the silver coins.

Once she is safely inside her bedroom, she locks the door behind her and unwraps the canvas bag. The button box appears undamaged, but how would she really know? She pulls the lever on the left side of the box and after a breathless moment when she is absolutely convinced the box is broken after all, the little shelf slides open without a sound and on it is a chocolate monkey the size of a jelly bean. She quickly stuffs the chocolate into her mouth and that gorgeous flavor takes her away again. She closes her eyes while it melts on her tongue.

The bag is ripped in several places and will have to be replaced, but Gwendy isn't worried about that. She looks around her bedroom and settles on the bottom of her closet, where her shoeboxes are stacked in messy piles. Her parents never bother with her closet these days.

She removes an old pair of boots from their oversized cardboard box and tosses them to the opposite end of the closet. She carefully places the button box inside and adds the pile of silver coins. Once the lid is securely back on the shoebox, she slides it—it's too heavy to pick up now; the cardboard would surely tear—into the shadows at the very back of her closet. Once that's done, she stacks other shoeboxes on top and in front of it.

She gets to her feet, backs up, and surveys her work. Convinced that she's done a competent job, she picks up the soaked canvas bag and heads for the kitchen to throw it away and grab some cereal for breakfast.

She lazes around the house the rest of the day, watching television and skimming her history book. Every thirty minutes or so—more than a dozen times in all—she gets up from the sofa, walks down the hallway, and peeks her head into her bedroom to make sure the box is still safe.

The next night is the prom, and she finds that she actually has to force herself to put on her pink gown and make-up and leave the house.

Is this my life now? she thinks as she enters the Castle Rock gym. *Is that box my life?*

$$15$$

SELLING THE SILVER COINS isn't back on Gwendy's radar until she sees the advertising flyer taped to the front window of the Castle Rock Diner. After that, it's pretty much all she can think about. There was that one trip to the coin shop, true, but it was mostly of an exploratory nature. Now, however, things have changed. Gwendy wants to attend an Ivy League university after she graduates from high school—and those places don't come cheap. She plans to apply for grants and scholarships, and with her grades she's sure she'll get something, but enough? Probably not. *Surely* not.

What *is* a sure thing are the 1891 Morgan silver dollars stacked inside a shoebox in the back of her closet. Over a hundred of them at last count.

Gwendy knows from leafing through back issues of *COINage* magazine at the drug store that the fair-trade price of the Morgans is not just holding steady; their value is still rising. According to the magazine, inflation and global unrest are driving the market in gold and silver coins. Her first idea was to sell enough of the coins (maybe in Portland, more likely in Boston) to pay for college and figure out how to explain the sudden windfall only when it becomes absolutely necessary. Maybe she'll say she found it. Hard to believe, but also hard to disprove. (The best-laid plans of sixteen-year-olds are rarely thought out.)

The Coin & Stamp Show flyer gives Gwendy another idea. A better idea.

The plan is to take two of the silver dollars, enough to test the waters, and bike down to the VFW first thing this weekend to see what she can get for them. If they actually sell, and for real money, then she'll know.

16

THE FIRST THING GWENDY notices when she walks into the VFW at ten-fifteen on Saturday morning is the sheer size of the place. It didn't look nearly as spacious from the outside. The dealer tables are arranged in a long, enclosed rectangle. The sellers, mostly men, stand on the inside of the rectangle. The customers, of whom there are already more than two or three dozen, circle the tables with wary eyes and nervous fingers. There doesn't seem to be a discernible pattern to the set-up—coin dealers here, stamp hucksters there—and more than a few of the merchants deal in both. A couple even have rare sports and tobacco cards fanned out across their tables. She is flabbergasted to see a signed Mickey Mantle card priced at $2,900, but in a way, relieved. It makes her silver dollars look like pretty small beans in comparison.

She stands in the entryway and takes it all in. It's a whole new world, exotic and intimidating, and she feels overwhelmed. It must be obvious to anyone watching her because a nearby dealer calls out, "Ya lost, honey? Anything I can help ya with?"

He's a chubby man in his thirties wearing glasses and an Orioles baseball cap. There's food in his beard and a twinkle in his eyes.

Gwendy approaches his table. "I'm just looking right now, thanks."

"Looking to buy or looking to sell?" The man's eyes drop to Gwendy's bare legs and linger there longer than they should. When he looks up again, he's grinning and Gwendy doesn't like that twinkle anymore.

"Just looking," she says, quickly walking away.

She watches a man two tables down examining a tiny stamp with a magnifying glass and tweezers. She overhears him say, "I can go seventy dollars and that's already twenty over my limit. My wife will kill me if I . . . " She doesn't stick around to see if he seals the deal.

At the far end of the rectangle, she comes to a table covered exclusively with coins. She spots a Morgan silver dollar in the center of the last row. She takes this as a good sign. The man behind the table is bald and old, how old she's not entirely sure, but at least old enough to be a grandfather. He smiles at Gwendy and doesn't glance at her legs, which is a good start. He taps the nametag attached to his shirt. "Name's Jon Leonard, like it says, but I go by Lenny to my friends. You look friendly, so is there anything special I can help you with today? Got a Lincoln penny book you want to finish filling out? Maybe looking for a buffalo nickel or a few commemorative state quarters? I got a Utah, very good condition and scarce."

"I actually have something I'd like to sell. Maybe."

"Uh-huh, okay, lemme take a look and I can tell you if we might do some business."

Gwendy takes the coins—each in its own little plastic envelope—out of her pocket and hands them to him. Lenny's fingers are thick and gnarled, but he slips the coins out with practiced ease, holding them by their thickness, not touching the heads and tails sides. Gwendy notices his eyes flash wider. He whistles. "Mind if I ask where you got these?"

Gwendy tells him what she told the coin dealer in Portland. "My grandfather passed away recently and left them to me."

The man looks genuinely pained. "I'm really sorry to hear that, honey."

"Thank you," she says, and puts her hand out. "I'm Gwendy Peterson."

The man gives it a firm shake. "Gwendy. I like that."

"Me too," Gwendy says and smiles. "Good thing, since I'm stuck with it."

The man turns on a small desk light and uses a magnifying glass to examine the silver dollars. "Never seen one in mint condition before, and here you got two of em." He looks up at her. "How old are you, Miss Gwendy, if you don't mind my asking?"

"Sixteen."

The man snaps his fingers and points at her. "Looking to buy a car, I bet."

She shakes her head. "One day, but I'm thinking of selling these to make some money for college. I want to go to an Ivy League school after I graduate."

The man nods his head with approval. "Good for you." He studies the coins again with the magnifying glass. "Be honest with me now, Miss Gwendy, your folks know you're selling these?"

"Yes, sir, they do. They're okay with it because it's for a good cause."

His gaze turns shrewd. "But they're not with you, I notice."

Gwendy might not have been ready for this at four-teen, but she's older now, and can hit the occasional adult curveball. "They both said I have to start fending for my-self sometime, and this might be a good place to start. Also, I read the magazine you've got there." She points. "*COINage?*"

"Uh-huh, uh-huh." Lenny puts down the magnifying glass and gives her his full attention. "Well, Miss Gwendy Peterson, a Morgan silver dollar of this vintage and in Near Mint condition can sell for anywhere from seven hundred and twenty-five dollars to eight hundred. A Morgan in *this* condition . . . " He shakes his head. "I honestly don't know."

Gwendy didn't practice this part—how could she?—but she really likes the old man, so she wings it. "My mom works at a car dealership, and they have a saying about some of the cars: 'Priced to sell.' So . . . could you pay eight hundred each? Would that be priced to sell?"

"Yes, ma'am, it would," he says with no hesitation. "Only are you sure? One of the bigger shops might be able to—"

"I'm sure. If you can pay eight hundred apiece, we have a deal."

The old man chuckles and sticks his hand out. "Then, Miss Gwendy Peterson, we have ourselves a deal." They shake on it. "I'll write you up a receipt and get you paid."

"Um . . . I'm sure you're trustworthy, Lenny, but I really wouldn't feel comfortable with a check."

"With me up in Toronto or down in D.C. tomor-row, who'd blame you?" He drops her a wink. "Besides, I got a saying of my own: Cash don't tattle. And what

Uncle Sammy don't know about our business won't hurt him."

Lenny slips the coins into their transparent envelopes and disappears them somewhere beneath the table. Once he's counted out sixteen crisp one hundred dollar bills—Gwendy still can't believe this is happening—he writes a receipt, tears out a copy, and lays it atop the cash. "I put my phone number on there too in case your folks have any questions. How far is home?"

"About a mile. I rode my bike."

He considers that. "Lotta money for a young girl, Gwendy. Think maybe you should call your parents for a ride?"

"No need," she says, smiling. "I can take care of myself."

The old man's eyebrows dance as he laughs. "I bet you can."

He stuffs the money and the receipt into an envelope. He folds the envelope in half and uses about a yard of scotch tape to seal it tight. "See if that'll fit nice and snug in your shorts pocket," he says, handing over the envelope.

Gwendy stuffs it into her pocket and pats the outside. "Snug as a bug in a rug."

"I like you, girl, I do. Got style and got sand. A combination that can't be beat." Lenny turns to the dealer on his left. "Hank, you mind watching my table for a minute?"

"Only if you bring me back a soda," Hank says.

"Done." Lenny slips out from behind his table and escorts Gwendy to the door. "You sure you're going to be okay?"

"Positive. Thanks again, Mr. Lenny," she says, feeling the weight of the money inside her pocket. "I really appreciate it."

"The appreciation is all mine, Miss Gwendy." He holds the door open for her. "Good luck with the Ivy League."

17

GWENDY SQUINTS IN THE May sunlight as she unlocks her bike from a nearby tree. It never occurred to her this morning that the VFW wouldn't have a bike rack—then again, how many vets did you see cruising around Castle Rock on bicycles?

She pats her pocket to make sure the envelope is still nice and snug, then straddles her bike and pushes off. Halfway across the parking lot, she spots Frankie Stone and Jimmy Sines, checking car doors and peering into windows. Some unlucky person was going to walk out of the Coin & Stamp Show today and find their car ransacked.

Gwendy pedals faster, hoping to slip away unnoticed, but she's not that lucky.

"Hey, sugar tits!" Frankie yells from behind her, and then he's sprinting ahead and cutting her off, blocking her exit from the parking lot. He waves his arms at her. "Whoa, whoa, whoa!"

Gwendy skids to a stop in front him. "Leave me alone, Frankie."

It takes him a moment to catch his breath. "I just wanted to ask you a question, that's all."

"Then ask it and get out of my way." She glances around for an escape route.

Jimmy Sines emerges from behind a parked car. Stands

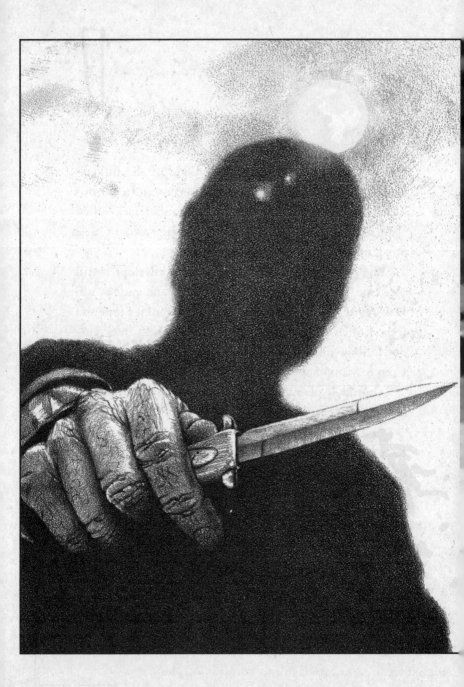

on the other side of her with his arms crossed. He looks at Frankie. "Sugar tits, huh?"

Frankie grins. "This is the one I was telling you about." He walks closer to Gwendy, trails a finger up her leg. She swats it away.

"Ask your question and move."

"C'mon, don't be like that," he says. "I was just wondering how your ass is. You always had such a tight one. Must make it hard to take a shit." He's touching her leg again. Not just a finger; his whole hand.

"These boys bothering you, Miss Gwendy?"

All three of them turn and look. Lenny is standing there.

"Get lost, old man," Frankie says, taking a step toward him.

"I don't think so. You okay, Gwendy?"

"I'm okay now." She pushes off and starts pedaling. "Gotta get going or I'm gonna be late for lunch. Thanks!"

They watch her go, and then Frankie and Jimmy turn back to Lenny. "It's two on one. I like those odds, old-timer."

Lenny reaches into his pants pocket and comes out with a flick knife. Engraved on its silver side are the only two words of Latin these boys understand: *Semper Fi.* His gnarled hand does a limber trick and presto, there's a six-inch blade glittering in the sunlight. "Now it's two on two."

Frankie takes off across the parking lot, Jimmy right behind him.

18

"IMAGINE THAT, GWENDY WINS again," Sallie says, rolling her eyes and tossing her cards onto the carpet in front of her.

There are four of them sitting in a circle on the Peterson's den floor: Gwendy, Sallie Ackerman, Brigette Desjardin, and Josie Wainwright. The other three girls are seniors at Castle Rock High and frequent visitors to the Peterson home this school year.

"You ever notice that?" Josie says, scrunching up her face. "Gwendy never loses. At pretty much anything."

Sallie rolls with it: "Best grades in school. Best athlete in school. Prettiest girl in school. And a card shark to boot."

"Oh, shut up," Gwendy says, gathering the cards. It's her turn to shuffle and deal. "That's not true."

But Gwendy knows it is true, and although Josie is just teasing in her usual goofy way (who else would aspire to be lead singer in a group called the Pussycats?), she also knows that Sallie isn't teasing at all. Sallie is getting sick of it. Sallie is getting jealous.

Gwendy first realized it was becoming an issue a few months earlier. Yes, she's a fast runner, maybe the fastest varsity runner in the county. Maybe in the entire state. Really? Yes, really. And then there are her grades. She always earned good ones in school, but in younger years she had to study hard for those grades, and even then, there were usually a handful of B's, along with all those A's on her report cards. Now she barely hits the books at all, and her grades are the highest in the whole junior class. She even finds herself writing down the wrong answers from time to time, just to avoid, ho-hum, another perfect test score. Or forcing herself to lose at cards and arcade games just to keep her friends from becoming suspicious. Regardless of her efforts, they know something is weird anyway.

Buttons aside, coins aside, little chocolate treats aside, the box has given her . . . well . . . *powers.*

Really? Yes, really.

She never gets hurt anymore. No strained muscles from track. No bumps or bruises from soccer. No nicks or scratches from being clumsy. Not even a stubbed toe or broken fingernail. She can't remember the last time she's needed a Band-Aid. Even her period is easy. No more cramps, a few drops on a sanitary pad, and done. These days Gwendy's blood stays where it belongs.

These realizations are both fascinating and terrifying to Gwendy. She knows it's the box somehow doing this— or perhaps the chocolate treats—but they really are one and the same. Sometimes, she wishes she could talk to someone about it. Sometimes, she wishes she were still friends with Olive. She might be the only person in the world who would listen and believe her.

Gwendy places the deck of cards on the floor and gets to her feet. "Who wants popcorn and lemonade?"

Three hands go up. Gwendy disappears into the kitchen.

19

THERE ARE BIG CHANGES in Gwendy's life during the fall and winter of 1978, most of them good ones.

She finally gets her driver's license in late September, and a month later on her seventeenth birthday, her parents surprise her with a gently used Ford Fiesta from the dealership where her mom works. The car is bright orange and the radio only works when it wants to, but none of that matters to Gwendy. She loves this car and plasters its meager back deck with big daisy decals and a NO NUKES bumper sticker left over from the sixties.

She also gets her first real job (she's earned money in the past babysitting and raking leaves, but she doesn't count those), working at the drive-in snack bar three nights a week. It surprises no one that she proves especially adept at her duties and earns a promotion by her third month of employment.

She is also named captain of the varsity outdoor track team.

Gwendy still wonders about Mr. Farris and she still worries about the button box, but not nearly with the same nervous intensity as she once did. She also still locks her bedroom door and slides the box out from inside her closet and pulls the lever for a chocolate treat, but not as often as she once did. Maybe twice a week now, tops.

In fact, she's finally relaxed to the point where she actually finds herself wondering one afternoon: *Do you think you might eventually just forget about it?*

But then she stumbles upon a newspaper article about the accidental release of anthrax spores at a Soviet bioweapons facility that killed hundreds of people and threatened the countryside, and she knows that she will never forget about the box and its red button and the responsibility she has taken on. Exactly what responsibility is that? She's not sure, but thinks it might be to just keep things from, well, getting out of hand. It sounds crazy, but feels just about right.

Near the end of her junior year, in March 1979, Gwendy watches television coverage of the nuclear meltdown at Three Mile Island in Pennsylvania. She becomes obsessed, combing over all the coverage she can find, mainly to determine how much of a danger the accident poses to surrounding communities and cities and states. The idea worries her.

She tells herself she will press the red button again if she has to and make Three Mile go away. Only Jonestown weighs heavy on her mind. Was that crazy religious fuck going to do it anyway, or did she somehow push him into it? Were the nurses going to poison those babies anyway, or did Gwendy Peterson somehow give them the extra crazy they needed to do it? What if the button box is like the monkey's paw in that story? What if it makes things worse instead of better? What if *she* makes things worse?

With Jonestown, I didn't understand. Now I do. And isn't that why Mr. Farris trusted me with the box in the first place? To do the right thing when the time came?

When the situation at Three Mile Island is finally contained and subsequent studies prove there is no further danger, Gwendy is overjoyed—and relieved. She feels like she's dodged a bullet.

20

THE FIRST THING GWENDY notices when she strolls into Castle Rock High on the last Thursday morning of the school year are the somber expressions on the faces of several teachers and a cluster of girls gathered by the cafeteria doors, many of them crying.

"What's going on?" she asks Josie Wainwright at the locker they share.

"What do you mean?"

"Kids are crying in the lobby. Everyone looks upset."

"Oh, that," Josie says, with no more gravity than if she were talking about what she'd eaten for breakfast that morning. "Some girl killed herself last night. Jumped off the Suicide Stairs."

Gwendy's entire body goes cold.

"What girl?" Barely a whisper, because she's afraid she already knows the answer. She doesn't know how she knows, but she does.

"Olive . . . uhh . . . "

"Kepnes. Her name is Olive Kepnes."

"*Was* Olive Kepnes," Josie says, and starts humming "The Dead March."

Gwendy wants to smack her, right in her pretty freckled face, but she can't lift her arms. Her entire body is numb. After a moment, she wills her legs to move and walks out of the school and to her car. She drives directly home and locks herself inside her bedroom.

21

IT'S MY FAULT, GWENDY thinks for the hundredth time, as she pulls her car into the Castle View Recreational Park parking lot. It's almost midnight and the gravel lot is empty. *If I'd stayed her friend . . .*

She's told her parents that she's sleeping over at Maggie Bean's house with a bunch of girlfriends from school—all of them telling stories and reminiscing about Olive and supporting each other in their grief—and her parents believe her. They don't understand that Gwendy stopped running with Olive's crowd a long time ago. Most of the girls Gwendy hangs out with now wouldn't recognize Olive if she were standing in front of them. Other than a quick "Hey" in the hallways at school or the occasional encounter at the supermarket, Gwendy hasn't spoken to Olive in probably six or seven months. They eventually made up after their fight in Gwendy's bedroom, but nothing had been the same since that day. And the truth of the matter is that had been okay with Gwendy. Olive was getting to be too damn sensitive, too high maintenance, just . . . too *Olive.*

"It's my fault," Gwendy mutters as she gets out of the car. She'd like to believe that's just adolescent angst—what her father calls Teenage It's All About Me Complex—but she can't quite get there. Can't help realizing that if she and Olive had stayed tight, the girl would still be alive.

There's no moon in the sky tonight and she forgot to bring along a flashlight, but that doesn't matter to Gwendy. She strikes off in the dark at a brisk pace and heads for the Suicide Stairs, unsure of what she's going to do once she gets there.

She's halfway across the park before she realizes she doesn't want to go to the Suicide Stairs at all. In fact, she never wants to see them again. Because—this is crazy, but in the dark it has the force of truth—what if she met Olive halfway up? Olive with her head half bashed in and one eye dangling on her cheek? What if Olive pushed her? Or talked her into jumping?

Gwendy turns around, climbs back into her cute little Fiesta, and drives home. It occurs to her that she can make damn sure no one jumps from those stairs again.

22

The Castle Rock Call
Saturday edition—May 26, 1979

Sometime between the hours of one a.m. and six a.m. on the morning of Friday, May 25, a portion of the Northeastern corner of the Castle View Recreational Park was destroyed. The historic stairway and viewing platform, as well as nearly one-half acre of state-owned property, collapsed, leaving a bewildering pile of iron, steel, earth, and rubble below.

Numerous authorities are still on site investigating the scene to determine if the collapse was a result of natural or man-made causes.

"It's just the strangest thing, and way too early for answers," Castle Rock Sheriff George Bannerman commented. "We don't know if there was a minor earthquake centered in this area or if someone somehow sabotaged the stairs or what. We're bringing in additional investigators from Portland, but they're not expected to arrive until tomorrow morning, so it's best we wait until that time to make any further announcements."

Castle View was recently the scene of tragedy when the body of a seventeen-year-old female was discovered at the base of the cliff . . .

23

GWENDY IS SICK FOR days afterward. Mr. and Mrs. Peterson believe grief is causing their daughter's fever and upset stomach, but Gwendy knows better. It's the box. It's the price she has to pay for pushing the red button. She heard the rumble of the collapsing rocks, and had to run into the bathroom and vomit.

She manages to shower and change out of baggy sweatpants and a t-shirt long enough to attend Olive's funeral on Monday morning, but only after her mother's prompting. If it were up to Gwendy, she wouldn't have left her bedroom. Maybe not until she was twenty-four or so.

The church is SRO. Most of Castle Rock High School is there—teachers and students alike; even Frankie Stone is there, smirking in the back pew—and Gwendy hates them all for showing up. None of them even liked Olive when she was alive. None of them even *knew* her.

Yeah, like I did, Gwendy thinks. *But at least I did something about it. There's that. No one else will jump from those stairs. Ever.*

Walking from the gravesite back to her parents' car after the service, someone calls out to her. She turns and sees Olive's father.

Mr. Kepnes is a short man, barrel-chested, with rosy cheeks and kind eyes. Gwendy has always adored him and shared a special bond with Olive's father, perhaps because they once shared the burden of being overweight, or perhaps because Mr. Kepnes is one of the sweetest people Gwendy has ever known.

She held it together pretty well during the funeral service, but now, with Olive's father approaching, arms outstretched, Gwendy loses it and begins to sob.

"It's okay, honey," Mr. Kepnes says, wrapping her up in a bear hug. "It's okay."

Gwendy vehemently shakes her head. "It's not . . . " Her face is a mess of tears and snot. She wipes it with her sleeve.

"Listen to me." Mr. Kepnes leans down and makes sure Gwendy is looking at him. It's wrong for the father to be comforting the friend—the *ex*-friend—but that is exactly what he's doing. "It has to be okay. I know it doesn't feel like it right now, but it *has* to be. Got it?"

Gwendy nods her head and whispers, "Got it." She just wants to go home.

"You were her best friend in the world, Gwendy. Maybe in a couple weeks, you can come see us at the house. We can all sit down and have some lunch and talk. I think Olive would've liked that."

It's too much, and Gwendy can no longer bear it. She pulls away and flees for the car, her apologetic parents trailing behind her.

The final two days of school are canceled because of the tragedy. Gwendy spends most of the next week on the den sofa buried beneath a blanket. She has many bad dreams—the worst of them featuring a man in a black suit and black hat, shiny silver coins where his eyes should be—and often cries out in her sleep. She's afraid of what she might say during these nightmares. She's afraid her parents might overhear.

Eventually, the fever breaks and Gwendy reenters the world. She spends the majority of her summer vacation working as much as she can at the snack bar. When she's not working, she's jogging the sunbaked roads of Castle Rock or locked inside her bedroom listening to music. Anything to keep her mind busy.

The button box stays hidden in the back of the closet. Gwendy still thinks about it—boy, does she—but she wants nothing to do with it anymore. Not the chocolate treats, not the silver coins, and most of all, not the goddamn buttons. Most days, she hates the box and everything it reminds her of, and she fantasizes about getting rid of it. Crushing it with a sledge-hammer or wrapping it up in a blanket and driving it out to the dump.

But she knows she can't do that. *What if someone else finds it? What if someone else pushes one of the buttons?*

She leaves it there in the dark shadows of her closet, growing cobwebs and gathering dust. *Let the damn thing rot for all I care,* she thinks.

24

GWENDY IS SUNBATHING IN the back yard, listening to Bob Seger & the Silver Bullet Band on a Sony Walkman, when Mrs. Peterson comes outside carrying a glass of ice water. Her mother hands Gwendy the glass and sits down on the end of the lawn chair.

"You doing okay, honey?"

Gwendy slips off the headphones and takes a drink. "I'm fine."

Mrs. Peterson gives her a look.

"Okay, maybe not fine, but I'm doing better."

"I hope so." She gives Gwendy's leg a squeeze. "You know we're here if you ever want to talk. About anything."

"I know."

"You're just so quiet all the time. We worry about you."

"I . . . have a lot on my mind."

"Still not ready to call Mr. Kepnes back?"

Gwendy doesn't answer, only shakes her head.

Mrs. Peterson gets up from the lawn chair. "Just remember one thing."

"What's that?"

"It will get better. It always does."

It's pretty much what Olive's father said. Gwendy hopes it's true, but she has her doubts.

"Hey, mom?"

Mrs. Peterson stops and turns around.

"I love you."

25

As it turns out, Mr. Kepnes was wrong and Mrs. Peterson was right. Things are not okay, but they do get better.

Gwendy meets a boy.

His name is Harry Streeter. He's eighteen years old, tall and handsome and funny. He's new to Castle Rock (his family just moved in a couple weeks ago as a result of his father's job transfer), and if it's not a genuine case of Love At First Sight, it's pretty close.

Gwendy is behind the counter at the snack bar, hustling tubs of buttered popcorn, Laffy Taffy, Pop Rocks, and soda by the gallon, when Harry walks in with his younger brother. She notices him right away, and he notices her. When it's his turn to order, the spark jumps and neither of them can manage a complete sentence.

Harry returns the next night, by himself this time, even though *The Amityville Horror* and *Phantasm* are still playing, and once again he waits his turn in line. This time, along with a small popcorn and soda, he asks Gwendy for her phone number.

He calls the next afternoon, and that evening picks her up in a candy-apple red Mustang convertible. With his blond hair and blue eyes, he looks like a movie star. They go bowling and have pizza on their first date, skating at the Gates Falls Roller Rink on their second, and after that they are inseparable. Picnics at Castle Lake, day trips into Portland to visit museums and the big shopping mall, movies, walks. They even jog together, keeping in perfect step.

By the time school starts, Gwendy is wearing Harry's school ring on a silver chain around her neck and trying to figure out how to talk to her mother about birth control. (This talk won't happen until the school year is almost two months old, but when it does, Gwendy is relieved to find that her mother is not only understanding, she even calls and makes the doctor's appointment for her—go, Mom.)

There are other changes, too. Much to the dismay of the coaching staff and her teammates, Gwendy decides to skip her senior season on the girls' soccer team. Her heart just isn't in it. Besides, Harry isn't a jock, he's a serious photographer, and this way they can spend more time together.

Gwendy can't remember ever being this happy. The button box still surfaces in her thoughts from time to time, but it's almost as if the whole thing was a dream from her childhood. *Mr. Farris. The chocolate treats. The silver dollars. The red button. Was any of it real?*

Running, however, is not negotiable. When indoor track season rolls around in late November, Gwendy is ready to rock and roll. Harry is there on the sidelines for every meet, snapping pix and cheering her on. Despite training most of the summer and into the fall, Gwendy finishes a disappointing fourth in Counties and doesn't qualify for States for the first time in her high school career. She also brings home two B's on her semester-ending report card in December. On the third morning of

Christmas break, Gwendy wakes up and shuffles to the hallway bathroom to take her morning pee. When she's finished, she uses her right foot to slide the scale out from underneath the bathroom vanity, and she steps onto it. Her instincts are right: she has gained six pounds.

26

GWENDY'S FIRST IMPULSE IS to sprint down the hallway, lock her bedroom door, and yank out the button box so she can pull the small lever and devour a magic chocolate treat. She can almost hear the voices chanting in her head: *Goodyear! Goodyear! Goodyear!*

But she doesn't do that.

Instead, she closes the toilet lid and sits back down. *Let's see, I bombed my track season, pulled a pair of B's for the semester (one of them just barely a B, although her parents don't know that), and I gained weight (six whole pounds!) for the first time in years—and I'm still the happiest I've ever been.*

I don't need it, she thinks. *More importantly, I don't* want *it.* The realization makes her head sing and her heart soar, and Gwendy returns to her bedroom with a spring to her step and a smile on her face.

27

THE NEXT MORNING, GWENDY wakes up on the floor of her closet.

She's cradling the button box in her arms like a faithful lover and her right thumb is resting a half-inch from the black button.

She stifles a scream and jerks her hand away, scrambling like a crab out of the closet. A safe distance away, she gets to her feet and notices something that makes her head swim: the narrow wooden shelf on the button box is standing open. On it is a tiny chocolate treat: a parrot, every feather perfect.

Gwendy wants more than anything to run from the room, slam the door behind her, and never return—but she knows she can't do that. So what *can* she do?

She approaches the button box with as much stealth as she can muster. When she's within a few feet of it, the image of a wild animal asleep in its lair flashes in her head, and she thinks: *The button box doesn't just* give *power; it is* power.

"But I won't," she mutters. *Won't what?* "Won't give in."

Before she can chicken out, she lunges and snatches the piece of chocolate from the little shelf. She backs out of the bedroom, afraid to turn her back on the button box, hurries down the hall into the bathroom, where she hurls the chocolate parrot into the toilet and flushes it away.

And for a while, everything is all right. She thinks the button box goes to sleep, but she doesn't trust that, not a bit. Because even if it does, it sleeps with one eye open.

28

Two life-changing events occur at the start of Gwendy's final semester of high school: her college application to study psychology at Brown University is granted an early acceptance, and she sleeps with Harry for the first time.

There've been several false starts over the past few months—Gwendy has been on the pill for at least that long—but each time she isn't quite ready, and gallant Harry Streeter doesn't pressure her. The deed finally goes down in Harry's candlelit bedroom on the Friday night of his father's big work party, and it is every bit as awkward and wonderful as expected. To make the necessary improvements, Gwendy and Harry do it again the next two nights in the back seat of Harry's Mustang. It's cramped back there, but it only gets better.

Gwendy runs outdoor track again when spring comes, and places in the top three in her first two meets. Her grades are currently A's across the board (although History is hovering in the danger zone at 91%), and she hasn't stepped on a scale since the week before Christmas. She's done with that nonsense.

She still suffers from the occasional nightmare (the one featuring the well-dressed man with the silver coin eyes continuing to be the most terrifying), and she still knows the button box wants her back, but she tries not to dwell

on that. Most days she is successful, thanks to Harry and what she thinks of as her new life. She often daydreams that Mr. Farris will return to take back possession of the button box, relieving her of the responsibility. Or that the box will eventually forget about her. That would sound stupid to an outsider, but Gwendy has come to believe that the box is in some way alive.

Only there will be no forgetting. She discovers this on a breezy spring afternoon in April, while she and Harry are flying a kite in the outfield of the Castle Rock High baseball field (Gwendy was delighted when he showed up at her house with the kite in tow). She notices something small and dark emerge from the tree-line bordering the school property. At first she thinks it's an animal of some sort. A bunny or perhaps a woodchuck on the move. But as it gets closer—and it seems to head directly at them— she realizes that it's not an animal at all. It's a hat.

Harry is holding the spool of string and staring up at the red, white, and blue kite with wide eyes and a smile on his face. He doesn't notice the black hat coming in their direction, not moving with the wind but against it. He doesn't notice the hat slow down as it approaches, then suddenly change direction and swoop a complete circle around his horrorstruck girlfriend—almost as if kissing her hello, so nice to see you again—before it skitters off and disappears behind the bleachers that run alongside the third base line.

Harry notices none of these things because it's a gorgeous spring afternoon in Castle Rock and he's flying a kite with the love of his young life at his side, and everything is perfect.

29

THE FIRST HALF OF May passes in a blur of classes, tests, and graduation planning. Everything from sizing caps and gowns, to sending out commencement notices in the mail, to finalizing graduation night party arrangements. Final exams are scheduled for the week of May 19th and the Castle Rock High School graduation ceremony will take place on the football field the following Tuesday, the 27th.

For Gwendy and Harry, everything is set. After the ceremony is finished, they will change clothes and head to Brigette Desjardin's house for the biggest and best graduation party in the school. The next morning, they leave for a week-long camping trip to Casco Bay, just the two of them. Once they return home, it will be work at the drive-in for Gwendy and at the hardware store for Harry. In early August, a ten-day vacation at the coast with Harry's family. After that, it's on to college (Brown for Gwendy; nearby Providence for Harry) and an exciting new chapter in their lives. They can't wait.

Gwendy knows she will have to make a decision about what to do with the button box once it's time to leave for college, but that's months in the future, and it's not a priority this evening. The biggest decision facing Gwendy at the moment is which dress to wear to Brigette's party.

"Good lord," Harry says, smiling. "Just pick one, already.

Or go as you are." *As she is* happens to be in bra and panties.

Gwendy gives him a poke in the ribs and turns to the next page in the catalog. "Easy for you to say, mister. You'll put on jeans and a t-shirt and look like a million bucks."

"You look like a *trillion* in your underwear."

They're lying on their stomachs on Gwendy's bed. Harry is toying with her hair; Gwendy is paging through the glossy Brown catalog. Mr. and Mrs. Peterson are at dinner with neighbors down the block and not expected back until late. Gwendy and Harry came in an hour ago, and Gwendy was mildly surprised to find she didn't need to use her key. The front door was not only unlocked but slightly ajar. (Her dad is big on locking up; likes to say Castle Rock isn't the little country town it used to be.) But everyone forgets stuff, plus Dad's not getting any younger. And with thoughts of the party to occupy them—not to mention thirty minutes of heaven in her bed beforehand— neither notices a few splinters sticking out around the lock. Or the pry marks.

"C'mon," Harry says now, "you're a knockout. It doesn't matter what you wear."

"I just can't decide whether to go strapless and dressy or long and flowy and summery." She tosses the catalog on the floor and gets up. "Here, I'll let you choose." She walks to the closet, opens the door . . . and smells him before she sees him: beer, cigarettes, and sweat-funk.

She starts to turn around and call to Harry, but she's too late. A pair of strong arms reach out from the shadows and hanging clothes and pull her to the floor. Now she finds her voice, "Harry!"

He's already off the bed and moving. He hurls himself

at Gwendy's attacker, and amidst a tangle of clothes hangers and blouses, they grapple across the floor.

Gwendy pushes herself back up against the wall and is stunned to see Frankie Stone, dressed in camo pants, dark glasses, and t-shirt, as if he thinks he's a soldier on a secret mission, rolling around her bedroom floor with her boyfriend. That's bad, but something else is worse: lying on the closet floor, half-buried in fallen clothes, is a scatter of silver dollars . . . and the button box. Frankie must have found it while he was waiting for her, or while he was waiting for Harry to leave.

Has he pushed any of the buttons?

Is Africa gone? Or Europe?

The two young men crash into the night table. Hairbrushes and makeup rain down on them. Frankie's Secret Agent Man shades fly off. Harry outweighs Frankie by at least thirty pounds, and pins the skinny little dipshit to the floor. "Gwen?" He sounds perfectly calm. "Call the police. I've got this skanky little motherf—"

But that's when it all goes to hell. Frankie is skinny, Frankie doesn't have much in the way of muscles, but that is also true of snakes. He moves like a snake now, first wriggling, then hoisting one knee into the crotch of Harry's boxers. Harry makes an *ooof* sound and tilts forward. Frankie pulls one hand free, makes finger-prongs, and jabs them into Harry's eyes. Harry screams, claps a hand to his face, and falls to one side.

Gwendy pushes herself up in time to see Frankie coming at her, grabbing for her with one hand and trying to get something out of the pocket of his camo pants with the other. Before he can touch her, Harry tackles him and they go reeling into the closet, falling and pulling down more dresses and skirts and pants and tops, so at first Gwendy can see nothing but a pile of clothes that appears to be breathing.

Then a hand emerges—a dirty hand with blue webbing tattooed across the back. It paws around aimlessly at first, then finds the button box. Gwendy tries to scream, but nothing comes out; her throat is locked tight. The box comes down corner first. Once . . . then twice . . . then three times. The first time it connects with Harry's head, the sound is muffled by clothes. The second time it's louder. The third time, the hit produces a sickening crack, like a breaking branch, and the corner of the box is coated with blood and hair.

The clothes heave and slide. Frankie emerges, still holding the button box in one tattooed hand. He's grinning. Behind him she can see Harry. His eyes are closed, his mouth hangs open.

"Don't know what this is, pretty girl, but it hits real good."

She darts past him. He doesn't try to stop her. She goes on her knees beside Harry and lifts his head with one hand. She cups the other palm in front of his nose and mouth, but she already knows. The box used to be light, but for a while tonight it was heavy, because it *wanted* to be heavy. Frankie Stone has used it to crush the top of Harry Streeter's skull. There is no breath on her palm.

"You killed him! You filthy son of a bitch, *you killed him!*"

"Yeah, well, maybe. Whatever." He seems uninterested in the dead boy; his eyes are busily crawling over Gwendy's body, and she understands he's crazy. A box that can destroy the world is in the hands of a crazy person who thinks he's a Green Beret or a Navy SEAL or something like that. "What is this thing? Besides where you store your silver dollars, that is? How much are they worth, Gwennie? And what do these buttons do?"

He touches the green one, then the violet one, and as his grimy thumb moves toward the black one, Gwendy does the only thing she can think of. Only she doesn't think, she just acts. Her bra closes in front, and now she opens it. "Do you want to play with those buttons, or with mine?"

Frankie grins, exposing teeth that would make even a hardened dentist wince and turn away. He reaches into his pocket again, and pulls out a knife. It reminds her of Lenny's, except there's no *Semper Fi* engraved on it. "Get over on the bed, Prom Queen. Don't bother taking off your panties. I want to cut them off you. If you lay real still, maybe I won't cut what's underneath."

"Did he send you?" Gwendy asks. She's sitting on her bottom now, with her feet on the floor and her legs drawn up to hide her breasts. With luck, one look at them is all this sick bastard is going to get. "Did Mr. Farris send you to take the box? Did he want *you* to have it?" Although the evidence seems to point to this, it's hard to believe.

He's frowning. "Mr. *who*?"

"Farris. Black suit? Little black hat that goes wherever it wants to?"

"I don't know any Mr. F—"

That's when she lashes out, once again not thinking . . . although later it will occur to her that the *box* might have been thinking for her. His eyes widen and the hand holding the knife pistons forward, driving through her foot and coming out the other side in a bouquet of blood. She shrieks as her heel slams into Frankie's chest, driving him back into the closet. She snatches up the box, and at the same time she pushes the red button, she screams, "*Rot in hell!*"

30

GWENDY PETERSON GRADUATES FROM Brown *summa cum laude* in June of 1984. There has been no running track for her since her senior spring in high school; the knife-wound in her foot got infected while she was in the hospital, and although it cleared eventually, she lost a piece of it. She still walks with a limp, although now it is barely discernable.

She goes out to dinner with her parents after the ceremony, and they have a fine time. Mr. and Mrs. Peterson even break their long abstinence with a bottle of champagne to toast their daughter, who is bound for Columbia grad school, or—perhaps—the Iowa Writers' Workshop. She thinks she might have a novel in her. Maybe more than one.

"And is there a man in your life?" Mrs. Peterson asks. Her color is high and her eyes are bright from the unaccustomed alcohol.

Gwendy shakes her head, smiling. "No man currently."

Nor, she thinks, will there be in the future. She already has a significant other; it's a box with eight buttons on top and two levers on the side. She still eats the occasional chocolate, but she hasn't taken one of the silver dollars in years. The ones she did have are gone, parceled out one or two at a time for books, rent (oh God, the luxury of a single apartment), and an upgrade from the Fiesta to a Subaru Outback (which outraged her mother, but she got over it eventually).

"Well," says Mr. Peterson, "there's time for that."

"Yes." Gwendy smiles. "I have plenty of time."

31

SHE'S GOING TO SPEND the summer in Castle Rock, so when her parents have gone back to their hotel, she packs up the last of her things, stowing the button box at the very bottom of her trunk. During her time at Brown, she kept the awful thing in a safe deposit box in the Bank of Rhode Island, something she wishes she had thought of doing sooner, but she was just a kid when she got it, a *kid*, goddammit, and what do kids know? Kids stow valuables in cavities under trees, or behind loose stones in cellars prone to flooding, or in closets. In *closets*, for Christ's sake! Once she gets to Columbia (or Iowa City, if the Writers' Workshop accepts her), it will go into another safety deposit box, and as far as she's concerned, it can stay there forever.

She decides to have a slice of coffee cake and a glass of milk before going to bed. She gets as far as the living room, and there she stops cold. Sitting on the desk where she has attended to her studies for the last two years, next to a framed picture of Harry Streeter, is a small, neat black hat. She has no doubt that it's the one she last saw on the day she and Harry were flying that kite on the baseball field. Such a happy day that was. Maybe the last happy one.

"Come on out here, Gwendy," Mr. Farris calls from the kitchen. "Set a spell, as they say down south."

She walks into the kitchen, feeling like a visitor in her own body. Mr. Farris, in his neat black suit and not looking a day older, sits at the kitchen table. He has a piece of the coffee cake and a glass of milk. Her own cake and milk are waiting for her.

He looks her up and down, but—as on that day ten years ago when she first met him at the top of the Suicide Stairs—without salacious intent. "What a fine young woman you've grown into, Gwendy Peterson!"

She doesn't thank him for the compliment, but she sits down. To her, this conversation seems long overdue. Probably not to him; she has an idea that Mr. Farris has his own schedule, and he always stays on it. What she says is, "I locked up when I went out. I always lock up. And the door was still locked when I came back. I always make sure. That's a habit I got into on the day Harry died. Do you know about Harry? If you knew I wanted coffee cake and milk, I suppose you do."

"Of course. I know a great deal about you, Gwendy. As for the locks . . . " He waves it aside, as if to say *pish-tush*.

"Have you come for the box?" She hears both eagerness and reluctance in her voice. A strange combination, but one she knows quite well.

He ignores this, at least for the time being. "As I said, I know a great deal about you, but I don't know exactly what happened on the day the Stone kid came to your house. There's always a crisis with the button box—a moment of truth, one could say—and when it comes, my ability to . . . see . . . is lost. Tell me what happened."

"Do I have to?"

He raises a hand and turns it over, as if to say *Up to you*.

"I've never told anyone."

"And never will, would be my guess. This is your one chance."

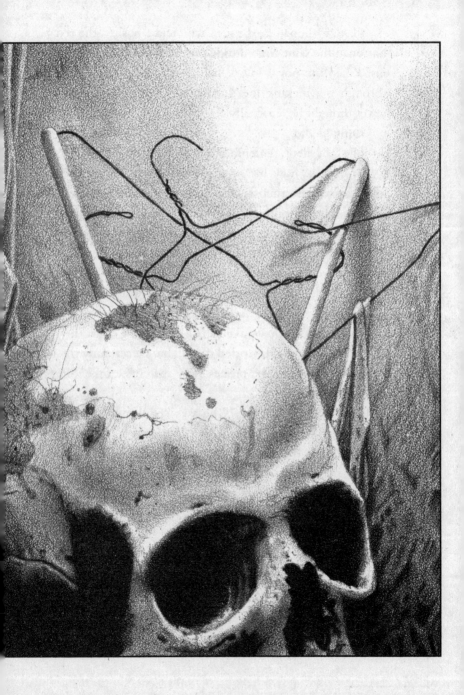

"I said I hoped he'd rot in hell, and I pushed the red button at the same time. I didn't mean it literally, but he'd just killed the boy I loved, he'd just stuck a knife right through my fucking foot, and it was what came out. I never thought he'd actually . . . "

Only he did.

She falls silent, remembering how Frankie's face began to turn black, how his eyes first went cloudy and then lolled forward in their sockets. How his mouth drooped, the lower lip unrolling like a shade with a broken spring. His scream—surprise? agony? both? she doesn't know— that blew the teeth right out of his putrefying gums in a shower of yellow and black. His jaw tearing loose; his chin falling all the way down to his chest; the ghastly ripping sound his neck made when it tore open. The rivers of pus from his cheeks as they pulled apart like rotting sailcloth—

"I don't know if he rotted in hell, but he certainly rotted," Gwendy says. She pushes away the coffee cake. She no longer wants it.

"What was your story?" he asks. "Tell me that. You must have thought remarkably fast."

"I don't know if I did or not. I've always wondered if the box did the thinking for me."

She waits for him to respond. He doesn't, so she goes on.

"I closed my eyes and pushed the red button again while I imagined Frankie gone. I concentrated on that as hard as I could, and when I opened my eyes, only Harry was in the closet." She shakes her head wonderingly. "It worked."

"Of course it worked," Mr. Farris says. "The red button is very . . . versatile, shall we say? Yes, let's say that. But in ten years you only pushed it a few times, showing you to be a person of strong will and stronger restraint. I salute you for that." And he actually does, with his glass of milk.

"Even once was too much," she says. "I caused Jonestown."

"You give yourself far too much credit," he says sharply. "*Jim Jones* caused Jonestown. The so-called Reverend was as crazy as a rat in a rainbarrel. Paranoid, mother-fixated, and full of deadly conceit. As for your friend Olive, I know you've always felt you were somehow responsible for her suicide, but I assure you that's not the case. Olive had ISSUES. Your word for it."

She stares at him, amazed. How much of her life has he been peering into, like a pervert (Frankie Stone, for instance) going through her underwear drawer?

"One of those issues was her stepfather. He . . . how shall I put it? He *fiddled* with her."

"Are you serious?"

"As a heart attack. And you know the truth about young Mr. Stone."

She does. The police tied him to at least four other rapes and two attempted rapes in the Castle Rock area. Perhaps also to the rape-murder of a girl in Cleaves Mills. The cops are less sure about that one, but Gwendy's positive it was him.

"Stone was fixated on you for *years*, Gwendy, and he got exactly what he deserved. He was responsible for the death of your Mr. Streeter, not the button box."

She barely hears this. She's remembering what she usually banishes from her mind. Except in dreams, when she can't. "I told the police that Harry kept Frankie from raping me, that they fought, that Harry was killed and

Frankie ran away. I suppose they're still looking for him. I hid the box in my dresser, along with the coins. I thought about dipping one of my high heel shoes in Harry's blood to explain the . . . the bludgeoning . . . but I couldn't bring myself to do it. In the end it didn't matter. They just assumed Frankie took the murder weapon with him."

Mr. Farris nods. "It's far from a case of all's well that ends well, but as well as can be, at least."

Gwendy's face breaks into a bitter smile that makes her look years older than twenty-two. "You make it all sound so good. As if I were Saint Gwendy. I know better. If you hadn't given me that goddamn box, things would have been different."

"If Lee Harvey Oswald hadn't gotten a job at the Texas Book Depository, Kennedy would have finished out his term," Mr. Farris says. "You can *if* things until you go crazy, my girl."

"Spin it any way you want, Mr. Farris, but if you'd never given me that box, Harry would still be alive. And Olive."

He considers. "Harry? Yes, maybe. *Maybe.* Olive, however, was doomed. You bear no responsibility for her, believe me." He smiles. "And good news! You're going to be accepted at Iowa! Your first novel . . . " He grins. "Well, let that be a surprise. I'll only say that you'll want to wear your prettiest dress when you pick up your award."

"What award?" She is both surprised and a little disgusted at how greedy she is for this news.

He once more waves his hand in that *pish-tush* gesture. "I've said enough. Any more, and I'll bend the course of your future, so please don't tempt me. I might give in if you did, because I like you, Gwendy. Your proprietorship of the box has been . . . exceptional. I know the burden it's been, sometimes like carrying an invisible packsack full of rocks on your back, but you will never know the good you've done. The disasters you've averted. When used with bad intent—which you never did, by the way, even your experiment with Guyana was done out of simple curiosity—the box has an unimaginable capacity for evil. When left alone, it can be a strong force for good."

"My parents were on the way to alcoholism," Gwendy says. "Looking back on it, I'm almost sure of that. But they stopped drinking."

"Yes, and who knows how many worse things the box might have prevented during your proprietorship? Not even I know. Mass slaughters? A dirty suitcase bomb planted in Grand Central Station? The assassination of a leader that might have sparked World War III? It hasn't stopped everything—we both read the newspapers—but I'll tell you one thing, Gwendy." He leans forward, pinning her with his eyes. "It has stopped a lot. A *lot*."

"And now?"

"Now I'll thank you to give me the button box. Your work is done—at least that part of your work is done. You still have many things to tell the world . . . and the world will listen. You will entertain people, which is the greatest gift a man or woman can have. You'll make them laugh, cry, gasp, *think*. By the time you're thirty-five, you'll have a computer to write on instead of a typewriter, but both are button boxes of a kind, wouldn't you say? You will live a long life—"

"*How* long?" Again she feels that mixture of greed and reluctance.

"That I will not tell you, only that you will die

surrounded by friends, in a pretty nightgown with blue flowers on the hem. There will be sun shining in your window, and before you pass you will look out and see a squadron of birds flying south. A final image of the world's beauty. There will be a little pain. Not much."

He takes a bite of his coffee cake, then stands.

"Very tasty, but I'm already late for my next appointment. The box, please."

"Who gets it next? Or can you not tell me that, either?"

"Not sure. I have my eye on a boy in a little town called Pescadero, about an hour south of San Francisco. You will never meet him. I hope, Gwendy, he's as good a custodian as you have been."

He bends toward her and kisses her on the cheek. The touch of his lips makes her happy, the way the little chocolate animals always did.

"It's at the bottom of my trunk," Gwendy says. "In the bedroom. The trunk's not locked . . . although I guess that wouldn't cause you any problems even if it was." She laughs, then sobers. "I just . . . I don't want to touch it again, or even look at it. Because if I did . . . "

He's smiling, but his eyes are grave. "If you did, you might want to keep it."

"Yes."

"Sit here, then. Finish your coffee cake. It really is good."

He leaves her.

32

GWENDY SITS. SHE EATS her coffee cake in small slow bites, washing each one down with a tiny sip of milk. She hears the squeak her trunk lid makes when it goes up. She hears the squeak when the lid is lowered again. She hears the *snap-snap* of the latches being considerately closed. She hears his footsteps approach the door to the hall, and pause there. Will he say goodbye?

He does not. The door opens and softly closes. Mr. Richard Farris, first encountered on a bench at the top of Castle View's Suicide Stairs, has left her life. Gwendy sits for another minute, finishing the last bite of her cake and thinking of a book she wants to write, a sprawling saga about a small town in Maine, one very much like her own. There will be love and horror. She isn't ready yet, but she thinks the time will come quite soon; two years, five at most. Then she will sit down at her typewriter—her button box—and start tapping away.

At last, she gets up and walks into the living room. There's a spring in her step. Already she feels lighter. The small black hat is no longer on her desk, but he's left her something, anyway: an 1891 Morgan silver dollar. She picks it up, turning it this way and that so its uncirculated surface can catch the light. Then she laughs and puts it in her pocket.

GWENDY'S
MAGIC FEATHER

RICHARD CHIZMAR

for Kara, Billy, and Noah
the Magic in my life

HOW GWENDY ESCAPED OBLIVION

by Stephen King

WRITING STORIES IS BASICALLY playing. Work may come into it once the writer gets down to brass tacks, but it almost always begins with a simple game of make-believe. You start with a what-if, then sit down at your desk to find out where that what-if leads. It takes a light touch, an open mind, and a hopeful heart.

Four or five years ago—I can't remember exactly, but it must have been while I was still working on the Bill Hodges trilogy—I started to play with the idea of a modern Pandora. She was the curious little girl, you'll remember, who got a magic box and when her damned curiosity (the curse of the human race) caused her to open it, all the evils of the world flew out. What would happen, I wondered, if a modern little girl got such a box, given to her not by Zeus but by a mysterious stranger?

I loved the idea and sat down to write a story called "Gwendy's Button Box." If you were to ask me where the name Gwendy came from, I couldn't tell you any more than I can tell you exactly when I did the original 20 or 30 pages. I might have been thinking about Wendy Darling, Peter Pan's little girlfriend, or Gwyneth Paltrow, or it might have just popped into my head (like the John

Rainbird name did in *Firestarter*). In any case, I visualized a box with a colored button for each of the earth's large land masses; push one of them and something bad would happen in the corresponding continent. I added a black one that would destroy everything, and—just to keep the proprietor of the box interested—little levers on the sides that would dispense addictive treats.

I may also have been thinking of my favorite Fredric Brown short story, "The Weapon." In it, a scientist involved in creating a super-bomb opens his door to a late-night stranger who pleads with him to stop what he's doing. The scientist has a son who is, as we'd now say, "mentally challenged." After the scientist sends his visitor away, he sees his son playing with a loaded revolver. The final line of the story is, "Only a madman would give a loaded gun to an idiot."

Gwendy's button box is that loaded gun, and while she's far from an idiot, she's still just a kid, for God's sake. What would she do with that box, I wondered. How long would it take for her to get addicted to the treats it dispensed? How long before her curiosity caused her to push one of those buttons, just to see what might happen? (Jonestown, as it turned out.) And might she begin to be obsessed with the black button, the one that would destroy everything? Might the story end with Gwendy—after a particularly bad day, perhaps—pushing that button and bringing down the apocalypse? Would that be so farfetched in a world where enough nuclear firepower exists to destroy all life on earth for thousands of years? And where, whether we like to admit it or not, some of the people with access to those weapons are not too tightly wrapped?

The story went fine at first, but then I began to run

out of gas. That doesn't happen to me often, but it *does* happen from time to time. I've probably got two dozen unfinished stories (and at least two novels) that just quit on me. (Or maybe I quit on them.) I think I was at the point where Gwendy is trying to figure out how to keep the box hidden from her parents. It all began to seem too complicated. Worse, I didn't know what came next. I stopped working on the story and turned to something else.

Time passed—maybe two years, maybe a little more. Every now and then I thought about Gwendy and her dangerous magic box, but no new ideas occurred, so the story stayed on the desktop of my office computer, way down in the corner of the screen. Not deleted, but definitely shunned.

Then one day I got an email from Rich Chizmar, creator and editor of *Cemetery Dance* and the author of some very good short stories in the fantasy/horror genre. He suggested—casually, I think, with no real expectation that I'd take him up on it—that we might collaborate on a story at some point, or that I might like to participate in a round-robin, where a number of writers work to create a single piece of fiction. The round-robin idea held no allure for me because such stories are rarely interesting, but the idea of collaboration did. I knew Rich's work, how good he is with small towns and middle-class suburban life. He effortlessly evokes backyard barbecues, kids on bikes, trips to Walmart, families eating popcorn in front of the TV . . . then tears a hole in those things by introducing an element of the supernatural and a tang of horror. Rich writes stories where the Good Life suddenly turns brutal. I thought if anyone could finish Gwendy's story, it would be him. And, I must admit, I was curious.

Long story short, he did a brilliant job. I re-wrote some of his stuff, he re-wrote some of mine, and we came out with a little gem. I'll always be grateful to him for not allowing Gwendy to die a lingering death in the lower righthand corner of my desktop screen.

When he suggested there might be more to her story, I was interested but not entirely convinced. What would it be about? I wanted to know. He asked me what I'd think if Gwendy, now an adult, got elected to the United States House of Representatives, and the button box made a reappearance in her life . . . along with the box's mysterious proprietor, the man in the little black hat.

You know when it's right, and that was so perfect I was jealous (not a lot, but a little, yeah). Gwendy's position of power in the political machinery echoed the button box. I told him that sounded fine, and he should go ahead. In truth, I probably would have said the same if he'd suggested a story where Gwendy becomes an astronaut, goes through a space warp, and ends up in another galaxy. Because Gwendy is as much Rich's as she is mine. Probably more, because without his intervention, she wouldn't exist at all.

In the story you're about to read—lucky you!—all of Rich's formidable skills are on display. He evokes Castle Rock well, and the regular Joes and regular Jills that populate the town ring true. We know these people, and so we care for them. We also care for Gwendy. To tell you the truth, I sort of fell in love with her, and I'm delighted that she's back for more.

Stephen King
May 17, 2019

1

ON THURSDAY, DECEMBER 16, 1999, Gwendy Peterson wakes up before the sun, dresses in layers for the cold, and heads out for a run.

Once upon a time, she walked with a slight limp thanks to an injury to her right foot, but six months of physical therapy and orthotic inserts in her favorite New Balance running shoes took care of that little problem. Now she runs at least three or four times a week, preferably at dawn as the city is just beginning to open its eyes.

An awful lot has happened in the fifteen years since Gwendy graduated from Brown University and moved away from her hometown of Castle Rock, Maine, but there's plenty of time to tell that story. For now, let's tag along as she makes her way crosstown.

After stretching her legs on the concrete steps of her rented townhouse, Gwendy jogs down Ninth Street, her feet slapping a steady rhythm on the salted roadway, until it runs into Pennsylvania Avenue. She hangs a sharp left and cruises past the Navy Memorial and the National Gallery of Art. Even in the heart of winter, the museums are all well illuminated, the gravel and asphalt walkways shoveled clean; our tax dollars hard at work.

Once Gwendy reaches the Mall, she notches it up a gear, feeling the lightness in her feet and the power in her legs. Her ponytail peeks out from underneath her winter cap, rustling against the back of her sweatshirt with every step she takes. She runs along the Reflecting Pool, missing the families of ducks and birds that make it their home during the warm summer months, toward the obelisk shadow of the Washington Monument. She stays on the lighted path, swinging a wide circle around the famous landmark, and heads east toward the Capitol Building. The Smithsonian Museums line both sides of the Mall here and she remembers the first time she visited Washington, D.C.

She was ten that summer, and she and her parents spent three long, sweaty days exploring the city from dawn to dusk. At the end of each day, they collapsed on their hotel beds and ordered room service—an unheard of luxury for the Peterson family—because they were too exhausted to shower and venture out for dinner. On their final morning, her father surprised the family with tickets to one of the city's pedicab tours. The three of them squeezed into the back of the cramped carriage eating ice cream cones and giggling as their tour guide pedaled them around the Mall.

Never in a million years did Gwendy dream she'd one day live and work in the nation's capital. If anyone questioned her of that likelihood even eighteen months earlier, her answer would have been a resounding no. *Life is funny that way,* she thinks, cutting across a gravel pathway in the direction of Ninth Street. Full of surprises—and not all of them good.

Leaving the Mall behind, Gwendy pulls frigid air into her lungs and quickens her stride for the final home stretch. The streets are alive now, bustling with early morning commuters, homeless people emerging from their cardboard boxes, and the rumble and grind of garbage trucks making their rounds. Gwendy spots the multi-colored Christmas lights twinkling from her bay window ahead and takes off in a sprint. Her neighbor across the street lifts a hand and calls out to her, but Gwendy doesn't see or hear. Her legs flex with fluid grace and strength, but her mind is far away this cold December morning.

2

EVEN WITH DAMP HAIR and barely a hint of make-up on her face, Gwendy is gorgeous. She draws a number of appreciative—not to mention a few openly envious—stares as she stands in the corner of the cramped elevator. Were her old friend, Olive Kepnes, still alive (even after all these years Gwendy still thinks of her almost every day), Olive would tell Gwendy that she looked like a million bucks and change. And she would be right.

Dressed in plain gray slacks, a white silk blouse, and low-heeled slip-ons (what her mother calls sensible shoes), Gwendy looks ten years younger than her thirty-seven years. She would argue vigorously with anyone who told her so, but her protests would be in vain. It was the simple truth.

The elevator dings and the doors slide open onto the third floor. Gwendy and two others sidestep their way out and join a small group of employees waiting in line at a cordoned-off security checkpoint. A burly guard wearing a badge and sidearm stands at the entrance, scanning identification badges. A young female guard is positioned a few yards behind him, staring at a video screen as employees pass between the vertical slats of a walk-through metal detector.

When it's Gwendy's turn at the front of the line, she

pulls a laminated ID card from her leather tote bag and hands it to the guard.

"Morning, Congresswoman Peterson. Busy day today?" He scans the bar code and hands it back with a friendly smile.

"They're all busy, Harold." She gives him a wink. "You know that."

His smile widens, exposing a pair of gold-plated front teeth. "Hey, I won't tell if you don't."

Gwendy laughs and starts to walk away. From behind her: "Tell that husband of yours I said hello."

She glances over her shoulder, readjusting the tote bag on her arm. "Will do. With any luck, he'll be home in time for Christmas."

"God willing," Harold says, crossing himself. Then he turns to the next employee and scans his card. "Morning, Congressman."

3

GWENDY'S OFFICE IS SPACIOUS and uncluttered. The walls are painted a soft yellow and adorned with a framed map of Maine, a square silver-edged mirror, and a Brown University pendant. Bright, warm lighting shines down on a mahogany desk centered along the opposite wall. Atop the desk are a hooded lamp, telephone, day-planner, computer and keyboard, and numerous stacks of paperwork. Across the room is a dark leather sofa. A coffee table covered with fanned-out magazines sits in front of it. A small table with a coffee station stands off to one side. There's also a three-drawer filing cabinet in the far corner and a small bookshelf lined with hardcover books, knickknacks, and framed photographs. The first of the two largest photos shows a tan and beaming Gwendy standing arm-in-arm with a handsome bearded man at the Castle Rock Fourth of July parade two years earlier. The second is of a much younger Gwendy standing in front of her mother and father at the base of the Washington Monument.

Gwendy sits at her desk, chin resting atop interlocked hands, staring at the photograph of her and her parents instead of the report sitting open in front of her. After a moment, she sighs and closes the folder, pushing it aside.

She taps a flurry of buttons on the keyboard and opens her email account. Scanning the dozens of notices in her mailbox, she stops on an email from her mother. The time-code shows it was received ten minutes earlier. She double-clicks on it and a digital scan of a newspaper article fills her monitor screen.

The Castle Rock Call
Thursday – December 16, 1999
STILL NO SIGN OF TWO MISSING GIRLS

Despite a countywide search and dozens of tips from concerned citizens, there has been no progress in the case of two abducted Castle County girls.

The latest victim, Carla Hoffman, 15, of Juniper Lane in Castle Rock, was taken from her bedroom on the evening of Tuesday, December 14. At shortly after six p.m., her older brother walked across the street to visit a classmate from school. When he returned home no more than fifteen minutes later, he discovered the back door broken open and his sister missing.

"We're working around the clock to find these girls," Castle Rock Sheriff Norris Ridgewick commented. "We've brought in officers from neighboring towns and are organizing additional searches."

Rhonda Tomlinson, 14, of nearby Bridgton, vanished on her way home from school on the afternoon of Tuesday, December 7...

Gwendy frowns at the computer screen. She's seen enough. She closes the email and starts to turn away—but hesitates. Tapping at the keyboard, she switches to SAVED MAIL and uses the Arrow button to scroll. After what feels like forever, she stops on another email from her mother, this one dated November 19, 1998. The subject line reads: CONGRATULATIONS!

She opens it and double-clicks on a link. A small, dark window with *Good Morning, Boston* written across it opens at the center of the monitor. Then a low resolution video comes to life and the *Good Morning, Boston* intro music is blaring from the computer speakers. Gwendy quickly turns down the volume.

Onscreen, Gwendy and popular morning show host, Della Cavanaugh, sit across from each other on straight-backed leather chairs. They each have their legs crossed and are wearing microphones clipped to their collars. A banner headline runs across the top of the video screen: HOMETOWN GIRL MAKES GOOD.

Gwendy cringes at the sound of her voice on the video, but she doesn't turn it off. Instead, she readjusts the volume, leans back in her chair, and watches herself being interviewed, remembering how utterly strange— and unsettling—it felt to tell her life story to thousands of strangers . . .

4

AFTER GRADUATING FROM BROWN in the spring of 1984, Gwendy spends the summer working a part-time job in Castle Rock before attending the Iowa Writers Workshop in early September. For the next three months, she focuses on classwork and starts writing the opening chapters of what will become her first novel, a multi-generational family drama set in Bangor.

When the workshop is over, she returns home to Castle Rock for the holidays, gets a tattoo of a tiny feather next to the scar on her right foot (more about that feather a little later), and begins to search for full-time employment. She receives a number of interesting offers and soon after decides on an upstart advertising and public relations firm in nearby Portland.

In late January 1985, Mr. Peterson follows behind Gwendy on the interstate—pulling a U-Haul trailer full of secondhand furniture, cardboard boxes stuffed with clothes, and more shoes than any one person should own— and helps her move into a rented second-floor downtown apartment.

Gwendy begins work the following week. She quickly proves to be a natural at the advertising game and over the course of the next eighteen months, earns a couple of promotions. By the middle of year two, she's traveling up and down the east coast to meet with VIP clients and is listed on company letterhead as an Executive Account Manager.

Despite her hectic schedule, the unfinished novel is never far from Gwendy's mind. She daydreams about it constantly and pecks away at it in every nook and cranny of free time she can muster: long flights, weekends, infrequent snow days, and the occasional weeknight when her workload allows.

At a holiday work party in December 1987, her boss, making polite conversation, introduces Gwendy to an old college friend and mentions that his star employee is not only a first-class account manager, but also an aspiring author. The old friend just happens to be married to a literary agent, so he calls his wife over and introduces her to Gwendy. Relieved to have a fellow book lover to talk to, the agent takes an immediate liking to Gwendy and by the end of the night, she convinces the aspiring author to send her the first fifty pages of her manuscript.

When the second week of January rolls around and Gwendy's phone rings one afternoon, she's shocked to find the agent on the line inquiring as to the whereabouts of those first fifty pages. Gwendy explains that she'd figured the agent was just being courteous and she didn't want to add one more unpublishable book to the slush pile. The agent assures Gwendy that she's never courteous when it comes to her reading material and insists that she send it right away. So, later that day, Gwendy prints the first three chapters of her novel, stuffs them into a FedEx overnight envelope and sends them on their way. Two days later, the agent calls back and asks to see the rest of the manuscript.

There's only one problem: Gwendy isn't finished writing the book.

Instead of admitting this to the agent, she takes the following day, a Friday, off from work—a first for Gwendy—and spends a long weekend drinking Diet Pepsi by the gallon and writing her ass off to finish the last half-dozen chapters. During her lunch break on Monday, Gwendy prints the almost three hundred remaining pages of the book and crams them into a FedEx box.

Several days later, the agent calls and offers to represent Gwendy. The rest, as they say, is history.

In April 1990, twenty-eight-year-old Gwendy Peterson's debut novel, *Dragonfly Summer*, is published in hardcover to rave reviews and less than impressive sales. A few months later, it wins the prestigious Robert Frost Award, given annually "to a work of exemplary literary merit" by the New England Literary Society. This honor sells maybe—and that's a hard *maybe*—a few hundred extra copies and makes for a nice cover blurb on the paperback edition. In other words, it's nothing to take to the bank.

That all changes soon enough with the release of Gwendy's second book, a suburban thriller called *Night Watch*, published the following autumn. Stellar reviews and strong word-of-mouth sales rocket it onto the *New York Times* bestseller list for four consecutive weeks, where it rests comfortably amidst mega-sellers by Sidney Sheldon, Anne Rice, and John Grisham.

The following year, 1993, sees the publication of Gwendy's third and most ambitious novel, *A Kiss in the Dark*, a hefty six-hundred-page thriller set on a cruise ship. The book earns a return trip to the bestseller list—this time for six weeks—and soon after the film version of *Night Watch* starring Nicolas Cage as the cuckolded suburban husband hits theaters just in time for the holidays.

At this point in her career, Gwendy's poised to make the leap to the big leagues of the entertainment industry. Her agent anticipates a seven-figure offer in the next book auction, and both *Dragonfly Summer* and *A Kiss in the Dark* are now deep in development by major film studios. All she has to do is stay the course, as her father likes to say.

Instead, she changes direction and surprises everyone.

A Kiss in the Dark is dedicated to a man named Johnathon Riordan. Years earlier, when Gwendy started working at the ad agency, it was Johnathon who took her under his wing and taught her the ropes of the advertising world. At a time when he could've easily viewed her as direct competition—especially with their proximity in age; Johnathon only being three years older than Gwendy—he instead befriended her and grew to become her closest ally, both in and outside the office. When Gwendy locked her keys in the car for the second time in as many days, whom did she call for help? Johnathon. When she needed serious dating advice, whom did she summon? Johnathon. The two of them spent countless evenings after work eating Chinese food straight out of the carton and watching romantic comedies at Gwendy's apartment. When Gwendy sold her debut novel, Johnathon was the first person she told, and when she did her first book signing, he was standing at the front of the line at the bookstore. As time passed and their relationship grew closer, Johnathon became the big brother Gwendy never had but always wanted. And then he got sick. And nine months later, he was gone.

This is where the surprise enters the picture.

Inspired by the AIDS-related death of her best friend, Gwendy resigns from the ad agency and spends the next eight months writing a non-fiction memoir about

Johnathon's inspiring life as a young gay man and the tragic circumstances of his passing. When she's finished, still not over the heartbreak, she immediately pours herself into directing a documentary based on Johnathon's story.

Family and friends are surprised, but not surprised. Most seem to explain her newfound passion with the simple, well-worn statement: "That's just Gwendy being Gwendy." As for her agent, although she never comes right out and says it—that would be unsympathetic, not to mention unkind—she is profoundly disappointed. Gwendy had been on the fast track to stardom and had veered off to tackle a topic as controversial and unseemly as the AIDS epidemic.

But Gwendy doesn't care. Someone important once told her: "You have many things to tell the world . . . and the world will listen." And Gwendy Peterson believes that.

Eyes Closed: Johnathon's Story is published in the summer of 1994. It garners positive reviews in *Publishers Weekly* and *Rolling Stone*, but is a slow mover in the national bookstore chains. By the end of August, it's demoted to bargain bins in the back of most stores.

The similarly titled documentary is another story altogether. Released shortly after the book, the film plays to packed festival audiences and goes on to win an Academy Award for Best Documentary. Nearly fifty million viewers watch as Gwendy gives her tearful acceptance speech. She spends the majority of the next few months doing interviews with national publications and appearing on various morning and late-night talk shows. Her agent is over the moon. She's back on the fast track again and more in demand than ever before.

Gwendy first meets Ryan Brown, a professional photographer from Andover, Massachusetts, during the making of the *Eyes Closed* documentary. The two strike up an easy friendship and, in an unforeseen turn of events for both, it grows into a relationship.

On a cloudless November morning, while hiking along the banks of the Royal River near Castle Rock, Ryan pulls a diamond ring out of his backpack, gets down on a knee, and proposes. Gwendy, tears and snot streaming down her face, is so caught up in the moment she finds herself unable to utter a single word. So, Ryan, ever the good sport, shifts to his other knee and asks again. "I know how much you like surprises, Gwennie. C'mon, what do you say? Spend the rest of your life with me?" This time Gwendy finds her voice.

They're married the following year at her parents' church in the center of Castle Rock. The reception is held at the Castle Inn and, despite Ryan's younger brother drinking too much and breaking his ankle on the dance floor, a good time is had by all. The father of the bride and the father of the groom bond over their mutual admiration of Louis L'Amour oaters, and the two mothers spend the entire day giggling like sisters. Most folks predict now that Gwendy is hitched, she'll settle down and concentrate on writing novels again.

But Gwendy Peterson does love surprises—and she has one more up her sleeve.

Born of simmering anger and frustration at the cruel and discriminatory manner in which many AIDS victims continue to be treated (she's particularly incensed that Congress recently voted to retain a ban on entry into the country for people living with HIV, even as more than two-and-a-half million AIDS cases have been reported

Peterson

EYES CLOSED: Jonathon's Story

Scribner

globally), Gwendy decides—with her husband's blessing—to run for public office.

Suffice to say, her agent is not pleased.

Gwendy pours her heart and soul into a grassroots campaign, and it quickly catches fire. Volunteers show up in unprecedented numbers and early fund-raisers exceed all expectations. As one notoriously stingy pundit notes: "Peterson, with boundless charisma and energy to match, has not only managed to mobilize the young vote and the undecided vote, she's found a way to stir the merely curious. And, in a state as tradition-steeped as Maine, that may well prove to be the key to a successful fall."

It turns out he's right. In November 1998, by a margin of less than four thousand votes, Gwendy Peterson upsets incumbent Republican James Leonard for the District One Congressional Seat of Maine. The following month, just days after Christmas, she makes the move to Washington, D.C.

So, there you have it, the story of how Gwendy finds herself eleven months and eight days into a two-year Congressional term, peddling her idealistic ideologies (as Fox News referred to them during last night's broadcast) to anyone who will listen, and often being referred to—with a not so subtle hint of derision—as the Celebrity Congresswoman.

The intercom on her desk buzzes, yanking Gwendy out of her time machine. She fumbles with the keyboard, closing the video window on her computer screen, and presses a blinking button on her telephone. "Yes?"

"Sorry to disturb, but you have a meeting with Rules and Records in seven minutes."

"Thanks, Bea. I'll be right out."

Gwendy glances at her wristwatch in disbelief. *Jesus, you just woolgathered away forty-five minutes of your morning. What's wrong with you?* It's a question she's asked herself a lot lately. She grabs a pair of manila folders from the top of the stack and hurries out of the office.

RICHARD CHIZMAR

141

5

AS IS OFTEN THE case in this corner of the world, an earlier meeting is running late, so Gwendy arrives with plenty of time to spare. Nearly two dozen House Representatives are crammed into the narrow hallway waiting to enter Conference Room C-9, so she positions herself by the water cooler in the outer lobby, hoping to review her notes in private. No such luck—it's been that kind of morning.

"Forget to do your homework last night, young lady?"

She clenches her jaw and looks up from the open folder.

Milton Jackson, longtime representative of the state of Mississippi, is seventy years old, looks ninety, and is the spitting image of what a buzzard would look like if it fluttered down from a telephone wire and slipped on a Men's Wearhouse suit. In other words, not pretty.

"Of course not," Gwendy says, offering her brightest smile. From day one at her new job, she recognized that Milton was one of those men who loathed anyone with a positive outlook on life or was simply happy, so she really turns it on. "Just doing some extra credit. And how are you this fine December morning?"

The old man squints at her, as if he's trying to figure out if it was a trick question. "Ahh, I'm okay," he finally grumbles.

"Leave her alone, Milt," someone says from behind them. "She's young enough to be your granddaughter."

This time Gwendy's smile is genuine as she turns to her friend. "I'd know that sweet voice anywhere. Good morning, Patsy."

"Heya, Gwennie. This old coot bothering you?" Patsy Follett is in her mid-sixties and as cute as she is petite. Even in the stylish high-heeled boots she's wearing, Patsy stands barely five feet tall. Her bobbed hair is dyed platinum and her make-up is, shall we say, plentiful.

"No, ma'am, we were just talking strategy for today's meeting." She looks at the congressman. "Isn't that right, Mr. Jackson?"

The old man doesn't respond. Just studies them from behind thick eyeglasses like they're flying insects splattered against the windshield of his brand new Mercedes.

"Speaking of strategy," Patsy says. "You still owe me a return call on that education budget, Milt."

"Yeah, yeah," he grumbles. "I'll have my secretary get back to you with a date."

Gwendy glances down at the floor and notices a piece of toilet paper stuck to the heel of one of the old man's loafers. She carefully reaches out with the tip of her shoe and nudges it free. Then, she slides the toilet paper against the wall so no one else will step on it.

"Or maybe you could just pick up the phone all by yourself and call me back later today," Patsy says, arching her eyebrows.

Milton scowls and elbows his way toward the front of the crowd without so much as a goodbye.

Patsy watches him go and lets out a thin whistle. "Boy,

that ugly mug of his is enough to make you want to skip breakfast. Maybe lunch, too."

Gwendy's eyes widen and she tries to hold back a giggle. "Be nice."

"An impossibility, dear girl. I am cranky as a hornet today."

A murmur ripples through the crowd and they finally start inching toward the entrance of the conference room.

"Guess it's that time again," Patsy says.

Gwendy puts out a hand, gesturing for her friend to go ahead of her. "What time is that?"

Patsy smiles, and her tiny, make-up–laden face lights up. "Time to fight the good fight, of course."

Gwendy sighs and follows her friend inside.

6

Two hours later, the door to the conference room bangs open and thirty representatives stream out, every last one of them looking like they could use a handful of Tylenol or, at the very least, a cold shower.

"Did you see Old Man Henderson's face?" Patsy asks as she and Gwendy enter the hallway. "I thought he was going to blow a gasket right there at the podium."

"I never saw anyone get so red—"

Someone bumps Gwendy hard from behind, knocking her aside, and keeps on hustling past. It's their chatty friend from this morning, Milton Jackson.

"Hey, nice manners, asshole," Patsy calls after him.

Gwendy tucks the manila folders under her arm and rubs her shoulder.

"You okay?"

"Oh, I'm fine," she says. "You shouldn't have yelled at him like that."

"Why not? The guy deserved it." She gives Gwendy a look. "You're not very good at losing your temper, are you?"

Gwendy shrugs. "I guess not."

"You should try it sometime. Might make you feel better."

"Fine. Next time that happens I'll call him . . . a walking example of why we need term limits."

"Sshhh," Patsy says, as they file into the elevator. "You're one of us now."

Gwendy laughs and presses the button for their floor.

"Any movement with the pharmaceutical people?" Patsy asks.

Gwendy shakes her head and lowers her voice. "Ever since Columbine everyone has shifted to gun control and mental health. And how can I blame folks for that? I just wish people around here had longer attention spans than kindergarteners. Three months ago, I almost had the votes. Today, it's not even close."

The elevator door slides open and they walk out into a mostly empty lobby. "Welcome to the grind, girlfriend. It'll circle back around. It always does."

"How long have you been doing this, Patsy?"

"I've represented the second district of the honorable state of South Carolina for sixteen years now."

Gwendy whistles. "How . . . ?" She pauses.

"How do I do it?"

Gwendy nods shyly.

Patsy puts a hand on the young congresswoman's shoulder. "Listen, honey, I know what you're thinking. How did you get yourself into this mess? It's not even been a year and you're frustrated and overwhelmed and looking for a way out."

Gwendy looks at her, saucer-eyed. "That's not what I—"

Patsy waves her off. "Trust me, we all went through it. It'll pass. You'll find your groove. And if you don't and you find your head slipping under water, give me a call. We'll find a way to fix it together."

Gwendy leans over and hugs her friend. It's a little like

146

embracing a child, she thinks. "Thank you, Patsy. I swear you're an angel."

"I'm really not. I'm old and fussy and don't much care for most of humanity, but you're different, Gwennie. You're special."

"I don't feel very special these days, but thank you again. So much."

Patsy starts to walk away, but Gwendy calls after her. "You really meant it? You've felt like this before?"

Patsy turns and puts her hands on her hips. "Honey, if I had a nickel for every time I've felt the way you're feeling, I still wouldn't have change for a quarter."

Gwendy bursts out laughing. "What does that even mean?"

Patsy shrugs her shoulders. "Beats me. My late husband used to say it whenever he wanted to sound clever and it's stuck with me ever since."

7

GWENDY WALKS INTO HER outer office feeling better than she has in days. It's almost as if a weight has been lifted from her chest and she can breathe again.

A gray-haired receptionist stops typing and looks up from her computer screen. "I left two messages on your desk and lunch should be here soon. Turkey club and chips okay?"

If Gwendy sometimes envisions (secretly, of course; she would never say these things out loud, not in a million years) Representative Patsy Follett as Tinkerbell, the wand-waving, miniature flying guardian angel of her childhood, then she most certainly imagines her receptionist, Bea Whiteley, as Sheriff Taylor's beloved Aunt Bea from the iconic television series, *The Andy Griffith Show.*

Although there's very little physical resemblance (for starters, Gwendy's Bea is African-American), there are a multitude of other similarities. First, there's the name, of course. How many women do you know named Bea or even Beatrice? And then there're the indisputable facts: Mrs. Whiteley is a natural caregiver, an outstanding cook, a person of devoted faith, and the sweetest, most good-natured woman Gwendy has ever known. Wrap all that up into a single human being and who do you have? Aunt Bea, that's who.

"You're a lifesaver," Gwendy says. "Thank you."

Bea picks up a sheet of paper from the corner of her desk. "I also printed your schedule for tomorrow." She gets up and hands it to Gwendy.

The congresswoman scans it with a frown. "Why does this feel like the last day of school before Christmas break?"

"Pretty sure the last day of school was a lot more fun than this." Bea sits down at her desk again. "How's your mom feeling?"

"Still good as of last night. Six weeks out from chemo. Markers in the normal range."

The older lady clasps her hands together. "God is good."

"Dad's driving her crazy, though. Want to hear the latest?" She doesn't wait for an answer. "He wants to withdraw all their savings and bury it in the back yard. He's convinced the bank's computer system's going to crash because of Y2K. Mom can't wait for him to start back at work again."

"All the more reason for you to get home. You flying out tomorrow night?" Bea asks.

Gwendy shakes her head. "Bumped my flight until Saturday morning. I need to wrap up a couple things before I go. How about you? When are you and Tim headed out?"

"We leave Monday to visit my sister in Colorado, and from there we go to see the kids on Wednesday. Speaking of the kids . . . would it be too much trouble to ask you to sign a couple of books for them? I'm happy to pay. I'm not asking for them for free or—"

Gwendy puts her hand out. "Will you please hush? I'd be happy to, Bea. It'd be my pleasure."

"Thank you, Mrs. Peterson. I'm very grateful." And she looks it, too, not to mention, relieved.

"Just go relax and enjoy that family of yours."

"All of us under the same roof for an entire week? It should be . . . interesting."

"It'll be a blast," Gwendy says.

Bea rolls her eyes. "If you say so."

"I say so." She walks into her office, laughing, and closes the door behind her.

RICHARD CHIZMAR

8

GWENDY TOSSES THE REPORTS back onto the stack and sits at her desk. She reaches for her day-planner, but her hand freezes in mid-air before it gets there.

There's a shiny silver coin sitting next to the keyboard.

Her outstretched hand begins to tremble. Her heart thumps in her chest, and it suddenly feels as if all the air has been sucked out of the room.

She knows before she looks that it's an 1891 Morgan silver dollar. She's seen them before.

A familiar voice, a man's voice, whispers in her ear: *"Almost half an ounce of pure silver. Created by Mr. George Morgan, who was just thirty years old when he engraved the likeness of Anna Willess Williams, a Philadelphia matron, to go on what you'd call the 'heads' side of the coin…"*

Gwendy whips her head around, but no one is there. She glances about her office, waiting for the voice to return, feeling as if she's just seen a ghost—and maybe she has. Nothing else in the room appears out of place. Reaching out with her other hand, she lets the tip of her index finger brush against the surface of the coin. It's cool to the touch, and it's real. She's not imagining it. She's not suffering some kind of stress-induced mental breakdown.

Heart in her throat, Gwendy uses her thumb to slowly slide the coin across the desk, closer to her. Then she leans down for a better look. The silver dollar is in mint condition and she was right—it's an 1891 Morgan. Anna Williams smiles up at her with unblinking silver eyes.

Pulling her hand back, Gwendy absently wipes it on the sleeve of her blouse. She gets up then and slowly wanders around the room, feeling as if she's just awakened from a dream. She bangs her knee against the rounded corner of the coffee table but she barely notices. Abruptly changing direction, she stops in front of the closet door, the only place where someone could possibly hide. After taking a steadying breath, she silently counts to three— and yanks open the door.

She recoils with her hands held in front of her face, nearly falling, but there's no one waiting inside. Just a handful of coats and sweaters hanging on wire hangers, a tangle of dress and running shoes littering the floor, and a brand-new pair of snow boots still in the box.

Exhaling with relief, Gwendy pushes the door shut and turns to face her desk again. The silver coin sits there, gleaming in the overhead lights, staring back at her. She's about to call for Bea when something catches her eye. She crosses to the filing cabinet in the corner. A bronze bust of Maine Civil War hero Joshua Chamberlain sits on top of it, a gift from her father.

Gwendy pulls open the top drawer of the cabinet. It's stuffed with folders and assorted paperwork. She closes it. Then she does the same with the second drawer: slides it open, quick inspection, close. Holding her breath, she bends to a knee and pulls open the bottom drawer.

And there it is: the button box.

A beautiful mahogany, the wood glowing a brown so rich that she can glimpse tiny red glints deep in its finish. It's about fifteen inches long, maybe a foot wide, and half

that deep. There are a series of small buttons on top of the box, six in rows of two, and a single at each end. Eight in all. The pairs are light green and dark green, yellow and orange, blue and violet. One of the end-buttons is red. The other is black. There's also a small lever at each end of the box, and what looks like a slot in the middle.

For a moment, Gwendy forgets where she is, forgets how old she is, forgets that a kind and gentle man named Ryan Brown was ever born. She's twelve years old again, crouching in front of her bedroom closet back in the small town of Castle Rock, Maine.

It looks exactly the same, she thinks. *It looks the same because it* is *the same.* There's no mistaking it even after all these years.

From behind her, there's a loud knock at the door. Gwendy almost faints.

9

"ARE YOU OKAY, CONGRESSWOMAN? I was knocking for a long time."

Gwendy steps back from the door and lets her receptionist into the office. Bea's carrying a small tray with the turkey club lunch on it. She places it on the desk and turns back to her boss. If Bea notices the silver coin sitting next to the keyboard, she doesn't mention it.

"I'm fine," Gwendy says. "Just a little embarrassed. I was doing some reading and I guess I dozed off."

"Must've been some dream you were having. It sounded like you were whimpering."

You don't know the half of it, Gwendy thinks.

"You sure you're okay?" Bea asks. "If you don't mind my saying, you look a little rattled and a lot pale. Almost like you've seen a ghost."

Bingo again, Gwendy thinks, and almost bursts out giggling. "I went for a longer than usual run this morning and haven't had much to drink. I'm probably just dehydrated."

The receptionist gives her a long look, clearly unconvinced. "I'll go grab a couple more waters then. I'll be right back." She turns and heads out of the office.

"Bea?"

She stops in the doorway and turns back.

"Did anyone stop by the office when I was at my meeting this morning?"

Bea shakes her head. "No, ma'am."

"You're certain?"

"Yes, ma'am." She looks around the room. "Is something wrong? Do you need me to call security?"

"No, no," Gwendy says, escorting the older lady the rest of the way out of the room. "But maybe you should call a doctor, since I can't seem to stay awake past lunchtime these days."

Bea once again offers a faint smile, not very convincingly, and hurries off.

Gwendy closes the door and walks a direct line back to the filing cabinet. She knows she doesn't have much time. Bending to a knee again, she slides open the bottom drawer. The button box is still there, practically sparkling in the overhead lights, waiting for her.

Gwendy reaches out with both hands and hesitates, her fingers hovering an inch or two above its highly polished surface. She feels the hairs on her arms begin to tingle, hears the faint whisper of *something* in the far corner of her brain. Steeling herself, she carefully lifts the box out of the drawer. And as she does, it all rushes back to her . . .

10

WHEN GWENDY WAS A young girl, her father hauled the old cardboard box marked SLIDES out of the attic every summer, usually some time around the Fourth of July. He set up his ancient slide projector on the coffee table in the den, positioned the pull-down screen in front of the fireplace, and turned off all the lights. He always made a big deal of the experience. Mom made popcorn and a pitcher of fresh lemonade. Dad narrated every slide with what he called his "Hollywood voice" and made shadow puppets during intermission. Gwendy usually sat on the sofa between her mother and father, but sometimes other neighborhood kids would join them, and on those occasions, she sat on the floor in front of the screen with her friends. Some of the kids grew bored and quickly made up excuses to leave ("Oops, I'm sorry, Mr. Peterson, I just remembered I promised my mom I'd clean my room tonight."), but Gwendy was never one of them. She was fascinated by the images on the screen, and even more so by the stories those images told.

As Gwendy's fingers close around the button box for the first time in fifteen years, it's as if a slideshow of vibrant, flickering images—each one telling its own secret story—blooms in front of her eyes. Suddenly, it's:

—*August 22, 1974, and a strange man in a black coat and a small neat black hat is reaching under a Castle View park bench and sliding out a canvas bag with a drawstring top. He pulls it open and removes the most beautiful mahogany box . . .*

—an early September morning, and Gwendy stands in front of her bedroom closet, dressing for school. When she's finished, she slips a tiny piece of chocolate into her mouth and closes her eyes in ecstasy . . .

—middle school, as Gwendy stares at herself in a full-length dressing room mirror, and realizes she isn't just pretty, she's gorgeous, and no longer wearing eyeglasses . . .

—sophomore year of high school and she's sitting on the den sofa, staring in horror as images of bloated, fly-covered corpses fill the television screen . . .

—late at night, the house graveyard quiet, and she's sitting cross-legged in the dark on her bed with the button box resting in her lap, eyes squeezed tight in concentration, using her thumb to press the red button, and then cocking her head at the open window, listening for the rumble . . .

—a mild spring evening and she's screaming hysterically as two teenaged boys crash into her night table, sending hairbrushes and make-up skittering across the bedroom floor, before reeling into the open closet, falling and pulling down dresses and skirts and pants from their plastic hangers, collapsing to the ground in a heap, and then a filthy hand with blue webbing tattooed across the back of it lifts the button box and brings it crashing down, corner first, into the crown of her boyfriend's skull . . .

Gwendy gasps and she's back in Washington D.C.—and without a moment to spare. She scrambles across her office floor on all fours and vomits into the wastebasket next to her desk.

11

DUE TO THE EXORBITANT cost of maintaining two residences in separate states, many first-year congressional representatives are forced to rent overpriced apartments (a large number of them located in leaky, unventilated basements) or share rented townhouses or condos with multiple roommates. Most do so without complaint. The hours are long, and they rarely find themselves at home anyway except to shower and sleep, or, if they're lucky, eat the occasional unrushed meal.

Gwendy Peterson suffers from no such financial dilemma—thanks to the success of her novels and the resulting movie adaptations—and lives alone in a three-story townhouse located two blocks east of the Capitol Building. Nevertheless, on a near daily basis, she feels no small amount of guilt because of her living situation, and is always quick to offer a spare bedroom should anyone need a place to stay.

Tonight, however, as she sits in the middle of her sofa with her legs curled beneath her, picking at a carton of shrimp lo mein and staring blindly at the television, she is over-the-moon grateful for her solo living arrangements and even more appreciative that she has no overnight guests.

The button box sits on the sofa next to her, looking out of place, almost like a child's toy in the sterile environment of the townhouse. It took Gwendy the better part of the afternoon to figure out how to smuggle the box out of her office. After several failed attempts, she finally settled on dumping her new boots onto the floor of the closet and using the large cardboard box they came in to conceal it under her arm. Fortunately, the security checkpoints set up throughout the building were put in place for arriving personnel only and not for those departing.

A commercial for the new Tom Hanks movie blares on the television, but Gwendy doesn't notice. She hasn't moved from the sofa in the past two hours except to answer the door when the deliveryman rang the bell. Dozens of questions sift through her mind, one after the other in rapid-fire succession, with a dozen more waiting in the shadows to take their place.

Two questions reoccur most frequently as if on a continuous loop:

Why is the box back?

And why now?

12

GWENDY HAS NEVER TOLD a soul about the button box. Not her husband, not her parents, not even Johnathon or the therapist she saw twice a week for six months back in her mid-twenties.

There was a time when the box filled her every waking thought, when she was obsessed with the mystery and the power contained within, but that was a lifetime ago. Now, for the most part, her memories of the box feel like scattered remnants of a recurring dream she once had during childhood, but whose details have long since been lost in the never-ending maze of adulthood. There's a lot of truth to the old adage: out of sight, out of mind.

She has, of course, thought about the box in the fifteen years since it vanished from her life, but—and she's just come to terms with this revelation in the last sixty minutes or so—not nearly as much as she probably should have, considering the immense role the button box played for much of her adolescence.

Looking back, there were weeks, perhaps even months, when it never once crossed her mind and then, boom, she would watch a news report about a mysterious, seemingly natural, disaster that occurred in some faraway state or country, and she would immediately picture someone sitting in a car or at a kitchen table with their finger resting on a shiny red button.

Or she would stumble upon a news teaser online about a man discovering buried treasure in the back yard of his suburban home and would click the link to see if any 1891 Morgan silver dollars were involved.

There were also those dark instances—thankfully rare—when she would catch a glimpse of old grainy video footage on television or hear a snippet of a radio discussion about the Jonestown Massacre in Guyana. When that happened, her heart would skip a beat and set to aching, and she would tumble into a deep black hole of depression for days.

And finally there were those times when she would spot a neat black bowler's hat bobbing up and down amidst a crowd on a busy sidewalk or glance over at an outdoor café table and spy the shiny dome of that black hat resting next to a mug of steaming coffee or a frosty glass of iced tea and, of course, her thoughts would rush back to the man in the black coat. She thought about Richard Farris and that hat of his more than all the rest of it. It was always the mysterious Mr. Farris that swam closest to the surface of her conscious mind. It was his voice she'd heard back in her office, and it is his voice she hears again now, as she sits on the sofa with her bare legs tucked beneath her: *"Take care of the box, Gwendy. It gives gifts, but they're small recompense for the responsibility. And be careful . . . "*

13

AND WHAT ABOUT THOSE gifts the box so willingly dispenses?

Although she didn't actually witness the narrow wooden shelf slide out from the center of the box with a silver dollar on it, she believes that's where the coin on her desk came from. Coin, box; box, coin; it all made perfect sense.

Does that mean pulling the other lever—*the one on the left side by the red button*, she remembers as if it were yesterday—will deliver a tiny chocolate treat? Maybe. And maybe not. You can never tell with the button box. She believed it had a lot more tricks up its sleeve fifteen years ago, and she believes it even more now.

She brushes her fingertip against the small lever, thinking about the animal-shaped chocolates, no two ever the same, each exotically sweet and no bigger than a jelly-bean. She remembers the first time she ever laid eyes on one of the chocolates—standing next to Richard Farris in front of the park bench. It was in the shape of a rabbit, and the degree of detail was astounding—the fur, the ears, the cute little eyes! After that, there was a kitty and a squirrel and a giraffe. Her memory grows hazy then, but she remembers enough: eat one chocolate and you were never hungry for seconds; eat a bunch of chocolates over a period of time and you *changed*—you got faster and stronger and smarter. You had more energy and always seemed to be on the winning side of a coin flip or a board game. The chocolates also improved your eyesight and erased your acne. Or had puberty taken care of that last one? Sometimes it was hard to tell.

Gwendy looks down and is horrified to see that her finger has strayed from the small lever on the side of the box to the rows of colored buttons. She jerks her hand back as if it's wrist-deep in a hornet's nest.

But it's too late—and the voice comes again:

"*Light green: Asia. Dark green: Africa. Orange: Europe. Yellow: Australia. Blue: North America. Violet: South America.*"

"And the red one?" Gwendy asks aloud.

"*Whatever you want,*" the voice answers, "*and you will want it, the owner of the box always does.*"

She gives her head a shake, trying to silence the voice, but it isn't finished yet.

"*The buttons are hard to push,*" Farris tells her. "*You have to use your thumb and put some real muscle into it. Which is a good thing, believe me. Wouldn't want to make any mistakes with those, oh no. Especially not with the black one.*"

The black one . . . back then she called it the Cancer Button. She shudders at the memory.

The phone rings.

And for the second time today, Gwendy almost faints.

14

"RYAN! I'M SO GLAD you called."

"I've been trying to get a . . . for days, sweetheart," he says, his voice momentarily gone amidst a blast of static. "Stupid phones here are worthless."

"Here" is the small island of Timor, located off the southern end of Southeast Asia. Ryan's been there since the first week of December with a *Time* magazine crew covering government unrest.

"Are you okay?" Gwendy asks. "Are you safe?"

"I stink like I've been living . . . barn the last couple weeks but I'm fine."

Gwendy laughs. Happy tears stream down her cheeks. She gets up from the sofa and starts pacing back and forth. "Are you going to make it home in time for Christmas?"

"I don't know, honey. I hope so but . . . are heating up here."

"I understand." Gwendy nods her head. "I hope you're wrong, but I understand."

"How's . . . doing?" he says, cutting out again.

"What? I didn't hear you, baby."

"How's your mom doing?"

Gwendy smiles—and then stops in her tracks.

She stares at the curtained window that occupies the upper half of the kitchen door, unsure if it's her imagination. A few seconds pass and she's just about convinced she's seeing things, when a shadow moves again. Someone's outside on the deck.

" . . . hear me?" Ryan says, startling her.

"Oh, she's doing fine," Gwendy says, inching into the kitchen and pulling open a drawer. "Gaining weight and going to her appointments." She takes out a steak knife and holds it against her leg.

"I'll have to make her . . . secret recipe pancakes when I . . . home."

"Just get your butt home in one piece, will you?"

He laughs and starts to say something else, and then there's an ear-piercing jolt of static—and dead air.

"Hello? Hello?" she says, pulling the phone away from her ear so she can look at the screen. "Shit." He's gone.

Gwendy places the cell phone on the counter, crouches, and edges closer to the door. When she reaches the end of the row of cabinets, she crab-walks the last couple of feet into position directly behind the door. Before she can lose her nerve, she lets out a banshee cry and springs to her feet, flipping on the outside light with one hand and using the other hand to flick aside the flowered curtains with the tip of the steak knife.

Whoever was standing outside of the door is gone. All that's left is her wide-eyed reflection staring back at her.

15

THE FIRST THING GWENDY does after retrieving her cell phone from the kitchen counter (even before she walks to the front door and double-checks the deadbolt) is to make sure nothing has happened to the button box. For one terrible, breathless moment, while she's crossing from the kitchen into the family room, she imagines that the figure at the back door was a diversionary tactic, and while she was busy conducting her counterattack, an accomplice was breaking into the front of the house and stealing away with the box.

Her entire body sags with relief when she sees the button box sitting on the sofa right where she'd left it.

A short time later, as she makes her way upstairs carrying the box, it occurs to her that she never once considered telling Ryan about it. At first, she tries to use the severed connection as an excuse, but she knows better. The button box came back to her and only her. Nobody else.

"It's mine," she says as she enters the bedroom.

And shivers at the intensity of her voice.

16

GWENDY SLEEPWALKS HER WAY through December 17, 1999, her final day at the office before Congress begins its three-week holiday break. She spends the first fifteen minutes convincing Bea that she feels well enough to be at work (the day before, the panicked receptionist was ready to call the paramedics when she found Gwendy vomiting into her trash can; luckily, Gwendy was able to convince her that it must've been something bad she ate for break-fast, and after agreeing to go home forty minutes early, the older woman finally relented) and the next eight-and-a-half hours resisting the urge to rush home and check on the button box.

She hated to leave the box back at the townhouse, especially after the scare at her kitchen door the night before, but she didn't have much of a choice. No telling how the X-ray machines at the security checkpoints would react to the box, and perhaps even more worrisome, no telling how the box would react to being X-rayed. Gwendy didn't have a clue what the inside of the button box looked like, or what its innards were made of, but she wasn't taking any chances.

Before she left for her two-block walk to the Capitol Building, she hid the box at the back of a narrow crawl-space underneath the staircase. She stacked cardboard boxes full of books on each side and in front of it, and laid a pile of winter coats on top of it all. Once she was satisfied, she closed the crawlspace's small door, locked up the townhouse, and started for work. She managed only to return home to check on the box twice before finally making it into the office.

Gwendy's last day passes in a blur of faceless voices and background noise. Several phone conferences in the morning and a pair of brief committee meetings in the afternoon. She doesn't remember much of what was said in any of them, or even what she ate for lunch.

When five o'clock rolls around, she locks her office and sets off to deliver Christmas gifts to a handful of co-workers—a set of scented candles and bath salts for Patsy, a cashmere sweater and bracelet for Bea, and a stack of signed books for Bea's children. After well-wishes and hugs goodbye, she heads for the lobby.

17

"I'm sure gonna miss your smiling face these next few weeks, Congresswoman."

"I'm going to miss you, too," Gwendy says, stopping at the security desk. She reaches into her tote bag and pulls out a small box covered in snowman wrapping paper. She hands it across the barrier to the barrel-chested guard. "Merry Christmas, Harold."

Harold's mouth drops open. He slowly reaches out and takes the gift. "You got me . . . this is really for me?"

Gwendy smiles and nods her head. "Of course. I would never forget my favorite head of security."

He looks at her in confusion. "Head of—?" And then he grins and those gold teeth of his wink at her in the fluorescent lights. "Oh, you're joking with me."

"Open your present, silly man."

His meaty fingers attack the wrapping paper and uncover a shiny black box with *Bulova* printed in gold lettering across the top of it. He opens the box and looks up in disbelief. "You bought me a watch?"

"I saw you admiring Congressman Anderson's last week," Gwendy says. "I thought you deserved one of your own."

Harold opens his mouth but no words come out. Gwendy is surprised to see that the guard's eyes have gone shiny and his chin is trembling. "I . . . this is the nicest present anyone has ever given me," he finally says. "Thank you."

For the first time today, Gwendy feels like maybe everything will be okay. "You're very welcome, Harold. I hope you and your family have a wonderful Christmas." She pats his arm affectionately and turns to leave.

"Not so fast," Harold says, raising a hand. He ducks behind the desk and comes back up with a wrapped gift of his own. He hands it to Gwendy.

She looks at him in surprise, and then reads the gift tag: *To Congresswoman Gwendy Peterson; From Harold & Beth*. "Thank you," she says, genuinely touched. "Both of you." She opens the present. It's a thick hardcover book with a bright orange dust jacket. She turns it over so she can see the front cover—and the room shifts, up, down, and up again, like she just sat down on a teeter-totter at the playground.

"You okay, Congresswoman?" Harold asks. "You already have a copy?"

"No, no," Gwendy says, holding up the book. "I've never read it, but I've always wanted to."

"Oh, good," he says, relieved. "I can barely make heads or tails of the jacket copy, but my wife read it and said it was fascinating."

Gwendy forces a smile on her face. "Thank you again, Harold. It really is a lovely surprise."

"Thank *you* again, Congresswoman Peterson. You shouldn't have, but I'm sure glad you did." He bursts out laughing.

Gwendy slips the book inside her leather tote and heads for the elevator. On the ride down, she takes another peek at the cover, just to make sure she's not losing her mind.

She's not.

The book Harold gave her is *Gravity's Rainbow*. It's the same novel Richard Farris was reading on the bench in Castle View twenty-five years earlier—on the day he first gave Gwendy the button box.

18

GWENDY IS LEANING TOWARD canceling her long-scheduled dinner plans with friends even before the copy of *Gravity's Rainbow* shows up, but Harold's well-meaning, yet not-so-pleasant surprise, cinches the deal. She goes straight home, unburies the button box from its hiding place, changes into sweatpants and a baggy sweater, and calls out for delivery.

While her friends—two former classmates from Brown—dine on filet mignon and grilled vegetables at historic Old Ebbitt Grill on Fifteenth (where you have to call weeks in advance for a table), Gwendy sits alone in her dining room, picking at the sorriest excuse for a garden salad she's ever seen and nibbling on a slice of pizza.

She's not really alone, of course. The button box is there, resting on the opposite end of the table, watching her eat like a silent suitor. A few minutes earlier, she looked up from her dinner and asked quite sincerely, "Okay, you're back. What do I do with you now?" The box didn't answer.

Gwendy's attention is currently focused on an evening news program playing on the den television, and she's not happy. She still can't believe Clinton lost to this idiot. "The President of the United States is a flipping moron," she says, stuffing a piece of lettuce that's closer to brown than it is green into her mouth. "You tell 'em, Bernie."

Anchorman Bernard Shaw, with his distinguished

salt-and-pepper hair and thick mustache, does just that: ". . . recap the sequence of events that has brought us to this potentially catastrophic standoff. Initially, spy-satellite photographs led U.S. officials to suspect that North Korea was developing a new nuclear facility near the Yongbyon nuclear center that was originally disabled by the 1994 accord. Based on these photographs, Washington demanded an inspection of the facility and Pyongyang countered by demanding the U.S. pay $300 million for the right to inspect the site. Earlier this week, President Hamlin responded angrily—and, many say, disrespectfully—in public comments directed at the North Korean leader, refusing to pay any such inspection fee and calling the proposal 'ludicrous and laughable.' Now, within the past hour, Pyongyang has released a written statement referring to President Hamlin as 'a brainwashed bully' and threatening to pull out of the 1994 accord. No response from the White House yet, but one unnamed official claims . . . "

"That's just great," Gwendy says, getting up from the table and tossing the remains of her salad into the trash. "A pissing contest between two egomaniacs. I'm going to get a lot of calls over this . . . "

19

GWENDY PULLS THE BLANKET over her chest and gives the box one last look before turning off the bedside lamp. Earlier in the evening, after brushing her teeth and washing her face, she placed the button box on the dresser next to her jewelry tray and hairbrushes. Now, she's wondering if she should move it closer. Just to be safe.

She reaches out to turn on the light again—but freezes when she hears the creak of a door opening on hinges that need oiling. She immediately recognizes the sound. It's her closet door.

Unable to move, she watches in terror as a dark figure emerges from inside the walk-in closet. She tries to bark out a warning—*Stop, I have a gun! I'm calling 911!;* anything that might buy her a little more time—but realizes that she's holding her breath. Suddenly remembering the button box on the dresser, she yanks off the thick blanket and scrambles across the bed.

But the intruder is too fast.

He lunges at her, strong arms grabbing her around the waist and wrestling her back onto the bed. She screams and flails at her attacker, clawing at his eyes, ripping off the ski mask he's wearing.

Gwendy sees his face in the glow of the television and gasps.

The intruder is Frankie Stone—somehow alive again

and looking exactly as he did almost twenty years earlier on the night he killed her boyfriend—baggy camo pants, dark glasses, and a tight tee-shirt, wearing that stupid grin of his, greasy brown hair staining his shoulders, shotgun pattern of acne scattered across his cheeks.

He flips her over and pins Gwendy against the mattress, and she can smell the stale, alcohol-tainted foulness of his breath as he hisses, "Give me the box, you dumb bitch. Give it to me right now or I'll eat you alive"—and then his jaws yawn open impossibly wide and the world goes dark as Frankie Stone closes his mouth and engulfs her.

20

GWENDY JERKS UPRIGHT IN bed, clutching a tangle of sweat-soaked sheets to her chest and gasping for breath. Her eyes dart to the closet door across the room—it's closed tight—and then to her dresser. The button box is exactly as she left it, sitting there in the dark with its watchful gaze.

21

"ARE YOU SURE YOU don't want me to stow your bag, Congresswoman Peterson?"

Gwendy looks at the co-pilot who had introduced himself just minutes earlier when she first boarded the eight-seat private plane, but she's already forgotten his name. "No, it's fine. I packed my laptop and I'll probably fiddle around with some work once we're in the air."

"Very well," he says. "We should be taking off in about twenty minutes." He gives her a reassuring smile—the kind that says, *Your life is in my hands, lady, but I slept great last night and only did a little bump of cocaine this morning, so hey it's all good*—and ducks back into the cockpit.

Gwendy yawns and looks out the window at the busy runway. The last thing she wants to do during the short flight is fiddle with her laptop. She's exhausted from not sleeping the night before and in a foul mood. Not even forty-eight hours have passed since the button box's return to her life, and she's already moved on from shock and curiosity to anger and resentment. She glances at her carry-on suitcase, tucked underneath the seat in front of her, and fights the urge to check on the box again.

Squeezing her eyes shut, she tries to silence the obsessive voice chattering away in the back of her head, and abruptly snaps them open again when she realizes she's dozing off. Sleeping with the box unsecured might not be such a smart idea, she decides.

"Is it safe?" she suddenly asks out loud, without intending to. She looks down at the suitcase again. The flight is less than ninety minutes long. What's the worst that can happen if she takes a little catnap? She doesn't know and she's not willing to find out. She can sleep when she gets home.

Is it safe? She's thinking of the old Dustin Hoffman movie now with the evil Nazi dentist. *Is it safe?*

When it comes to the button box, Gwendy knows the answer to that question. The box is never safe. Not really.

"We're number two for take-off, Congresswoman," the co-pilot says, peeking out from the cockpit. "We should have you on the ground in Castle Rock a few minutes before noon."

22

If Gwendy's being honest with herself—and as the King Air 200 climbs high in the clouds above a muddy twist of Potomac River she's determined to be exactly that—she has to admit that her crummy mood this morning is coming from one overwhelming source: a long-forgotten memory from her youth.

It was a mild and breezy August day shortly before the start of her tenth-grade year in high school, and Gwendy just finished running the Suicide Stairs for the first time in months. When she reached the top, she sat and rested on the same Castle View bench where years earlier she'd first met a man named Richard Farris. She stretched her legs for a moment, and then she leaned her head back and closed her eyes, enjoying the feel of the sun and the wind on her face.

The question that had bloomed in her mind while sitting on the bench that long ago summer day resurfaced—and rather rudely—earlier this morning as Gwendy was busy cushioning the button box in her carry-on bag with rolled up wads of socks and sweaters: *How much of her life is her own doing, and how much the doing of the box with its treats and buttons?*

The memory—and the central thought contained within that memory—was almost enough to make Gwendy scream

in rage and fling the box across the bedroom like a toddler in the midst of a temper tantrum.

No matter how she looks at it, Gwendy knows she's led what most people would call a charmed life. There was the scholarship to Brown, the writers' workshop in Iowa, the fast-track job at the ad agency, and of course, the books and movies and Academy Award. And then there was the election, what many pundits called the biggest political upset in Maine history.

Sure, there were failures along the way—a lost advertising account here, a film option that didn't pan out there, and her love life before Ryan could probably best be described as a barren desert of disappointment—but there weren't too many, and she always bounced back with an ease of which others were envious.

Even now, glaring at the button box resting securely between her feet, Gwendy believes with all her heart that the bulk of her success can be attributed to hard work and a positive attitude, not to mention thick skin and persistence.

But what if what she believes to be true . . . simply isn't?

23

A LIGHT SNOW IS falling from a low-hanging, slate gray sky when Gwendy lands at the Castle County Airport out on Route 39. Nothing heavy, just a kiss on the cheek from the north that will leave yards and roadways coated with an inch or so of slush by dinnertime.

She called ahead before boarding the plane and asked Billy Finkelstein, one of only two full-timers at Castle County Airport, to jump her car battery back to life and pull her Subaru hatchback out of one of the three narrow hangars that run alongside the wooded shoulder of Route 39.

Billy is true to his word, and the car's waiting for her in the parking lot, both the engine and heater running hard. She thanks Billy, sliding him a tip even though it's against the rules, and nods hello to his boss, Jessie Martin, one of her father's old bowling partners. She loads her carry-on into the front passenger seat and tosses her tote bag on top of it.

On her way home, Gwendy makes a pair of quick phone calls. The first is to her father to let him know she landed safely and that she'll be there for dinner tonight. Mom's asleep on the sofa, so she doesn't get to speak to her, but Dad's pleased as punch and looking forward to seeing Gwendy later.

The second call is to Castle County Sheriff Norris

Ridgewick's cell phone. It rings straight to voicemail, so she leaves a message after the beep: "Hey, Norris, it's Gwendy Peterson. I just got back into town and figured we ought to touch base. Give me a buzz when you can."

As she presses the END button on her phone, Gwendy feels the Subaru's back tires momentarily loosen their grip on the road. She carefully steers back into the center of the lane and drops her speed. *That's all you need,* she thinks. *Hit a telephone pole, knock yourself unconscious, and have the button box discovered by some nineteen-year-old snowplow driver with a tin of Red Man in his back pocket and frozen snot crusted on his lip.*

24

THERE ARE ONLY TWO ways up to Castle View in 1999: Route 117 and Pleasant Road. Gwendy steers the Subaru onto Pleasant, climbing past a winding half-mile stretch of single homes—ranchers, Cape Cods, and saltbox colonials; many of them decorated for Christmas—and takes a left after the new American Legion playground onto View Drive. She drives another couple hundred yards and then makes a right into the snow-covered parking lot of Castle View Condominiums. Several years ago, she and Ryan were among the first half-dozen folks to purchase a unit in the newly built complex. Despite their busy travel schedules, they've been happy there ever since.

Gwendy swings into a reserved spot in the front row and turns off the engine. Circling to the passenger side to pull out her suitcase, she glances down a series of gently sloping hills to a fenced-off precipice where she once ran a zigzagging metal staircase called the Suicide Stairs. Standing out like a dark scar on the snowy hillside is the wooden bench where she first met the stranger in the black hat.

Gwendy punches in a four-digit security code to gain entrance to her building and climbs the stairs to the second floor. Once inside Unit 19B, she shrugs off her jacket, leaving it on the foyer floor, unzips her suit-case and takes out the button box, carries it down the hallway to the bedroom, places it on her husband's side of the bed, and curls up next to it. Thirty seconds later, she's snoring.

25

GWENDY OPENS HER EYES to the dark silence of her bedroom, disoriented by the lack of daylight at the window, and momentarily forgets where she is. She hustles into the bathroom to pee and experiences a sharp spike of panic in her chest when she remembers dinner with her parents.

After stashing the button box inside a fireproof safe in the office she shares with Ryan, she spends the next five minutes searching for her keys. She finally finds them in the pocket of her jacket on the floor and rushes out the door, determined not to be late.

Driving faster than she should on the slick roads, she's a block away from her parents' house when she thinks about the box again. "It should be safe in the safe," she says out loud and laughs.

The safe was originally her husband's idea. Convinced that they both needed a place to store their valuables, he supervised the purchase and installation of the SentrySafe a few months after they moved into the condo. Of course, several years later, there was nothing inside the thing except for a handful of contracts, old insurance papers, an envelope containing a small amount of cash, and a signed Ted Williams baseball inside a plastic cube—and now the button box.

I can't keep lugging it around with me everywhere I go, Gwendy thinks, turning onto Carbine Street. *Can't keep it in the condo either, not when Ryan gets back.* She'd stored the button box in a safe deposit box at the Bank of Rhode Island during her four years at Brown, and that worked out just fine. Maybe she'd drop by Castle Rock Savings and Loan at the beginning of next week, see what they have available.

Gwendy spots her parents' Cape Cod ahead in the distance and breaks into a smile. Her father has really outdone himself this year. Green and red and blue Christmas bulbs outline the gutters of the roof and spiral up and down the front porch railings. A huge inflatable Santa Claus, illuminated by a series of bright spotlights, dances in the breeze at the center of the front yard. An inflatable red-nosed reindeer grazes in the snow at Santa's feet.

He did all this for Mom, Gwendy realizes, pulling into the driveway and parking behind her father's truck. Still smiling, she gets out and walks to the door. She's home again.

26

MR. PETERSON IS PREPARING chicken and dumplings for dinner, Gwendy's favorite, and the three of them catch up on everything from the two missing girls to across-the-street neighbor Betty Johnson's sudden conversion to bleach blonde to the New England Patriots three-game losing streak. Mrs. Peterson, looking better than Gwendy has seen her look in months, complains about still needing to take daily naps and her husband's constant coddling, but she does so with a grateful smile and an affectionate squeeze of Mr. Peterson's forearm. She's wearing a different wig tonight—a shade darker and a couple inches longer—than the one she was wearing the last time Gwendy was home, and it not only makes her look healthier, it makes her appear years younger. Her face lights up when Gwendy tells her so.

"Any more news from Ryan?" Mrs. Peterson asks, as her husband gets up and goes into the kitchen to silence the oven timer.

"Not since he called two nights ago," Gwendy says.

"You still think he'll make it home in time for Christmas?"

Gwendy shakes her head. "I don't know, Mom. It all depends on what happens over there. I've been keeping an eye on the news but they haven't reported much yet."

Mr. Peterson walks into the dining room carrying a

plate stacked high with biscuits. "Saw President Hamlin on the tube earlier this evening. I still can't believe our Gwendy gets to work with the Commander-in-Chief."

Mrs. Peterson gives her daughter a smile and rolls her eyes. She's heard this spiel before. Many times. They both have.

"Have you spoken with him lately?" he asks eagerly.

"A bunch of us were in a meeting with him and the vice president last week," Gwendy says.

Her father beams with pride.

"Trust me, it's not all that it's cracked up to be."

As is often the case, she's tempted to tell her father the reality of the situation: that President Hamlin is a sexist bore of a man who rarely looks Gwendy in the eyes, instead focusing on her legs if she's wearing a dress or her chest if she's wearing pants; that she purposely never stands too close to the Commander-in-Chief because of his tendency to touch her on the arms and shoulders when he speaks to her. She's also tempted to tell him that the President's as dumb as a donut and has horrible breath, but she doesn't say any of these things. Not to her father, anyway. Now her mother is a different story.

"I liked what he said about North Korea," Mr. Peterson says. "We need a strong leader to deal with that madman."

"He's acting more like a petulant child right now than a leader."

Her father gives her a thoughtful look. "You really don't like him, do you?"

"It's not that . . . " she says. *Careful, girl.* "I just don't care for his policies. He's cut healthcare funds for the poor every year he's been in office. He cut federal funding for AIDS clinics and reinforced anti-gay legislation across the board. He spearheaded a movement to reduce budgets for the arts in public schools. I just wish he cared more about people and less about winning every argument."

Her father doesn't say anything.

Gwendy shrugs. "What can I say? He's just a muggle, Dad."

"What's a muggle?" he asks.

Mrs. Peterson touches his arm. "From Harry Potter, dear."

He looks around the table. "Harry who?"

This time his wife smacks him on the arm. "Oh, stop it, you smart aleck."

They all crack up laughing.

"Had you going for a minute," he says, winking.

For the next several hours, Gwendy relaxes and the button box hardly crosses her mind. There's one brief moment, when she's standing at the kitchen window overlooking the backyard, and she spots the old oak tree towering in the distance and remembers once hiding the box in a small crevice at the base of its thick trunk. But the memory's gone from her head as quickly as it arrives, and within seconds, she's back in the den watching *Miracle on 34th Street* and working on a crossword puzzle with her father.

27

". . . INITIALLY OCCURRED WHEN ANTI–INDEPENDENCE militants launched an attack on a crowd of unarmed civilians."

An expression of grim sincerity is etched on the Channel Five newscaster's face, as a banner headline reading BREAKING NEWS: CRISIS IN TIMOR scrolls across the bottom of the screen. "There are early reports of violence and bloodshed spreading throughout the countryside, the worst of the fighting centered in the capital city of Dili. The fighting erupted after a majority of the island's eligible voters chose independence from Indonesia. Over two hundred civilian casualties have already been reported with that number expected to rise."

Gwendy sits at the foot of the bed, dressed in a long flannel nightgown, the button box propped up on a pillow beside her, its twin rows of multi-colored buttons looking like teeth in the glow of the television.

The anchorman promises more breaking news from Timor just as soon as it becomes available, and then Channel Five goes to commercial.

At first, Gwendy doesn't move, doesn't even seem to breathe, and then she turns to the box and in an odd, toneless voice says, "Curiosity killed the cat." She uses her pinky to pull the lever on the right side of the box.

A narrow wooden shelf slides out from the center with

a silver dollar on it. Gwendy picks up the shiny coin and, without looking at it, places it beside her on the bed. The shelf slides back in without a sound.

"But satisfaction brought it back," she recites in that same odd voice and pulls the other lever.

The wooden tray slides out again, this time dispensing a tiny piece of chocolate in the shape of a horse.

She picks up the chocolate with two steady fingers and looks at it with amazed wonder. Lifting it to her face, she closes her eyes and breathes in the sweet, otherworldly aroma. Her eyes open lazily and gaze at the chocolate with a look of naked desire. She licks her lips as they begin to part—

—and then she's fleeing to the bathroom, hot tears streaming from her eyes, and flushing the chocolate horse down the toilet.

28

THE FIRST PERSON GWENDY sees when she walks into the Castle Rock Diner on Sunday morning is Old Man Pilkey, the town's retired postmaster. Hank Pilkey is going on ninety years old and has a glass left eye as the result of a fly-fishing accident. Rumor has it his second wife, Ruth, got drunk on moonshine and caused the injury while they were honeymooning in Nova Scotia. When Gwendy was young, she was terrified of the old man and dreaded tagging along with her parents to the post office on Saturday mornings. It wasn't that she was spooked or even grossed out by the shiny prosthetic eyeball. She was simply a nervous wreck that she'd go into some kind of weird staring trance and cause the old guy discomfort or, even worse, embarrassment.

Fortunately, years of practice have helped to ease Gwendy's fears, and when she swings open the diner's front door—a pair of HAVE YOU SEEN THIS GIRL? posters taped to the outside of the thick glass—at a few minutes before ten and Old Man Pilkey spots her with a toothless grin, hops down from his stool in front of the long Formica counter and opens his saggy arms in greeting, Gwendy looks him in the eye and hugs him back with genuine affection.

"There's our hometown hero," he croaks, gripping

her shoulders with bony fingers and holding her at arm's length so he can get a good look at her.

Gwendy laughs and it feels good after the long night she's just had. "How are you, Mr. Pilkey?"

"Fair to middling," he says, easing back onto the stool. "Fair to middling."

"And how's Mrs. Pilkey?"

"Ornery as ever, and twice as sweet."

"Fair words to describe the both of you," Gwendy says and gives him a wink. "Enjoy your Sunday, Mr. Pilkey."

"You do the same, young lady. My best to your folks."

Gwendy walks to an empty table by the window, nodding hello to several other townspeople, many of them dressed in church clothes, and sits down. Gazing around the diner, she estimates she knows two-thirds of the people in there. Maybe more. She also estimates that maybe half of them voted for her last November. Castle Rock's her hometown, but it's still—and probably always will be—a Republican hotspot.

"I thought that was you."

Gwendy looks up, startled.

"Jesus, Norris. You scared me."

"Sorry about that," he says. "Whole damn town's on edge." He gestures to the empty chair. "Mind if I sit?"

"Please," Gwendy says.

The sheriff sits down and adjusts his gun belt on his hip. "I got your message. Was planning to call you back this morning, but I needed coffee first. Late night."

Norris Ridgewick is two years older than Gwendy and has occupied the Castle County Sheriff's Office since taking over for Alan Pangborn in late 1991. Standing a hint over five-foot-six and weighing in at an even one hundred and fifty pounds (wearing his uniform, shoes, and side-arm), the sheriff doesn't make much of a physical impression, but he more than makes up for it by being resourceful and kind. Gwendy has always believed that Norris carries a deep well of sadness within him—most likely due to losing his father when he was just fourteen years old and his mother a decade later. Gwendy likes him a lot.

"Why so late?" she asks. "Anything new with the girls?"

The sheriff's eyes wander around the diner. Gwendy follows his gaze and notices many of the other diners have stopped eating and are staring at them. "Not much," he says, lowering his voice. "We're checking out some leads with the Tomlinson girl. A part-time teacher at her school. A custodian at the dance studio she attended. But neither are exactly what I'd call . . . prime suspects."

"And the Hoffman girl?"

He shrugs and waves to get a waitress's attention. "That one's even tougher. We've got the timeframe down to just under fourteen minutes. That's how long the brother was out of the house. In those fourteen minutes, someone smashed the glass on the back door, entered the house, took Carla Hoffman from her bedroom, and disappeared without a trace."

"Without a trace," Gwendy repeats in a whisper.

He nods. "Or much of a struggle, evidently. No prints on the door or anywhere inside the house. It'd snowed that morning but the kids had a snowball fight in the yard, so it was a mess. No chance of boot- or footprints. Could've come by car, but none of the neighbors saw or heard anything."

"Anything coming in on the tip-line?" she asks. "I saw the Hoffmans put up a reward."

"Bunch of calls . . . but only a handful worth following up on, which we're doing."

"Nothing else?"

The sheriff shrugs. "We're trying our damnedest to find a connection between the two girls, but so far it's not there. They live in different neighborhoods, attend different schools, have different hair color, body types, hobbies. No sign that they knew each other or had close mutual friends. Neither has a boyfriend or has ever been in any kind of trouble."

"What are the chances the two disappearances aren't related?"

"Doubtful."

"What's your gut say?"

"My gut says I need coffee." He glances around for the waitress again.

Gwendy gives him an irritated look.

"What?" he asks. "You believe in all that gut instinct mumbo jumbo?"

"I do," she says.

The sheriff pulls in a deep breath, lets it out. He glances out the window before meeting Gwendy's eyes again. "Lotta weird shit has happened in the Rock over the years, you know that. The Big Fire in '91, boogeyman Frank Dodd murdering those folks, Sheriff Bannerman and those other men getting killed by that rabid Saint Bernard, hell, even the Suicide Stairs. You believe it was an earthquake that knocked them down, I got a bridge to sell you."

Gwendy sits there and offers up her best poker face, an

expression she's nearly perfected after less than a year in Washington D.C.

"I hope to hell I'm wrong," he says, sighing heavily, "but I have a feeling we're never gonna see those girls again. Not alive anyway."

29

AFTER BREAKFAST, GWENDY STROLLS across the street to the Book Nook and picks up the Sunday editions of both *The New York Times* and *The Washington Post*. The owner of the bookstore, a stylish woman in her mid-fifties named Grace Featherstone, greets her with a hug and several minutes of colorfully worded grievances relating to President Hamlin. Gwendy stands at the counter, unable to get a word in, nodding enthusiastically. When the older woman finally takes a breath, Gwendy pays for the newspapers and a pack of mints. Then she goes outside and sits in her car, scanning both publications for news about Timor, or more importantly, photographs from Timor.

Several years earlier, Ryan was sent to Brazil to help cover a story about a number of seaside villages that had been taken over and eventually destroyed by a local drug lord. He spent three weeks hiding in the jungle with armed guerillas, unable to contact home in any fashion. During this time, the only way Gwendy was able to confirm Ryan's safety was by locating his photo credits in the daily newspapers and a handful of websites on the Internet. Ever since, in similarly trying times, this method became Gwendy's safety net of last resort. Just seeing Ryan's name printed in tiny type next to one of his photographs was enough to calm her heart for the next day or two until the next photo made an appearance.

Gwendy checks and double-checks both papers—her fingertips growing dark with smudged ink, the passenger seat and dashboard disappearing beneath a mountain of loose pages and advertising circulars—but doesn't find any photographs. Each newspaper carries a brief article, but they're buried on inside pages and are mostly rehashes of old stories. The Associated Press recently reported online that a United Nations force consisting of mainly Australian Defense Force personnel was deployed to East Timor to establish and maintain peace. After that, not much else was known.

30

GWENDY SPENDS THE MAJORITY of Sunday afternoon Christmas shopping with her mom. Their first stop is the Walmart, where Gwendy picks up a couple of jigsaw puzzles for her father and Mrs. Peterson snatches the last remaining Sony Walkman on the shelf for Blanche Goff, her longtime neighbor and friend "to use on her morning strolls around the high school track."

Gwendy's cell phone rings as they're walking to the parking lot. It's her father checking in to see how Mom is faring. Gwendy gives her mother a look and tells him everything's fine and promises to keep an eye on her. Before she hangs up, Mrs. Peterson grabs the phone from her daughter's hand and says, "Just watch your football games and leave us alone, you old nag." The two of them climb into the Subaru, stashing their bags in the back seat and giggling like a couple of teenagers.

The truth is Gwendy *has* been keeping close tabs on her mother, and so far she's delighted with what she's seen. Mrs. Peterson is still a bit frail and she's definitely slower on her feet, but all that's to be expected after everything she's been through. More important, to Gwendy at least, is the fact that her mother's cheery attitude and whip-smart sense of humor are back, not to mention that sweet smile of hers. There'd been barely a glimpse of those things during the eight weeks of chemotherapy.

After Walmart, the two women grab a light lunch at Cracker Barrel and head to the mall out on Route 119. The two-story shopping mall is as crowded and noisy as a Friday night football game—it seems like half of Castle Rock's teenage population is there that afternoon—but they don't let it take away from their fun. Gwendy and her mom spend the next couple hours knocking off the final items on their gift lists, eating double-scoop ice cream cones while people-watching in the food court, and singing along to the never-ending selection of Christmas carols playing over the mall's sound system.

At their final stop of the day, Gwendy leaves her mom sitting on a bench outside of Bart's Sporting Goods, and goes inside to purchase a rain-suit for Ryan to wear kayaking. It was his only gift request before he left, and she's determined to have it waiting for him under the tree. Gwendy is stuffing the credit card receipt into her bag and not looking where she's going when she bumps into another shopper on her way out of the store.

"I am so sorry," Gwendy says and then looks up and sees who it is. "Oh my God, Brigette!"

The tall, blonde woman laughs and picks up the shopping bag that was jostled from her hand. "Same old Gwendy, always running somewhere."

Brigette Desjardin was two years ahead of Gwendy at Castle Rock High. Back in those days, they ran indoor track together and spent a lot of time at each other's houses.

"I haven't seen you since what . . . the Fourth of July parade?" Gwendy asks, giving her friend a hug.

"You ran into me that day, too."

Gwendy covers her mouth. "Oh my God, you're right, I did. I am so sorry." Gwendy had knocked a glass of lemonade right out of Brigette's hand and all over her brand-new sundress. "I never used to be so darn clumsy, but I think I'm making up for lost time these past few years."

"That's okay, Gwen," says Brigette, laughing. "I think I know a way you can make it up to me."

"Tell me."

Brigette raises her eyebrows. "Well, you probably haven't heard, but I was elected president of the PTA in September."

"That's terrific," Gwendy says with sincere admiration. "Congratulations."

"Oh, whatever." Brigette rolls her eyes and smiles. "Miss Big-Shot Senator."

"I'm not a—"

"Anyhoo, I'm in charge of the New Year's Eve celebration this year—weather permitting, we're holding it outside in the Common—and I was wondering . . . "

Gwendy doesn't say anything. She can guess what's coming next.

". . . if you might stop by and say a few words?"

One of her mother's favorite sayings flits through her mind: *Don't choose the easy thing to do, choose the* right *thing to do.*

"It would only be for three or four minutes, but I understand if you can't or don't want to or you already have other—"

Gwendy places a hand on her old friend's shoulder. "I'd be happy to."

Brigette squeals and throws her arms around Gwendy. "Thank you, thank you! You have no idea what this means to me."

RICHARD CHIZMAR

"Just make sure you're not holding a mug of hot chocolate when you see me coming."

Brigette giggles, relaxing her bear hug. "Deal."

"I'll give you a call next week so you can tell me when and where to show up."

"Perfect. Thank you again *so* much." She starts walking away, and then turns back. "A very merry Christmas to you and your family."

"Merry Christmas. I'm glad I ran into you."

Gwendy turns and starts wading through the crowded promenade. Halfway to the bench where she'd left her mom, Mrs. Peterson comes into view and Gwendy raises a hand to wave—but she never gets that far.

Her mother isn't alone.

A stab of terror piercing her chest, Gwendy starts pushing her way through the crowd.

31

"Who was that?" Gwendy nearly shouts, frantically scanning the throng of shoppers behind the bench. "Who were you just talking to?"

Mrs. Peterson looks up in surprise. "What . . . what's wrong?"

"The man with the black hat, the one you were just talking to . . . did you know him?"

"No. He said he's visiting with friends in town. He asked me a couple of questions and went on his way."

"What friends?"

"I didn't ask him that," Mrs. Peterson says. "What's going on, Gwen?"

Up on her tip-toes now, still searching the crowd. "What kind of questions did he ask?"

"Well, let me think . . . he asked how I liked it here in Castle Rock. I told him I'd lived here my entire life, that it was home."

"What else?"

"He wanted to know if I could recommend a good restaurant for dinner. He said he hadn't had a decent hot meal in weeks and was very hungry, which I thought was rather odd considering how nicely he was dressed."

"What else?"

"That was it. It was a very brief conversation."

"What did he look like? Can you describe him?"

"He was . . ." She thinks for a moment. "Tall and thin and probably about your age. I think he had blue eyes."

Mrs. Peterson stands and picks up her shopping bags from the bench. "Now are you going to tell me what's going on, or do I have to start worrying about you, too?"

Thinking fast, Gwendy looks at her mom with that same blank poker face. "There's a reporter who's been bothering me these past few weeks. He's persistent and not a very nice man. For a minute, I was afraid he followed me all the way up here from DC."

"Oh, dear," Mrs. Peterson says, and Gwendy immediately feels horrible for lying to her. "This gentleman seemed very kind, but I guess you can never really tell, can you?"

Gwendy gives her a quick nod. "It's getting harder and harder, that's for sure."

32

THE COLD AIR FEELS good in Gwendy's lungs and the burn in her legs is like catching up with an old friend. After dropping off her mom at the house, she wanted nothing more than to drive home to the condo and head straight upstairs to bed, but her brain had other ideas. Especially after the scare she experienced at the mall.

She follows Pleasant Road down the winding hill, the street well lit and cheery with yard after yard of twinkling Christmas lights, until it runs into Route 117. The road grows darker here, just the occasional pole lamp casting dim globes of sickly yellow light onto the ground below, and she picks up her pace, heading for the old covered bridge that stretches across the Bowie Stream.

Running is usually just as much an act of meditation for Gwendy as it is a form of exercise. On those rare bad weather days when she's forced to work out on the treadmill or StairMaster at the YMCA, she often listens to music on her Sony Walkman—usually something upbeat and peppy like Britney Spears or the Backstreet Boys; a fact Ryan never fails to give her grief about—but during her outside jaunts, she almost always prefers to run in silence. Just her and her innermost thoughts, the familiar sounds of the city or the countryside, and the rhythmic slap of her shoes punishing the asphalt.

Tonight she's thinking about her husband.

Of course, she's worried about him and anxious he won't make it home in time for Christmas, but she knows those concerns are out of her control and even a little bit selfish. Ryan has a job to do, a sometimes dangerous job he loves with all his heart, and she supports that passion unconditionally—as he does hers. It's part of what makes them work so well together. On a daily basis, they may prefer the simplicity of each other's company—a walk in the woods, a game of gin rummy at the kitchen table, a late night double-feature at the drive-in—to crowded black tie events and fancy art openings, but when work calls they each know the drill. True passion is almost always accompanied by sacrifice.

So why all the angst this time? Gwendy wonders, as she approaches the old bridge. It's not like this is their first rodeo. Ryan's gone away on dozens of other assignments since they've been together.

A steady stream of likely answers trickles through her mind as she runs: it's because of the holidays; it's because her mother is still recovering from a life-altering illness; it's because the button box is back in her life and she doesn't have a clue what to do with it.

Gwendy considers the question a little longer, then checks off All Of The Above and picks up her stride, focusing on the road ahead.

The streetlight attached to the covered bridge's outer planking is dark, most likely having served as target practice for some bored townie with a .22 rifle. The entrance looms ahead like a dark, hungry mouth, but Gwendy doesn't break pace. She glides into the heart of the pitch-dark tunnel, rapid footsteps echoing around her, reminding

her, just as they did when she was a little girl, of the old fairy tale about the evil troll living under the bridge.

It's just a story, she tells herself, pumping her arms. *Nothing's going to reach out and grab you. Nothing's going to leap down from the rafters and—*

She's a few yards away from reaching the exit when she hears a noise in the darkness behind her. A furtive scratching like claws scrambling across pavement. A finger of dread tickles the length of her spine. She doesn't want to turn and look, but she can't help herself. A pair of close-set eyes, unblinking and coal-red, watches her from deep within the shadows. Gwendy feels her legs begin to falter and wills them to keep moving, her breath coming fast and ragged. By the time she looks away, she's clear of the bridge and back under the stars on Route 117.

Probably just a stupid raccoon, Gwendy thinks, sidestepping around a pothole in the road. Pulling cool air deeply into her lungs, she keeps running, a little faster now, and doesn't look back.

33

WITH ALL OF HER Christmas shopping completed and the bulk of her work correspondence caught up, Gwendy spends the Monday and Tuesday before Christmas settling into an almost scandalously lazy routine. For her, anyway.

On Monday morning, she sleeps in (waking almost ninety minutes later than her usual 6:00 AM, having forced herself not to set her alarm the night before) and remains in bed until nearly noon, catching up on news programs and movies on cable. After a luxuriously long bubble bath, she makes a light lunch and retires to the sunroom, where she stretches out on the loveseat and alternates between staring out the floor-to-ceiling windows and daydreaming, and reading the new Ridley Pearson thriller deep into the afternoon. Once the December sun begins its inevitable slide toward the horizon, she marks her page, leaves the thick paperback on an end table, and goes upstairs to change clothes. Then she grabs her keys and heads to her parents' house for dinner.

After nearly three months of being waited on in her own kitchen, Mrs. Peterson is finally feeling strong enough to cook again. Under the watchful eye of her husband, Mrs. Peterson prepares and serves a steaming hot casserole of beef stroganoff and a Christmas tree-shaped platter stacked with homemade rolls. The food is delicious, and

Mrs. Peterson is so openly and endearingly pleased with herself, her smiles bring tears to her husband's eyes.

After dinner, Gwendy and her father shoo Mrs. Peterson into the den while they clear the table and wash the dishes. Then they join her in watching *A Christmas Carol* on television and crack open a new jigsaw puzzle.

At a few minutes before nine, Gwendy bids her folks goodnight and drives back to the condo. She considers going for a run, but decides against it, working the three-digit combination on the safe instead, and taking out the button box.

It keeps her company at the foot of the bed while she changes into a nightgown and brushes her teeth. She finds herself talking to it more and more now, just as she did when she was younger. The box doesn't answer, of course, but she's almost certain that it listens—and watches. Before she puts it away for the night, she sits on the edge of the mattress, places the box in her lap, and pulls the lever by the red button. The narrow shelf slides out and on it is a tiny chocolate monkey. She admires the fine detail, and then slowly lifts it to her nose and inhales. Her eyes flutter closed. When she opens them again, she gets up and walks at a deliberate pace to the bathroom where she flushes the chocolate down the toilet. Unlike last time, there is no panic and there are no tears. "See?" she says to the box as she reenters the bedroom, "I'm in control here. Not you." And then she returns the button box to the safe and goes to sleep.

Tuesday is more or less a repeat performance of the day before, and there are moments when Gwendy can't help but think of scenes from *Groundhog Day*, that silly movie Ryan likes so much.

She starts the day by again sleeping in and lounging in bed for most of the morning. Then she takes a long bath, finishes the Pearson novel shortly after lunch, and devours the first four chapters of a new John Grisham.

She's not in much of a holiday mood, but she forces herself to haul out the artificial tree and boxes of ornaments from the crawlspace. She sets up the tree in the corner of the family room and hangs last year's wreath on the front door. When dusk descends upon Castle Rock, she goes upstairs to change and heads to her parents' for another dose of Mom's home cooking. Lasagna and salad are on the menu tonight, and Gwendy eats two generous servings of each. After dinner, she and her father once again take care of the dishes, and then join Mrs. Peterson in the den. Tonight's feature is *White Christmas*, and when the movie's over and the credits are rolling, Mr. Peterson shocks both his wife and daughter by rolling up his pant legs, doing his best Bing Crosby imitation, and performing the "Sisters" routine in its entirety. Mrs. Peterson, hardly believing her eyes, collapses onto the sofa laughing so hard she ends up having a coughing fit, prompting her husband to hightail it into the kitchen for a glass of cold water. She takes a big drink, starts hiccupping, and lets out a tremendous belch—and the three of them burst out in delirious laughter all over again. The party breaks up a short time later, and Gwendy heads home, snow flurries dancing in the beams of her car's headlights.

She takes her time driving across town and walks into her condo at precisely nine-thirty, juggling and almost dropping the stack of Tupperware containers her mom sent home with her. There's enough leftover lasagna, stroganoff, and cheesecake in there to last well into the New

Year. She's struggling to open the refrigerator when her cell phone rings. Gwendy glances at the counter where she left the phone next to her keys and turns her attention back to the refrigerator. She slides the largest container onto the top shelf next to half-empty cartons of milk and orange juice, and is trying to make room on a lower shelf when the phone rings again. She ignores it and jams in the other two containers, one after the other. The phone rings a third time as Gwendy is closing the refrigerator door, and it's almost as if a lightning bolt reaches down from the heavens and strikes some sense into her.

She lunges for the cell phone, knocking her keys onto the floor.

"Hello? Hello?"

At first there's nothing—and then a burst of loud static.

"Hello?" she says again, disappointment washing over her. "Is anyone—"

"Hey, baby girl . . . I was just about to hang up."

Every muscle in her body goes limp, and she has to lean against the table to keep from falling. "Ryan . . . " she says, but it comes out in a whisper.

"You there, Gwen?"

"I'm here, honey. I'm so happy to hear your voice." The tears come now, gushing down her face.

"Listen . . . I don't know how long this line's gonna last. We haven't even been able to file our reports with the magazine or any of the newspapers . . . yesterday . . . fires all over the place."

"Are you okay, Ryan? Are you safe?"

"I'm okay. I wanted to tell you . . . taking care of myself and doing my best . . . get home to you."

"I miss you so damn much," she says, unable to keep the emotion from her voice.

"I miss you, too, baby . . . know when I'll be able to call again, but I'll keep trying . . . by Christmas."

"You're breaking up."

Staccato bursts of static hijack the line. Gwendy pulls the phone away from her ear and waits for them to decrease in intensity. Amidst the noise, she hears her husband's faint voice: ". . . love you."

She presses the phone back to her ear. "Hello? Are you still there? Please take care of yourself, Ryan!" She's nearly shouting now.

The line crackles and then goes silent. She holds it tight against her ear, listening and hoping for one more word—anything—but it doesn't come.

"I love you more," she finally whispers, and ends the call.

34

FORTY-EIGHT HOURS OF LAZINESS (she tries to tell herself she wasn't actually being lazy, she was simply relaxing and decompressing—but she's not buying it) is all Gwendy can tolerate. On Wednesday, she wakes up at dawn and goes for a run.

A sleety, granular snow is falling and the roads are slick with ice, but Gwendy pushes forward, the hood of her sweatshirt cinched tight around her face. Running through downtown Castle Rock is usually a comforting experience for Gwendy. She jogs her normal route—down Main Street, avoiding the unshoveled sidewalks, past the Common, the library, and the Western Auto, circling the long way around the hospital and heading uptown past the Knights of Columbus hall and back toward View Drive—and she feels a sense of rightness in her world, a sense of *belonging*. She's traveled all over the country for her work—first as an ad exec, then as a writer/filmmaker, and finally as a public servant—but there's only one Castle Rock, Maine. Just as her mother had told the stranger in the black hat at the mall, this is home.

But something feels off today.

This morning she feels like a visitor traveling through a foreign and unfriendly landscape. Her mind is cluttered and distracted, her legs sluggish and heavy.

At first she blames this feeling on the way her phone

call with Ryan ended the night before—so abrupt and un-settled. After hanging up, she cried herself to sleep with worry.

But when she passes in front of the sheriff's station as she makes her way uptown, she realizes it's something else entirely. For the first time, she understands how much she's dreading the difficult task that awaits her later that morning.

35

GWENDY'S FIRST IMPRESSION OF Caroline Hoffman is that she's a woman who is used to getting her own way.

When Gwendy walks into the stationhouse at 9:50 AM (a full ten minutes early for the meeting), she's hoping the Hoffmans haven't arrived yet so she and Sheriff Ridgewick will have time to discuss the investigation.

Instead, the three of them are waiting for her in the conference room. There's no sign of Sheila Brigham, the longtime dispatcher for the Castle Rock Sheriff's Department, so Deputy George Footman escorts Gwendy inside and closes the door behind her.

Sheriff Ridgewick sits on one side of a long, narrow table, a chair standing empty next to him. Mr. and Mrs. Hoffman sit side-by-side across from him, a second empty chair separating them. They make an interesting couple. Frank Hoffman is slight in stature, bespectacled, and dressed in a wrinkled brown suit that has seen better days. He has dark circles under his eyes and a slender nose that has been broken more than once. Caroline Hoffman is at least three or four inches taller than her husband, and thick and broad across the shoulders and chest. She could be a female lumberjack, something not unheard of in this part of the world. She's wearing jeans and a gray Harley Davidson sweatshirt with the sleeves rolled up. A tattoo of a boat anchor decorates one meaty forearm.

"Sorry to keep you waiting," Gwendy says, taking a seat beside the sheriff. She places her leather tote on the table in front of her, but quickly removes it and puts it on the floor when she realizes it's dripping wet from melting snow. She uses the sleeve of her sweater to wipe up the small puddle left behind.

"Morning, Congresswoman," Sheriff Ridgewick says.

"Can we get started now?" Mrs. Hoffman asks, glaring at the sheriff.

"Sure thing."

Gwendy leans forward and extends her hand, first to Mr. Hoffman and then to his wife. "Good morning, I'm Gwendy Peterson. I'm very sorry to meet you both under these circumstances."

"Good morning," Mr. Hoffman says in a surprisingly deep voice.

"We know who you are," Mrs. Hoffman says, wiping her hand on her pant leg, like she touched something unsavory. "Question is, how you gonna help us?"

"Well," Gwendy says, "I'll do whatever I can to help locate your daughter, Mrs. Hoffman. If Sheriff Ridgewick needs—"

"Her name is Carla," the big woman interrupts, eyes narrowing again. "Least you can do is say her damn name."

"Of course. I'll do whatever I can to help find Carla. If the sheriff needs additional personnel, I'll make sure he has it. If he needs more equipment or vehicles, I'll make sure he has that, too. Whatever it takes."

Mrs. Hoffman looks at Sheriff Ridgewick. "What the sheriff needs is someone to come in here and show him how to do his job properly."

Gwendy bristles. "Now wait a minute, Mrs. Hoffman—"

The sheriff touches Gwendy's forearm, silencing her. He looks at the Hoffmans. "I know you folks are desperate for answers. I know you're unhappy with the way the investigation is progressing."

Mrs. Hoffman snickers. "Progressing."

"But I assure you me and my men are working around the clock to chase down every single scrap of possible evidence. No one will rest until we find out what happened to your daughter."

"We're just so worried," Mr. Hoffman says. "We're both sick with worry."

"I understand that," the sheriff says. "We all do."

"Jenny Tucker over the hair salon says your guys were checking out the Henderson farm yesterday," Mrs. Hoffman says. "Wanna tell me why that is?"

The sheriff sighs and shakes his head. "Jenny Tucker's the biggest gossip in town. You know that."

"Doesn't make it not true."

"No, it doesn't. But in this case it's *not* true. Far as I know, no one's been out to the Henderson place."

"Why not?" she presses. "From what I hear he did time in Shawshank when he was younger."

"Hell, Mrs. Hoffman, half the hard-grit laborers in Castle County served time at one point or another. We can't go searching all their houses."

"Tell us this," she says, cocking her head to the side like an agitated rooster. "And give us a straight answer for a change. What *do* you have? After a full week of walking around in circles, what *do* you have?"

Sheriff Ridgewick lets out a deep breath. "We've talked about this before. I can't tell you anything more than I already have. In order to protect the integrity of the investigation—"

Mrs. Hoffman slams a heavy fist down on the table, startling everyone in the room. "Bullshit!"

"Caroline," Mr. Hoffman says, "maybe we should—"

Mrs. Hoffman turns on her husband, eyes burning. The thick veins in her neck look like they're going to explode. "They got nuthin', Frank. Just like I told ya. They ain't got a goddamn thing."

Gwendy has been listening to all of this with a sense of disconnected awe, almost as though she were sitting in the front row of a studio audience at an afternoon talk show—but something inside her awakens now. She raises a hand in an effort to take control of the room and says, "Why don't we all just take a minute and start over again?"

Glaring at Gwendy, Mrs. Hoffman suddenly jerks to her feet, knocking over her chair. "Why don't ya save that happy horseshit for the folks 'round here who were dumb enough to vote for ya?" She kicks the chair out from under her feet, spittle spraying from the corners of her mouth. "Coming in here with your fancy clothes and five-hundred-dollar boots, trying to shine us on like we're stupid or somethin'!" Flinging open the door, she storms out.

Gwendy stares after Mrs. Hoffman with her mouth hanging open. "I didn't mean to . . . I was just trying . . . "

Mr. Hoffman stands. "Congresswoman, sheriff, you'll have to excuse my wife. She's very upset."

"It's no problem at all," Sheriff Ridgewick says, escorting him to the door. "We understand."

"I apologize if anything I said made matters worse," Gwendy says.

Mr. Hoffman shakes his head. "Things can't get much worse, ma'am." He looks closely at Gwendy. "Do you have children of your own, Congresswoman?"

Gwendy tries to swallow the lump that rises in her throat. "No. I don't."

Mr. Hoffman looks down at the ground and nods, but he doesn't say anything further. Then he shuffles out of the room.

Sheriff Ridgewick stares after him and turns back to Gwendy. "That went well."

Gwendy looks around the conference room, unsure of what to do next. It all happened so fast her head is swirling. She finally blurts out, "I bought these boots at Target."

36

GWENDY MOPES AROUND THE condo for the rest of the afternoon, watching cable news and drinking too much coffee. She left the sheriff's office hours earlier feeling depressed and incompetent in equal measures, like she let everyone in the room down. She obviously said something to stoke Mrs. Hoffman's ire, and the sheriff was doing just fine handling the two of them before she went and opened her big mouth. And that smartass comment about her clothes and boots . . . it bothered Gwendy. It shouldn't have, she knows that, but it did. Since returning to Castle Rock after all those years away, she'd grown used to the occasional snide dig. It came with the territory. So why did she let it get to her like that?

"Well, don't just sit there," she says to the button box. "Figure it out and get back to me."

The box ignores her. It sits there—on the end table, next to a half-empty mug of coffee and an outdated *TV Guide*—and answers her with stubborn silence. She grabs the remote and turns up the volume on the television.

President Hamlin stands at the edge of the White House lawn, his arms crossed in defiance, the Marine One helicopter whirring in the background. ". . . and if they continue to make these threats against the United States of America," he says, flashing his best tough-guy look at the camera, "we will have no alternative but to fight power with power. This great country will not back down."

Gwendy watches in disbelief. "Jesus, he thinks he's in a movie."

Her cell phone rings. She knows it's too soon to hear from Ryan again, but she scrambles across the sofa and snatches it up anyway. "Hello?"

"Hey, Gwen. It's Dad."

"I was just thinking about you guys," she says, muting the television. "Need me to bring anything for dinner?"

There's a slight pause before he answers. "That's why I'm calling. Would you be terribly upset if we canceled tonight?"

"Of course not," she says, sitting up. "Is everything okay?"

"Everything's fine. Mom's just kind of dragging after her doctor's appointment this afternoon. To tell you the truth, so am I."

"Do you want me to pick up something from Pazzano's and drop it off? I'd be happy to."

"That's sweet of you, but no, we're good. I'm going to reheat some lasagna and we're hitting the sack early."

"Okay, but call me if you change your mind. And give Mom my best."

"I will, honey. Thanks for being such a great daughter."

"'Night, Dad."

Gwendy hangs up and looks at the Christmas tree standing in the corner. A string of lights has gone out. "Yeah, some great daughter . . . I completely forgot she even had a doctor's appointment today." She gets up and takes a couple of steps into the middle of the room, and then stops. Suddenly, she wants to cry, and not just your garden variety sniffles, either. She feels like dropping to her knees, burying her face in her hands, and sobbing until she passes out.

A tightness growing in her chest, Gwendy slumps onto the sofa again. *This is pathetic*, she thinks, wiping away tears with the heels of her hands. *Absolutely pathetic. Maybe a hot bath and a glass of wine will—*

And then she looks at the button box.

37

GWENDY CAN'T REMEMBER THE last time she went on two runs in the same day. If she had to guess, she'd say it was the summer when she was twelve years old, the same summer Frankie Stone started calling her Goodyear and she finally decided to do something about her weight. She ran pretty much everywhere that summer—to the corner store to pick up eggs and bread for her mother, to Olive's house to listen to records and tear through the latest issue of *Teen* magazine, and of course, every morning (even on Sundays) she ran the Suicide Stairs up to Castle View Park. By the time school started in September, Gwendy had lost almost fifteen pounds of baby fat and the button box was hidden away in the bottom of her bedroom closet. After that, life would never be the same for her.

Tonight, she jogs at a fast clip along the centerline of Route 117, enjoying the feel of her heart pounding in her chest. The snow stopped falling several hours earlier, right around dinnertime, and the plows are busy clearing side streets at this late hour. The main roadways are eerily empty and hushed. At the bottom of the hill, she passes a group of men wearing hardhats and orange vests with CRPW stenciled on them: *Castle Rock Public Works*. One of them drops the shovel he's working and gives her an enthusiastic round of applause. She flashes the man a smile and a thumbs-up, and keeps on trucking.

The tiny piece of chocolate the button box dispensed was in the shape of an owl, and Gwendy stared in rapt fascination at the amazing details—the staggered lines of each feather, the pointy tip of its beak, the pools of dark shadow that made up its eyes—before popping it into her mouth and allowing it to dissolve on her tongue.

There was a moment of complete *satisfaction*—at what, she didn't know, maybe *everything*—and then a rush of startling clarity and energy spread throughout her body. All of a sudden, she not only no longer felt like crying, her entire body felt lighter, her vision seemed clearer, and the colors in the condo appeared brighter and more vibrant. Was this what it was like when she was younger? She couldn't exactly remember. All she knew was that it suddenly felt like she'd sprouted wings and could fly up into the sky and touch the moon. She immediately changed into workout clothes and running shoes, and headed outside.

No, not immediately, she reminds herself, as she cruises past the Sunoco station toward Main Street and the center of town.

Something else happened first.

In the midst of all those good feelings, those *wonderful* feelings, she suddenly found herself fixating on the red button at the left side of the box, and then slowly reaching out with a finger and touching it, caressing its glassy surface, and the thought of actually pressing it and erasing President Richard Hamlin from the face of the earth wormed inside the basement of her brain like the wisp of a forgotten dream just before waking.

227

Whoa, girl, a little voice whispered inside her head. *Be careful what you daydream because that box can hear you thinking. Don't you doubt it, not even for a second.*

Then, and only then, did she carefully withdraw her finger and go upstairs to change into running gear.

38

THE NEXT DAY DAWNS clear and cold. A brisk wind blows in from the east, swirling amongst the treetops and drifting mounds of snow against the tires of parked cars and the sides of buildings. In the glare of morning sun, the blanket of ice-crusted snow is almost too brilliant to look at.

Gwendy pulls her car to the shoulder of the narrow back road and takes off her sunglasses. A half-dozen sheriff's department vehicles are parked in a staggered line in front of her. A group of uniformed officers huddle between two of the cars, heads down, lost in conversation. An open field of maybe fifteen or twenty acres bordered by deep woods stretches out along the right side of the road. Thick trees crowd the other side, blocking the sun's rays and dropping the temperature there by at least ten degrees.

Sheriff Ridgewick spots her car and disengages from the other men. He starts walking in her direction, so Gwendy gets out and meets him halfway.

"Thanks for coming on short notice," he says. "I thought you'd want to be here."

"What's going on?" she asks, zipping up her heavy jacket. "Did you find the girls?"

"No." He looks out across the open field. "Not yet. But we did find the sweatshirt Carla Hoffman was wearing the night she disappeared."

She looks around. "All the way out here?"

He nods and points at the northeast corner of the field. Gwendy follows his finger and, squinting, she can just make out a couple of dark figures camouflaged by the backdrop of trees. "One of my men spotted it this morning. Wind was blowing so hard it was actually moving across the field. That's what caught his attention. That and the color."

"Color?"

"We knew from talking to Carla's older brother that she'd been wearing a pink Nike sweatshirt the night she was taken. The officer saw something small and pink tumbling across the field and pulled over. At first he thought it was just a plastic grocery bag. Wind blows hard like today, these trees act like a kind of wind tunnel and all kind of crap flies through here. Empty cans. Fast food litter. Plastic bags, paper bags, you name it."

"Sounds like your officer deserves a raise for checking it out."

"He's a good man." The sheriff looks closely at Gwendy. "All of my men and women are."

"So what happens next?"

"Evidence is out there now looking at the sweatshirt. Deputy Footman's pulling in some additional bodies to conduct a search of the surrounding area. You're welcome to help if you'd like. Half the town will probably show up if we let 'em."

Gwendy nods her head. "I think I will. I have a hat and gloves in the car."

"Helluva way to spend the day before Christmas Eve." He sighs deeply. "Anyway, probably another hour or so before we get started. Might as well get inside and run the heater." He starts back toward the other men. "There's coffee and donuts in one of the patrol cars if you want."

Gwendy doesn't acknowledge the offer. She's staring at the snow-covered field, her brow furrowed. "Sheriff . . . if your deputy found the sweatshirt blowing around on top of the snow, and it just stopped snowing yesterday afternoon sometime, that means the sweatshirt was left sometime in the last . . . " She thinks. "Sixteen hours, give or take."

"Maybe," he says. "Unless it was somewhere under cover and the wind shook it loose after the snow stopped."

"Huh," Gwendy says. "I didn't think of that."

"All I know is there are no houses within three miles of us and this stretch of road is mainly used by hunters. The sweatshirt either found us by accident or we were meant to find it." He glances at the men huddled between the cars and then looks back at Gwendy. "My money's on the second one."

39

SHERIFF RIDGEWICK IS RIGHT about one thing: half the town of Castle Rock shows up for the search. At least, that's how it appears to Gwendy as she takes her place in the long, arcing line of locals, most of the women dressed in colorful winter coats and boots, most of the men wearing the standard autumn uniform of an adult New England male—camouflage. As they begin fanning out across the field, Gwendy looks around and sees old folks walking alongside young couples, and young couples walking alongside college and high school kids. Even under these dreary circumstances, the sight brings a brief smile to her face. For all of its dark history and idiosyncrasies, Castle Rock is still a place that takes care of its own.

The sheriff's instructions to the group are simple enough: walk slowly, side by side, with no more than five or six feet separating you from the person on your right and the person on your left; if you find something, anything, don't touch it and don't get too close, call for one of the officers and they'll come running.

Gwendy stares at the snow-covered terrain in front of her, willing her feet to move deliberately, despite the frigid temperature pushing her to pick up the pace. Her cheeks burn and her eyes water from the constant gusts of wind. For the first time that morning, her thoughts stray to the button box. She knows that eating the chocolate was a mistake, a moment of weakness, and is determined not to allow it to happen again. Sure, it made her feel better last night—okay, it did much more than that, if she's being perfectly honest with herself. And when she looked in the bathroom mirror this morning—feeling more rested and purer in soul than she's felt in months—and noticed the dark circles that had taken up residence under her eyes the past few weeks had vanished, all of a sudden the magic chocolates didn't seem like such a bad idea after all.

But then she remembered her finger brushing against the smooth surface of the red button and that little voice whispering inside her head—*Be careful what you daydream because that box can hear you thinking*—and she shuddered at the memory and tried her best to push it far, far away.

"Gwendy, dear," a voice says, startling her from her thoughts. "How is your mother doing?"

Gwendy cranes her head forward and looks first to her right, and then to her left. An older woman, a few spots down the line, lifts a gloved hand and waves.

"Mrs. Verrill! I didn't even see you there."

The woman smiles back at her. "That's okay, dear. It's hard to tell who's who all bundled up like this."

"Mom's doing much better. Thank you for asking. She's back in the kitchen and ready to kick my father out of the house so she can have some peace and quiet."

Mrs. Verrill lifts a hand to her mouth and chuckles. "Well, please tell her I said hello and that I would love to stop by and see her sometime."

"I'll do that, Mrs. Verrill. I'm sure she'd be thrilled to see you."

"Thank you, dear."

Gwendy smiles and returns her focus to the field of

untouched snow stretching out before her. She guesses it's maybe another fifty or sixty yards before they reach the tree line. *Then what?* she thinks. *Do we turn around or plow ahead?* She must have missed that part of Sheriff Ridgewick's—

Sensing that the man walking to her immediate right is staring at her, Gwendy glances in his direction. She's right; his brown eyes are closely studying her. The man is young, early twenties, and underdressed in an untucked flannel shirt and Buffalo Bills baseball cap. He suddenly grins and looks right past her. "I told you it was her, Pops."

"Excuse me?" she says, confused.

A quiet voice from her left says, "I thought for sure she was too young to be a governor . . . or senator."

Gwendy looks from her left to her right and back again. "I'm . . . I'm not either one."

The older man scratches at his unshaven chin. "Then what are ya?"

"I'm a—"

"She's a congresswoman," the young man says with a look of embarrassment. "I told you that."

"I'm afraid you two have lost me," Gwendy says, exasperated. "Have we met before?"

"No, ma'am. My name is Lucas Browne and that there's my father."

"Charlie," the other man says, placing his hand on his stomach and giving a little bow. "Third generation Castle Rock."

"Wait a minute, so your name is . . . Charlie Browne?"

He bows again. "At your service."

The younger man groans and blushes an even deeper shade of red.

They're actually kind of charming, Gwendy thinks.

"Anyway, I saw you standing there when the sheriff was talking," Lucas says. "I nudged my Pops and told him who you were." He looks at his father with a raised chin. "But he didn't believe me."

"I didn't, I admit it," he says, hands raised. "I thought you had to be a lot older to work high up in the government like that."

Gwendy gives him a big smile. "Well, I'll take that as a compliment. Thank you."

Beaming, the older man puffs his chest out. "My boy there, he's the smart one in the family. Two years of college down in Buffalo . . . before he ran into a bit of trouble. But he'll go back and finish what he started one day soon. Ain't that right, son?"

Lucas, suddenly looking like he'd rather be anywhere else in the world right then, nods his head. "Yes, sir. One day."

"Well, it's a pleasure to meet you both," Gwendy says, anxious to move on from the conversation. "It's always nice to get to know—"

"What's that?" Lucas asks, pointing at a small dark object emerging from the trees in front of them. A murmur of raised voices travels down the line of searchers. People start pointing. Someone on the far left flank breaks formation and chases after the object, slipping and sprawling face-first in the snow. Several people sarcastically cheer.

At first, Gwendy thinks it's a plastic grocery bag, like the sheriff had described earlier. It's the right size and shape, and it's riding the wind's currents, up, down, swirling in tight little circles, tumbling wildly to the ground, and then surfing back up again.

But then, halfway across the open field, the object appears to inexplicably change direction in mid-flight. Banking hard to the right, it heads directly toward her

—and Gwendy flashes back to a blustery golden-hued April afternoon she once spent at the side of a boy she loved, flying kites and holding hands and feeling like their happiness would last forever and—

at that moment, she understands it's a hat swooping toward her in the whipping wind—a small, neat black hat.

The dark object suddenly veers to the left, hurtling away from her at terrific speed, and for one fleeting, hopeful moment, Gwendy believes she's wrong, it's just a grocery bag after all—but then the wind squalls again and it loops back around, coming closer and closer, swerving and somersaulting across the frozen ground directly at her feet—

—where Lucas Browne leaps forward and stomps on it, abruptly halting its long journey.

"Would you look at that?" Charlie Browne says, eyes wide as 1891 silver dollars. He bends down to pick it up.

"Stop!" Gwendy shouts. "Don't touch it!"

The older man jerks his hand back and looks up at her. "Why not?"

"It . . . it could be evidence."

"Oh, yeah," he says, straightening up and smacking himself a good one on the side of his head.

A small crowd has gathered around them by now.

"What is it?"

"Is that what I think it is?"

"Did you see that sucker move? Almost like someone was working a remote control."

Deputy Footman sidesteps his way through the group of onlookers. "What've you got there?"

"Sorry about that, officer," Lucas says, removing his boot from the object. "Only way I could stop it."

The deputy doesn't say anything. He drops to a knee in the snow and carefully examines the object.

It's not a grocery bag, of course.

It's a hat—a small, neat black hat.

Faded with age, tattered and worn around the edges of the brim, a ragged three-inch tear slicing across the top of the crushed dome.

"This thing's been out here forever," the deputy says, rising to his feet. "It's no help to us." He walks away, and the crowd begins to dissipate.

Gwendy doesn't move. Biting her lip, she stares down at the black hat, almost hypnotized by the sight of it, unaware that Charlie Browne and his son are watching her. *Is Farris sending some kind of a message? Or is he playing games with me? Making up for lost time?*

She bends down to get a better look at the filthy hat— and a gust of wind picks it up and swoops it away from her, sending it hurtling toward the road. It climbs and climbs, then plummets to the ground, rolling on its side like a child's Frisbee for several yards before lifting up and taking flight once again.

Gwendy stands in the middle of the snow-covered field, eyes lifted to the sky, and watches as the black hat disappears into the trees beyond the road. When she turns around, the staggered human chain of searchers has moved on without her.

40

HOMELAND CEMETERY IS THE largest and prettiest of Castle Rock's three graveyards. There are tall iron gates out front with a lock, but it's used only twice a year—on graduation night at the high school and on Halloween. Sheriff George Bannerman is buried in Homeland, as is Reginald "Pop" Merrill, one of the town's most infamous—and unsavory—citizens.

Gwendy drives through the ornate gates just as dusk is settling over the land, and she can't decide whether the cemetery, with its rolling hills and stone monuments and lengthening shadows, appears tranquil or menacing. Maybe both, she decides, parking along the central lane and getting out. Maybe both.

Knowing where she's going, she walks a direct route, punching her way through knee-deep snow to a scattering of grave markers that rest atop a steep hillside skirted by a small grove of pine trees. There are smudges of naked earth here where the tree's thick branches have prevented snow from accumulating below. The treetops sway back and forth overhead, whispering secrets to each other in the cold breeze.

Gwendy stops in front of a small marker in the last row. The trees grow close together, blocking the day's dying light and casting the ground in shadow, but she knows what's carved onto the headstone by memory:

OLIVE GRACE KEPNES
1962-1979
Our Loving Angel

She drops to a knee in the snow, only several inches deep here, and traces the grooves with her bare fingertips. As always, she thinks whoever was in charge of the inscription did a pretty shitty job of it. Where were the exact dates of Olive's birth and death? Those were important days to remember and should have been included. And what did "Our Loving Angel" have to say about the *real* Olive Kepnes? Nothing. It said nothing at all to keep her memory alive. Why didn't it mention that Olive had an infectious laugh and knew more about Peter Frampton than anyone else in the world? Or that she was a connoisseur of all types of candy and bad horror movies on late night television? Or that she wanted to be a veterinarian when she grew up?

Gwendy kneels in the snow—feet numb despite her waterproof boots thanks to hours of fruitless searching earlier in the afternoon—and visits with her old friend until the pools of shadow melt together into one, and then she says goodbye and slowly walks back in the dark to her car.

41

GWENDY LOCKS THE CAR and is halfway up the sidewalk to her condo when she hears footsteps behind her.

She glances over her shoulder, scanning the length of parking lot. At first she doesn't see anyone, even though she can still hear the hurried footfalls. Then she spots him: a man, lost in the shadows between streetlights, striding toward her. Maybe thirty yards away and moving fast.

Gwendy hurries to the entrance and punches in her security code with shaky fingers. She tries to open the door but it doesn't budge.

She looks behind her again, panicking now. The man is closer. Maybe fifteen yards away. She can't be a hundred percent certain in the dark, but it looks like he's wearing a ski mask, obscuring his face. Just like in her dream.

Gwendy punches in the code again, concentrating on each button. The door buzzes. She flings it open, steps inside, and slams it shut behind her, sprinting up the stairs to the second floor. As she fumbles with her keys outside the door to her condo, she hears someone rattling the entrance door downstairs, trying to get in.

She finally gets the door unlocked and rushes inside. After locking the deadbolt, she hurries to the front window and takes a peek outside.

The parking lot is empty. The man is nowhere in sight.

42

"MORNING, SHEILA," GWENDY SAYS, a little too eager for the early hour. "I'm here to see Sheriff Ridgewick."

The scarecrow-thin woman with bright red hair and matching eyeglasses looks up from the magazine she's reading. "Hey there, Gwendy. Sorry I missed you the other day. Heard there was some fireworks."

Sheila Brigham has manned the glass-walled dispatch cubicle at the Castle County Sheriff's Department for going on twenty-five years now. She's also in charge of the front desk and coffee maker. Sheila started on the job fresh out of community college, when bell-bottoms were all the rage and George Bannerman was patrolling The Rock. She got married and raised a family here, and took good care of Alan Pangborn during his decade-long stint, and, unlike most folks, didn't let the fire of '91 scare her away, even though she'd spent nearly three weeks in a hospital bed in the aftermath of that disaster.

"I'm afraid I didn't inspire much confidence in our elected officials," Gwendy says.

Sheila waves a dismissive hand. "Don't worry yourself none about that. Carol Hoffman's mean as a hornet on a good day—and she doesn't have many of those."

"Still, I feel horrible. That poor woman."

Sheila makes a grunting sound. "You want to feel sorry for someone, feel sorry for that husband of hers."

"Can't argue with you there."

She picks up her magazine again. "You can go on back. He's waiting for you."

"Thank you. Merry Christmas, Sheila."

She makes that same grunting sound and returns her attention to reading.

The door to Sheriff Ridgewick's office is open, so Gwendy walks right in. He's sitting behind his desk talking on the telephone. He holds up a finger, mouths "one minute," and gestures for her to sit down. "I understand that, Jay, I do. But we don't have time. I need it yesterday." His face darkens. "I don't care. Just get it done."

He hangs up and looks at Gwendy. "Sorry about that."

"No problem," she says. "Now what's all the secrecy about? Why couldn't you just tell me on the phone?"

The sheriff shakes his head. "Don't like that cell phone of yours. Last thing we need right now is a leak."

"You're as paranoid as my father. He's whipped himself into a frenzy. Thinks all the world's technology's going to collapse when the clock strikes midnight next week."

"Tell that to Tommy Perkins. He claims he picks up a half-dozen cell phone conversations every day on that shortwave of his."

Gwendy laughs. "Tom Perkins is a dirty-minded, senile old man. You really believe what he says?"

The sheriff shrugs. "How else did he know about Shelly Piper being pregnant before the rest of the town?"

"Probably did the deed himself, the old perv."

The sheriff's jaw drops, his mouth forming a perfect O. "Gwendy Peterson."

"Oh, hush," she says, waving a hand at him. "And stop stalling, Norris. Is the news that bad?"

The smile fades from his face. "I'm afraid it is."

"Tell me."

He gets up and closes the door. Returning to his desk, he opens a drawer and takes out a large envelope. "Take a look," he says, handing it to Gwendy.

She opens the flap and slides out a pair of glossy color photographs. It's hard to tell what the three small white objects are in the first photo, but the second shot is a close-up view and much clearer. "Teeth?" she says, looking at the sheriff.

He nods in response.

"Where'd they come from?"

"They were found inside the pocket of Carla Hoffman's pink sweatshirt."

43

GWENDY'S STILL THINKING ABOUT the three small teeth hours later as she showers and gets ready to attend Christmas Eve mass with her parents.

Forensics have already confirmed that the teeth are archetypal for a female Carla Hoffman's age, and Sheriff Ridgewick's in touch with the girl's dental office to determine if they have X-rays on file. Carla's parents know about the sweatshirt but haven't been told about the gruesome discovery made inside the pocket. "It's our first concrete piece of evidence," the sheriff had confided to Gwendy. "We need to see where it leads before news of it gets blabbed all over town."

The discovery of the teeth had pushed thoughts of last night's terrifying encounter in the parking lot out of Gwendy's mind, but they return to her now, twenty-four hours later, as she's selecting a dress for church.

The whole thing feels like a bad dream. The man was wearing a mask, she's sure of that now. But at this time of year, ski masks are common. Other than that, she doesn't remember much of anything. Dark clothing, maybe jeans, and some kind of shoes or boots with a heel. She definitely heard him before she saw him. Another thing, she hadn't noticed any strange cars in the lot, so he either parked somewhere nearby and came in on foot, or he lived close by.

But why would anyone want to do that? she thinks, settling on a long black dress and a pair of leather boots. *Was he just trying to scare her? Or was it more than that? For that matter, did he even know it was* her? *Maybe the whole thing was just a prank. Or had nothing to do with her at all.*

Gwendy also wonders why she chose not to say anything about it to Sheriff Ridgewick this morning, although she has a theory about that. It all points back to the chocolate owl she ate a couple of nights earlier. It's true that eating the chocolate immediately infused her with a sense of calm energy and clearness of vision—both the internal and external variety—but it did more than that: it gave her back her sense of balance in the world; a sense of confidence that was sorely lacking these past few months. Missing Ryan, floundering at her job, worrying about her mom and a President with the IQ of a turnip and the temperament of a schoolyard bully . . . all of a sudden, she felt like she could shoulder her share of the load again, and more. *All thanks to some kind of wonder drug . . . or candy,* she thinks. It was an uneasy feeling to have, and in some ways it made her feel even guiltier about eating the chocolate. After all, she wasn't a lost and insecure teenager like the first time the button box came into her life. She was an adult now with years of experience at handling the curve balls life threw at her.

She's strapping on her seat belt and pulling out of the parking lot on her way to meet her parents at church when that dreaded question rears its ugly head once again: *How much of her life is her own doing, and how much the doing of the box with its treats and buttons?*

Gwendy has never been less sure of the answer.

44

FOR AS LONG AS Gwendy can remember, the Petersons have attended the 7:00 PM Christmas Eve mass at Our Lady of Serene Waters Catholic Church, and then gone crosstown to the Bradleys' annual holiday party afterward. When she was a little girl, Gwendy would often spend the drowsy drive home with her head resting against the cool glass of her back-seat window, searching the night sky for a glimpse of Rudolph's glowing red nose.

The church service tonight lasts a little more than an hour. Hugh and Blanche Goff, the Petersons' longtime next-door neighbors, arrive a few minutes late. Gwendy happily scoots over to make room for them in the pew. Mrs. Goff smells like mothballs and peppermint breath mints, but Gwendy doesn't mind. The Goffs were never able to have children of their own, and she's like a surrogate daughter to them.

Gwendy closes her eyes and loses herself in Father Lawrence's sermon, his soothing voice as much a part of her childhood memories as Saturday morning swims with Olive Kepnes at the Castle Rock Rec Pool. Few of the priest's stories are new to her, but she finds his words and delivery comforting nonetheless. Gwendy watches the simple joy in her mother's face as Mrs. Peterson sings along with the choir and, a short time later, stifles a giggle when

Mr. Goff breaks wind during Holy Communion, earning a gentle elbow to the ribs from her father.

When the service is over, the Petersons file out with the rest of the congregation and stand outside of the church's main entrance, mingling with friends and neighbors. The most boisterous greetings are reserved for Gwendy's mom, as this is her first time back at church in weeks. There is one exception, however. Father Lawrence wraps Gwendy up in a bear hug and actually lifts her off the ground. Before he disappears back into the rectory, he makes her promise to come back soon. Once the crowd thins out, Gwendy walks Mr. and Mrs. Goff to their car in the parking lot, and then she follows her parents to the Bradleys' mansion on Willow Street.

Anita Bradley—as Castle Rock gossips have enviously whispered for going on three decades now—married old and married rich. After her husband Lester, a wildly successful lumber tycoon nineteen years her senior, suffered a fatal heart attack in early 1991, many locals thought that once the funeral services were completed and legal matters attended to, Anita would pack up house and head for the sunny shores of Florida or maybe even an island somewhere. But they were wrong. Castle Rock was her home, Anita insisted, and she wasn't going anywhere.

As it turns out, her staying was a very good thing for the town. Anita has spent the almost nine years since her husband's death donating her time and money to a long list of local charities, volunteering her sewing expertise to help out the Castle Rock High School Theatrical Society, and serving as the head of the library's Board of Trustees. She also makes a ridiculously delicious apple pie, which she sells at Nora's Bake Shop all summer long.

248

A smiling and moderately tipsy Anita—her long, thick gray hair styled into some kind of gravity-defeating, triple-decker, power tower—welcomes the Peterson family inside her home with dainty hugs and papery soft (not to mention, sandpapery dry) kisses on their cheeks. The three-story Bradley house sprawls more than seven thousand square feet atop the rocky hillside and is filled with room after room of turn-of-the-century antiques. Gwendy has always been terrified of breaking something valuable. She takes her parents' coats and, adding her own, leaves them draped over a Victorian sofa in the library. Then she heads into the bustling, high-ceiled great room, searching for familiar faces, anxious to make an appearance and get back home again.

But, as is often the case in Castle Rock, familiar faces her age prove difficult to find. Most of Gwendy's close friends from high school never returned to The Rock after attending college. Like her, many of them took jobs in nearby Portland or Derry or Bangor. Others moved to distant states, only returning for occasional visits with parents or siblings. Brigette Desjardin is one of only a small handful of exceptions to this rule, and appears to be the only one in attendance here at the Bradleys' annual Christmas party. Gwendy bumps into her by the punch bowl—there are no unfortunate spills this time around—and enjoys a spirited but brief conversation with Brigette and her husband Travis before a PTA friend of Brigette's drunkenly interrupts them. Gwendy smiles and moves on.

Of course, there are plenty of others waiting to speak with Gwendy. While familiar faces are scarce, friendly—and merely curious—faces are not. It seems as if everyone there wants a photo or a quick word or two with the

Celebrity Congresswoman, and the barrage of questions comes fast and furious:

Where's your husband? Where's Ryan? ("Overseas working on assignment.")

How's your mom feeling? ("Much better, thank you, she's here somewhere, I'm actually trying to find her.")

What's President Hamlin really like? ("Ummm . . . he's a handful.")

How's it going down there in DC? ("Oh, it's going okay, trying to fight the good fight every day.")

Why aren't you drinking? Hold on, let me grab you something. ("No, thanks, really, I'm kind of tired and not much of a drinker.")

What about those missing girls? ("It's terrible and it's frightening, and I know the sheriff and his people are doing everything humanly possible to find them.")

I saw you running the other night. Don't you ever get tired of all that running? ("Actually, no, I find it relaxing—that's why I do it.")

How worried should I be about what's going on with North Korea? Do you think we're going to war? ("Don't lose any sleep over it. A lot of awfully bad things would have to happen for the United States to go to war, and I don't believe it's going to happen.") Gwendy's not so sure about this last one, but she figures it's part of her job to keep her constituents calm.

By the time she locates her parents sitting in a corner on the opposite side of the room talking to a co-worker from Dad's office (the man also requests a "real quick photo," which Gwendy dutifully smiles for), she feels like she's just finished an all-day publicity whirlwind for one of her book releases. She also has a splitting headache.

Once they're alone, she tells her parents she's exhausted and asks if they'll be okay at the party without her. Her mom fusses that Gwendy needs to stop working so hard and orders her right home to bed. Her father gives her a sarcastic look and says, "I think we can survive without your guiding light for one night, kiddo. Go home and get some rest." Gwendy swats him on the arm, kisses them both goodnight, and starts across the room toward the library to get her coat.

That's when it happens.

A muscular hand reaches out from the sea of people and grabs Gwendy by the shoulder, spinning her around.

"Well, well, well, look who it is."

Caroline Hoffman suddenly looms in front of her, bloodshot eyes narrowed into slits. The hand gripping Gwendy's shoulder begins to squeeze. Her free hand balls into a meaty fist.

Gwendy glances around the room, looking for help . . . but Mr. Hoffman is nowhere in sight, and none of the other partygoers seem to have noticed what's happening. "Mrs. Hoffman, I don't know what—"

"You make me sick, you know that?"

"Well, I'm sorry you feel that way, but I don't know—"

The hand squeezes harder.

"Let go of me," Gwendy says, shrugging the woman's hand off of her. She can smell Mrs. Hoffman's breath—and not beer, the hard stuff. The last thing she wants to do is antagonize her. "Listen, I appreciate the fact that you're upset and you don't like me very much, but this isn't the time or the place."

"I think it's the perfect time and place," Mrs. Hoffman says, an ugly sneer spreading across her face.

"For what?" Gwendy asks heavily.

"For me to kick your stuck-up little ass."

Gwendy takes a step back, raising her hands in front of her, in shock that this is actually happening.

"Is everything okay?" a tall man Gwendy has never seen before asks.

"No," she says, voice trembling. "No, it's not. This woman has had too much to drink and needs a ride home. Can you help her find someone? Or perhaps you can call her husband?"

"I'd be happy to." The man turns to Mrs. Hoffman and tries to take her arm. She shoves him away. He slams into a couple behind him, knocking the other man's wine-glass out of his hand. It tumbles to the floor and shatters—and now everyone in the room is staring at the tall stranger and Mrs. Hoffman.

"What are y'all gawking at?!" she slurs, the color rising in her chubby cheeks. "Buncha blue-ballers!"

"Oh, my," someone behind Gwendy says.

Gwendy takes advantage of the distraction and quickly slips away into the library where she digs out her coat from the now massive pile on the sofa. She puts it on, rubbing away furious tears, and starts pacing in front of the sofa. *How dare she put her hands on me? How dare she say those things?* Pacing faster now, she can feel the heat intensifying throughout her body. *All I was trying to do was help her rude ass and she acts like—*

A loud crash comes from the next room.

And then cries of alarm.

Gwendy hurries back into the great room, afraid of what she might find.

Caroline Hoffman is lying unconscious on the hard-wood floor, her arms splayed above her head. A nasty gash on her forehead is bleeding heavily. A crowd has gathered around her.

"What happened?" Gwendy asks no one in particular.

"She fell," an old man, standing in front of her, says. "She'd calmed down some and was walking out on her own and she just spun around and fell and hit her head on the table. Darnedest thing I've ever seen."

"It was almost like somebody pushed her," another woman says. "But there wasn't anybody there."

Remembering the flush of anger she'd just experienced and a long-forgotten dream about Frankie Stone, Gwendy stumbles out of the house in a daze and doesn't look back.

Head spinning, it takes her several minutes to remember where she parked her car. When she finally locates it near the bottom of the Bradleys' long driveway, she gets in and drives home in silence.

45

WHEN GWENDY GETS HOME fifteen minutes later, she changes into a nightgown, washes her face and brushes her teeth, and goes directly to bed. She doesn't turn on the television, she doesn't put her cell phone on charge, and for the first time since its return, she leaves the button box locked inside the safe overnight.

46

GWENDY DOESN'T CHECK ON the button box the next morning, either. Another first for her.

Christmas dawns dark and gloomy with a suffocating layer of thick clouds hanging over Castle Rock. The weather forecast calls for snow by nightfall, and the town DPW trucks are already busy dropping salt as Gwendy makes her way down Route 117 to her parents' house. Almost all of the homes she passes still have their Christmas lights glowing at ten-thirty in the morning. For some reason, instead of looking cheerful and festive, the dim lights and murky sky provide a depressing backdrop to her drive.

Gwendy expects to pass the day in the same blue mood she went to bed with but is determined to hide it from her parents. They have enough on their plate without her ruining their Christmas celebration.

But by the time the brunch table is cleared and presents are exchanged in the living room, Gwendy finds herself in a surprisingly cheery mood. Something about spending Christmas morning in the house she grew up in makes the world feel safe and small again, if only for a short time.

As they do every year, Mr. and Mrs. Peterson fret about Gwendy going overboard and spoiling them with gifts— "We asked you not to do that this year, honey, we didn't have much time to get out and shop!"—but she can tell they're surprised and pleased with her choices. Dad, still dressed in a robe and pajamas, sits in his recliner with his legs up, reading the instructions for his brand-new DVD player. Mom is busy modeling her L.L.Bean jacket and boots in the full-length hallway mirror. A stack of jigsaw puzzles, assorted shirts and sweaters, a TiVo so Mom can digitally record her shows, a men's L.L.Bean winter jacket, and subscription gift cards to *National Geographic* and *People* magazine sit under the tree, next to Ryan's unopened presents.

Gwendy is equally pleased with her own gifts, particularly a gorgeous leather-bound journal her mother found in a small shop in Bangor. She's sitting on the living-room sofa, relishing the texture of the thick paper against her fingertips, when her father reaches out with a large red envelope in his hand.

"One more little present, Gwennie."

"What's this?" she asks, taking the envelope.

"A surprise," Mrs. Peterson says, coming over and sitting on the arm of her husband's recliner.

Gwendy opens the envelope and slides out a card. A glittery Christmas tree decorates the front of it. A little girl with pigtails stands at the foot of the tree, looking up with wonder in her eyes. Gwendy opens the card—and a small white feather spills out and flutters to the carpet at her feet.

"Is that—?" she starts to ask, eyes wide, and then she reads what her father has written inside the card . . .

You have ALWAYS
believed in magic,
dear Gwendy, and magic
has ALWAYS believed
in you.

. . . and she can no longer find the words to finish.

She looks up at her parents. They're both sitting there with goofy grins on their faces. Happy tears are forming in her mother's eyes.

Gwendy bends down and picks up the feather, stares at it with disbelief. "I just can't . . . " She turns the feather over in her hand. "How did you . . . *where* did you find it?"

"I found it in the garage," her father says proudly. "I was looking for a 3/8 inch screw in one of those cabinets you liked to play with so much when you were little, the ones with all the little drawers?"

Gwendy mutely nods her head.

"Slid out the last drawer in the last row, and there it was. I couldn't believe it myself."

"You must have hidden it there," her mother says. "What? Almost thirty years ago."

"I don't remember," Gwendy says. She looks up at her parents and this time she's the one wearing the big goofy grin. "I can't believe you found my magic feather . . . "

47

When Gwendy is ten years old, her family spends a week in upstate New York visiting with one of Mr. Peterson's first cousins. It's July and the cousin (Gwendy can no longer remember his name nor the names of his wife or three children; as best as she can recall, they never saw them again except at the occasional wedding or funeral) has a summer home on a lake, so there's plenty to do. Canoeing, swimming, fishing, jumping off tire swings, even water skiing. There's also a small town nearby with a mini golf course and water slide for the tourists.

Gwendy looks forward to the trip all summer long. She starts saving her money as soon as the school year ends, stashing away the quarters she makes from helping her father clean the garage and dusting the house from top to bottom for her mother. By the time she packs her own suitcase and climbs into the back seat for the seven-hour drive, she's managed to save almost fifteen dollars in loose change. Her plan is to hold onto most of the money until the final two days of the trip, and then splurge on herself. Candy, comics, ice cream, maybe even a pocket transistor radio with an earphone if she has enough left over.

But it doesn't work out that way.

Within minutes of their arrival, Mr. and Mrs. Peterson disappear into the cabin for a "grand tour" and Gwendy finds herself standing by the car surrounded by a group of local kids, including the cousin's three children, who are all spending the summer at the lake. The boys are shirtless and tan and look wild with their messy hair and sugar-spiked eyes. The girls are long-legged and aloof and mostly older.

Nervous and not knowing what else to say, Gwendy eventually unzips her suitcase and shows the kids her plastic marble bag filled with quarters. Most of them are indifferent, and a few even laugh at her. But one of the older boys doesn't laugh; he seems interested, and maybe even impressed. He waits until the other kids all run off, whooping and hollering into the back yard, and then he approaches Gwendy.

"Hey, kid," he says, looking around. "I got something you might be interested in."

"What?" Gwendy asks, even more nervous now that she's alone with a boy—a cute, older boy.

He reaches into the back pocket of his cut-off jean shorts and when his hand swims back into view, it's holding something small and fluffy and white.

"A feather?" Gwendy asks, confused.

A look of disgust comes onto the older boy's face. "Not just any old feather. It's a magic feather."

Gwendy feels her heart flutter. "Magic?"

"That's right. It once belonged to an Indian chief who used to live around here. He was also a medicine man, a very powerful one."

Gwendy swallows. "What does it do?"

"It does . . . magic stuff," he says. "You know, like bringing you good luck and making you smarter. Stuff like that."

"Can I hold it?" Gwendy asks almost breathlessly.

"Sure, but I'm getting kinda tired of taking care of it. I've had it for a few years now. You interested in taking it off my hands?"

"You want to give it to me?"

"Not give," he says. "Sell."

Gwendy doesn't miss a beat. "How much?"

The boy lifts a dirty finger to his lips, thinking. "I guess ten dollars is a fair enough price."

Gwendy's shoulders sag a little. "I don't know . . . that's a lot of money."

"Not for a magic feather it ain't." He starts to put the feather back in his pocket. "No biggie, I'll just sell it to someone else."

"Wait," Gwendy blurts. "I didn't say no."

He looks down his nose at her. "You didn't say yes either."

Gwendy glances at the plastic bag filled with quarters and then looks at the feather again.

"Tell you what," the boy says. "You're new around here, so I'll cut you a deal. How's nine dollars sound?"

Gwendy feels as if she's just won the grand prize at the spinning wheel booth at the Castle Rock Fourth of July carnival. "Deal," she says at once, and starts counting out nine dollars in quarters.

48

DRIVING HOME LATER THAT Christmas night, Gwendy thinks about her father's words from earlier: "We all poked fun at you about that feather, Gwen, but you didn't care. You *believed*. That's what mattered then, and that's what matters now: you've always been a believer. That beautiful heart of yours has led you down some unexpected roads, but your faith—in yourself, in others, in the world around you—has always guided you. That's what that magic feather of yours stands for."

49

UNFORTUNATELY, EVEN AFTER THE surprise appearance of her long-lost magic feather, Gwendy's good mood doesn't last, and by nine o'clock, she's slumped in front of the television, missing her husband terribly. A hollow ache has crept into her heart, and no amount of meditation or happy-sappy positive thinking can ease it. She stares at her cell phone, willing it to ring, but it remains silent on the sofa beside her.

The button box sits on the coffee table next to her Grisham book, the small white feather, and a cup of hot tea. Normally, Gwendy would be worried about spilling her drink and getting it on the box. Tonight she doesn't give a damn.

Once she got back to the condo, Gwendy called Sheriff Ridgewick to wish him a Merry Christmas and ask about Caroline Hoffman. He picked up on the first ring and assured her that Mrs. Hoffman was doing just fine. Some stitches and a concussion—and one doozy of a hangover. The hospital kept her overnight and released her earlier this afternoon. Her husband was waiting to drive her home.

The phone call started the shift in Gwendy's mood—she could still picture the dark angry gash on the woman's forehead; the glassy, excited stares of the partygoers gathered around her—and then when she stumbled upon the tattered deck of playing cards Ryan left behind, the downward spiral began in earnest.

On their second official date, many years ago in downtown Portland, Ryan confided in her that he'd always wanted to be a magician. Gwendy was charmed by the thought and implored him to show her a magic trick. After dinner, and much convincing on Gwendy's part, they stopped at a drug store and picked up a pack of Bicycle playing cards. The two then sat on a bench in the park and Ryan demonstrated three or four different tricks, each one more elaborate than the last. Gwendy was impressed with his skills, but it was much more than that. It was *deeper* than that. This childlike wonder was a part of Ryan she'd never known existed when they were just friends, a part of his true self. That was the first time Gwendy thought: *I might be falling in love with this guy.*

Twenty minutes earlier, when Gwendy bent over to pick up her bookmark and discovered the old pack of cards sitting in a nest of dust bunnies underneath the corner of the sofa, her first reaction was one of calm gratitude: *Hey, I'm glad I found you, Ryan will be looking for you when he gets home.*

And then those four words exploded inside her head: *WHEN HE GETS HOME!*

Oh my God, he forgot his damn cards, she thought, her stomach roiling. *He never went anywhere without taking them with him. He says they're his good luck charm. He says they remind him of home and keep him safe.*

Gwendy picks up her book from the coffee table, and then immediately puts it down again. She can't focus. She glances at the television screen, jiggling her foot with nervous tension. "If he's not going to call, at least let there be something on the news. Anything. Please." She knows she talks to herself too much, but she doesn't care. No one is around to hear her.

She turns her head and stares at the button box. "What are you looking at?"

Leaning forward, she runs her finger along the rounded edge of the wooden box, keeping a fair distance from the buttons. "You made me hurt that woman last night, didn't you?"

She feels *something* then, a slight vibration in her fingertip, and pulls her hand back. Before she realizes what she's saying: "What's that? You can help me get Ryan home?"

Sure, she thinks hazily. *Find out from the news where the rebel forces are located in Timor. Once you've pinpointed their location, push the red button. Once they're gone, the uprising's over, and Ryan comes home again. Simple.*

Gwendy shakes her head. Blinks her eyes. The room feels like it's swaying, ever so slightly, like she's riding on a ship in uneasy seas.

And, hey, while you're at it, why not do something about that jerk-off president of yours, too?

Is she thinking these thoughts or *listening* to them? It's suddenly hard to tell. "Destroy North Korea?" she asks dimly.

You need to be careful there. You do that and someone will most likely assume the U.S. military's responsible. Someone like China, let's say, and they'll want to retaliate, won't they?

"Then what are you proposing?" Her voice sounds very distant.

Not proposing anything, dear woman, just food for thought is all. But what if that president of yours were to up and disappear?

*Now that's not such a bad idea, huh? And just think, it's only a
red button away.*

Gwendy leans forward again, her eyes fixed on something far away. "Murder in the name of peace?"

*You could certainly call it that, couldn't you? Personally, I
rather think of it along the lines of that age-old question: if it were
possible, would you travel back in time and assassinate Hitler?*

Gwendy reaches out with both hands and picks up the
button box. "Richard Hamlin's a lot of things, most of
them bad, but he's no Adolf Hitler."

Not yet, anyway.

She places the box in her lap and leans back into the
sofa cushion. "Tempting, but who's to say the vice president will be any better. Guy's a certified fruitcake."

Then why not get rid of the lot of them? Start over fresh.

Staring at the rows of colored buttons. "I don't
know . . . that's a lot to think about."

*Okay then. Perhaps it would be easier to start with
something . . . less far-reaching. A bitch-cow of a woman named
Caroline Hoffman? How about a certain ill-mannered congressman from the state of Mississippi?*

"Maybe . . . " Gwendy slowly reaches out with her
right hand—

And that's when the phone rings.

50

GWENDY SHOVES THE BUTTON box off her lap and onto the sofa. Snatches up her cell phone. "Hello? Ryan? Hello?"

"I'm sorry, Mrs. Peterson," a quiet voice says. "It's Bea. Bea Whiteley."

"Bea?" she says absently. It feels like the room swims back into focus, although she can't for the life of her remember it appearing out of focus in the first place. "Is everything okay?"

"Everything's fine. I just wanted to . . . first, I want to apologize for calling so late on Christmas. I didn't even think about the three-hour time difference until the phone started ringing."

"No need to apologize, Bea. I'm wide awake."

"It sounds like Ryan didn't make it home."

Gwendy settles back into the sofa. She glances at the button box and then quickly looks away. "No, he didn't. I'm hoping to hear from him soon, though."

"I'm sorry."

"Thank you." She can hear laughter in the background. "Sounds like your grandchildren are having a Merry Christmas."

"Running around here like a bunch of wild animals."

Gwendy laughs.

"Mrs. Peterson, I called to thank you."

"For?"

"The beautiful notes you wrote inside your books to my children. Nobody's ever said those kinds of things about me before, except for maybe my own family. I just wanted to tell you how much it meant to me."

"It was my pleasure, Bea. I meant every word."

"It was such a surprise," Bea says, sniffling. "I swear I've never seen my daughter look at me the way she did today. Like she was so proud of me."

"She has every right to be proud," Gwendy says, smiling. "Her mother's an amazing woman."

"Well, thank you again so much. I . . . " She hesitates.

"Is there something else?"

When Bea Whiteley speaks again, her voice sounds odd and tentative. "I was wondering . . . is everything else there okay, Mrs. Peterson?"

"Everything's fine," she says, sitting up and glancing at the button box again. "Why do you ask?"

"I feel silly saying it out loud, but . . . just before I called, I couldn't shake the feeling that something was wrong . . . that you were in some kind of trouble."

A shiver passes through Gwendy. "Nope, everything's fine. I've just been sitting here watching television."

"Okay . . . good." She sounds genuinely relieved. "I'll let you be now. Merry Christmas, Mrs. Peterson, and thank you again."

"Merry Christmas, Bea. I'll see you in a couple of weeks."

51

GWENDY WAKES UP EARLY the next morning with what feels like a mild hangover, despite having not touched a drop of alcohol the night before. She downs a bottle of water and knocks out a hundred sit-ups and fifty push-ups on the bedroom floor, hoping to get her blood pumping and chase away the headache. She'd slept restlessly, with unremembered dreams lurking just below her consciousness—but even without the details, she senses they were unpleasant and frightening.

The snow stopped falling a short time before daylight, leaving behind four or five inches in Castle County and most of western Maine. The traffic man on Channel Five warns travelers looking for a post-Christmas getaway to adjust their schedules for delays. Gwendy calls her father and informs him that she's coming over to shovel the driveway and sidewalk, and she's not taking no for an answer. Surprisingly, he agrees without an argument and tells her he'll have hot coffee and leftover sausage-and-egg casserole from yesterday's brunch waiting for her on the table when she arrives.

Gwendy throws on warm clothes and laces up her boots, then heads downstairs to clean off her car. Once she's finished scraping the windows and brushing off the roof, she climbs inside the Subaru and immediately turns down the heat. She's already sweating.

On her way down the hill, she spots a group of children having a snowball fight at the Castle View Rec Park. She can hear their excited shouts and squeals of delight even with the windows up. She smiles and tries to remember how long it's been since she's plunked someone with a snowball. Too long, she decides.

Ten minutes later, she turns onto Carbine Street and spots the flashing red and yellow lights of an ambulance in the distance. Her first pang of concern is for Mrs. Goff—she suffers from occasional bouts of vertigo and has fallen before. Last spring, she'd spent two weeks in the hospital nursing a broken hip. As she gets closer, Gwendy realizes the ambulance is parked in her parents' driveway and someone on a stretcher is being loaded into the back. She stomps on the brakes and fishtails to the curb.

Her father stumbles out the front door of the house, carrying Mrs. Peterson's purse in one hand and a jacket in the other. His face is drawn and pale.

"Dad!" Gwendy shouts, jumping out of the car and meeting him on the snow-covered sidewalk. "What happened? Is Mom okay?"

They both turn and watch as the ambulance pulls away, disappearing down the street.

"I don't know," he says weakly. "She started having cramps shortly after I talked to you. At first, she thought it was because she ate too much last night, but then the pain got worse. She was curled up in a ball on the bed, crying. I was about to call you when she started vomiting blood. That's when I called the ambulance. I didn't know what else to do."

Gwendy takes her father by the arm. "You did the right thing. Are they taking her to Castle County General?"

He nods, his eyes big and ready to fill with tears.

"Come on," she says, guiding him toward the curb. "I'll drive you."

52

THERE ARE ONLY A handful of other people sitting on the bright orange, plastic-molded seats outside of the emergency room at 10:00 AM. An older bald man nursing a sore neck from a fender-bender earlier that morning, a teenage boy with a deep cut on his lip and another under his swollen and darkening right eye from a sledding mishap, and a young Asian couple holding a pair of fussing, pink-faced twins on their laps.

When Mr. Peterson sees his wife's oncologist, Doctor Celano, emerge via the swinging doors marked NO ENTRANCE, he immediately gets to his feet and meets him in the middle of the waiting room. Gwendy scrambles to catch up.

"How is she, Doc?" he asks.

"We gave her some pain medication, so she's resting comfortably. There's been no more vomiting since the ambulance."

"Do you know what's wrong?" Gwendy asks.

"I'm afraid her tumor markers are up again," the doctor says, a solemn expression coming over his face.

"Oh, Jesus," Mr. Peterson says, sagging into his daughter's shoulder.

"I know it's difficult, but try not to get too alarmed, Mr. Peterson. Her blood tests from Wednesday's appointment just came back this morning. I pulled them up on the computer when I heard the ambulance call, and they're showing an uncomfortable increase—"

"An uncomfortable increase?" Mr. Peterson says. "What does that mean?"

"It means that most likely the cancer has returned. To what extent, we don't know yet. We're going to admit her today and run a series of tests."

"What kind of tests?" Gwendy asks.

"We've already drawn more blood this morning. Once she's settled into a room, we'll schedule abdominal and chest scans."

"Tonight?" Mr. Peterson asks.

He shakes his head. "Not on a Sunday, no. We'll let her get some rest and wheel her over to Imaging in the morning."

Mr. Peterson looks past the doctor to the swinging doors. "Can we see her?"

"Soon," Doctor Celano says. "They're transporting her to the second floor anytime now. Once she's in her room, I'll come back down and get you myself."

"Does she know yet?" Gwendy asks.

The doctor nods. "She asked me to be honest with her. I believe her exact words were: 'Do not blow sunshine up my rear. Give it to me straight.'"

Mr. Peterson shakes his head, eyes shiny with tears. "That sounds like my girl."

"Your girl's a fighter," Doctor Celano says. "So try to be as strong for her as you can. She'll need you. The both of you."

53

GWENDY OPENS THE DOOR to the house she grew up in, the only real honest-to-God house she's ever lived in—with an actual garage and sidewalk and yard—and walks inside. The interior is dark and silent. She immediately turns on the overhead light in the foyer. Her father's car keys lie on the hardwood floor, dropped in panic and unnoticed. She picks them up and returns them to their spot on the foyer table. Walking into the living room, she turns on the lamps at each end of the sofa. *That's better*, she decides. Everything looks to be in its proper place. You would never even know by looking around what kind of chaos the morning had brought.

She walks upstairs, running her hand along the polished wood bannister where four empty red stockings hang. Halfway down the carpeted hallway, she glances into her parents' bedroom, and that's when any semblance of normalcy inside the house is shattered into a million jagged pieces. The bed sheet and blankets are pushed into a heap on the floor. One of the pillows and a significant portion of the white mattress sheet are streaked with dark splashes of blood and bite-sized chunks of a half-digested meal. Her father's pajamas lie in a pile on the floor at the entrance to the small walk-in closet. The entire room smells sour, like food that has been left in the sun too long and gone bad.

Gwendy stands in the doorway, taking it all in, and then she springs into action. She makes quick work of the bed, stripping the sheets, blankets, and pillowcases. Bundling them together with her father's discarded pajamas, she runs them to the basement, holding her breath, and dumps the dirty sheets and PJs into the washer. Once that's done, she returns upstairs and sprays the bedroom with a can of scented air-freshener she finds in the bathroom. Then she takes down clean sheets and pillowcases from the top shelf of the closet and remakes the bed.

Standing back and examining her work, she remembers the reason she came to the house in the first place. She finds an overnight bag and packs a change of clothes for her father, a clean nightgown for her mother, and several pairs of socks. She doesn't know why she adds the extra socks, but she figures better safe than sorry. Next she goes into the bathroom and gathers toiletries. Adding them to the bag, she zips it up tight and heads into the hallway.

Something—a feeling, a memory, she's not really sure—makes her stop outside the doorway to her old bedroom. She peers inside. Although it's long been converted into a combination guest room and sewing room, Gwendy can still picture her childhood bedroom with crystal clarity. Her beloved vanity stood against that wall, her desk, where she wrote her first stories, in front of the window. Her bookshelf right there next to a Partridge Family trashcan, her bed against the wall over there, beneath her favorite Billy Joel poster. She leans into the room and gazes at the long, narrow closet where her mother now stores swathes of cloth and sewing supplies. The same closet where she hid the button box all those years. The same closet where the first boy she ever loved had died violently right in front of her eyes, his head bashed to a bloody pulp by that monster Frankie Stone.

And that cursed box.

"What do you want from me?" she asks suddenly, her voice strained and harsh. She walks farther into the room, turns in a slow circle. "I did what you asked and I was just a goddamn child! So why are you back again!" She's shouting now, her face twisted into an angry mask. "Why don't you show yourself and stop playing games?"

The house responds with silence.

"Why me?" she whispers to the empty room.

54

MONDAYS ARE NOTORIOUSLY BUSY days at Castle County General Hospital, and December 27 is no exception. The nurses and orderlies are understaffed by nearly ten percent thanks to the holiday weekend and three members of the custodial crew call out sick because of the flu—but life marches on around here.

Gwendy sits alongside the bed in Room 233 and watches the steady rise and fall of her mother's chest. She's been sleeping peacefully for nearly a half-hour now, which is the only reason Gwendy's alone in the room with her. Twenty minutes earlier, she finally managed to shoo her father into the hallway and downstairs to the cafeteria to get himself breakfast. He hadn't left his wife's side since they were reunited yesterday afternoon and was hesitant to go, but Gwendy insisted.

The John Grisham novel sits unopened on Gwendy's lap, a coupon for granola bars marking her page. She listens to the intermittent beeping of the machines and watches the constant drip of saline and remembers dozens of other hospital rooms very much like this one. The windowless third-floor room at Mercy Hospital where her dear friend Johnathon had taken his final breaths, dozens of photographs and homemade get-well cards affixed to the wall above his head. So many other rooms in so many other hospitals and AIDS clinics she'd once visited. So many brave human beings, young and old, male and female, all united by one basic purpose: survival.

Ever since those days, Gwendy has loathed hospitals—the sights, smells, sounds—all while maintaining the utmost respect for those who fight for their lives there, and the doctors and nurses who aid them in that fight.

". . . *you will die surrounded by friends, in a pretty nightgown with blue flowers on the hem. There will be sun shining in your window, and before you pass you will look out and see a squadron of birds flying south. A final image of the world's beauty. There will be a little pain. Not much.*"

Richard Farris once spoke those words to her, and she believes them to be true. She doesn't know when it will happen, or where, but that doesn't matter to her. Not anymore.

"If anyone deserves that kind of a goodbye, it's you, Mom." She looks down at her lap, stifling a sob. "But I'm not ready yet. I'm not ready."

Mrs. Peterson, eyes still closed, chest still rising and falling, says: "Don't worry, Gwennie, I'm not ready either."

"Oh my God," Gwendy almost screams in surprise, her book tumbling from her lap to the floor. "I thought you were sleeping!"

Mrs. Peterson half-opens her eyes and smiles lazily. "I was until I heard you going on and on."

"I am *so* sorry, Mom. I've been doing that, talking out loud to myself, like some kind of crazy old cat lady."

"You're allergic to cats, Gwendy," Mrs. Peterson says, matter-of-factly.

Gwendy looks closely at her mom. "Oh-kay, and that must be the morphine talking."

Mrs. Peterson lifts her head and looks around the room. "You actually convinced your father to go home?"

"Not a chance. But I did make him go to the cafeteria and get something to eat."

She nods weakly. "Good job, honey. I'm worried about him."

"I'll take care of Dad," Gwendy says. "You just worry about getting better."

"That's in God's hands now. I'm so tired."

"You can't give up, Mom. We don't even know how bad it is. It could be—"

"Who said anything about giving up? That's not going to happen, not as long as I have you and your father by my side. I have too much to live for."

"Yes," Gwendy says, nodding. "You sure do."

"All I meant is . . . " She searches for the right words. "If I'm supposed to beat this thing again, if there's any chance at all, then I'll beat it. I believe that. No matter how hard of a fight awaits me. But . . . if I'm *not* supposed to . . . if God decides this is my time, then so be it. I've lived a wonderful life with more blessings than any one person should possess. How can I possibly complain? Anyway, that's all I meant . . . that's the only way they're going to stuff me in the ground."

"Mom!" Gwendy exclaims.

"What? You know I don't want to be cremated."

"You're impossible," Gwendy says, taking down her backpack from the windowsill. "I brought you some of those little fruit juices you like so much and some snacks. Also brought you a surprise."

"Oh, goodie, I like surprises."

She unzips her backpack. "Eat and drink first, then the surprise."

"When did you get so bossy?"

"Learned from the best," Gwendy says and sticks out her tongue.

"Speaking of surprises—and I don't know why in the world I woke up thinking about this just now—but do you remember the year we tried to surprise your father for his birthday?" She scoots herself up in bed, eyes wide open and alert now, and takes a sip from the small carton of juice.

"When we decorated the garage with all those balloons and streamers?" Gwendy asks.

Mrs. Peterson points a finger at her. "That's the one. He was away fishing all afternoon. We crammed everyone inside and the big plan was to hit the door opener as soon as he pulled into the driveway."

Gwendy starts giggling. "Only we didn't know he'd fallen off a log and landed in the mud on the way back to his truck."

Mrs. Peterson nods. "We'd swiped the automatic door opener from his truck so he'd had no choice but to get out." Now she's chuckling right along with her daughter.

"We were all hiding in the dark and when we heard the truck pull up and the driver's door open and close . . . "

"I hit the button and up goes the garage door and there's your father . . . " Mrs. Peterson starts laughing and can't finish.

"Standing there with his fishing pole in one hand and his tackle box in the other," Gwendy says, "and he's naked as a jaybird from the waist down, those pale skinny legs of his caked with mud." Gwendy throws her head back and laughs.

Mrs. Peterson places a hand over her heart and struggles to get the words out. "I'm covering your eyes with one hand and waving your father back to his truck with the other. I look over and see the expression on poor Blanche Goff's face . . . " She snorts out a giggle. "I thought she was going to have a heart attack sitting right there in her lawn chair."

And then both women are clutching their sides and howling with laughter—and neither one of them is able to get another word out.

55

WHEN MR. PETERSON WALKS out of the elevator and hears raucous laughter coming from somewhere down the hallway, his eyes narrow with annoyance. *Whoever's making all that racket better not wake up my wife or there's going to be hell to pay.*

It's not until he turns the corner by the nurses' station and sees the door to Room 233 standing wide open with a cluster of smiling nurses gathered outside that he realizes it's his wife and daughter making the racket.

"What's going on in here?" he asks, walking into the room with a puzzled expression on his face.

Mrs. Peterson and Gwendy take one look at him—and burst out in another fit of laughter.

56

TWENTY MINUTES LATER, AN orderly raps on the door. He's a big fellow with a warm smile and a thicket of dreadlocks crammed into a bursting-at-the-seams hairnet. "Sorry to break up the party, folks, but I'm here to take Mrs. Peterson down to Imaging."

"Winston!" Mrs. Peterson says, her face lighting up. "I thought your shift was over."

"No, ma'am." He shakes his head. "Not until I'm finished taking care of my favorite patient."

Visibly touched, she says, "Thank you, Winston."

"I'll be right here when you get back," Mr. Peterson says, squeezing his wife's hand.

She looks up at him with those beautiful blue eyes of hers and gives him a little squeeze back. "I'm ready," she says to the orderly.

"I'll be here, too," Gwendy says, doing her best not to cry.

"I know you will." Mrs. Peterson pulls her other hand out from underneath the blanket and holds up a small white feather. Her hand looks very thin and delicate. "Thanks again for the loan, sweetheart. I'll take good care of it."

Gwendy smiles, but doesn't risk saying another word.

57

BACK HOME, GWENDY SLIDES the button box into the safe and pushes the heavy door shut behind it, listening for the audible *click* as the lock engages. Then she spins the dial, once, twice, three times, and gives the handle a good hard yank just to make sure. She's almost to her bedroom when the doorbell rings.

Freezing in the hallway, she holds her breath, willing whomever it is to go away.

The doorbell rings again. A double-ring this time.

Gwendy, still dressed in the clothes she'd worn to the hospital earlier, pulls her cell phone out of her sweater pocket. She punches in 9-1-1 and hovers her finger over the SEND button. Creeping down the hallway, she eases into the foyer, careful not to make any noise, and peeks out the peephole.

The doorbell rings again—and she almost screams.

Stepping back, she unlocks the deadbolt and swings the door open.

"Jesus, Sheriff. You could have called before you—"

"Another girl's gone missing. Right down the road from here."

"What? When?"

"Call came in about an hour ago." Sheriff Ridgewick reaches down to his belt and adjusts the volume on his radio. "The girl's father said she was ice skating at the pond with friends. Some of the older kids had a bonfire going and maybe twenty-five or thirty people were there. Another parent was supposed to be watching her, but she got to talking with a neighbor, and you know how that goes. No one noticed the girl was missing until it was time to go."

"Your men checked the ice?" Gwendy asks, knowing it's a dumb question even before it leaves her mouth.

"We did," he says, nodding. "But it's been solid for at least six weeks now. No way she fell in."

"So now what? You search the area—and what else?"

"I've got officers combing the surrounding woods and side streets. We also set up roadblocks in a couple of locations, but if whoever took her stuffed her in the trunk and started driving right away, they're long gone by now. The rest of my people are knocking on doors up and down View Drive, asking folks if they've seen anything suspicious the past few days."

Gwendy's face drops. "I think you better come in, Sheriff." She takes a step back to give him room. "I have something I need to tell you, and I don't think you're going to like it."

58

THE BLONDE REPORTER FROM Channel Five holds the microphone in front of Sheriff Ridgewick's face as he speaks. She's wearing a fluffy light blue winter beanie that matches her coat and her makeup is perfect, despite the whipping wind and freezing cold temperature. The sheriff, eyes watering and cheeks raw, looks tired and miserable.

". . . is currently underway for Deborah Parker, a resident of the nineteen-hundred block of View Drive. Miss Parker is fourteen years old and a freshman at Castle Rock High School."

A color photograph of a smiling teenage girl with metal braces and dark brown curly hair appears in the upper right-hand corner of the television screen.

"She's five-foot-two-inches tall, weighs one hundred and five pounds, and has brown hair and brown eyes. She was last seen earlier this evening at approximately 7:30 PM ice skating with friends at Fortier Pond. If anyone has any information as to Deborah Parker's whereabouts or witnessed anything out of the ordinary in the Castle View area, please contact the Castle Rock Sheriff's Department at . . . "

59

GWENDY HAS NEVER LAID eyes on the man standing outside of the sheriff's office before, but she can smell his press
credentials a mile away. It also helps that she can see the
mini-recorder he's palming in his left hand.

"Congresswoman Peterson," he says, cutting her off
by the entrance. "Any comment on the missing girls?"

"And you are?" she asks.

He pulls a laminated ID card out from under his jacket
and extends it as far as the lanyard will permit. "Ronald
Blum, *Portland Press Herald*."

"I'm here this morning to be briefed by Sheriff
Ridgewick. I'll leave it to him to issue any official state-
ments." She starts to walk away.

"Is it true that there've been other unsuccessful recent
attempts to abduct young girls here in Castle Rock?"

Gwendy pulls opens the door and lets it swing closed
in the reporter's face. He shouts something else, but she
can't make it out through the heavy glass.

The stationhouse is buzzing this morning. A handful
of officers sit at their desks talking on the telephone and
jotting down notes. Several others are gathered in front of
a bulletin board, examining a large map of Castle Rock.
There's a line at the coffee machine and another in front
of the Xerox copier. Gwendy spots Sheila Brigham in her
cubicle and heads that way.

The veteran dispatcher is busy talking to someone on her headset, and judging by the annoyed look on her face, she's been stuck on the line for quite some time. She sees Gwendy approach and covers the microphone with her hand. "Go on back. It's a shit-show here today."

Gwendy waves thank you and walks down the narrow hallway. This time the door to Sheriff Ridgewick's office is closed. She knocks three times for luck.

"Come in," a muffled voice says.

She opens the door and steps inside. The sheriff is standing at the window, staring outside. "That reporter get you on the way in?"

She nods. "I didn't have much to say."

"I appreciate that," he says, turning around and looking at her.

"He asked if there'd been any other attempted abductions in Castle Rock recently. I almost fainted, but I don't think he noticed."

"He's just fishing," the sheriff says, leaning back against his desk.

"I guess, but it was very unsettling after what I told you last night."

"He doesn't know anything about that. Nobody does. Yet."

"You'll tell the others today?"

He nods. "The State Police are sending additional detectives later this morning. We're setting up a task force, so I'll be sharing your story during the initial briefing."

"Let me know if you need me to be there to face the music in person."

"That won't be necessary," he says almost casually. "What I'll say is, you thought the whole thing was a prank until you got to thinking about it later on. That's when you realized that maybe the guy had been wearing a mask. So you told me all about it this morning. You didn't see a vehicle and are unable to provide a physical description of the man other than dark clothes and shoes with some sort of a heel."

She looks at him with gratitude. "Thank you, Norris."

"Don't mention it," he says, waving her off. "No need for the whole damn world to discover how hard-headed you are."

Gwendy laughs. "Now you sound like my mother."

60

WHEN GWENDY WALKS INTO Room 233 on the second floor of Castle County General and sees the tears streaming down both her mother and father's faces, her heart drops.

Mrs. Peterson is sitting on the edge of the hospital bed with her bare legs dangling over the side. She's holding hands with her husband and leaning her head against his shoulder. She looks very much like a young girl. Doctor Celano stands at the foot of the bed, reading from an open chart. When he hears the door open, he turns to Gwendy with a big, toothy grin on his face.

"I'm sorry I'm late," Gwendy says, confused. "I got held up in a meeting."

Her father looks up at her. His eyes are watery and dancing and he's also wearing a broad smile.

"What's going on?" Gwendy asks, feeling like she just stepped into the Twilight Zone.

"Oh, honey, it's a miracle," her mother says, holding out her arms.

Gwendy goes to her and gives her a hug. "What is? What's happening?" Her mother only squeezes tighter.

Mr. Peterson nods to the doctor. "Tell her what you just told us."

Doctor Celano raises his eyebrows. "All of the scans came back clean. No sign of a tumor anywhere."

"What? That's great news, right?" Gwendy asks, afraid to get her hopes up.

"I'd say so."

"But what about the blood results?"

The doctor waves the medical chart at her. "The blood work we took yesterday morning also came back clean. Your mother's numbers are squarely in the normal range."

"How is that possible?" Gwendy asks in disbelief.

"I wondered the same thing myself," Doctor Celano says, "so I put in a request right away for additional blood work and rushed the lab for the results."

"I was curious what was going on," Mrs. Peterson says, laughing. "They took three more tubes before breakfast, and I told the nurse she was turning into a vampire."

"The new tests came back normal. Again," the doctor says, closing the chart and holding it at his side.

Gwendy stares at him. "Could it be a mistake?"

"A mistake was made, but not yesterday or today. I'm positive these results are accurate." The doctor sighs heavily and the smile disappears from his face. "With that said, I want to assure you that I'll get to the bottom of what went wrong in regards to Mrs. Peterson's initial blood work on the 22nd. It was a reprehensible error, and I *will* find out where it occurred."

"But what about the stomach pain? The vomiting?"

"That's a bit of a mystery, I'm afraid," the doctor says. "My best guess is she ate something that didn't agree with her and the force of the vomiting agitated scar tissue that was caused by the chemotherapy. It's happened to patients of mine before."

"So what . . . what does this all mean?" Gwendy asks.

"It means she's not sick!" Mr. Peterson says, putting an

291

arm around Gwendy's shoulder and giving her a shake. "It means we can take her home!"

"Today?" Gwendy says, looking at the doctor. She still can't believe this is happening. "Right now?"

"As soon as we're finished with her discharge papers."

Gwendy gazes at Doctor Celano for a moment, and then looks back at her parents. Their faces are alight with happiness. "I'm starting to think that feather of yours really is magic," her father says.

And then all three of them are laughing again and holding on to each other for dear life.

61

IN MOST OF EASTERN Maine, news of an approaching nor'easter—still four or five days out but already gaining strength at a monstrous rate—fills the airwaves and front pages of newspapers over the next forty-eight hours. There's very little panic in this part of the world, even when it comes to the bigger storms—but there *is* an underlying sense of dread. Blizzards mean accidents—both on the roads and closer to home. There will be broken bones and frostbite; overturned cars in ditches and downed power lines. Elderly folks will be rendered housebound, unable to venture out to grocery stores and pharmacies; meals and refills will be missed and illnesses will slither under drafty door cracks with insidious stealth and take hold. The youngsters won't fare much better, as they gleefully abandon whatever common sense they possess in the first place to rush headlong outside into the storm to build forts and wage snowball wars and hurtle down tree-speckled hills at breakneck speeds on flimsy slivers of drugstore plastic. If town folks are lucky, no one will need a mortician. But then again nor'easters aren't usually harbingers of anything even close to resembling good luck.

This time, in the western half of the state, it's a different story altogether. The approaching blizzard is relegated to page two or even three, and only discussed in detail during the weather portion of most television

newscasts. The three missing Castle County girls domi-
nate local media coverage from early morning drive-time
to the eleven o'clock nightly news. Family members and
friends, schoolmates and even teachers are interviewed, all
offering a slightly modified version of the same somber
story: the three girls are kind and talented and have never
been in any kind of trouble; they certainly didn't run away
from home. Sheriff Norris Ridgewick and State Police
Detective Frank Thome are also constant on-air presences.
They continue to offer the same grim-faced reassurances
that their respective departments are doing everything humanly possible to locate the missing girls and the same
passionate requests for information from the public. Their
singular message and lack of originality in delivering that
message prompts one local reporter to write that both men
"are reading from the same uninspired script."

Despite the lack of recovered bodies or anything else
resembling proof, the Portland press have already begun
to throw around the "serial killer" moniker and have
dredged up no fewer than three sidebar articles relating to
Frank Dodd and his stint as "The Castle Rock Strangler"
in the early 1970s.

In Castle Rock, there are no mentions of Boogeyman
Dodd in the press—although there are plenty of whispers in the bars and restaurants and stores; in a small
town like The Rock, the whispering never ends. The
December 30, 1999 edition of *The Castle Rock Call* features
large photos of each of the three girls above the front-
page fold and a banner headline running just below that
reads: MANHUNT TURNS UP NO CLUES – TASK
FORCE PUZZLED.

Gwendy Peterson takes one look at the newspaper and

tosses it unread onto her parents' dining-room table. "Let's go, slowpokes!" she yells upstairs. "We're going to be late!"

Gwendy and her father have spent the past two days taking excellent care of Mrs. Peterson—at least that's what they would claim if asked. Mrs. Peterson, on the other hand, would tell a completely different story; without hesitation or filter, she'd tell you they've spent the past two days driving her bat-shit crazy.

Despite the doctor's words of assurance—both at the hospital and during a follow-up phone call yesterday afternoon—Mr. Peterson insisted that his wife remain on the family-room sofa for the remainder of the week, resting and recovering under a pile of blankets.

"Recovering from what?" Mrs. Peterson retorted. "I ate something bad and puked. Big deal. End of story."

For once, Gwendy took her father's side of the argument, and the two of them wore a path in the carpet leading to and from the sofa, trying to make sure she was comfortable and adequately entertained. In the process, they also wore out Mrs. Peterson's patience. After two days spent reading a half-dozen magazines from cover to cover, watching hours of television, knitting, and working on another jigsaw puzzle until she was seeing double, Mrs. Peterson finally lost it, shortly after lunch, hurling the television remote at her husband and declaring, "Stop babying me, dammit! I feel fine!"

And it seems like she really does. Only one short nap yesterday, and nothing at all so far today. The color has returned to her face and her appetite—as well as her spunky attitude—is back to normal. In fact, a short time ago, she not so subtly hinted (insisted) that Gwendy and Mr. Peterson take her out to dinner tonight, and not just any old restaurant, either. She has Gwendy call her favorite Italian bistro, Giovanni's, in neighboring Windham, and make a reservation for three (which they'll be late for if they don't leave the house in the next few minutes).

Gwendy turns at the sound of footsteps and can't believe her eyes. "Wow," she says, getting up from the table. "You look like a million bucks, Mom."

"A billion," a smiling Mr. Peterson says, coming down the stairs behind her.

Mrs. Peterson is wearing a dark blue dress underneath a long gray sweater. For the first time in months, she has on lipstick and eye shadow. Gold earrings dangle from her ears and a single pearl necklace hangs around her neck.

"Thank you," Mrs. Peterson says primly. "If you keep up the compliments, I will consider forgiving the both of you."

"In that case," Mr. Peterson says, extending his arm toward the front door, "your chariot awaits."

62

THE DRIVE FROM CASTLE Rock to Windham takes forty-five minutes but dinner is worth every mile of it. Both Gwendy and Mrs. Peterson order stuffed shrimp a la Guiseppi, side salads, and cups of seafood bisque. Mr. Peterson decides on chicken cacciatore and devours an entire loaf of Italian bread all by himself before his entrée arrives. "You keep that up," Mrs. Peterson tells him, "and we'll be visiting *you* in the hospital."

After they finish eating, Mr. and Mrs. Peterson take to the dance floor and slow dance to back-to-back ballads sung by a Frank Sinatra look-alike set up on a small stage by the bar. At the conclusion of the last song, Mr. Peterson dips his wife over his bended knee, before pulling her close for a kiss on the cheek. They return to the table giggling like a couple of high-school sweethearts.

"You sure you don't want to give it a whirl, Gwennie?" her father asks, sliding out Mrs. Peterson's chair for her. "I still have a little gas left in the tank."

"I'm stuffed. I think I'll just sit here until I float away."

"Will there be dessert for anyone?" the waitress says from over Mrs. Peterson's shoulder.

"Not me," Gwendy says, groaning.

Mr. Peterson pats his full belly. "None for me, either."

"No, thank you, dear," Mrs. Peterson says, and as her husband asks the waitress for the check, she turns to Gwendy. "I think I'll just have one of those yummy chocolates of yours when I get home instead."

63

GWENDY JOGS UP THE last hilly stretch of Pleasant Road, sticking as close to the shoulder as she can. After two close calls this morning, she's especially wary of the increased traffic, even at such an early hour. It's been three long days since fourteen-year-old Deborah Parker disappeared from Fortier Pond, but the neighborhood is still bustling with a combination of police and sheriff vehicles, volunteer searchers, and curious lookie-loos, mostly out-of-towners with their noses pressed against the glass of their windshields.

Gwendy's schedule on this chilly final day of the twentieth century is remarkably clear (a fact she grudgingly attributes to a lack of anything resembling a healthy social life). After she finishes her run and showers, she plans to catch up on some overdue email correspondence, then swing by her parents' house for a quick check-in—Mr. and Mrs. Peterson are going next door to the Goff's later this evening for dinner—and then it's back home for an exciting afternoon of John Grisham before it's finally time to leave for Brigette Desjardin's PTA New Year's Eve party. She's already prepared a five-minute speech for the occasion and is hoping she doesn't have to stick around for much longer than that.

As she turns the corner and her building comes into

view, Gwendy's thoughts turn to the button box and the miniature chocolate animals.

So far, she's given her mom a total of seven pieces of chocolate—the first one a tiny turtle she smuggled into the hospital along with several cartons of fruit juice, and the most recent an adorable little pig when they got home from the restaurant last night.

Before pulling the lever on the left side of the box and slipping the bite-sized chocolate turtle into a sandwich bag and stuffing it into the zippered pocket of her backpack to take to the hospital, Gwendy agonized long and hard over the decision. She knew from firsthand experience that the button box dispensed not-so-tiny doses of magic along with its animal treats—but she also knew the gifts were rarely delivered without consequence. *So what exactly was going to happen the first time she gave someone else one of the chocolates? How about a whole bunch of them?* Gwendy didn't know the answers, but in the end, she was willing to roll the dice.

It wasn't until the other morning at the hospital when Doctor Celano gave them the miraculous news that she finally felt at peace with her decision. How could she not after that? But if Gwendy was holding onto any lingering doubts—and, okay, maybe there *were* just a few—it was the graceful dip at the end of that last slow dance and the dreamy look on her mother's face when Mr. Peterson planted the tender kiss on her cheek that sent those doubts packing once and for all. Gwendy knew she would remember that moment and her parents' laughter for the rest of her life (however long that might be).

Gwendy offers a cheerful good morning to her

across-the-hall neighbor exiting the building and bounds up the stairs to the second floor, feeling light on her feet. She unzips her pocket and pulls out her key and cell phone. She's reaching for the doorknob when she notices the MESSAGE light blinking on her telephone.

"No, no, no," she says, realizing she forgot to turn on her ringer. She pushes the button to retrieve her messages and holds the phone up to her ear.

"Hey, honey, I can't believe I got through! Been trying for days! I miss you so—"

The message cuts off in mid-sentence.

Gwendy stares at her phone in disbelief.

"Come on . . . " She fumbles with the buttons, trying to find out if there's another message. There isn't. She hits the REPEAT button and stands in front of her door, listening to those four seconds of Ryan's voice. Over and over again.

64

GWENDY SITS CROSS-LEGGED ON the bed, wet hair wrapped in a towel, and hits SEND on the email she just finished writing. Once the modem disconnects from dial-up, she closes her laptop. A look of concern on her face, she swings her legs off the bed and starts to get dressed. She's tying her shoes when the phone rings.

"Hello?" Trying not to get her hopes up.

"Gwendy, it's Patsy Follett. I catch you at a bad time?"

"Patsy!" she says, excited to hear the congresswoman's voice. "I just responded to your email."

"And I just opened it and read it. Figured it'd be easier to call."

"Well, how are you?" Gwendy asks. "Happy New Year!"

"Happy New Year to you, too. I was doing great until I talked to my friend in the Senate this morning. Then, not so great."

"You really think we're going to be called back early?"

"That's what he said. Some kind of emergency session because of President Big Mouth and Korea. First time it's happened since Harry flippin' Truman."

"That means there's more going on behind the scenes than the news is telling us."

"Evidently," Patsy says with disgust in her voice. "I

gotta admit this is the first time I've actually been scared the idiot's going to get us in another war."

Gwendy looks across the bedroom at the button box on the dresser. She walks over to it.

"I lose you, Gwen?"

"No, no, I'm right here. Just thinking."

65

GWENDY ONLY STAYS AT her parents' house for a short time that afternoon, just long enough to talk Patriots football with her dad (he thinks Pete Carroll has to go after another fourth-place finish; she believes he deserves one more year to turn things around) and help her mom pick out an outfit for the New Year's Eve dinner later that night at the Goffs.

She's already outside on the front porch digging in her coat pockets for her car keys when Mrs. Peterson swings open the door and stops her. "Hold on a second. I need to talk to you about something."

Gwendy turns around. "You need to get back inside, Mom, before you catch a cold. It's freezing out here."

"This'll only take a second."

It's bad news, Gwendy thinks, reading the expression on her face. *I knew it was too good to be true.*

"I'm afraid I have some bad news."

"Oh, Mom," Gwendy says. "What is it?"

"I should've told you before now, but I kept chickening out."

Gwendy goes to her. "Just tell me what's wrong."

"I've checked my bag, I've looked everywhere, I even called the hospital . . . but I can't find your magic feather anywhere."

Gwendy stares at her—and starts laughing.

"What?" Mrs. Peterson asks. "What's so funny?"

"I thought . . . I thought you were going to tell me you were sick again, that the hospital had made another mistake."

Mrs. Peterson places a hand over her heart. "Dear God no."

"The feather will turn up if it's supposed to," Gwendy says, opening the door. "It did once before. Now get inside, you silly woman."

66

ON HER WAY HOME from Carbine Street, Gwendy sees Sheriff Ridgewick's cruiser parked on the shoulder of Route 117 with its hazard lights blinking. She hits her turn signal and pulls over behind him.

As she gets out of the car, she spots the sheriff climbing out of a snowy ravine that runs alongside the highway. He's up to his hips in drifting snow and cussing up a blue streak.

"What would your constituents think if they heard you talking like that?"

The sheriff looks up at her with snow in his hair and daggers in his eyes. "They'd think I've had a shitty-ass day, which I have."

Gwendy extends a hand to help. "What were you doing down there, anyway?"

"Thought I saw something," he says, taking her hand. He pops out of the ditch and starts stomping his boots on the gravel shoulder. He looks up at her. "I was just about to call you before I pulled over."

"What's up?"

He rubs a hand over his chin. "We received a padded envelope at the stationhouse about an hour ago. No return address. Postmarked yesterday in Augusta."

Gwendy feels her face flush. She knows what's coming next.

"The orange ski hat Deborah Parker was wearing the afternoon she went ice-skating was inside the envelope. And stuffed inside the hat . . . three more teeth, presumably hers."

Gwendy gapes at him, unable to find the words.

"To make matters worse, I just got off the phone a little while ago with that reporter from the *Portland Herald*. Someone leaked. He knows about the teeth we found in the sweatshirt and he knows about the package."

"But you said it was only delivered an hour ago."

He nods. "That's right."

"So how . . . ?"

Sheriff Ridgewick shrugs. "Someone needed the money I guess. Anyway, he's working on an article for tomorrow morning's paper and he's already calling the guy 'The Tooth Fairy.'"

"Jesus."

"Ayuh," he says grimly. "Shit's about to hit the fan."

67

GWENDY'S BRIEF SPEECH AT the PTA New Year's Eve party goes over well and earns her a spirited round of applause from the audience, along with the usual smattering of cat-calls. Castle Rock may be proud of its hometown-girl-made-good, but there are still plenty of folks around here who don't believe a woman should be representing their voice in the nation's capital, much less a thirty-seven year-old woman who happens to be a Democrat. That's what many of the old-timers down at the corner store call "adding insult to injury."

When Brigette originally explained that the plan was for everyone inside the Municipal Center to file outside to Castle Rock Common at 11:00 PM so the big midnight countdown could take place in the center of town by the clock tower, Gwendy believed it was the very epitome of a bad idea. It would be dark and freezing cold. People would be tired and cranky. She predicted that most folks would probably just head for their cars and the warmth of their living rooms at that point to celebrate the ball dropping with Dick Clark and assorted celebrity guests on television.

But she was dead wrong, she admitted now.

The PTA volunteers had created quite the festive winter wonderland on the Common, hanging dozens of strings of twinkling white Christmas lights in the trees and shrubbery, around the railing and the roof of the bandstand, and along the white picket fence that bordered the woods at the northern edge of the Common. Red and green streamers hung from lampposts and street signs. A hot chocolate and coffee booth had been set up by the entrance, and someone had even dressed up the War Memorial, draping a bright red ribbon around the WWI soldier's neck and scrubbing the splatters of birdshit off his pie-dish helmet.

Conspicuous in their absence were the number of HAVE YOU SEEN THIS GIRL? posters missing from nearby telephone poles and lampposts and the windows of the handful of buildings that bordered the Common. For a few hours on one night only, talk of the missing girls had been pushed to the background and folks were focusing on the positive and hopeful. Tomorrow morning, the posters and the chatter would undoubtedly return.

At 11:45 PM, as Gwendy stands in line waiting for hot chocolate, the place is positively hopping. Kids dart past her in eager packs, shouting and laughing, tossing snowballs at each other and sliding on stray patches of ice, while their parents and neighbors wander around, flitting from huddled group to huddled group, chatting, gossiping, sneaking sips of whiskey from hidden flasks, and making grandiose plans for 2000 to be the best year ever. Gwendy spots Grace Featherstone from the Book Nook talking to Nanette from the diner over by the bandstand. Brigette is holding court with a number of her PTA minions by the picnic tables, no doubt making sure everything's set for midnight and the big countdown. Gwendy saw Mr. and Mrs. Hoffman earlier inside the hall, but did her best to avoid them—going so far as to hide in the bathroom for much longer than was probably necessary. So far, so good, in that regard—she hasn't seen either one of them again since.

The line inches forward, and she notices a tall man with a bushy mustache wearing a Patriots cap leaning against a lamppost by the fountain. He appears to be watching her, but Gwendy can't be sure she isn't imagining it. She thinks she remembers seeing him earlier in the audience during her speech.

"That you, Mrs. Gwendy Peterson?"

She turns around. It takes her a second to recognize the older man standing behind her, but then it comes to her in a flash. "Well, hello again, Mr. Charlie Browne."

"Just Charlie, please."

"Enjoying the New Year's Eve festivities?"

"I was enjoying it a lot more when we were inside and I wasn't freezing my giblets off."

Gwendy tosses her head back and laughs. "Good thing the wind isn't blowing, or we'd look like a bunch of ice sculptures out here."

He grunts and looks around. "You see my boy around anywhere? That clock strikes midnight and I'm outta here."

Gwendy shakes her head. "Sorry, I haven't seen him."

"There you are," Brigette says, arriving in a perfume-scented flurry. "I was looking for you. What are you doing waiting in line?" She waves furiously at one of the women in the booth. "Can I get a hot cocoa ASAP for the congresswoman?"

"Brigette, no," Gwendy says, horrified. People are staring at them, some of them pointing.

"Here you go," a dark-haired woman says, hustling over with a steaming Styrofoam cup.

Gwendy doesn't want to accept it, but she has no choice. "Thank you. You really didn't have to do that."

"Nonsense," Brigette says, taking her by the arm and leading her away. "I want you right next to me at midnight."

"Happy New Year, Mr. Browne," Gwendy says over her shoulder. "It was nice seeing you again."

"Happy New Year, Congresswoman," he says, smirking, and Gwendy doesn't know if it's her imagination or not, but she's almost positive his tone is no longer a friendly one.

"Three more minutes," Brigette says, glancing at her watch. She spots her husband standing across the Common talking to two other men. "Travis! Travis!" She points at the clock tower. "Over there!"

He nods dutifully and starts in that direction.

The miniature clock tower is located at the very heart of the Castle Rock Common. It stands twenty-two feet high and its face measures three feet across its center. Erected during the town's reconstruction period in the aftermath of the Big Fire, there's an engraved metal plaque positioned at the stone base of the tower that reads: *In honor of the indomitable spirit of the citizens of Castle Rock — 1992*.

A burly woman wearing what looks like several layers of flannel shirts flashes a look of relief as they approach. "Thank goodness, I was starting to get worried." She hands Brigette a microphone. A long black cord snakes from the bottom of the mic to a large speaker propped up on a picnic table behind them.

Gwendy smiles at the woman. "Happy New Year."

"Happy New Year," she says shyly, and quickly looks away.

Travis walks up beside them, grinning and smelling like aftershave and whiskey. "All ready to go, ladies?"

"Almost," Brigette says. She turns on the microphone and a whine of feedback erupts from the speaker. People groan and cover their ears. The woman in the flannel shirts scurries to adjust several knobs at the top of the speaker until the sound diminishes and finally dissipates.

"One minute til midnight!" Brigette announces, giddily. "One minute until midnight!"

A crowd starts to gather at the foot of the clock tower, the younger kids swarming toward the front, most of them wearing glow-in-the-dark necklaces and carrying party horns or noisemakers. Many of the adults are wearing glittery cardboard hats with Y2K! or 2000! or HAPPY NEW YEAR! printed across the brims at jaunty angles.

"Thirty seconds!" Brigette shouts, her tone bordering on hysterical, and for the first time tonight, Gwendy wonders how much her friend has had to drink.

Studying the crowd, she sees Grace and Nanette and Milly Harris, the church organist, huddled together off to the side. All three are staring up at the clock and counting down. Charlie Browne is standing toward the back by himself with his foot propped up on a bench. He's wearing scuffed cowboy boots and a green plastic derby with a fake yellow flower poking out from the top. He grins and gives Gwendy a big wave. She gratefully waves back, thinking she must've been wrong about him before.

Maybe ten yards behind Mr. Browne is the mustached stranger in the Patriots cap. He's scanning the crowd, but it's hard to get a good look at his face because the brim of his hat is tilted so low.

"TEN, NINE, EIGHT, SEVEN, SIX . . ." Brigette

lowers the microphone from her mouth. The roar of the crowd has grown louder than her amplified voice.

"FIVE . . . FOUR . . . THREE . . . TWO . . . ONE . . . "

The crowd erupts. "HAPPY NEW YEARRRR!"

A cacophony of drunken hooting and hollering, blowing horns and honking noisemakers fills the air. Confetti is tossed by the handfuls. Someone on the other side of the Common shoots off a string of bottle rockets. Brilliant explosions of red, white, and blue sparks light up the night sky and shower down upon the snow-covered ground. Everywhere around Gwendy, people are embracing and kissing. She thinks of Ryan, the way his whiskers tickle her chin when he kisses her, and a deep ache blooms in the center of her chest.

Brigette untangles herself from her husband's arms, and then it's Gwendy's turn. "Happy New Year!" she shouts above the clatter, hugging Gwendy tight. "I'm so glad you're here!"

"Happy New Year!" Gwendy says, her face awash in the glow of fireworks.

"My turn next." Travis is standing behind his wife, arms held open wide, looking at Gwendy. "Happy New Year!"

Gwendy leans over and hugs him and the side of her face brushes against the cold skin of Travis's cheek. "Happy New—" she starts to say, and then something changes.

Everything changes.

Suddenly Travis appears very clear to her, very *bright* and in focus, almost as if he's somehow lit from within, and everything else around him falls away. She notices the tiny scar on Travis's chin and immediately *understands* that

314

the neighbor's dog, Barney, snapped at Travis when he was eight years old because he'd been throwing rocks at it from across the chain-link fence. This was in Boston, where Travis grew up. She stares at the thick, wavy texture of his hair and suddenly *understands* that he's having an affair with his hair dresser, a single woman named Katy who lives in a trailer on the outskirts of town with her three-year-old son. Her dear old friend Brigette knows nothing about it . . .

. . . and then Gwendy's vision blurs and Travis suddenly swirls out of view, like he's being sucked into the maw of a pitch-black vortex, and everything else around him swims back into focus.

"—you okay?" Travis asks. He's standing a few feet away, staring at her with concern in his eyes.

Gwendy blinks and looks around. "I'm fine," she says. "Felt a little light-headed for a minute there."

"Christ, I thought you were having a seizure or something," he says.

"Come on," Brigette says, taking her by the arm. "Let's sit down."

"Honest, I'm fine." She wants out of there, and she wants out of there right now. "I think it's time I head home. It's been a long day."

"Are you sure you should be driving? Travis could take—"

"I'm good," Gwendy says, forcing a smile. "I promise."

Brigette gives her a lingering look. "Okay, but please be careful."

"Will do," Gwendy says, waving goodbye. "I'll talk to you tomorrow."

What in the hell was that all about? she thinks, cutting

across the Common on the way to her car. She doesn't even know how to describe what just happened, but she knows she's never experienced anything remotely like it before. It's almost as if a door had opened, and she'd stepped inside. But opened to what? Travis's soul? It sounded hokey, like something out of a science fiction novel, but it also made a certain amount of sense to her, the same way that the button box made a certain amount of sense to her now.

Was what happened some kind of a bizarre side effect because of the chocolates she'd given to her Mom? And why Travis? She barely knew the guy, and he certainly wasn't the only person she'd come in contact with tonight. She shook hands with dozens of other people.

A dark figure suddenly steps out of the shadows in front of her. "Are you okay, Mrs. Peterson?"

Startled, Gwendy jerks to a stop. It's the stranger in the Patriots cap, and he's standing close enough to reach out and touch her. She's trapped in between buildings now, and it's darker here without the streetlights.

"I'm fine," she says, trying to sound unafraid. "You really should be more careful about ambushing people like that. Especially with everything that's going on around here."

"I apologize," the man says in a pleasant tone. "I saw what happened and was concerned."

"You saw what happened," Gwendy repeats with an edge to her voice. "And why were you watching me in the first place, Mr. . . . ?"

"Nolan," the man says, pulling open his coat to reveal a badge clipped to his belt. "Detective Nolan."

Gwendy's eyes widen and she feels a flush spread across her cheeks. "And now I feel very foolish."

The detective holds up his hands. "Please don't, ma'am. I should have identified myself right away."

"Did Sheriff Ridgewick ask you to keep an eye on me?"

"No, ma'am," he says. "Way he talks about you, I'm pretty sure the sheriff thinks you can take care of yourself."

Gwendy laughs. She can picture Norris saying exactly those words. "Well, have a good night, detective. Thanks for checking on me."

He nods mutely and starts walking back in the direction of the Common.

Gwendy turns toward the street and, in the time it takes to recognize the man walking toward her, she decides to conduct an experiment. "Hey, there, Mr. Gallagher," she says. "Happy New Year." She tugs the glove off her right hand and extends it toward him.

"Happy New Year to you, too, young lady." Gwendy's eighth grade algebra teacher shakes her hand with a firm grip. She can feel the rough callouses on his palm. "You should stop by the school one day. The kids would love to see you."

"I'll do that," she says, waiting for something, *anything*, out of the ordinary to happen.

But it doesn't.

So she keeps walking until she reaches Main Street where she parked her car. She's thinking about the button box and its chocolate treats and not looking where she's going when her feet suddenly go out from under her. One minute she's striding confidently past the Castle Rock Diner, catching a fleeting glimpse of her reflection in the darkened front window, and the next she's skidding across an icy patch of sidewalk, her arms flailing above her head.

317

Someone grabs her around the waist.

"Oh my God," she says, steadying herself.

"That was a close one, Mrs. Peterson." Lucas Browne lets go of her waist and reaches down to the sidewalk. He comes back up holding her glove. "You dropped this." He smiles and hands it to her and their bare fingers touch . . .

. . . and Main Street suddenly falls away, the cars and storefronts and streetlights disappearing, and all she can see is *him*, in brilliant, almost luminescent, detail. And just like that she *knows*. Lucas Browne is the Tooth Fairy. She stares at his hand and watches as his gloved fingers wrap around a stainless steel instrument, reach into a dummy mouth full of fake teeth set up on a brightly lit table, *UB School of Dental Medicine* stitched across the breast of the long white lab coat he's wearing . . . and then those same fingers, filthy now, gripping a pair of rusty workroom pliers, and he's standing over a cowering Deborah Parker, her long hair spiked with sweat, her eyes wide and frightened, the tips of his cowboy boots splattered with fat drops of blood . . .

And then the darkness swallows him away, and the streetscape sharpens into focus again and Lucas Browne is standing on the sidewalk in front of her.

"What just happened?" he asks, eyes narrowing. "Are you okay?"

"I'm . . . I'm fine," she says. "Thank you. You saved me from a nasty fall." Her voice sounds dull and distant.

A young couple, walking arm-in-arm, passes by then. The teenage boy, a James Dean wannabe with his leather jacket and cigarette dangling from his mouth, nods at them. "What's up, Lucas?"

Lucas doesn't answer, doesn't even look at the

guy—just watches Gwendy cross the street with that same wary look on his face.

Gwendy unlocks the car and climbs inside, hurriedly locking the door behind her. Her hands are shaking and her heart feels like it's going to burst inside her chest. She starts the engine and pulls away without letting it warm up. When she glances toward the sidewalk, Lucas Browne is still standing there, watching her.

68

SHERIFF RIDGEWICK PICKS UP on the first ring. "Hello?"

"It's Lucas Browne!" Gwendy nearly shouts. "Lucas Browne's the Tooth Fairy!"

"Gwendy? Do you know what time it is?"

"Listen to me, Norris. Please. I think Deborah Parker's still alive, but I don't know how much time she has."

"Okay, start over and tell me how you know this."

"I just ran into Lucas Browne on Main Street and—"

"What were you doing on Main Street at this time of night?"

"I was walking to my car after the New Year's Eve party," she says, her frustration building, "but that's not important. Lucas Browne went to dental school in Buffalo."

"How exactly do you know that? For that matter, how do you know Lucas Browne?"

"I met him and his father when we were searching the field that day. His father told me Lucas went to college in Buffalo, but he came home early after he got into some kind of trouble."

"And Lucas told you it was dental school when you saw him tonight?"

She doesn't answer right away. "Something like that." She takes a deep breath. "Norris, he was wearing cowboy boots. I think there was blood on them."

Rustling in the background now. "Where are you?"

"I just turned on 117. Headed home."

"Turn around," he says, and she can hear a door opening and closing. "Meet me at the station. Don't call anyone else."

"Hurry, Norris."

69

GWENDY PULLS UP A chair and sits next to Sheila Brigham inside the dispatch cubicle, listening to the radio calls as they come in. She recognizes Sheriff Ridgewick right away, although his voice sounds much deeper over the airwaves, and State Trooper Tom Noel, who was a year behind her at Castle Rock High and grew up two blocks away from Carbine Street. The others are strangers to her, their words terse and clipped, but Gwendy can hear the excitement simmering in their voices.

The sheriff and Deputy Footman are in the lead car, followed by a large convoy of Castle County Sheriff's Department, Castle Rock Police Department, and Maine State Police vehicles. They've just crossed over the old railroad bridge on Jessup Road and will be splitting up and surrounding the Browne's ranch house in a matter of minutes.

Despite numerous requests and a half-hearted attempt at bribery (involving one of Mr. Peterson's prized fly fishing rods), the sheriff refused to allow Gwendy to ride along with him or his men—the press would have a field day, he argued, especially if something went wrong and she were injured—so this is the closest she'll get to the action.

She stares at the radio with nervous anticipation, tapping her foot on the ugly green carpet and chewing her fingernails. Sheila has already scolded her twice for not being able to sit still, but Gwendy can't help it. She's running on fumes and nearly a half-dozen cups of coffee. It's almost ten o'clock in the morning and she hasn't slept a wink. In fact, she didn't even make it home last night.

Shortly after 1:00 AM, not long after meeting Gwendy at the stationhouse, Sheriff Ridgewick got in touch with a Detective Tipton of the Buffalo Police Department. Files were pulled. Phone calls made. Doors knocked on. By 6:00 AM, a senior official from the Administration Office at the University of Buffalo verified that Lucas Tillman Browne of Castle Rock, Maine was dismissed from the School of Dental Medicine—just before the conclusion of his third semester—after numerous female students filed sexual harassment and stalking complaints against him. Shortly after 8:00 AM, State Police detectives learned from the Tomlinsons and the Parkers that both families had hired handyman Charles Browne the previous spring to power-wash the aluminum siding on their houses. In both instances, Mr. Browne had been accompanied by his son. It'd been so long ago the families had simply forgotten. This treasure trove of new information led to a search warrant being issued for the Browne residence and the surrounding property.

"I've got eyes on a single male subject," the radio squawks, and Gwendy can picture Sheriff Ridgewick sitting in the driver's seat of his cruiser, squinting through a dirty windshield. *"Check that, two male subjects in the garage. Second man's working under the truck."*

"*Copy that. We're in position out back.*"

"*All good at the fence line. He comes this way, we got 'em.*"

"*Approaching subjects now. Detective Thome is at my twelve o'clock blocking the driveway. Stand by.*"

Three-and-a-half minutes later: "*Warrant has been served. Both subjects cooperating. Detectives entering the residence. Stand by.*"

The radio goes mostly silent then. Someone requests a new pair of gloves be brought inside the house. Another officer asks if he and his men should continue to turn away traffic at the intersection. Deputy Portman responds in the affirmative.

Gwendy pulls in a deep breath, lets it out. Sheila takes a bite of her donut and stares intently at the radio monitor, the expression on her face unchanged.

"How in the world are you so calm?" Gwendy asks, breaking the silence. "I'm dying over here."

Sheila gives her a dry look, smudges of white powder stuck in the corners of her mouth. "Twenty-five years on the job, honey. Seen and heard it all by now. You wouldn't believe the things I've seen!" She takes another bite of donut and continues with her mouth full. "I'll tell you this, though . . . if you don't stop chewing on those nails of yours, you're gonna have to walk across the street to the drugstore in about five minutes and buy yourself some Band-Aids."

Gwendy lowers her pinky finger from her mouth and crosses her arms like a sullen teenager.

"*Sheila, come back,*" the radio squawks.

She wipes powdery fingers on her blouse and keys the mic. "Right here, Sheriff."

325

There's a crackle of static, and then: *"I've got a message for our visitor."*

"Roger that. She's sitting right next to me gnawing on her fingers."

"Tell her . . . we got our man."

70

"TURN IT UP, GWEN," her father says, sitting down on the arm of his recliner. He's staring at the television screen with rapt fascination.

"I'll be making a few brief comments," Sheriff Ridgewick says into the tangle of microphones set up outside the stationhouse, "and then I'll hand it over to State Police Detective Frank Thome to answer any questions."

He flips open a notepad and starts reading. "Earlier today, the Castle County Sheriff's Department and the Maine State Police executed a search warrant on a residence located at 113 Ford Road in northern Castle Rock. A number of personal items belonging to Rhonda Tomlinson were discovered under a loose floorboard in one of the bedrooms. After interviewing multiple residents of the home, a suspect, Lucas Browne, age twenty, was placed into custody. After receiving permission from the owner of the residence, Charles Browne, age fifty-nine, to search a family-owned cabin located near Dark Score Lake, officers discovered fourteen-year-old Deborah Parker shackled and unconscious inside the cabin's dirt cellar. She has been reunited with her family and is currently receiving medical treatment at a local hospital."

The sheriff looks up from his notepad, the dark circles under his eyes telling the rest of the story. "After an extensive search of the property surrounding the cabin, officers were able to locate the remains of Rhonda Tomlinson and Carla Hoffman buried a short distance away. Both families have been notified and the victims' remains will be transported to the Castle County Morgue in due course pending further investigation. Lucas Browne has been charged in the abductions and murders of Miss Tomlinson and Miss Hoffman and the abduction and torture of Miss Parker. Additional charges are pending. Lucas Browne remains in custody at this time at the Castle County Sheriff's Department. Detective Thome will now take your questions."

Sheriff Ridgewick steps away from the makeshift podium and stares down at the ground.

"Well." Mr. Peterson sighs. "Far from a happy ending, but it's the best we could've hoped for I suppose."

"Those poor families," Mrs. Peterson says, making the sign of the cross. "I can't even imagine what they're going through."

Gwendy doesn't say anything. The last eighteen hours have been a whirlwind—and her brain and body are still struggling to recover.

Earlier in the afternoon, the sheriff confided in her with great detail the horrors they'd discovered inside the Brownes' house and cabin: a pair of Ziploc sandwich baggies found under a second loose floorboard in Lucas's bedroom, the first containing assorted jewelry belonging to Lord-knows-how-many-women, and the second baggie containing fifty-seven teeth of various shapes and sizes. In the cellar of the cabin, they found a macabre toolkit consisting of a selection of bloodstained pliers, an electric drill, and several power saws. Gwendy wondered how long it would take for the press to get hold of this information.

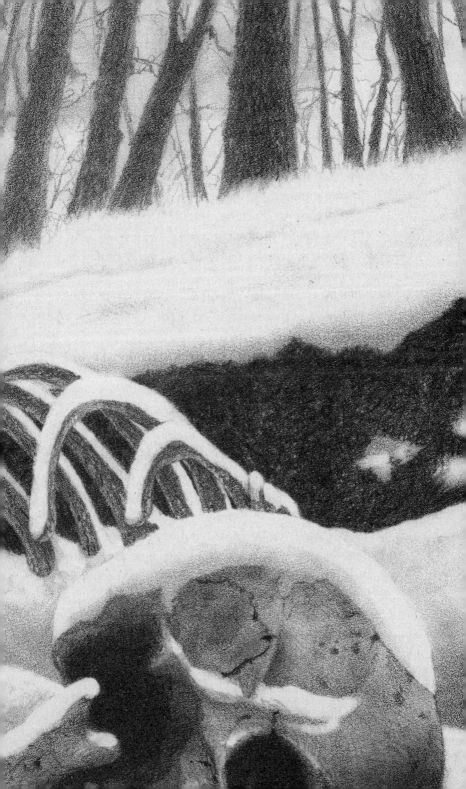

"Good for Norris Ridgewick," Mr. Peterson says, still staring at the television. "About time the people in this town gave him his due."

Gwendy's cell phone rings. "I better take this." She gets up from the sofa and walks into the kitchen. "Hello?"

"Got a minute?"

"Were your ears burning, Sheriff?"

"Every day for the last two weeks," he says, wearily.

"We just watched a replay of your press conference. You did well."

"Thanks." He pauses. "I still feel strange not mentioning your part in the investigation. Feels wrong to get all the credit."

"I figure a lot of that credit is overdue around here."

"I wouldn't say that."

"I would."

"I do have one question for you."

Here it comes. "What's that?" she asks.

"I know the whole dental school thing tipped it off for you. And the cowboy boots. But how did you *really* know?"

Gwendy doesn't answer right away. When she does, her words are carefully chosen and as honest as she can make them. "It was just a strong . . . feeling. He gave off this seriously creepy vibe, a kind of *hunger*, you could feel it wafting off him."

"So you're saying it was . . . gut instinct?"

She can picture him rolling his eyes. "Something like that."

"Well, whatever it was, I'm grateful. You saved that girl's life."

"*We* did, Norris."

"Are you home right now? I want to drop off the report I just finished writing. Make sure we're on the same page."

"I'm at my parents' house, but I could swing by the station after dinner."

"That'll be too late. You mind if I bring it by there?"

"That's fine. I'll be here." And she thinks, *If he tries to shake my hand, I'll just tell him I'm coming down with a bug, better not to touch me. Just like I told my parents earlier this afternoon.*

"Great, give me fifteen minutes."

But it only takes ten.

Gwendy is leaning across the dining room table, looking for a corner piece of the latest jigsaw puzzle—the nighttime skyline of New York City—when the doorbell rings.

"That's Norris," she says, getting up from the table.

"Make sure you invite him in," Mrs. Peterson says.

Gwendy walks into the foyer. "You must have been speeding—" she says, swinging open the door. The words die in her throat. "Ryan?"

Her husband is standing on the porch, a bouquet of flowers in one hand, his camera bag in the other. His face is clean-shaven and tanned, and his eyes are twinkling with nervous anticipation. He looks like a little boy bouncing on his heels and grinning.

"I know how you like surprises," he says.

Gwendy squeals with excitement and throws herself into his arms. He drops the camera bag and picks her up with his free hand, spinning her around. Her lips find his, and as he twirls her around and around on the porch of the house she grew up in, she thinks: *There's nothing bad in this man, only* home.

71

FOR THE FIRST TIME in her life, Gwendy wants to tell someone about the button box.

She glances over at Ryan in the driver's seat. She hates keeping such a big secret from him—*any* secret, for that matter—but she worries that it could be dangerous for her husband to know about the box. She also doesn't like the idea of him not having a choice in the matter. If she decides to tell him, he's stuck with the knowledge—and the responsibility—whether he wants it or not. How is that any better than what Richard Farris has done to her? Twice now!

"Penny for your thoughts," he says, checking his rearview mirror and signaling to change lanes. "You're awfully quiet. Worried about the emergency session?"

She nods her head. "Yes." And it's the truth.

"You'll do great, honey."

"I honestly don't even know what I'm supposed to do, what my role in all this will be."

"You'll listen and learn, and then you'll step up and lead. It's what you always do."

She sighs and stares out the window. Frozen ponds and farm buildings, snow-swirled into gray ghosts, blur past in the distant fields. "Hopefully we can talk some sense into the man. But I'm not holding my breath."

"If I know you, you won't rest until you do."

The call came in the night before. On the other end of the line was the Speaker of the House himself, Dennis Hastert. His message was brief and to the point: both the House and Senate would reconvene on Monday, January 3 at 9:00 AM, five days ahead of schedule. Gwendy thanked him for the call and hung up and then told Ryan. They'd only left her parents' house a couple of hours earlier, and he hadn't even had time to unpack his bags yet.

She was afraid to leave the button box inside the safe at the condo—what if Ryan decided to go home without her at some point and he opened it?—and Castle Rock Savings and Loan was closed because it was Sunday, so she had no choice but to take the box along with her.

As soon as that problem was solved, another complication rose in its place: because of the short notice, she was unable to arrange for a private plane out of Castle County Airport and was forced to fly out of a larger commuter airpark just south of Portland. But the extra drive and the inevitable questions from Ryan ("Since when do we fly private?") were worth the hassle if only to avoid the X-ray machines at the airport.

"How about I drop you out front with the luggage?" Ryan asks, steering the car off the exit ramp and onto the access road for Portland South Airpark. "I'll go park in the garage and meet you inside."

"Sounds good. We should have plenty of time."

Ryan pulls up to the section of curb marked UNLOADING ZONE in front of the main building— unlike the Castle County Airport, this place actually has more than one, not to mention multiple runways and a three-story parking garage—and unloads the luggage from the trunk, including Gwendy's carry-on containing the button box. He leaves Gwendy standing at the curb and drives across the street to the garage.

She looks around and sees two large families waiting in line with their suitcases at Baggage Check (in this case, a makeshift fiberglass booth with a pair of oversized grocery carts parked beside it). Several young children are doing their best to squirm out of their parents' grip, and one little girl, her face beet-red and stained with tears, appears on the verge of a major tantrum. A lone, harried-looking airport employee is ticketing the mountain of expensive luggage with the efficiency and speed of a sloth. If he has any help on this second day of January, it's currently nowhere in sight.

Gwendy sighs, feeling sorry for the guy, and sits down on a nearby bench. She arranges the three large suitcases in front of her on the sidewalk and places her carry-on next to her, resting an arm atop it for safekeeping.

"Excuse me, madam, is anyone sitting here?"

"Not at all," she says, looking up. "Feel free to—"

Richard Farris is standing in front of her, looking almost like a mirror image of the man she'd first met twenty-five years earlier on a bench in Castle View Park. His face hasn't aged a day, and he's wearing dark jeans with a button-down dress shirt (light gray this time instead of white), a dark jacket as if from a suit, and of course that small neat black hat of his is perched atop his head.

"How . . . where did you come from?" she says in a low, awed voice.

He sits down at the other end of the bench, smiling warmly. The carry-on suitcase rests between them.

Gwendy thinks about pinching herself on the arm to make sure she's not dreaming, but she's suddenly afraid to move. "Was that you at the mall with my mom? Did you . . . why did you leave the box with me again?" She's speaking fast now, weeks of frustration and anxiety surging into her voice. "I thought you said—"

Farris holds up a hand, silencing her. "I understand you have questions, but my time here is limited, so let us palaver for a spell before we're interrupted." He scoots a little closer to the center of the bench. "Regarding the return of our old friend, the button box . . . let's just say I found myself in a bit of a jam and needed to tuck it away somewhere safe for a short time." He looks at her with discernible affection in his light blue eyes. "You, Gwendy Peterson, were the safest place I could think of."

"I guess I'll take that as a compliment."

"As it was intended, dear girl. I told you long ago, your proprietorship of the button box was exceptional the first time I left it in your possession. And I have full trust it was once again."

"I wouldn't be so sure," she says. "I was a mess the whole time. I didn't know what to do. Push the button, not push the button." She lets out a long breath. "In the end, I did the best I could."

"And that's all one can ask for in any such endeavor. Knowing you as I do, I believe you did quite well this time around, too." He rests his hand on the carry-on suitcase, drumming his long, slender fingers along the zipper. "Ignoring the temptation of the buttons is a difficult chore during the best of times. Not many are able to resist. But, as you well know by now, when left alone, the box can be a strong force for good."

"But I didn't leave it alone," she says with a whine in her voice she remembers well from adolescence. "Not completely. I pulled the lever . . . a lot."

Farris nods his head ever so slightly.

"Will my mother be okay? The chocolates cured her, didn't they?" And then almost as an afterthought: "I had to try."

"Hospitals have been known to make mistakes, particularly when it comes to those pesky blood tests. Samples get contaminated; glass tubes get mislabeled. Happens all the time. I trust you left her with a sufficient supply?"

"I did," she says, sounding like a guilty teenager.

A minivan pulls to the curb in front of them. The side door slides open and a woman and young girl climb out carrying suitcases. They both say cheerful goodbyes to the driver, the door slides shut, and the van drives away. The woman and girl walk to the back of the line at Baggage Check and never once glance in their direction on the bench.

"What happened with Lucas Browne and my friend's husband . . . the awful things I saw in my head . . . the box did that, right? Was it because of the chocolates? Will it happen again?"

"That's not up to me. When it comes to the button box, some things—*many* things—remain beyond my reach."

She gapes at him. "But if you don't know the answers, then who does?"

Farris doesn't respond, just studies her through squinting eyes that appear almost gray now. The hat lays a thin line of shadow over his brow. Finally, he says: "I do, however, have one resolution for you that I believe you've been anxious about for quite some time now."

"What?" Gwendy asks, and the whiny tone is back. The idea that Richard Farris is not, in fact, the omnipotent force behind the button box's power, but rather some kind of glorified *courier*, not only pisses Gwendy off but also terrifies her.

He leans closer, and for one tense moment, Gwendy fears he's going to reach out and take her hand. "Your life is indeed your own. The stories you've chosen to tell, the people you've chosen to fight for, the lives you've touched . . . " He waves his hand through the air in front of his face. "All your own doing. Not the button box's. You have *always* been special, Gwendy Peterson, from the day you were born."

Gwendy forgets to breathe for a moment. She feels an enormous weight crumble from atop her shoulders, from around her heart. "Thank you," she manages, voice trembling.

Farris cocks his head, as if listening to a faraway voice. "Alas, my time is up. Your husband is on his way. Lovely man he is, too—a storyteller in his own right."

"What about the box?" Gwendy blurts.

"Already taken care of."

She looks at him, momentarily confused, and then she picks up her carry-on bag and gives it a shake.

It feels empty. It *is* empty.

"How did you—?"

Farris laughs. "You should know better by now than to ask such silly questions, young lady."

It feels strange to be called "young lady" by a man who appears to be roughly the same age as she. Then again, every minute of this experience feels strange, almost dreamlike.

"I must go," he says, standing, and Gwendy's certain he's going to take out his old-fashioned watch from the pocket inside his coat and check the time—but he doesn't. "Although I slowed his progress quite a bit, your husband's a dedicated man and he'll be here shortly." He looks down at Gwendy with that same glimmer of affection shining in his eyes. "And then the two of you shall check your bags and soar up and away into a long and prosperous and happy life together."

"If we ever make it through that line," Gwendy says jokingly.

"What line?" he asks.

She looks up and points. "That one." But now there's no one waiting in front of the Baggage Check booth. Not a single person.

"What the . . . ?"

When she turns back to the bench, Richard Farris is gone.

She gets to her feet and looks around—but he's nowhere in sight. The sidewalk and road are empty. He just vanished into thin air. But not before leaving a goodbye present for her.

Sitting on top of Gwendy's carry-on bag is a very familiar small white feather.

72

"ALL SET," RYAN SAYS, jogging across the street. They pick up their suitcases and head down the sidewalk toward Baggage Check.

"What took you so long?" Gwendy asks.

"Elevator was out of order. Had to walk down three floors. Then I realized I'd forgotten to lock the damn car, so I had to walk all the way back up again."

Gwendy laughs. "My little worrywart."

"Learned it from you," he says, sticking his tongue out at her.

She puts a hand on his arm, stopping him, suddenly serious. "I was thinking about what you said. In the car."

He gives her a questioning look.

"You were right," she says. "When I get there tomorrow, I'll listen and learn, and then I'll do the work. Whatever it takes. However long it takes."

He leans close to her so their foreheads are touching. "Now that sounds like the Gwendy Peterson I know."

"How may I help you, folks?" the smiling man sitting inside the booth asks.

"We're on Flight 117," Ryan says, checking the paperwork. "Scheduled to take off at 3:10. We'd like to check three bags please."

The man picks up a clipboard and scribbles something on a sheet of paper. "Can I see your IDs, please?"

Ryan pulls out his wallet and shows the man his driver's license. Gwendy fishes her license out of the side pocket of her purse and slides it across the counter. The man picks it up, double-checks the name, and then hands it back to her. "That'll do it," he says. He walks out from behind the booth and places their bags into one of the oversized carts. Unclipping a walkie-talkie from his belt, he keys the button and says, "Flight 117 baggage pick-up. Come and get 'em, Johnny."

A muffled voice answers, "Copy that, boss, be there in a flash."

Gwendy and Ryan start walking up the sidewalk toward the main building, but Gwendy turns back after a couple of steps and returns to the luggage cart. She throws her empty carry-on bag in with the others. Then she reaches into her coat pocket. "Here you go, sir. Happy New Year." She tosses something to the man inside the booth.

He reaches up and snags it. Staring down at the shiny silver coin lying heads-up in his palm, his face brightens. "Hey, now, thank you very kindly, ma'am."

Gwendy laughs. She turns around and takes Ryan's hand and they walk into the airport together.

ACKNOWLEDGMENTS

Bev Vincent read the earliest version of this short novel and, despite his busy schedule, supplied invaluable feedback in record time. Bev also kept the secret and calmed my nerves on a near daily basis. Billy Chizmar read that same early draft and emailed me from his college dorm room in Maine with some simple advice that made the backstory hum a lot smoother. As usual, Robert Mingee caught my last-minute mistakes and cleaned me up for public viewing. Brian Freeman and the good folks at CD did what they always do when I disappear into my writing cave for weeks at a time: they took care of business and let me focus on the words. Ed Schlesinger of Simon & Schuster came on board at the eleventh hour and his insightful notes undoubtedly made *Gwendy's Magic Feather* a better book.

I'm indebted to all of these fine people for their wisdom and encouragement. Just remember, I'm old and stubborn, so any mistakes you stumble upon are mine and mine alone.

I also want to thank artists extraordinaire Ben Baldwin and Keith Minnion for returning for another round and giving such beautiful life to Gwendy's story. I put Gail Cross of Desert Isle Design through the ringer on this project and, as usual, she came through with flying colors.

Much appreciation to my agent Kristin Nelson for all

STEPHEN KING

her hard work on this book and for always asking "What's next?"

Finally, I'm immensely grateful to my friend, Steve King, not only for his generous and thorough edit of *Gwendy's Magic Feather*, but also for trusting me to return to Castle Rock and Gwendy Peterson's life.

GWENDY'S FINAL TASK

STEPHEN KING AND RICHARD CHIZMAR

For Marsha DeFilippo,
a friend to a couple of writers.

1

IT'S A BEAUTIFUL APRIL day in Playalinda, Florida, not far from Cape Canaveral. This is the Year of Our Lord 2026, and only a few of the people in the crowd standing on the east side of Max Hoeck Back Creek are wearing masks. Most of those are old people, who got into the habit and find it hard to break. The coronavirus is still around, like a party guest who won't go home, and while many fear it may mutate again and render the vaccines useless, for now it's been fought to a draw.

Some members of the crowd—again, it's mostly the oldies, the ones whose eyesight isn't as good as it once was—are using binoculars, but most are not. The craft standing on the Playalinda launch pad is the biggest manned rocket ever to lift off from Mother Earth; with a fully loaded mass of 4.57 million pounds, it has every right to be called Eagle-19 Heavy. A fog of vapor obscures the last 50 of its 400-foot height, but even those with fading vision can read the three letters running down the space-craft's side:

T

E

T

And those with even fair hearing can pick up the ap-plause when it begins. One man—old enough to remem-ber hearing Neil Armstrong's crackling voice telling the world that the Eagle had landed—turns to his wife with tears in his eyes and goosebumps on his tanned, scrawny arms. The old man is Douglas "Dusty" Brigham. His wife is Sheila Brigham. They retired to the town of Destin ten years ago, but they are originally from Castle Rock, Maine. Sheila, in fact, was once the dispatcher in the sheriff's office.

From the Tet Corporation's launch facility a mile and a half away, the applause continues. To Dusty and Sheila it sounds thin, but it must be much louder across the creek, because herons arise from their morning's resting place in a lacy white cloud.

"They're on their way," Dusty tells his wife of fifty-two years.

"God bless our girl," Sheila says, and crosses herself. "God bless our Gwendy."

2

EIGHT MEN AND TWO women walk in a line along the right side of the Tet control center. They are protected by a plexiglass wall, because they've been in quarantine for the last twelve days. The techs rise from behind their computers and applaud. That much is tradition, but today there's also cheering. There will be more applause and cheers from the fifteen hundred Tet employees (the patches on their shirts, jackets, and coveralls identify them as the Tet Rocket Jockeys) outside. Any manned space mission is an event, but this one is extra special.

Second from the end of the line is a woman with her long hair, now gray, tied back in a ponytail that's mostly hidden beneath the high collar of her pressure suit. Her face is unwrinkled and still beautiful, although there are fine lines around her eyes and at the corners of her mouth. Her name is Gwendy Peterson, she's sixty-four, and in less than an hour she will be the first sitting U.S. senator to ride a rocket to the new MF-1 space station. (There are cynics among Gwendy's political peers who like to say MF stands for a certain incestuous sex act, but it actually stands for Many Flags.)

The crew are carrying their helmets for the time being, so nine of them have a free hand to wave, acknowledging the cheers. Gwendy—technically a crew member—can't wave unless she wants to wave the small white case in her other hand. And she doesn't want to do that.

Instead of waving she calls, "We love you and thank you! This is one more step to the stars!"

The cheers and applause redouble. Someone yells, "*Gwendy for President*!" A few others take up the call, but not that many. She's popular, but not *that* popular, especially not in Florida, which went red (again) in the last general election.

The crew leaves the building and climbs into the three-car tram that will take them to Eagle Heavy. Gwendy has to crane her neck all the way to the reinforced collar of her suit to see the top of the rocket. *Am I really going up in that?* she asks herself, and not for the first time.

In the seat next to her, the team's tall, sandy-haired biologist leans toward her. He speaks in a low murmur. "There's still time to back out. No one would think the worse of you."

Gwendy laughs. It comes out nervy and too shrill. "If you believe that, you must also believe in Santa Claus and the Tooth Fairy."

"Fair enough," he says, "but never mind what people would think. If you have any idea, any at all, that you're going to freak out and start yelling '*Wait, stop, I've changed my mind*' when the engines light up, then call it off now. Because once those engines go, there's no turning around and no one needs a panicked politician onboard. Or a panicky billionaire for that matter." He looks to the car ahead of them, where a man is bending the ear of the Ops Commander. In his white pressure suit, the man bears a resemblance to the Pillsbury Doughboy.

The three-car tram starts to roll. Men and women

in coveralls applaud them on their way. Gwendy puts the white case down and holds it firmly between her feet. Now she can wave.

"I'll be fine." She's not entirely sure of that but tells herself she has to be. *Has* to. Because of the white case. Stamped in raised red letters on both sides are the words **CLASSIFIED MATERIAL**. "How about you?"

The bio-guy smiles, and Gwendy realizes that she can't remember his name. He's been her training partner for the last four weeks, only minutes ago they back-checked each other's suits before leaving the holding area, but she can't remember his name. This is NG, as her late mother would have said: not good.

"I'll be fine. This'll be my third trip, and when the rocket starts to climb and I feel the g-force pressing down? Speaking just for myself, it's the best orgasm a boy ever had."

"Thank you for sharing," Gwendy says. "I'll be sure to put it in my first dispatch to the down-below." It's what they call Earth, the down-below, she remembers that, but what's Bio Boy's damn name?

In the pocket of her jumper she's got a notebook with all sorts of info in it—not to mention a very special bookmark. The names of all the crew members are in there, but no way can she get at the notebook now, and even if she could, it might—almost certainly *would*—raise suspicions. Gwendy falls back on the technique Dr. Ambrose gave her. It doesn't always work, but this time it does. The man next to her is tall, square-jawed, blue-eyed, and has a tumble of sandy hair. The women think he's hot. What's hot? Fire's hot. If you touch it, you might get a—

Bern. That's his name. Bern Stapleton. Professor Bern

Stapleton who also happens to be Major Bern Stapleton, Retired.

"Please don't," Bern says. She's pretty sure he's talking about his orgasm metaphor. There's nothing wrong with her short-term memory, at least not so far.

Well . . . not *too* wrong.

"I was joking," Gwendy says, and pats his gloved hand with her own. "And stop worrying, Bern. I'll be fine."

She tells herself again that she must be. She doesn't want to let down her constituents—and today that's all of America and most of the world—but that's minor compared to the locked white box between her boots. She can't let *it* down. Because there's a box inside the box, made not of high-impact steel but of mahogany. It's a foot wide, a bit more than that in length, and about seven inches deep. There are buttons on top and levers so small you have to pull them with your pinky finger on either side.

They have just one paying passenger on this flight to the MF, and it's not Gwendy. She has an actual job. Not much of one, mostly just recording data on her iPad and sending it back to Tet Control, but it's not entirely a cover for her real business in the up-above. She's a climate monitor, her call designation is Weather Girl, and some of the crew jokingly refer to her as Tempest Storm, the name of a long-ago ecdysiast.

What is that? she asks herself. *I should know.*

Because she doesn't, she resorts to Dr. Ambrose's technique again. The word she's looking for is like paint, isn't it? No, not paint. Before you paint you have to get rid of the *old* paint. You have to . . .

"Strip," she murmurs.

"What?" Bern asks. He has been distracted by a bunch

of applauding men standing beside one of the emergency trucks. Which please God won't have to roll on this fine spring day.

"Nothing," she says, thinking, *An ecdysiast is a stripper.*

It's always a relief when the missing words come. She knows that all too soon they won't. She doesn't like that, is in fact terrified of it, but that's the future. Right now she just has to get through today. Once she's up there (where the air's not just rare but nonexistent), they can't just send her home if they discover what's wrong with her, can they? But they could screw up her mission if they found out. And there's something else, something that would be even worse. Gwendy doesn't want to even think about it but can't help herself.

What if she forgets the real reason she's up there? The real reason is the box inside the box. It sounds melodramatic, but Gwendy Peterson knows it's true: the fate of the world depends on what's inside that box.

3

THE SERVICE-AND-DELIVERY STRUCTURE BESIDE Eagle
Heavy is a crisscross latticework of steel beams housing
a huge open elevator. Gwendy and her fellow travelers
mount the nine stairs and get inside. The elevator has a capacity of three dozen and there's plenty of room to spread
out, but Gareth Winston stands next to her, his considerable belly pooching out the front of his white pressure suit.

Winston is her least favorite person on this trip to the
up-above, although she has every confidence he doesn't
know it. Over a quarter-century in politics has taught
Gwendy the fine art of hiding her feelings and putting
on a you're-so-darn-fascinating face. When she was first
elected to the House of Representatives, a political veteran
named Patricia "Patsy" Follett took Gwendy under her
wing and gave her some valuable advice. That particular
day it was about an old buzzard from Mississippi named
Milton Jackson (long since gone to that great caucus room
in the sky), but Gwendy's found it useful ever since: "Save
your biggest smiles for the shitheads, and don't take your
eyes off theirs. The women will think you love their
earrings. The men will think you're smitten with them.
None of them will know that you're actually watching
their every move."

"Ready for the biggest joyride of your life, Senator?"

Winston asks as the elevator begins its slow 400-foot trundle up the side of the rocket.

"Ready-ready-Teddy," Gwendy says, giving him the wide smile she reserves for shitheads. "How about you?"

"Totally excited!" Winston proclaims. He spreads his arms and Gwendy has to take a step back to keep from being bopped in the chest. Gareth Winston is prone to expansive gestures; he probably feels that being worth a hundred and twenty billion dollars (not as much as Jeff Bezos, but close) gives him the right to be expansive. "Totally thrilled, totally up for it, totally *stoked*!"

He is, needless to say, the paying passenger, and in the case of space flight that means paying through the nose. His ticket was $2.2 million, but Gwendy knows there was another price, as well. Mega-billions translates into political clout, and as it gears up for a manned Mars mission, TetCorp needs all the political allies it can get. She just hopes Winston survives the trip and gets a chance to use his influence. He's overweight and his blood pressure at last check was borderline. Others in the Eagle crew may not know that, but Gwendy does. She has a dossier on him. Does *he* know she knows? It wouldn't surprise Gwendy in the least.

"To call this the trip of a lifetime would be an understatement," he says. He's speaking loudly enough for the others to turn around and look. Operation Commander Kathy Lundgren gives Gwendy a wink, and a small smile touches the corners of her mouth. Gwendy doesn't have to be a mind reader to know what that means: *Better you than me, sister.*

As the slow-moving elevator passes the lower **T** in

TET, Winston gets down to business. Not for the first time, either. "You're not here just to send back rah-rah dispatches to your adoring fans, or to look down at the big blue marble and see how the fires in the Amazon are affecting wind currents in Asia." He looks meaningfully down at the white box with its CLASSIFIED stamp.

"Don't sell me short, Gareth. I took meteorology classes in college and boned up all last winter," Gwendy says, ignoring both the comment and the implied question. Not that he's afraid to ask outright; he already has, several times, both during their four weeks of preflight training and their twelve days of quarantine. "It turns out that Bob Dylan was wrong."

Winston's broad brow creases. "Not sure I'm following you, Senator."

"You actually *do* need a weatherman to know which way the wind blows. The fires in the Amazon and those in Australia are making fundamental changes in Earth's weather patterns. Some of those changes are bad, but some may actually be working in the environment's favor, strange as that seems. They could put a damper on global warming."

"Never believed in all that stuff myself. Overblown at best, nonexistent at worst."

Now they are passing the **E**. *Get me away from this guy*, Gwendy thinks . . . then realizes that if she didn't want to be in close quarters with a guy like Gareth Winston, she should have avoided this trip altogether.

Only she couldn't.

She looks up at him, maintaining what she thinks of as the Patsy Follett Smile. "Antarctica is melting like a

Popsicle in the sun and you don't think global warming is real?"

But Winston won't be led away from what interests him. He may be an overweight blowhard, but he didn't make all those mega-billions by being stupid. Or distractable. "I would give a great deal to know what's in your little white box, Senator, and I have a great deal to give, as I'm sure you know."

"Ooo, that sounds suspiciously like a bribe."

"Not at all, just a figure of speech. And by the way, since we're going to be space-mates very shortly, can I call you Gwendy?"

She maintains the brilliant smile, although it's starting to hurt her face. "By all means. As for the contents of this . . ." She lifts the box. "Telling you would get us both in very big trouble, the kind that lands you in a federal facility, and it's really not worth it. You'd be disappointed, and I'd hate to let down the fourth richest man in the world."

"Third richest," he says, and gives her a smile that equals Gwendy's in brilliance. He waggles a gloved finger at her. "I won't give up, you know. I can be very persistent. And no one is going to put me in prison, dear." *Oh my,* Gwendy thinks. *We've progressed from Senator to Gwendy to dear in the course of one elevator ride. Of course, it's a very slow elevator.* "The economy would collapse."

To this she makes no reply, but she's thinking that if the box inside the box—the button box—fell into the wrong hands, *everything* would collapse.

The sun might even gain a new asteroid belt between Mars and Venus.

4

AT THE TOP OF the gantry there's a large white room where the space travelers stand, arms raised and doing slow pirouettes, as a disinfecting spray that smells suspiciously like bleach wafts over them. It's their last cleansing.

Not long ago there was another room in here, a small one, with a sign on the door reading WELCOME TO THE LAST TOILET ON EARTH, but Eagle Heavy is a luxury liner equipped with its own bathroom. Which, like the three cabins, is actually little more than a capsule. One of the private cabins is Gareth Winston's. Gwendy reckons he deserves it; he paid enough for it. The second is Gwendy's. Under other circumstances she might have protested this special treatment, U.S. senator or not, but considering her main reason for being on this trip, she agreed. Mission Control Director Eileen Braddock suggested that the six members of the crew without flight responsibilities (Ops Commander Kathy Lundgren and Second Ops Sam Drinkwater) draw straws for the remaining cabin, but the crew voted unanimously to give it to Adesh Patel, the entomologist. His live specimens have already been loaded. Adesh will sleep in a cramped bunk surrounded by bugs and spiders. Including (*Oh, ag,* Gwendy thinks) a tarantula named Olivia and a scorpion named Boris.

The lavatory belongs to all, and no one is any happier about that than their mission commander. "No more diapers," Kathy Lundgren told Gwendy during quarantine. "*That*, my dear Senator, is what I call one giant leap for mankind. Not to mention womankind."

"*Ingress*," the loudspeakers on Mission Control boom. "*T-minus two hours and fifteen minutes. Green across the board.*"

Kathy Lundgren and Second Ops Sam Drinkwater face the other members of the crew. Kathy, her auburn hair sparkling with tiny jewels of disinfectant mist, addresses all eight, but it seems to Gwendy that she pays special attention to the senator and the billionaire.

"Before we begin our final prep, I'll summarize our mission's timeline. You all know it, but I am required by TetCorp to do this once more prior to entry. We will achieve Earth orbit in eight minutes and twenty seconds. We will circle the earth for two days, making either thirty-two or thirty-three complete circumnavigations, the orbits varying slightly to create a Christmas bow shape. Sam and I will be charting space junk for disposal on a later mission. Senator Peterson—Gwendy—will begin her weather monitoring activities. Adesh will no doubt be playing with his bugs."

General laughter at this. David Graves, the mission's statistician and IT specialist, says, "And if any of them get free, out the hatch they go, Adesh. Along with you." This provokes more laughter. To Gwendy they sound pretty loosey-goosey. She hopes she sounds that way herself.

"On Day Three, we'll dock with Many Flags, which

just now is pretty much deserted except for a Chinese enclave—"

"Spooky," Winston says, and makes an *ooo-OOOO* sound.

Kathy gives him a flat look and continues. "The Chinese keep to themselves in Spoke 9. We're in Spokes 1, 2, and 3. Spokes 4 to 8 are currently not occupied. If you see the Chinese at all, it will be while they're running the outer ring. They do a lot of that. You'll have plenty of room to spread. We're going to be up there for an additional nineteen days, and room to spread is an incredible luxury. Especially after forty-eight hours in Eagle Heavy.

"Now here comes the important part, so listen to me carefully. Bern Stapleton is a veteran of two previous trips. Dave Graves has made one. Sam, my second in command, has made five, and I've made seven. The rest of you are newbies, and I'll tell you what I tell all newbies: This is your final chance to turn around. If you have even *the slightest doubt* about your ability to pull your weight from ingress to final egress, you must say so now."

Nobody speaks up.

Kathy nods. "Outstanding. Let's get this show on the road."

One by one they cross the access arm and are helped into the spacecraft by a quartet of white-suited (and disinfected) service personnel. Lundgren, Drinkwater, and Graves—who'll be overseeing the flight from a bank of touch screens—go first.

Below them, on the second level, Dr. Dale Glen, physicist Reggie Black, and biologist Bern Stapleton seat themselves in a row.

On the third and widest level, where eventually more

paying passengers will sit (or so TetCorp hopes) are Jafari Bankole, the astronomer who'll have little to do until they're in the MF station, entomologist Adesh Patel, passenger Gareth Winston, and last but not least, the junior senator from Maine, Gwendy Peterson.

5

GWENDY SEATS HERSELF BETWEEN Bankole and Patel. Her flight chair looks like a slightly futuristic La-Z-Boy recliner. Above each of them are three blank screens, and for a panicky moment Gwendy can't remember what they're there for. She's supposed to do something to light them up, but what?

She looks to her right in time to see Jafari Bankole plugging a lead into a port in the chest of his suit, and things come into focus. *Keep it together, Gwendy.*

She plugs in and the screens above her first light up, then boot up. One shows a video feed of the rocket on its launch pad. One shows her vital signs (blood pressure a little high, heart rate normal). The third shows a rolling column of information and numbers as Becky, Eagle Heavy's computer, runs an ongoing series of self-checks. These mean nothing to Gwendy, but presumably they mean something to Kathy Lundgren. Also to Sam and Dave Graves, of course, but it's Kathy—plus Eileen Braddock, the Mission Control director—who will be watching the readouts with the greatest attention, because either one of them can scrub the mission if they see something they don't like. That decision, Gwendy knows, would cost upward of seventeen million dollars.

Right now all the numbers are green. Above the marching columns is a countdown clock, also in the green.

"Hatch closed," Becky tells them in her soft, almost human voice. "Conditions remain nominal. T-minus one hour, forty-eight minutes."

"Downrange check," Kathy says from two levels above Gwendy.

"Weather downrange . . . ," Becky commences.

"Belay that, Becky." Kathy can't turn her head much because of her suit, but she waves an arm. "You give it to me, Gwendy."

For a terrible moment Gwendy has no idea what to do or how to respond. Her mind is a mighty blank. Then she sees Adesh Patel pointing below her seat and things click into place again. She understands that stress is making her condition worse and tells herself again that she has to calm down. *Must.* She's a lot less terrified about sitting on megatons of highly combustible rocket fuel than she is of the relentless neurological decay going on in the gray sponge between her ears.

She grabs the iPad out of its clips beneath her seat, PETERSON stamped on the cover. She thumbprints it and swipes to the current weather app. The cabin's superb WiFi overrides the diagnostic screen above her. What takes its place is a weather map similar to one on a TV newscast.

"It's grand downrange," she tells Kathy. "High pressure all the way, clear skies, no wind." And, she knows, it would take hurricane-force winds to knock Eagle Heavy off course once it was really rolling. Most weather concerns have to do with lift-off and reentry.

"How about the up-above?" Sam Drinkwater calls back to her. There's a smile in his voice.

"Thunderstorms seventy miles up, with a slight

chance of meteor showers," Gwendy returns, and everyone laughs. She turns off her tablet, and the diagnostic screen resumes.

Jafari Bankole says, "If you would like the porthole seat, Senator, there is still time for us to switch."

There are two portholes on the third level—again, with an eye to future tourism. Gareth Winston, of course, has one of them. Gwendy shakes her head. "As the crew astronomer, I think you should have an observation post. And how many times have I told you to call me Gwendy?"

Bankole smiles. "Many. It just does not come naturally to me."

"Understood. Appreciated, even. But as long as we're crammed together in the world's most expensive sardine can, will you give it your best shot?"

"All right. You are Gwendy, at least until we dock with the Many Flags station."

They wait. The minutes drain away (*the way my mind is draining away*, Gwendy can't help thinking). At T-minus 40, Becky tells them the service structure is retracting on its gigantic rails. At T-minus 35, Becky announces, "Fuel loading has commenced. All systems remain nominal."

Once upon a time—actually just ten or twelve years ago, but things move fast in the twenty-first century—the fuel was loaded before the human cargo, but SpaceX changed that, and a lot of other things. There are no more flight controls, just the ubiquitous touch screens, and Becky is really running the show (Gwendy just hopes the Beckster isn't a female version of HAL 9000). Lundgren and Drinkwater are basically just there for what Kathy calls "the dreaded holy-shit moment." Dave Graves is actually more important; if Becky has a nervous breakdown, he can fix it. Probably. Hopefully.

"Helmets," Sam Drinkwater says, putting on his. "Let me hear your roger."

One by one they respond. For a moment Gwendy can't remember where the catches are, but then it comes to her and she locks down.

"T-minus 27," Becky informs. "Systems nominal."

Gwendy glances at Winston, and is meanly pleased to see that some of his rich-guy bonhomie has evaporated. He's looking out his porthole at blue sky and a corner of the Mission Control building. There's a red patch on the fleshy cheek Gwendy can see, but otherwise he looks pale. Maybe thinking this wasn't such a good idea, after all.

As if catching her thought, he turns to her and gives her a thumbs-up. Gwendy returns the gesture.

"Got your special box all secure?" Winston asks.

Gwendy has it beneath one knee, where it won't fly away unless she does. And she's secured with a five-point harness, like a jet fighter pilot.

"Good to go." And then, although she's no longer sure what it means—if it means anything: "Five-by-five."

Winston grunts and turns back to the window.

On her left, Adesh has closed his eyes. His lips are moving slightly, almost certainly in prayer. Gwendy would like to do the same, but it's been a long time since she had any real confidence in God. But there is *something*. That she's sure of, because she cannot believe that any power on Earth made the strange device currently hidden inside a steel container that can only be opened with a seven-digit code. Why it has ended up in her hands again is a question to which she supposes she knows the answer, or at least part of it. Why she's saddled with it while suffering the first stages of early-onset Alzheimer's is less understandable. It's also hideously unfair, not to mention absurd, but since when did questions of fairness ever enter into human events? When Job cried out to God, the Almighty's response was mighty cold: *Were you there when I made the world?*

Never mind, Gwendy thinks. *Third time is the charm, last time pays for all. I'll do what I have to do, and I'll hold on to my mind long enough to do it. I promised Farris, and I keep my promises.*

At least she always has.

If not for the innocent people with me, she thinks, *for the most part good people, brave people, dedicated people (maybe with the exception of Gareth Winston), I'd almost wish we'd blow up on the launching pad or 50 miles downrange. That would take care of everythi—*

Except it wouldn't; that's something else that's slipped her increasingly unreliable mind. According to Richard Farris, the author of all her misery, it wouldn't take care of everything any more than weighting the goddamned button box down with rocks and dropping it into the Marianas Trench would take care of everything.

It had to be space. Not just the final frontier but the ultimate wasteland.

Give me strength, Gwendy prays to the God whose existence she highly doubts. As if in response, Becky—the god of Eagle Heavy—tells them they are now at T-minus 10 minutes, and all systems remain green.

Sam Drinkwater says, "Visors down and locked. Let me hear your roger."

They snap down their visors, firing off their responses. At first everything looks dark to Gwendy, and she remembers her polarizing visor also came down. She shoves it up with the heel of her gloved hand.

"Initiate oxygen flow, let me hear your roger."

The valve is somewhere on her helmet, but she can't remember where. God, if only she could get to her notebook! She looks at Adesh in time to see him twist a knob on his helmet's left side, just above the pressure suit's high collar. Gwendy copies him and hears the soft shush of air into her helmet.

Remember to turn it off once we achieve orbit, she tells herself. *Cabin air after that.*

Adesh is giving her a questioning look. Gwendy makes a clumsy **O** with her thumb and forefinger. He gives her a smile, but Gwendy is afraid he saw her hesitation. Again she thinks of her mother's NG: not good.

6

TIME IN TRAINING HAS been slow. Time in quarantine has been slow. The walk-out, the elevator ride, the insertion, all slow. But as those last earthbound minutes begin, time speeds up.

In her helmet—too loud, and Gwendy can't remember how to turn it down—she hears Eileen Braddock in Mission Control say, "T-minus five minutes, terminal countdown begins."

Kathy Lundgren: "Roger that, Mission Control, terminal countdown."

Use your iPad, Gwendy thinks. *It controls everything in your suit.*

She touches the suit icon, finds the volume control, and uses her finger to decrease the blare. *See how much you remember?* she thinks. *He'd be proud.*

Who would be proud?

My handsome hubby. She has to fish for his name, which is appalling.

Ryan, of course. Ryan Brown is her handsome hubby.

Sam Drinkwater: "Eagle is in auto idle. All fuel is on."

On her iPad and on the screen above her, T-minus 3:00 gives way to 2:59 and 2:58 and 2:57.

A gloved hand grips hers, making Gwendy startle. She looks around and sees Jafari. His eyes ask her if it's okay or if she'd like him to let go. She nods, smiles, and tightens her grip. His lips form the words *All will be well*. Winston has his bought-and-paid-for porthole, but it's going to waste, at least for now. He's staring straight ahead, his lips pressed so tightly together that they're almost not there, and Gwendy knows what he's thinking: *Why did this seem like a good idea? I must have been crazy.*

Kathy: "Arm for launch?"

Sam: "Roger that, armed for launch. Eleven minutes from stars in the daytime, folks."

Seemingly only seconds later, Eileen from Mission Control: "Crew okay? Let me hear you roger."

One by one they reply. Gareth Winston is last, his *roger* a dry croak.

Kathy Lundgren, sounding as cool as the other side of the pillow: "Flight termination armed. T-minus one minute. Are we go for launch?"

Sam Drinkwater and Eileen Braddock answer together: "Go for launch."

With the hand not holding Jafari's, Gwendy feels for the steel box. It's there, it's safe. Only the box inside it is *not* safe. The box inside is the most dangerous thing on Earth. Which is why it must *leave* Earth.

Eileen Braddock: "First Ops Commander Lundgren, you have the bird."

"Roger that, I have the bird."

On the screen above Gwendy, the final ten seconds begin to count off.

She thinks: *What is my name?*

Gwendy. My father wanted a Gwendolyn and my mother wanted a Wendy, like in *Peter Pan*. They compromised. Hence, I am Gwendy Peterson.

Gwendy thinks: *Where am I?*

Playalinda, Florida, the Tet Corporation's launch complex. At least for a few more seconds.

Why am I here?

Before she can answer that question, a vast rumble begins 450 feet below where she sits reclined in her ergonomic chair. Eagle's cabin begins to vibrate—gently, at first, then more strongly. Gwendy has a fragmentary memory of being five or six and sitting on top of their washing machine as it goes into its final spin cycle.

"We are firing green," Sam Drinkwater says.

A second or two later Kathy says, "Lift-off!"

The roar is louder, the vibration more intense. Gwendy wonders if that's normal or if something has gone wrong. On the center screen above her she now sees Mission Control and the rest of the complex through a red-orange bloom of fire. How far below is it? Fifty feet? A hundred? A shudder runs through the craft. Jafari's grip tightens.

This isn't right. This can't be right.

Gwendy closes her eyes, asking herself again why she's here.

The short answer is because a man—if he *is* a man—told her that she had to be. At this moment, waiting for her life and all the others' to end in a vast explosion of cryogenic liquid oxygen and rocket-grade kerosene, she can't remember the man's name. A crack has opened in the bottom of her brain and everything she has ever known has started to leak into the darkness below it. All she can remember is that he wore a hat. Small and round.

Black.

7

THIS IS THE THIRD time the button box has come into Gwendy Peterson's life. The first time it was in a canvas bag with a drawstring top. The second time she found it in the bottom drawer of a filing cabinet in her Washington, D.C., office. During her freshman term as Maine's second district representative, that was. The third time was in 2019, while she was running for the Senate, a campaign that Democratic committee insiders felt had as much chance of succeeding as the Charge of the Light Brigade. Each time it was brought by a man who always dressed in jeans, a white shirt, a black suitcoat, and a small bowler hat. His name was Richard Farris. On the first occasion, the button box was in her possession all through her adolescence. On the second, her custodianship was much shorter, but she believed it saved her mother's life (Alicia Peterson died in 2015, years after cancer should have killed her).

The third time was . . . different. *Farris* was different.

Gwendy retired from the House of Representatives in 2012, although she could have gone on getting elected well into her eighties, perhaps even into her nineties, if she had so chosen. "You're like Strom Thurmond," Pete Riley, head of the Maine Democratic Committee once told her. "You could have gone on getting reelected even after you were dead."

"Please, no comparisons to that guy," Gwendy had said.

"Okay, how about John Lewis? Whoever you use for a comparison—hell, Margaret Chase Smith from right up the road in Skowhegan spent thirty-three years in D.C.—the point is the same: you're the fabled automatic. And we need you."

But what Gwendy needed to do was write books. Fiction was her first love. She had published only five novels, and time was marching on. Retirement from public service opened up that side of her life and made her happy in a way life under the Capitol dome never had. She published *Bramble Rose* in 2013 and then, in 2015, a serial killer novel called *Desolation Street*. That one, featuring a charming maniac who harvested the teeth of his victims, was set in D.C. but based on certain events in her hometown.

She was considering another book, one full of romance and family secrets, when Donald Trump was elected president. Many in Maine's second district rejoiced, feeling the Washington swamp would be drained, the budget would be balanced, and the flood of "bad hombre" illegal immigrants from South America would finally be dammed up. For lifelong Democrats—the kind of people who avoided Fox News as if it might give them rabies—it was the beginning of a four-year nightmare. Gwendy's own father, perhaps the most apolitical member of the Democratic party in the entire state of Maine, looked at Gwendy with sober eyes the day after the election and said, "This is going to change everything, Gwennie. And probably not in a good way."

She was deep into the novel, this one set in Maine at

the time of the Bradley Gang massacre in Derry, when Pete Riley came to see her again. The poor man looked as if he'd lost twenty pounds between election night in 2016 and that early winter day a little over two years later. He kept it simple and he kept it brief. He wanted Gwendy to run against Paul Magowan for the Senate in 2020, which he called "the year of perfect eyesight." He said only Gwendy would have a chance of beating the Republican businessman, who expected his campaign to be little more than a formality on the way to a foregone conclusion.

"If nothing else, you could slow his roll and give some hope to all the good folks suffering TD."

"Which is what?"

"Trump Depression. Come on, Gwendy, open your mind to this. Give it fair consideration."

Fair consideration was one of her trademark phrases, used at least once at every town hall gathering during her political career. If Pete expected it to turn the key in her lock, he was disappointed. "You're joking. You have to be. Aside from the fact that I'm writing a new book—"

"And I'm sure it will be as good or better than the others," Pete said, flashing his most winning Clark Gable smile.

"Don't bother blowing smoke up my skirt," Gwendy (who that day was wearing a pair of old Levis) said. "Better men than you have tried and failed. What I was going to say is that aside from the new book, where there's a lot of hot sex that I'm enjoying vicariously, that idiot Magowan won by fifteen points in '14. And after spending two years with his lips firmly attached to Donald Trump's ass, he's got an eighty percent approval rating."

"Bullshit," Pete said. "Republican propaganda. You know it is."

"I know nothing of the kind, but let's say it is. I was quite popular during my run in the House, I'll give you that, but memories are short. Magowan is the man of the hour, and I'm the woman of yesterday. There's a tide in politics, and right now it's running strong conservative. You know that as well as I do. I probably wouldn't lose by fifteen points, but I'd lose."

Pete Riley went to the window of Gwendy's small study and looked out with his hands stuffed deep in his pockets. "Okay," he said, not looking at her. "Barring a miracle, you'd lose. I think we've settled that point. So lose. Make a pretty concession speech about how the voters have spoken but the fight continues and blah blah blah. Then you can go back to writing about Derry, Maine, in the 1930s. But this isn't the '30s, it's 2018, and you know what?"

He turned back to her like a good defense attorney addressing the jury.

"Yeats's blood-dimmed tide is also running. People are turning away from women's rights, from science, from the very notion of equality. They're turning away from *truth*. Politics aside, somebody needs to stand up and make them look at all the stuff it's easier and more comfortable not to believe in. You always did that, *always*. I'm asking you to do it again."

"To be your noble Joan of Arc and let the good people of Maine burn me at the stake?"

"Nobody is going to burn you alive," Pete said . . . not knowing that eight years later Gwendy would be atop a flaming torch called Eagle Heavy and more than half expecting to be transformed into superheated atoms at any moment. "You're going to lose an election. But in the meantime, you could make that fat prick Magowan sweat bullets. Get him on the debate stage and make people see that he's sticking up for ideas that aren't just bad, they're unworkable and downright dangerous. *Then* you can go back to writing your books."

Gwendy had been ready to be angry with Pete, but she saw he was at least partly right. She was being melodramatic. Which, she supposed, went with writing fiction full of secrets and hot sex. "Take one for the team, in other words. Would that be accurate?"

He gave her the big Clark Gable grin. "Hole in one."

"Let me think about it," she'd said.

Probably a mistake.

8

BUT NOT AS BIG as this one, Gwendy thinks as the roar of the engines increases to a bellow. Jafari Bankole's grip has become paralyzing, even through the thickness of their two gloves. She goes to CREW on her iPad with her free hand, highlights Jafari's name with the pad-sensitive tip of her index finger (it's easier to remember stuff when you're not trying, she has discovered), and speaks to him comm to comm, so it's private. "Let up a little, Jaff, okay? You're hurting."

"Sorry, sorry," he says, and relaxes his grip. "This is . . . such a very long way from Kenya."

"And from western Maine," Gwendy says.

The cabin's shudder-shake begins to lessen, and her recliner starts to turn slightly on its gimbals. Or is it? Maybe what's really happening is that the altitude of the cabin is changing. Tilting.

Gwendy punches for Ops Comm so she can listen to Kathy, Sam, and Mission Control.

"Three hundred fifty miles downrange and the sound barrier is just a happy memory," Eileen says. She sounds calm, and why not? Eileen is safe on the ground.

"Roger that," Kathy says. She also sounds calm, which is good.

"Looking fine, Eagle Heavy. Nominal burn, all three engines."

"Roger." Sam Drinkwater this time.

The cabin's tilt is gradually becoming more pronounced, and the ride has become smooth. For the time being, at least.

"You are go for throttle up, Eagle Heavy."

Kathy and Sam together: "Roger."

Gwendy can't hear any real difference in the engine roar, but an invisible hand settles on her chest. Ahead of her, Dale Glen, the mission's doctor, appears to be making notes on his iPad, and never mind the pad-sensitive fingertip; he has stripped his glove off. *He could be in his Missoula consulting room*, Gwendy thinks.

She goes to FLIGHT INFO on her pad. They are less than two minutes into the flight but already 22 miles high and traveling at 2,600 miles an hour. For a woman who considers driving at 80 on the Maine state turnpike living dangerously, she finds the number hard to comprehend, but there's no doubt about the increasing pressure on her body. Gravity doesn't want to let go.

There's a thud, followed by a bright flash in the porthole to her left, and for a moment she thinks it's all over. Jafari's hand clamps down again.

"Solid booster rocket has separated," Sam says, to which Dave Graves responds, "Hallelujah. Swivel those jets, BoPeep."

"Call me that again and I'll tear your face off," Kathy says. "Let me hear your roger."

"Roger that," Dave says, grinning.

The tilt of the cabin increases. Outside, the blue sky has darkened to violet.

"Three main engines all firing beautifully," Kathy says, and Gwendy sees Bern Stapleton lift his hands with the thumbs up. A moment later he's in her helmet, comm to comm. "Enjoying the ride, Senator?"

And because for the moment it's just the two of them, she says, "Best orgasm a girl ever had."

He laughs. It's loud. Gwendy winces. She needs to turn down the sound, but how does she do that? She knew a little while ago, she even did it, but now she can't remember.

It's on your iPad. Everything is.

Before she can turn down the volume, Bern has clicked off and Ops Comm returns. Below and now far behind, Eileen Braddock is telling them they've passed the point of negative return.

Kathy: "Roger that, negative return."

No going back now, Gwendy thinks, and her fear is replaced by a feeling of what-the-hell exultation that she never would have expected. *Space or bust.*

She motions for Jafari to raise his visor and she raises her own. Not protocol, but it's only for a few seconds, and she has something she wants to say. Needs to say.

"Jaff! We're going to see the stars!"

The astronomer smiles. "God's grace, Gwendy. God's grace."

9

After Pete Riley's visit, Gwendy began to read up on Paul Magowan, the Republican junior senator from Maine. The more she read, the more disgusted she became. The younger Gwendy Peterson would have been outright horrified, and even at fifty-eight, with several trips around the political block in her resume, she felt at least some horror.

Magowan was an avowed fiscal conservative, declaring he wouldn't allow tax-and-spend progressives to mortgage the futures of his constituents' grandchildren, but he had no problem with clear-cutting Maine's forests and removing the commercial fishing bans in protected areas. His attitude seemed to be that the grandchildren he was always blathering about could deal with those things when the time came. He promised that with the help of President Trump and other "friends of the American economy," he was also going to get Maine's textile mills running again "from Kittery to Fort Kent."

He waved aside such issues as acid rain and polluted rivers—which had given up such wonders as two-headed salmon in the mid-twentieth century, when the mills had been booming 24/7. If he was asked how the product of those mills could compete with cheap Chinese imports, Magowan told voters, "We're going to ban all Chinese imports except for moo-shu pork and General Tso's chicken."

People actually laughed and applauded this codswallop.

While she was watching that particular video on YouTube, Gwendy found herself remembering what Pete Riley had said on his exploratory trip in December of '18: *People are turning away from women's rights, from science, from the very notion of equality. They're turning away from truth. Somebody needs to stand up and make them look at all the stuff it's easier and more comfortable not to believe in.*

She decided she was going to be that somebody, but when Pete called her in March of 2019, she told him she still hadn't decided.

"Well, you better hurry up," Pete told her. "It gets late early in politics, as you well know. And if you're going to take a shot at this, I want to be your campaign manager. If you'll let me, that is."

"With that smile of yours, how could I say no?" Gwendy asked.

"Then I need to start positioning you."

"Ask me again in April."

Pete made a low moaning sound, as if she'd stepped on his foot. "That long?"

"I need to deliberate. And talk to my husband, of course." Although she was pretty sure she knew what Ryan's reaction would be.

What she needed to do was to finish her book, *City of Night* (a title already used by John Rechy, but too good not to use again), and clear the decks. Then she was going to

383

go after Senator Paul Magowan with everything she had. As someone with absolutely no chance of winning, she felt good about that.

When she told Ryan, he reacted pretty much as she had expected. "I'm going to go out and buy a bottle of wine. The good stuff. We need to celebrate. *Ladies and gentlemen, Gwendy Peterson is BACK!*"

10

OUTSIDE THE PORTHOLE NEAREST to Gwendy, the sky is now dark. More than dark. "Blacker than a raccoon's asshole," Ryan might have said. The cabin rotates further, her chair compensates, and all at once her three monitor screens are directly ahead of her instead of over her head. The roaring of the engines stops, and all at once Gwendy is floating against her five point restraining harness. It reminds her of how it feels when a roller-coaster car takes its first dive, only the feeling doesn't stop.

"Crew, helmets can come off," Sam says. "Unzip your suits if you want to but keep them on for now."

Gwendy unlocks her helmet, takes it off . . . and watches it float, first in front of her and then lazily upward. She looks around and sees three other helmets floating. Gareth Winston snatches his down. "What the hell do I do with it?" He sounds shaky.

Gwendy remembers this, and Winston should; God knows they had enough dress rehearsals.

Reggie Black says, "Under your seat. Your compartment, remember?"

"Right," Winston says, but doesn't add a thank-you; that doesn't seem to be in his vocabulary.

Gwendy stows her helmet, opening the hatch by feel and waiting until she hears the small click as the helmet's magnetized circle finds the corresponding circle on the side of her personal stowage area, which is surprisingly large. There's also room for her pressure suit when the time comes, but for the time being the only thing she wants to put in there is the steel box with its dangerous cargo. She takes it from beneath her knee, places it in the compartment, and discovers she has to hold it down so it won't float back up like a helium balloon.

Steel floats, she marvels. *Holy God, I'm in a place where steel floats.*

"Senator Peterson," Kathy calls. "Gwendy. Come up here. I want to show you something. Do you remember how to move around?"

She doesn't. It's gone. It shouldn't be, but it is.

Reggie Black, the mission physicist, bails her out. "One or two slow strokes," he says. "Easy, so you—"

Now she remembers. "So I don't bump my head on the DESTRUCT button." A joke they learned in training.

"Exactly so," Adesh says, beaming. "Must not bump that one, no!"

Winston says nothing. Gwendy can see he's miffed not to have been invited up top first; he is, after all, the paying passenger. The guy may be worth an obscene amount of money, but with his lower lip stuck out the way it is now, he looks like a petulant child.

Gwendy unbuckles and laughs when she rises slowly from her seat. She pulls her knees up to her chest as she was taught during training and goes into a lazy forward roll. She extends her legs. She could be lying on her stomach in bed, except of course there *is* no bed. And she doesn't have to stroke. Jafari closes his hand around her ankle and gives her a gentle push. Laughing, delighted, she floats toward the top of the cabin (only it's now the front of the cabin),

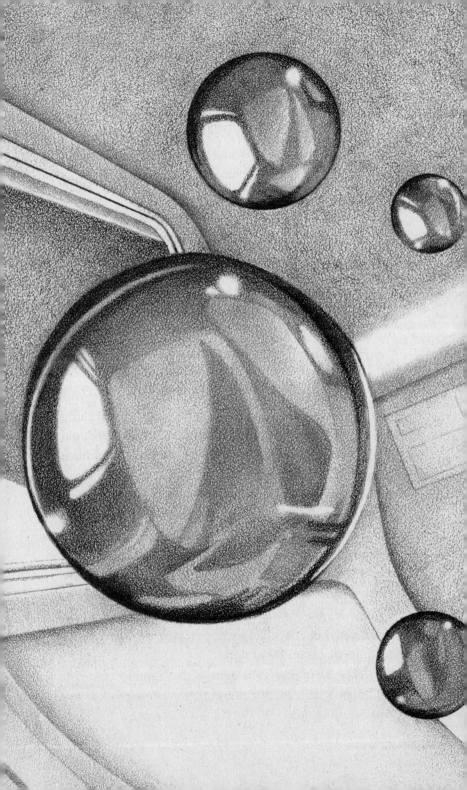

over the heads of Reggie, Bern, and Dr. Glen. *It's like being in a dream*, she thinks.

She grabs the back of David Graves's seat and pulls herself in between Kathy and her second in command, whose name has slipped her mind. It's something about water, but she can't remember what.

There are no portholes in the control area, but there's a narrow slit window four feet long and six inches wide. "You can see this better on your center screen," Kathy says quietly, "and of course on your tablet, but I thought you might like your first look this way. Since you're part of the reason these missions are still flying."

I had my own reason, Gwendy thinks. *Space exploration, advancing human knowledge, sure. But now there's something else.*

For one horrifying moment she can't remember what that something else is, even though it's the biggest thing in her life. Then that concern is driven from her mind by what she's seeing below her . . . and yes, it's definitely below.

The home world hangs in the void, blue-green and wearing many scarves of white cloud. She has seen pictures, of course, but the reality, the firsthand *reality*, is staggering. Here, in all the black nothing of empty space, is a world teeming with improbable life, beautiful life, lovely life.

"That's the Pacific Ocean," the second in command says quietly, and now that she's not trying, she can remember his name: Sam Drinkwater.

"How can America be gone so fast, Sam?"

"Speed will do that. Hawaii just passing below us. Japan coming up."

She can see a whirlpool down there, white twisting away in the middle of the blue, and remembers the monsoon she saw while checking the weather dump on her computer early that morning when she couldn't sleep. But this is no computer screen; this is a God's eye view.

"Pure beauty is what it is," she responds to Sam, and begins to cry. Her tears rise and hang above her, perfect floating diamonds.

11

Of course the opposition was laying for her.

They could do that, because Gwendy was the only viable candidate for the Democratic nomination. She announced her intentions in August of 2019, with her husband by her side. She spoke from the Castle Rock bandstand on the town common, where she'd announced her candidacy for the House of Representatives each time she ran. There were reporters and camera crews from all the Maine television stations in attendance, plus bloggers and even a national guy, who probably just happened to be in the area: Miguel Almaguer, from NBC News. There was also an excellent turnout of locals, who cheered their fannies off. Gwendy even spotted some homemade signs. Her favorite, waved by her old friend Brigette Desjardin, read HEY, MAINE! SENDY GWENDY!

The coverage of her speech was good (local NPR stations ran the whole ten minutes that night). Paul Magowan's comment on the late news was typically condescending: "Welcome to the race, little lady—at least you'll have your books to fall back on when it's over."

The Magowan campaign would hold most of its advertising for another full year, because Mainers don't really get interested in the local races until three or four months before the election, but they fired an opening salvo on August 27, the day after Gwendy's announcement. Full-page newspaper advertisements and sixty-second TV spots began with the statement that "Maine's Favorite Writer Is Running for the United States Senate!"

Printed below it in the newspaper ads and narrated on TV for the reading challenged was a selection from *Bramble Rose*, published in 2013 by Viking. Gwendy was sourly amused by the portentous tones of the narrator in the TV ad.

"Andrew embraced her from behind with one hand planted firmly on her bare midriff. With his other he stroked her **bleep** *until she began to breathe hard.*

" 'I want you to **bleep** *me now,' she said, 'and don't stop until I* **bleep***.'*

He carried her to the bedroom and threw her down on the four-poster. Panting, she turned on her side and grasped his **bleep***, breathing, 'Now, Andy. I can't wait any longer.' "*

Below this in the print ads, and across an especially unflattering picture of Gwendy in the TV ads (mouth open, eyes squeezed half shut, looking mentally disabled), was a question: *ISN'T THERE ALREADY ENOUGH PORNOGRAPHY IN WASHINGTON?*

Gwendy was amused by the sheer scurrilousness of this attack. Her husband was not. "You ought to sue them for defamation of character!" Ryan said, throwing down the Portland *Current* in disgust.

"Oh, they'd love me to get down in the dirt with them," Gwendy said. She picked up the newspaper and read the excerpt. "Do you know what this proves?"

"That Magowan will stoop to anything?" Ryan was still fuming. "That he's low enough to put on a tall hat and crawl under a rattlesnake?"

"That's good, but not what I was thinking of. It proves that context is everything. *Bramble Rose* is a better book than this suggests. Maybe not a lot, but still."

When asked about the so-called pornography in the weeks that followed, Gwendy responded with a smile. "Based on Senator Magowan's voting record, I'm not sure he could tell you the difference between porn and politics. And since we're on the subject of porn, you might want to ask him about his pal Donald Trump's romance with Stormy Daniels. See what he's got to say about that."

What Magowan had to say about Stormy Daniels, it turned out, was not much, and eventually the whole issue blew away, as teapot tempests have a way of doing. Both campaigns dozed as the autumn of 2019 burned away Indian summer and brought on the first cold snap. Magowan might bring back the carefully culled passage from her book when the election run started in earnest, but based on her sharply worded retort, he might not.

Gwendy and Ryan helped serve Thanksgiving dinner that year to a hundred homeless people at the Oxford Street shelter in Portland. They got back to Castle Rock late and Ryan went right to bed. Gwendy put on her pajamas, almost got in beside him, then realized she was too wired to sleep. She decided to go downstairs and have a juice glass of wine—just two or three swallows to calm the post-event jitters she still felt even after years in the public eye.

Richard Farris was sitting in the kitchen, waiting for her.

Same clothes, same round black hat, but otherwise how he'd changed. He was old.

And *sick*.

12

When Gwendy turns around to stroke her way back from officer country to the crew's launch area, she almost bumps heads with Gareth Winston, who is floating just behind her. "Make way for the big fella, Senator."

Gwendy turns on her side, grabs a handhold, and pulls herself back to her seat while Winston crams between Graves and Drinkwater. He peers out through the slit for a few moments, then says, "Huh. View's better from the porthole."

"Enjoy it, then," Kathy says. "Suggest you let those who don't have a porthole come up and have a peek."

Dave Graves is checking a run of computer figures and murmuring with Sam, but he takes a moment to give Gwendy a look, eyebrows waggling. Gwendy isn't sure he's communicating *Three weeks with this guy should be fun*, but she's pretty sure that's what it is. Gwendy has met plenty of rich people in Washington. They are attracted to power like bugs to a bug-light, and most of them are pretty much okay; they want to be liked. She thinks Gareth is an exception to the general rule.

She grabs her seatback, does a neat little twist (in zero-g, her sixty-four-year-old body feels forty again), and settles in. She buckles her harness and unzips her suit to the waist. She takes her notebook from the elasticized pocket of her red Eagle jumpsuit, not because she needs it at this moment but just to verify it's there. The book is crammed with names, categories, and information.

Some of it she doesn't need yet, but she's read enough about what's wrong with her to know she will as the mental rot in her brain advances. *1223 Carbine Street.* Her address. *Pippa*, the name of her father's ageing dachshund. *Homeland Cemetery*, where her mother is buried. A list of her medications, presumably now stored in her tiny cabin along with the scant wardrobe she was allowed to bring. No telephone numbers, her iPhone won't work up here (although Eileen Braddock assured her such service was only a year or two away), but a complete list of her phone's functions, plus a list of her duties as Eagle's weather officer. That may be a make-work job, but she intends to do it well.

The most important thing in her memory book (that's how she thinks of it) is halfway through, written in red ink and boxed: *1512253*. It's the code that opens the otherwise unopenable steel case. The idea of forgetting that number, and thus finding herself unable to get to the button box inside, fills Gwendy with horror.

Adesh has pulled himself over to look out of Winston's porthole, and Jafari Bankole is looking over his shoulder. There's currently no Earth to look at from that one, but Dr. Glen has pulled himself down to look out the other side. "Amazing. *Amazing*. It's not like looking at photos, or even film footage, is it?"

Gwendy agrees and opens her notebook to the crew page, because she has forgotten the doc's first name. Also, Reggie Black—what's his job? She knew only minutes ago, but it's slipped away.

A feather floats up from her book. Winston, now swimming his way back, reaches for it.

"Don't touch that," Gwendy says sharply.

He pays no attention, simply plucks it out of the air, looks at it curiously, then hands it to her. "What is it?"

"A feather," Gwendy says, and keeps herself from adding, *Are you blind?* She has to live with this man, after all, and his support of the space program is vital. If they find signs of life in the solar system—or beyond—that might not be the case, but for now it is. "I use it as a bookmark."

"Lucky charm, perhaps?"

The shrewdness of this startles her and makes her a little uneasy. "How did you guess?"

He smiles. "You have the same feather tattooed on your ankle. Saw it in the gym while you were on the treadmill."

"Let's just say I like it."

Winston nods, seeming to lose interest. "Gentlemen? May I have my seat back? And my porthole?" He puts a slight but unmistakable emphasis on *my*.

Adesh and Jafari move out of his way, a couple of swimming trout making way for an overfed seal.

"It's marvelous," Adesh murmurs to Gwendy. She nods.

Once she's got some clear space to maneuver, Gwendy releases her harness again and takes off her pressure suit. She does an involuntary forward roll in the process and thinks that weightlessness isn't all it's cracked up to be. Once the suit is stowed under her seat, folded on top of the steel case, she descends to the next and last level down, which will be the passenger common room on later orbital flights . . . and perhaps on flights to the moon. Such an amenity is brand new, and it won't be there on craft that go directly to the MF station. This is its maiden run.

The area is shaped like a great big Contac capsule and surprisingly roomy. There are two large viewscreens set into the floor, one showing empty black space and the other featuring the vast shoulder of Mother Earth with its gauze of atmosphere (faintly dirty, Gwendy can't help but notice). Two of the cabins are on the port side, the other and the head on the starboard. The shiny white doors can't help but remind her of morgue lockers on some of the TV crime shows she enjoys. A sign on the toilet says ALWAYS REVIEW PROCEDURE BEFORE OPERATING.

Gwendy doesn't need the john yet, so she gives a lazy kick of her feet and floats to the cabin with SEN. PETERSON on the door. The latch is like the one on a refrigerator. She pulls it and uses the grip over the door to yank herself inside. The cabin—actually more of a nook— is also in the shape of a cold capsule but much smaller. Claustrophobic, really. This time she's reminded of the crew quarters in World War II submarine films. There's a bunk with a harness to keep the sleeper from floating up to the curved ceiling a foot or so above, a miniscule fridge big enough for three or four bottles of juice or soda (maybe a sandwich, if you really crammed), and—of all things—a Keurig coffee maker. *Coffee in your cabin*, she thinks. *The height of space travel luxury.*

On top of the tiny fridge, held in place by a magnet, is a steel-framed photograph of Gwendy and Ryan and her parents, the four of them on the beach at Reid State Park, laughing with their arms around each other.

Gwendy will soon start her weather duties, but for now she needs to mentally refocus and review the crew information. She lies down on her bunk and buckles herself in. Servos are humming somewhere, but otherwise her little cold capsule is eerily silent. They may be circling the planet at thousands of miles an hour, but there's no sense of movement. She opens her red notebook and finds the crew pages. Names and thumbnail bios. Reggie Black is the physicist, of course he is. And Dr. Glen's first name is Dale. Easy-peasy, clear as a freshly washed window . . . but it could be gone again in an hour, maybe just fifteen minutes.

I'm crazy to be here, she thinks. *Crazy to be covering up what's wrong with me. But he gave me no choice. It has to be you, Gwendy, he said. I have no one else. So I agreed. In fact, I was sort of excited by the prospect. Only . . .*

"Only then, I was all right," Gwendy whispers. "At least I thought I was. Oh God, please get me through this."

Here in the up-above, after what she has seen below her—Earth so fragile and beautiful in the black—it's easier to think He or She might really be there.

13

"WHAT—" GWENDY BEGAN, MEANING to finish with either *are you doing here* or *is wrong with you*, she didn't know which, and Farris didn't give her time.

He put a finger to his lips and whispered: "Hush." He lifted his eyes toward the ceiling. "Don't wake your husband. Outside."

He struggled to his feet, swayed, and for a moment she was sure he was going to fall. Then he caught his balance, breathing hard. Inside his cracked lips—and were those fever blisters on them?—she saw yellowish teeth. Plus gaps where some were missing.

"Under the table. Take it. Hurry. Not much time."

Under the table was a canvas bag. She hadn't seen that bag since she was twelve, forty-five years ago, but she recognized it immediately. She bent down and picked it up by the drawstring top. Farris walked unsteadily to the kitchen door. There was a cane leaning beside it. She would have expected such a fabulous being—someone straight out of a fairy tale—to have a fabulous walking stick, maybe topped with a silver wolf's head, but it was just an ordinary cane with a curved handle and a scuffed rubber bicycle grip over the base. He leaned on it, fumbled for the doorknob, and almost fell again. Black suit coat, black jeans, white shirt: those garments, which had once fitted him with casual perfection, now bagged on him like cast-off duds on a cornfield scarecrow.

She took his arm (so thin under the coat!) to steady him and opened the door herself. That door and all the others were locked when she and Ryan left, and the burglar alarm was set, but now the knob turned easily and the alarm panel on the wall was dark, not even the message WAITING in its window.

They went out on the screened back porch, where the wicker furniture hadn't yet been taken in for the cold season. Richard Farris tried to lower himself into one of the chairs, but his legs wouldn't cooperate and instead he just dropped, letting out a pained little grunt when his butt hit the cushion. He gasped a couple of times, stifled a cough with his sleeve (which was caked with the residue of many previous coughs), then looked at her. His eyes were the same, at least. So was his little smile.

"We need to palaver, you and me."

It wasn't what he'd said the first time she met him; close, but no cigar. Back then he'd said they *ought* to palaver. *Needing to*, she thought, *takes it to a whole new level*.

Gwendy shut the door, sat down in the porch swing with the canvas bag between her feet, and asked what she would have asked in the kitchen, had he not reminded her that she had a husband upstairs.

"What's wrong with you? And why are you here?"

He managed a smile. "Same Gwendy, right to the point. What's wrong with me hardly matters. I'm here because there's been what that little green fellow Yoda would call 'a disturbance in the Force.' I'm afraid I must ask you—"

He began to cough before he could finish. It racked

his thin body and she thought again how like a scarecrow he was, now one blown about on its pole by a strong autumn wind.

She started to get up. "I'll get you a glass of wa—"

"No. You won't." He brought the spasm under control. Coughing that hard should have raised a flush in his cheeks, but his face remained dead pale. His eyes were set in dark circles of sick.

Farris fumbled in his suit coat and brought out a bottle of pills. He started to cough again before he could get the cap off and the bottle dropped from his unsteady fingers. It came to rest against the drawstring bag. Gwendy picked it up. It was a brown pharmacy bottle, but there was no information on the label, just a series of runes that made her strangely dizzy. She closed her eyes, opened them again, and saw the word DINUTIA, which meant nothing to her. The next time she blinked, the dizzying runes were back.

"How many?"

He was coughing too hard to reply but held up two fingers. She pushed the cap off and brought out two small pills that looked like the Ranexa her father took for his angina. She put them in Farris's outstretched hand (there were no lines on it; the palm was perfectly smooth), and when he popped them in his mouth, she was alarmed to see tiny beads of blood on his lips. He swallowed, took a breath, then another, deeper one. Some color bloomed in his cheeks, and when it did she could see a little of the man she'd first met on Castle View, near the top of the Suicide Stairs, all those years ago.

His coughing eased, then stopped. He held out his hand for the bottle. Gwendy looked inside before putting the cap on. There were only half a dozen pills left. Maybe eight. He returned the bottle to his inner coat pocket, sat back, and looked out at the darkened backyard. "That's better."

"Is it heart medicine?"

"No."

"A cancer drug?" Her mother had taken both Oncovin and Abraxane, although neither of them looked like the little white pills Farris had taken.

"If you really must know, Gwendy—you were always curious—there are many things wrong with me and they're all crowding in at once. The years I was forgiven—there have been many—are rushing back like hungry diners into a restaurant." He offered his charming little smile. "I'm their buffet."

"How old *are* you?"

Farris shook his head. "We have more important things to talk about, and my time is short. There's trouble, and the thing inside that canvas bag is responsible. Do you remember the last time we spoke?"

Gwendy does, vividly. She was at Portland South Airpark, sitting on a bench while Ryan went to park the car. Her luggage, including the button box in her carry-on bag, was piled around her. Richard Farris sat down and said they should palaver a spell before they were interrupted. And so they did. When the palaver was done, the button box was gone from her bag. Presto change-o, now you see it, now you don't. And the same was true of Farris himself. She had turned her head for a moment, and when she looked back, he was gone. She'd thought then she would never see him again.

"I remember."

"Twenty years ago that was." He kept his voice low, but the rasp was gone, his fingers were no longer trembling, and his color was good. *All just for the time being*, Gwendy thought—she had nursed her mother through her last illness, and her father was now in slow but steady decline. Pills could only do so much, and for so long. "You were a lowly House of Representatives backbencher then, one among hundreds. Now you're gunning for a seat of genuine power."

Gwendy gave a quiet laugh. She was sure Richard Farris knew a great deal, but if he thought she was going to beat Paul Magowan and ascend to the United States Senate, he understood jack shit about Maine politics.

Farris smiled as if he knew exactly what she was thinking (an uncomfortable idea, which didn't make it wrong). Then the smile faded. "The first time you had the box, your proprietorship lasted six years. Remarkable. It's passed through seven sets of hands just since that day at the airport."

"The second time I had it was barely the blink of an eye," Gwendy said. "Long enough to save my mother's life—I still believe that—but not much longer."

"That was an emergency. This is another." Farris toed the canvas bag between her slippered feet with an expression of distaste. "This thing. This goddamned thing. How I hate it. How I *loathe* it."

Gwendy had no idea how to reply to that, but she knew how she felt: scared. Her mother's old saying came to mind: this is NG.

"Every year it gains power. Every year its ability to do good grows weaker and its ability to do evil grows stronger. Do you remember the black button, Gwendy?"

"Of course I do." Speaking through numb lips. "I used to call it the Cancer Button."

He nodded. "A good name for it. That's the one with the power to end everything. Not just life on Earth but Earth itself. And each year the proprietors of the box feel a stronger compulsion to push it."

"Don't say that." She sounded watery, on the verge of tears. "Oh please, Mr. Farris, don't say that."

"Do you think I want to?" he asked. "Do you think I even want to be here, tasking you with this—excuse the language—this fucking thing for a third time? But I have to, Gwendy. There is simply no one else I trust to do what needs to be done, and no one else who may—I say *may*—be able to do it."

"What is it you want me to do?" She would find out that much, at least, and then decide. If she could, that was; if he left the button box with her, she'd be stuck with it.

No, she thought, *I won't. I'll weight the bag with rocks and throw it into Castle Lake.*

"Seven proprietors since the year 2000. Each held it a shorter time. Five committed suicide. One took his whole family with him. Wife and three kiddos. Shotgun. He kept telling the police negotiator, 'The box made me do it, it was the button box.' Of course they had no idea what he was talking about because by then it was gone. I had it back."

"Dear God," Gwendy whispered.

"One is in a mental asylum in Baltimore. He threw the button box into a crematorium furnace. Which did no good, of course. I committed him myself. The seventh, the last, only a month ago . . . I killed her. I didn't want to, I was responsible for what she became, but I had no choice."

He paused. "Do you remember the colors, Gwendy? Not the red and the black, I know you remember those."

Of course she remembered. The red button did whatever you wanted, for good or ill. The black one meant mass destruction. She remembered the other six just as well.

"They stand for the continents of the earth," she said. "Light green, Asia. Dark green, Africa. Orange, Europe. Yellow, Australia. Blue is for North America, and violet is for South America."

"Yes. Good. You were a quick study even as a child. Later you may not be, but if you fight it . . . fight it hard, for all you're worth . . ."

"I'm not following you." Gwendy thought that the effect of the pills he'd taken was beginning to wear off.

"Never mind. The last proprietor was a woman named Patricia Vachon, from Vancouver. She was a schoolteacher working with mentally disabled children, and like you in many ways, Gwendy. Level-headed, strong-willed, dedicated, and with a moral fiber that went bone-deep. Rightness as opposed to righteousness, if you see what I mean."

Gwendy did.

"If existence is a chess game, with black pieces and white ones, Patricia Vachon stood firmly on the side of the white. I thought she might even be the White Queen, as you once were. Patricia had lovely dark skin, but she was of the white. The *light*. Do you understand?"

"Yes."

Gwendy wasn't very good at the kind of chess played on a board—Ryan always beat her on the occasions when she let him talk her into a game—but she had been very

STEPHEN KING

good at real-life chess during her years in the House of Representatives. There, she was always thinking three moves ahead. Sometimes four.

"I thought she was perfect," Farris continued. "That she'd be able to take care of the box for years, perhaps even until we were able to decide how to dispose of it once and for all."

"We? Who is *we*?"

Farris paid no attention. "I was wrong. Not about her, but about the box. I underestimated its growing power. I shouldn't have, not after what happened to the others who came after you, Gwendy, but the Vachon woman seemed so *right*. Yet in the end the box destroyed her, too. Even before I put a bullet in her head, she was destroyed. I'm responsible."

Tears began to trickle down Farris's seamed cheeks. Gwendy observed them with incredulity. He was no longer the man she knew. He was . . .

Broken, she thought. *He's broken. Probably dying.*

"She was going to push the black button. She was struggling mightily—*heroically*—against the impulse, but she actually had her thumb on it when I shot her. And pushing down. Luckily, one might say providentially, the buttons are hard to push. Very hard. As I'm sure you remember."

Gwendy certainly did. The first time she tried to push one—it was the red button, as a kind of experiment—she thought they were dummies and the whole thing was a joke. It wasn't, unless you considered the hundreds dead in the South American country of Guyana as a joke. How much of the Jonestown massacre was actually her fault she still didn't know, and wasn't sure she wanted to.

"How did you get there in time to stop her?"

"I monitor the box. Every time it's used, I know. And usually I know when the proprietor is even thinking of using it. Not always, but there's another way I can keep track."

"When the levers are pulled?"

Richard Farris smiled and nodded.

There were two levers, one on each side of the box. One dispensed Morgan silver dollars, uncirculated and always date-stamped 1891. The other dispensed tiny but delicious chocolate animals. They were hard to resist, and Gwendy realized that made them the perfect way to monitor how often the proprietor was using the box. Handling it. Picking up its . . . what? Cooties? Germs? Its capacity to do evil?

Yes, that.

"Proprietors who pull the levers too frequently to get the chocolates or the dollars raise red flags. I knew that was happening with the Vachon woman, and I was disappointed, but I thought I had more time to find another proprietor. I was wrong. When I reached her, she had already pushed one of the other buttons. Probably just to take the pressure off for a little while, poor woman."

Gwendy felt cold all over. The hair on the back of her neck stirred. "Which one?"

"Light green."

"When?" Her first thought was of the Fukushima disaster, when a tsunami caused a Japanese nuclear reactor to melt down. But Fukushima was at least seven years ago, maybe more.

"Near the end of this October. I don't blame her. She held on as long as she could. Even while her thumb was on that light green button, trying to overcome a compulsion too strong to resist, she was thinking, *Please, no explosion. Please, no earthquake. Please, no volcano or tidal wave.*"

"You heard this in your head. Telepathically."

"When someone touches one of the buttons, even the lightest caress, I go online, so to speak. But I was far away, on other business. I got there as quickly as I could, and I was in time to stop her before she could push the one you call the Cancer Button, but I was too late to stop her from pushing the Asia button."

He ran a hand through his thinning hair, knocking his little round hat askew, making him look like someone in an old-time musical about to start tap-dancing.

"This was just four weeks ago."

Gwendy spun her mind back, trying to think of a disaster that had occurred in one of the Asian countries during that timespan. She was sure there'd been plenty of tragedy and death, but she couldn't think of a mega-disaster strong enough to displace Donald Trump from the lead story on the evening news.

"Maybe I should know, but I don't," she said. "An oil refinery explosion? Maybe a nerve gas attack?" Knowing either would be too small. Things like the red button handled the small stuff.

Jonestown, for instance.

"It could have been much, much worse," Farris said. "She held back as well as she could, and against mighty forces from the black side of the board. But it's bad enough. Only two people have died so far, one of them the owner of what in Wuhan Province is called a wet market. That's a place where—"

"Where meat is sold, I know that." She leaned forward.

"Are you talking about a sickness, Mr. Farris? Something like MERS or SARS?"

"I'm talking a *plague*. Only two dead now, but many more are sick. Some are carrying the disease and don't even know it. The Chinese government isn't sure yet, but they suspect. When they do know, they'll try to cover it up. As a result it's going to spread. It's going to be very, very bad."

"What can I do?"

"That's what I'm going to tell you. And I'll help, if I can."

"But you're—"

She doesn't want to finish, but he does it for her. "Dying? Oh yes, I suppose I am. But do you know what that means?"

Gwendy shook her head, for a moment thinking of her mother, and a night when they looked up at the stars.

Farris smiled. "Neither do I, dear girl. Neither do I."

14

WHEN GWENDY PETERSON WAS a young girl, she and her best friend Olive Kepnes played a game called "mermaids" at the Castle Rock Community Pool. They waded side-by-side into the shallow end until the water, chilly even in August, reached the middle of their chests. Then they took turns sitting on the bottom while the other girl remained standing and recited a series of secret, made-up words. Once her breath gave out and she resurfaced, the underwater girl—the mermaid—would try to guess what had been said. There were no winners or losers in this game. It was simply for fun.

When Gwendy opens her eyes to the bright overhead lights, the memory notebook pinned against her chest by one tightly clenched fist, Olive Kepnes and this long-ago game is the first thought that pops into her head. The voice coming from the other side of the shiny white door, no more than a half-dozen feet away, sounds distant and garbled, like she's hearing it from underwater.

She lifts her head and looks around, her eyes settling on the black and silver Keurig coffee maker. She blinks at it in confusion. She knows she's on a rocket ship traveling through space—she remembers that much—but what in the blue blazes is a coffee machine doing there?

She tries to sit up and experiences a flash of ice-cold panic when she discovers the restraints holding her in place, and then an immediate flood of relief when she realizes she must have dozed off in her bunk. She unbuckles the harness and floats upward from the narrow mattress. *Just like Tinkerbell*, she thinks in a moment of pure amazement.

There's a hollow knock at the door and the muffled voice comes again. Gwendy doesn't recognize it—in fact, is unable to determine if it's male or female—but it sounds like someone is saying, *"My dog is lost in the hay."* Even in the swirling gray mist of her half-awake stupor, she's pretty sure that's not right.

Whoever it is outside the door thumps again, a loud triple-knock this time, and then there's that same voice. *"I went fishing in the bay,"* it murmurs, with even more urgency this time around.

Gwendy slips the notebook into her pocket, then gives a single lazy kick and glides across the capsule-shaped cabin. As she reaches out to unlatch the door, it occurs to her that there's no peephole centered at eye level like there is on her front door back home in Castle Rock. This bothers her for some reason and she hesitates, suddenly afraid. *Is this what it feels like to lose your mind?*

Holding her breath, she pulls open the heavy white door. Adesh Patel and Gareth Winston are floating above the common room floor, the pair of large viewscreens lapping at the bottom of their boots like dark hungry mouths. Mother Earth, still surrounded by that gauzy haze Gwendy noticed earlier, winks at her from hundreds of miles away and keeps right on spinning.

Adesh, brown eyes wide with concern, swims closer and asks, "Gwendy, are you okay?"

It had been the entomologist's voice she'd heard calling out from the other side of the cabin door. Winston, bobbing up and down a few feet behind him, looking like a plump marshmallow in his unzipped pressure suit and grinning that I'm-better-than-you-and-you-know-it grin of his adds, "Sounds like you were having a whopper of a nightmare, Senator."

Gwendy speaks a little too cheerfully to come across as entirely convincing. "I'm fine, boys. Just dozed off and took a little catnap. Space travel does that to a girl."

15

"A PLAGUE . . . from China?" Gwendy stared at the skeleton of a man sitting across from her on the screened-in back porch. "How bad? Will it come here to the States?"

"Everywhere," Farris answered. "There will be body bags stacked like cordwood outside of hospital loading docks. Funeral homes will bring in fleets of refrigerated trucks once the morgues begin to fill up."

"What about a vaccine? Won't we be able to—"

"Enough," he hissed, flashing a glimpse of decaying teeth. "I told you, I don't have much time."

Gwendy leaned back in the wicker porch swing, cinching her robe tight across her chest. *I don't have much time.* She thought once again: *He's dying.*

"And I don't have a choice, do I?"

"You, Gwendy Peterson, of all people should know that you always have a choice." He let out a deep, wavering breath.

And that's when Gwendy figured it out—what had been nagging at the back of her brain ever since they'd first come outside onto the porch. The temperature in Castle Rock had dropped to single digits on Thanksgiving evening; she and Ryan had heard a weather report on the radio as they were pulling into the driveway no more than an hour ago. She was shivering, and every time she opened her mouth a fleeting misty cloud appeared in front of her face—*fairy breath* they used to call it when they were kids—yet when Farris spoke, there was nothing, not even a trace.

"I wouldn't call it much of a choice," she said, glancing at the canvas bag resting between her feet. "I'm stuck with the damn thing no matter what I say."

"But what you choose to *do* with it is entirely up to you." He coughed into his hand, and when he pulled it away, she once again noticed a fine spray of blood across his knuckles.

"You said the box was going bad, that it killed the last seven people you entrusted it with. What makes you think I'll be any different?"

"You've always been different." He held up a slender finger in front of her face. "You've always been *special*."

"Bullshit," she said mildly. "It's a suicide mission and you know it."

Farris's cracked lips curled into a gruesome imitation of a smile, and then just as abruptly the smile disappeared. He cocked his head, staring off to the side, listening to something only he could hear.

"Who's coming?" Gwendy asked. "Where are they from? What do they want?"

"They want the button box." When he turned around again, it was the Richard Farris she'd first met on a bench in Castle View Park staring back at her—if only in his eyes, which were now strong and clear and focused with intensity. "And they're very angry. Listen to me carefully."

He leaned forward, bringing with him a whiff of rotting carrion, and before Gwendy could shrink away, he reached over and took her hand in his. She shuddered, staring down at their intertwined fingers, thinking: *He doesn't feel human. He's not human.*

In a surprisingly sturdy voice, Richard Farris explained what needed to be done. From the first word to the last, it took him maybe ninety seconds. When he was finished, he released her hand and slumped back into the patio chair, the remaining color draining rapidly from his face.

Gwendy sat there motionless, staring out at the dark expanse of backyard. After awhile she looked at him and said, "What you're asking is impossible."

"I sincerely hope not. It's the only place they can't come for it. You have to try, Gwendy, before it's too late. You're the only one I trust."

"But how in the—"

Sitting upright, he raised a hand to stop her from speaking. He turned his head and peered next door into the deep pool of shadows beneath a weeping willow tree.

Gwendy got to her feet and slowly walked closer to the wire screen, following his gaze. She saw and heard nothing in the frozen darkness. A few seconds later, the wood-framed screen door to the back porch banged closed behind her. She turned and looked without much surprise. The wicker chair was empty. Richard Farris had left the building. Like Elvis.

"I ONLY GOT THERE right at the end," Adesh says, keeping his voice low, "but it sounded like you were whimpering. I thought perhaps you had injured yourself."

Both he and Gwendy are once again strapped into their flight chairs on the third deck of Eagle Heavy. The steel box marked **CLASSIFIED MATERIAL** is tucked safely beneath her seat. Gwendy cradles her iPad in her ungloved hands, the screen silent and dark.

"Winston said you sounded frightened and were calling out . . . something about a 'black box.' He claims he couldn't understand the rest of it."

Gwendy doesn't remember falling asleep and dreaming, but the very idea that Gareth Winston could be telling the truth makes her feel light-headed and causes her stomach to perform an uneasy cartwheel. She carries too many deep, dark secrets inside to start talking in her sleep now.

She steals a glance at Jafari Bankole, who's busy studying one of the overhead monitors, and at the opposite end of the craft, Gareth Winston, now buckled in tight and snoring loudly in his flight seat next to the porthole. *His* porthole. *Is he really asleep?* For the second time since boarding, the same crystal clear thought surfaces inside Gwendy's muddled head: *That man is smarter than he appears*.

"What was he doing down there in the first place?"

"He said he was going to use the toilet, and maybe he

did," Adesh tells her, leaning close enough for Gwendy to smell cinnamon on his breath. He drops his voice to a whisper. "But when I went down a short time later to check on my specimens, I found him standing there with his hand in the proverbial cookie jar."

Gwendy waits for him to continue, dreading what's coming next.

"He was fiddling with the latch on your cabin door."

NG, Gwendy thinks. *Not good at all.*

A smile comes onto Adesh's round face, and not a friendly one. "When he finally turned around and saw me, his eyes bugged out—pardon the pun—and he practically jumped out of his pressure suit. That's the nice thing about being weightless. No one can hear you coming."

"Well, I'm grateful you came along when you did. I . . . I . . ."

And just like that her brain short-circuits and shuts down. All the information that was stored there just a moment earlier suddenly vanishes as if an invisible eraser has been swept across the inside of her head. *Where has it gone?* She doesn't know that. All she *does* know is that her name is Gwendy Peterson and she's a passenger on a spaceship and she's trying to save the world. But save it from what? She has no memory at all of that, nor what she was just talking about or whom the person is she was just talking to. The abrupt and overwhelming sense of loss— of abandonment—frightens her so badly that sudden tears bloom in the corners of her eyes.

"Senator Peterson? Gwendy? Are you okay?" Adesh asks. His eyes narrowed in concern, he appears on the verge of calling out for help.

"I'm . . ." she begins to answer, and then, just like that,

everything is back where it's supposed to be. She's talking to Adesh Patel, the Bug Man, about Gareth Winston, the nosy and noisy lout sleeping just over yonder. Winston's a billionaire with a capital "B," and Gwendy isn't sure he can be trusted. Judging from the look on Adesh Patel's face, the Bug Man's not entirely convinced Gwendy can be trusted, either.

"I'm fine," she finally says. "I was in the middle of a thought and something my late mother used to say came along and hijacked my brain. I'm not sure why, but it's happening more and more often these days."

Adesh's brown eyes immediately soften. "Oh, Gwendy, I'm so sorry you lost her."

It's a nasty trick on Gwendy's part and she knows it— but she has no regrets. "Don't be. Please. It was a lovely thought and I'm glad I had it." She thumbprints her iPad and the blank screen flashes to life. "I just wish I had better control over when those sorts of memories resurface. It can be a bit . . . embarrassing."

"Please, don't be embarrassed. I'm sure you miss her terribly."

Gwendy sighs. "And you would be right about that." She musters a halfhearted smile. "To tell the truth, I'm more embarrassed that it's my first day in the up-above and I'm already off schedule." She studies the readout on her iPad. "I'm not due for a sleep break for another six hours."

Adesh wrinkles his brow and *pish-toshes* her. "You took a twenty-minute nap. So what?" He looks around furtively and gives his stomach a couple of gentle pats. "I'll let you in on a little secret. It's still an hour or so until my first designated meal, and I've already snuck two protein bars."

"You did no such thing!"

"I most assuredly did."

She takes a peek at the level above them. "You better not let the boss hear you say that."

"What happens on third level stays on third level," he says, shrugging his shoulders against the restraining belts.

Gwendy puts a hand to her mouth and stifles a giggle. Throughout the four weeks of intense training and twelve days of close-quarters quarantine, she's gotten to know several of her fellow crew members rather intimately. While Kathy Lundgren and Bern Stapleton are like old and trusted friends by now, she feels like she's barely scratched the surface with many of the others, including the Indian gentleman they call the Bug Man. She knows that Adesh Patel is quiet and polite and brilliant. He's traveled the world and speaks several languages. He's happily married to a beautiful woman named Daksha, which means "The Earth" in their traditional culture, and they have fourteen-year-old twin sons. She's seen a number of photographs, and the family is always smiling. She also knows that neither of the boys wants to follow in their parents' footsteps and become doctors. Instead, they're determined to become professional baseball players with lucrative shoe contracts and seven-digit social media followings—a fact the humble entomologist admits often keeps him awake at night.

After today Gwendy believes she's learned something else, something very important, about Adesh Patel. He has a kind heart to go along with his kind chestnut eyes, and she likes him a great deal. She believes she can trust him on this journey—and she needs all the allies she can get. Even those—perhaps even especially those—with a pet scorpion and a creepy tarantula.

Across the deck, Gareth Winston begins snorting in his sleep, a cacophony of wet, gurgling, slobbering sounds, not unlike what you might hear from a pair of horny prize hogs going at it in the midst of rutting season.

Gwendy and Adesh gape in astonishment at the blubbering billionaire, then glance at each other and crack up. Jafari looks up from his iPad. "What? What did I miss?" The mystified expression on the astronomer's face makes them laugh even harder. "What? Tell me."

There's a sudden buzzing sound and Kathy Lundgren's amused face appears on the middle screen of the three overhead monitors. "Hate to be a buzzkill, folks, but some of us are trying to get a little work done up here." She gives them a friendly wink. "A bit quieter, please."

"My apologies," Gwendy says, her cheeks flushing. "I started the whole thing."

"No worries, Senator. I'm glad you're enjoying the trip."

Kathy's face disappears from the screen and is immediately replaced by a series of data charts and multicolored graphs.

"What's all the ruckus about?"

The three crew members turn and stare across the deck. Gareth Winston is rubbing sleep from his eyes with one chubby, balled-up fist. His usually neat short brown hair is sticking up in sweaty spikes. Before any of them can manage an answer, he whips his head around and peers excitedly out the nearby porthole. *His* porthole. "Hey! Are we there yet?"

17

THE MORNING AFTER RICHARD Farris's surprise Thanksgiving visit dawned clear and cold in the town of Castle Rock, Maine. Overnight, a storm sweeping across the upper half of the state took an unexpected dip to the south and slowed its roll just long enough to clip Castle County on its way out to sea, dropping six inches of wet snow on the frozen streets and lawns. Gwendy could hear the plows working even before she opened her eyes.

Slipping out of bed shortly before seven, after a brief stint of troubled sleep, Gwendy got dressed in the dark and left her husband dreaming peacefully beneath the covers. Before she stepped into the hallway, she took a single backward glance at the only man she'd ever truly loved. *No more secrets after today*, she silently promised, easing the door closed behind her.

Trying hard to remain calm, Gwendy checked the alarm system (the panel display was back to reading READY TO ARM; no big surprise there) and turned on the coffeemaker in the kitchen before heading out to the garage.

Using the old wooden stepladder her father had passed down to her the previous summer, Gwendy slowly ascended the rungs until she was able to reach the highest row of metal shelving that ran along the length of the garage's cluttered back wall. She scooted aside an old Tupperware container labeled FISHING TACKLE & BOBBERS, and—breathing heavy with the effort; at fifty-seven, she wasn't nearly as spry as she once was— carefully took down a cardboard box marked SEWING SUPPLIES. Once she was safely down, she placed the box on the cold concrete floor at her feet, dropped to a knee, and opened the flaps. Gooseflesh immediately broke out across her forearms.

The button box, snug in its canvas bag, was waiting for her inside.

She felt the short hairs on the back of her neck begin to tingle, and heard that familiar faint whisper of *something* in the far corner of her brain. She quickly closed up the box, got to her feet, and backed away.

This goddamned thing. How I hate it. How I loathe *it.*

She shivered, listening to the echo of Farris's voice in the dim silence of the garage, remembering his pale sickly face, scarecrow limbs, rotting and missing teeth.

And then his final words came to her, practically pleading by then: *It's the only place they can't come for it. You have to try, Gwendy, before it's too late. You're the only one I trust.*

"Why me?" she asked, barely recognizing the sound of her own voice.

She waited for an answer, but none came. Certainly not God, asking her if she was there when He made the world.

Summoning her courage, she climbed the ladder again and returned the cardboard box to its hiding place on the

top shelf. Locking the garage door—she couldn't remember the last time she'd done that—she went back inside to the kitchen and poured herself a mug of hot coffee. She sipped it staring out the window above the sink at the snow-covered backyard, once again promising herself that she was going to tell Ryan everything. She was too old and too frightened to go it alone this time around—*third time's a charm*, she thought—but it was more than that. She owed her husband the truth after all these years, and it would feel good to finally tell it. Damn good.

But that conversation would have to wait until later tonight.

She had a busy day to get through first.

Every year, bright and early on Black Friday morning, her old friend Brigette Desjardin would swing by the house and pick her up. They'd grab a quick breakfast at the Castle Rock Diner before heading off on a ninety-minute road trip to Portland. Once there, they'd lace up their Reeboks and spend the day braving the overflow crowds at not one, not two, but all three of the city's massive shopping malls. They usually returned home late in the evening, the trunk and back seat of Brigette's bright red BMW crammed full of shopping bags and gift boxes, bragging about the great deals they'd gotten and complaining about swollen feet from all the walking and chapped lips from all the talking. And all the greeting: that, too, because a surprising number of people still recognized Gwendy from her stint in the House. For some of those folks, Gwendy Peterson was practically an old family friend; she'd been part of their lives for that long. Political demi-celebrity aside, Christmas shopping with Brigette was a holiday tradition Gwendy always enjoyed and looked forward to. And she liked people, for the most part.

This year would obviously be a different story. All of a sudden, thanks to the man in the little black hat, she had more important matters to worry about than shoe sales and triple value coupons.

She considered bailing out altogether—in fact, she picked up the telephone and went so far as to punch in half of Brigette's number, only to hang up. A last-minute cancellation would give rise to more questions than she was prepared to answer. No, she told herself, she'd just have to "suck it up, buttercup," as her father liked to say.

Ryan had his own Black Friday activities to participate in. First up, a Chinese buffet for lunch with the guys on the bowling team, followed by a three-game, best-average-score-takes-all competition at the Rumford Rock 'N Bowl (the annual winner was awarded a two-foot-high, gold-plated trophy resembling a kicking donkey's backside; Ryan had taken it home three years running). After bowling, they would head over to Billy Franklin's bachelor pad, where they'd feast on catered Mexican food and watch college football on the big-screen television. Ryan usually rolled home around eight or nine at night suffering from a serious case of dragon breath and immediately rushed upstairs in search of the big plastic container of Tums. He'd spend half the night moaning and groaning in the bathroom and wake up the next morning swearing that he wasn't going back next year. They could keep their damn trophy. The two of them would have a good laugh about it over breakfast—just toast and a big glass of ice water for Ryan—knowing full well that he didn't mean a word of it.

So, yes, she decided, she'd suck it up, buttercup, and they'd both get through their respective busy days. Then they'd come home, change into their PJs, grab a bottle of good red wine and a couple of glasses, and rendezvous in the bedroom. And after all these years, she'd tell him everything.

Only it didn't turn out that way.

Gwendy held up her end of the deal just fine. At first, as was to be expected, she was distracted and quiet. She barely touched her omelet, home fries, and toast at breakfast. Once they got in the car, she found herself staring out the window at the passing countryside, daydreaming about the button box and Richard Farris's pale, waxy skin. And those perfectly smooth, unlined hands of his; she couldn't stop thinking about those. She did her best to keep up with the conversation—nodding when she sensed it was appropriate and tossing in the occasional comment or two—but Brigette wasn't fooled. Halfway to Portland, she turned down the car radio and asked Gwendy if something was wrong. Gwendy shook her head and apologized, claiming she had a lingering headache from the previous night and hadn't gotten much sleep (at least that much was true). She made a show of popping three Advil tablets and singing along with Barry Manilow's "I Write the Songs" when it came on the radio—and that seemed to do the trick for Brigette.

By the time they parked the car and waded into the frenzy, Gwendy actually found herself smiling and laughing. Brigette, with that childlike enthusiasm and goofy sense of humor of hers, had a way of turning back the clock and making the rest of the world melt away. Gwendy often told her husband that spending an afternoon with Brigette Desjardin was a little like stepping into a time machine and traveling back to the late 1970s. Her simple enjoyment of life was contagious.

Both women scored major coups at the first boutique they entered—a half-price carryall purse for Gwendy; a pair of knee-high leather boots for Brigette—and that set the tone for the rest of the day. They spent the next eight hours giggling and gossiping like a couple of happy teenagers.

Often—actually more often than she would have expected—Gwendy was approached by men and women who said they were going to vote for her. One of them, an older woman with perfectly coifed pink hair, touched her on the elbow and whispered, "Just don't tell my husband."

After grabbing soup and salads for dinner at a bursting-at-the-seams Cracker Barrel just off I-95, Gwendy finally made it home at 7:45 p.m. She immediately shucked her clothes, leaving them in a messy pile on the bathroom floor, and slipped into a warm bubble bath. An hour later, dressed in her favorite silk pajamas, which Ryan had smuggled home from an assignment in Vietnam, she dozed off on the family room sofa with a true crime paperback laying open in her lap.

Some time later she was awakened by a ringing doorbell. *Big dummy forgot his keys*, she thought, getting up from the sofa. She glanced at the antique grandfather clock on her way to the foyer and was surprised to see that it was after midnight. Still, she wasn't worried until she looked into the peephole and saw Norris Ridgewick standing on the porch. Norris, who once upon a time held the title of Castle County Sheriff for almost two decades, had retired a year earlier and now spent most of his days fishing at Dark Score Lake.

She yanked open the door and immediately knew from the look in her old friend's eyes that Ryan was not coming home tonight. Or ever. Before Ridgewick could manage a single word, Gwendy let loose a sob that tore at her chest and stumbled back to the sofa with tears streaming down her cheeks.

Norris plodded into the house, head down, and closed the door behind him. Sitting down on the arm of the sofa, he placed a hand on Gwendy's shoulder. As he explained what had happened—a hit-and-run, her husband of so many years taken in mere instants—Gwendy scooted to the far side of the couch and curled into a fetal position, hugging her legs tight to her chest.

"He wouldn't have suffered," Norris said, and then added the very thing she had been thinking: "I know that's no consolation."

"Where?" Thinking it must have been in the Rock 'N Bowl's parking lot, probably some guy in a pickup truck pulling out too fast after too many beers, maybe reaching down to tune the radio.

"Derry."

"*Where?*" Thinking she must have misheard. Derry was over a hundred miles north of the Rock 'N Bowl and Billy Franklin's Rumford apartment.

Norris, perhaps thinking she wanted the actual location, consulted his notebook. "He was crossing Witcham Street. Near the bottom of what they call Up-Mile Hill."

"Witcham Street in Derry? Are you sure?"

"Sorry to say, dear, but I am."

"What was he doing there?" Still not able to believe this news. It was like a stone lodged in her throat. No, lower: on her heart.

Norris Ridgewick gave her an odd look. "You don't know?"

Gwendy shook her head.

In the days following her husband's funeral, Gwendy found herself searching for an answer to that question with a dogged persistence that bordered on obsession. She discovered from talking to several members of Ryan's bowling team that he had called them early on Black Friday and canceled on the annual tournament, as well as Billy Franklin's after party. He gave no reason, just claimed that something important had come up.

None of it made any sense to Gwendy. It surely wasn't work-related—Ryan was supposed to be taking it easy until after the New Year, a fact she confirmed in a phone call with his editor—much less an assignment that would've required him to make the two-hour drive to Derry on the day after Thanksgiving.

What she knew about Derry wasn't good. It was a dark and dreary town with a violent history. There were an unsettling number of child murders and disappearances lurking in its past, as well as detailed documentation of strange sightings and weird goings-on. Toss in a series of deadly floods and the fact that Derry was home to one of the most blatantly anti-LGBT communities in the state, and you had yourself a place that most non-locals avoided like poison sumac.

A woman Gwendy had become close with during a long-ago fund-raising campaign claimed that back when she was a teenager living in Derry, she'd once been chased down a dark street by a giggling man dressed as a circus clown. The man had had razors for teeth and huge round silver eyes . . . or so she said. She was only able to get away from him by running into the Derry Police Station screaming her terrified head off. While the officer in charge fetched a glass of water and tried his best to calm her, two other policemen went outside to search for the man. They returned fifteen minutes later—faces flushed, eyes wide, breathing heavy—claiming that they hadn't seen a thing. The streets were deserted. But they had sounded scared, the woman told Gwendy. And they had looked it, too. She was certain they weren't telling the truth. The officer in charge drove the girl home later that night in his squad car and watched her from the driveway until she was safely inside.

And there was this: when Gwendy was growing up, her father claimed on more than one occasion—usually after reading something troubling in the newspaper or drinking too many cans of Black Label beer—that Derry was haunted. When he was in his early twenties, years before he married Gwendy's mom, he'd lived for six months in a cramped studio apartment overlooking the canal that split the town in two. He'd spent his days peddling cheap insurance policies door to door. He'd despised his time in Derry and fled the town as soon as the opportunity presented itself. Although usually practical to his bones, Alan Peterson told his daughter he believed that some places were built on bad ground, thereby ensuring they would forever remain cursed. He insisted that Derry was one of those places.

Many longtime residents of Maine wore their well-earned reputation for coming across as surly and mistrusting to outsiders—if not downright hostile at times—as a sort of badge of honor. Gwendy knew this and accepted it, even going so far in years past as to poke fun at the stereotype in several of her novels, as well as a handful of political speeches. *"I told that flatlandah to git his ass on back down the rud to N'Yawk"* was always good for a warm-up laugh before getting down to business.

But even she was shocked—and angered—by the treatment she received upon her subsequent visit to Derry. In the company of the investigating detective, Ward Mitchell, she spent half an hour at the intersection of Witcham and Carter Streets, where Ryan had died. Mitchell at least was polite—she was, after all, a high-profile politician who'd just lost her husband—but he answered her questions without a hint of warmth. Witnesses? *None.* Ryan's cell phone? *No sign.* She thanked him, bid him a happy New Year, and sent him on his way.

She parked her rental in a nearby garage and set off on foot. Stopping at a handful of shops and restaurants, as well as a rundown bar named the Falcon—many of these establishments bearing red-white-and-blue PAUL MAGOWAN FOR SENATE signs in their front windows—she introduced herself to the employees and explained what had happened to her husband just a few weeks earlier. Then she pulled out a photograph of Ryan from her purse and showed it to them, politely asking if anyone had happened to see or speak with him.

In response, she received any number of ill-mannered grunts and dismissive head shakes. And no one whispered that they were going to vote for her.

Giving up on the local townspeople, Gwendy's final stop of the afternoon was a return visit to the Derry Police

431

Station, where Detective Mitchell greeted her coolly. "I forgot something—what about surveillance video?"

He shook his head. "No cameras anywhere downtown. Oh, maybe in a few stores, but that's all of it. This isn't a nanny state, you know, like California."

"If it had happened in California," Gwendy said tartly, "you might have a license plate, Detective. Has that occurred to you?"

"Very sorry for your loss, Ms. Peterson," he said, pulling a pile of paperwork toward him. His cheap sport coat pulled open and she saw his gun in a shoulder rig. Something else, too. A Magowan campaign button on the breast pocket of his shirt.

"You've been a great help, Detective."

He ignored the sarcasm. "Always glad to assist."

After describing her unsettling visit to Norris Ridgewick at lunch two days later, Gwendy found herself giving serious consideration to Norris's suggestion that she hire a private detective to look further into the matter. He even gave her a business card of someone he knew and trusted. She meant to call and set up an appointment, but before she knew it Christmas was there, and New Year's Eve, and she had her elderly father to take care of.

Not to mention a Senate campaign to run. Shortly after Ryan's death, Pete Riley had called to ask her (dread in his voice) if she wanted to declare herself out of the race. "I'd understand if you did. I'd hate it, but I'd understand."

There were a great many issues that she cared about—Magowan's pledge to resume clear-cutting the forests up north was a major one—but it was the button box she was thinking about when she replied. "I'm running."

"Thank God. Just don't say I'm in it to win it. That didn't work so well for Hilary."

She gave a dutiful laugh, although it wasn't funny. What neither of them said was that the election was less than a year away and early polls had Gwendy Peterson lagging by almost twelve points.

The gray days of winter arrived. The first nor'easter of 2020 blasted Castle Rock during the third week of January, dumping nearly two feet of snow and toppling trees and telephone poles. Most of the town lost power for three days, and a sophomore girl from Castle Rock High lost her right eye in a sledding accident. January turned into February, February into March. The sun rose each morning, and so did Gwendy Peterson. She was too old and out of shape to start jogging again, but she began walking a daily three-and-a-half-mile route, usually in the frigid hours just after dawn when the streets were silent and still. She stopped dyeing her hair and let the gray grow out. She also started writing a new book about a haunted town. A thousand words here, five hundred words there, even scribbling a short chapter on a Dunkin' Donuts napkin during one of her campaign stops. Anything to blunt the keen edge of her grief.

And all of that time, hidden away in a cardboard box marked SEWING SUPPLIES, the button box waited. Sometimes, when the house was as quiet as a church, Gwendy could hear it talking out there in the garage, that faint whisper of *something* echoing deep in the corners of her brain. When that happened, she usually told it to shut the hell up and turned up the volume on the television or the radio. Usually.

Did the idea of pressing the red button and blasting the

433

town of Derry (and all those awful people) off the face of the planet ever enter Gwendy's consciousness? As a matter of fact it did, and on more than one occasion. How about the shiny black button? Did she ever think about pressing the old Cancer Button and ending the whole shebang? Was she ever so tempted in her grief? The sorry truth: she was.

But Gwendy also remembered what Richard Farris had told her that nightmarish evening on the screened-in back porch—the box's last seven proprietors all dead, many of their families in the ground right alongside them—and it occurred to her that perhaps what the button box wanted most of all was a voluntary act of madness and mass destruction from its most faithful guardian. Talk about a win—the win of *all* wins—for the bad guys. And exactly who *were* the bad guys?

Around that time, the plague that Farris had warned her about—the media was calling it the coronavirus or COVID-19, depending on which channel you watched; Gwendy couldn't help but think of it as the Button Box Virus because she knew it had been responsible—finally made landfall in the United States. Only a handful of people had died so far, but many others had fallen sick and were being admitted to hospitals. Schools and colleges all across the country were sending students home to learn online. Concerts and sporting events were being canceled. Half the country was wearing masks and practicing safe social distancing; the other half—led by a frozen-like-a-deer-in-the-headlights President Trump—believed it was all a big hoax designed to steal their constitutional rights. So far, there was no sign of the stacked-up body bags that Farris had told her about, but Gwendy had no doubt they were coming. And soon.

Some late nights, when she was feeling particularly small and alone, curled up like an orphaned child on her side of the spacious king-size bed or lying awake in a hotel room after a campaign stop, unable to find sleep despite a warm bath and several glasses of wine, Gwendy was certain that the button box was responsible for taking Ryan away from her. *A life for a life*, she thought. *It saved my mother and took my lover.* The goddamn box had always been like that—it preferred to keep things square.

In March of 2020, she got a phone call on her personal cell, a number known to only a handful of people. Perhaps a dozen in total. UNKNOWN CALLER showed in the window. Because spammers were now required to display an actual callback number (legislation she had enthusiastically voted for), Gwendy took the call.

"Hello?"

Breathing on the other end.

"Say something, or I'm hanging up."

"It was a Cadillac that hit your husband." The voice was male, and although he wasn't using one of those voice-distorting gadgets, he was clearly trying to disguise his voice. "Old. Fifty, maybe sixty years, but in beautiful shape. Purple. Or could have been red. Fuzzy dice hanging from the rearview."

"Who is this? How did you get this number?"

Click.

Gone.

Gwendy closed her eyes and ran a review of all the people who had her private cell number (in those days she was still capable of such a mental task). She came up empty. It was only later that she realized she had also given her number to Ward Mitchell of the Derry PD. She doubted it had been him, with his chilly eyes and Magowan campaign button, but it would have been entered into the department's computer system, and she had an intuition that it had been a cop who called her . . . but she never found out who.

Or why.

18

BERN STAPLETON HANDS THE iPad back to Jafari Bankole. The astronomer looks at the screen and shakes his head in disbelief. "I swear I tried that. Twice."

"Probably you did," Stapleton says. "These gadgets are fancy as hell, but they're not perfect." He glances over at Senator Peterson, who's strapped in her flight chair, busy tapping away at her own mini computer. "Let me know if you need anything else, Jaff."

"Thank you," Bankole says, already engrossed in the seemingly endless rows of shifting numbers.

This is Stapleton's third trip to the up-above, which is why he's currently making his rounds on level three of Eagle Heavy. All four crew members on the lower deck are first-timers, what the veterans call Greenies. Stapleton knows from experience that four weeks of training, no matter how rigidly organized, just isn't enough time.

"How're tricks, Senator?"

Gwendy looks up from her iPad screen. "Just finished performing my assigned duties as weather girl, and now I'm checking my emails. Pretty typical afternoon. What are you up to?" Despite her sassy tone, she's genuinely curious. She'd noticed Stapleton speaking quietly with Adesh Patel a few minutes earlier, their heads mere inches apart, and it worried her. Were they discussing her little episode from earlier? Sneaking glances at her when she wasn't looking? She doesn't think that's the case, but even the possibility makes her uneasy.

"Thought I'd make sure the rookies were pulling their weight," Bern says. "Speaking of that . . ." He looks around. "Where's Winston?"

Gwendy hooks a thumb toward level four. "Either in the bathroom again or hiding in his cabin. I think he's already grown bored with the view from his precious porthole."

"How about you?" Stapleton asks. "You bored yet?"

Gwendy's entire face brightens—and the years fall away. Stapleton stares in amazement, thinking, *This is what Gwendy Peterson looked like as a little girl.* "You're kidding, right?" She holds up her iPad for him to see. "The interior temperature of our current destination, specifically Spoke One of the Many Flags Space Station, is a comfortable seventy-three degrees Fahrenheit. I was curious, so I checked." She taps the screen—once, twice, three times. "TetCorp plans to take a ship very much like the one we're presently flying in to Mars in the next couple of years. Do you know what the current temperature on the surface of Mars is at this exact moment?"

Stapleton actually does know, but he doesn't dream of saying so. Not with Senator Gwendy Peterson looking at him with the cheery (and wonder-filled) eyes of a twelve-year-old. Instead, he shakes his head.

"It's the middle of the night on Mars, and almost two hundred degrees below zero." She lowers the iPad to her lap. "Makes Maine feel like a beach in the Bahamas."

He laughs and gives a gentle kick of his legs to remain in place. "So what was all the commotion about earlier? I heard Kathy had to shut the party down."

"That was my fault. Winston was over there snoring like a banshee, and it got me to laughing." She shrugs her shoulders. "Once I started, I couldn't stop."

"Sometimes first impressions are correct ones," he says, glancing at the billionaire's empty flight seat.

Gwendy nods, recalling Winston's booming voice and obnoxious behavior during their four weeks of close-quarters training. "I keep reminding myself to give the man the benefit of the doubt, but it's not been easy."

"Maybe this will help." He lowers his voice. "Kathy told me that Winston is responsible for more than half of St. Jude's annual funding, but the press doesn't print a word about it, because he doesn't want them to know. Shocking, huh?"

"Well, if in fact that's true," she says, wondering why the information was missing from her dossier, "then God bless Gareth Winston, and he certainly deserves the bene-fit of my doubt. May heavenly choirs sing his name."

"Hopefully, you'll still feel that way after spending nineteen days with him on MF-1." He grins. "If you're really lucky, you and Winston might even get partnered up to take a spacewalk together."

Gwendy flashes her training partner a scorching look—but doesn't say anything. She's thinking about Richard Farris's plan for the button box at that moment, and praying she can pull it off.

"I better head back. Reggie and Dale get upset if I leave them alone for too long." He begins to drift slowly upward, then stops himself by grabbing hold of one of the ship's support beams. "Almost forgot to ask. You ready for your video chat?"

In just over two hours, Gwendy has a video conference

scheduled with top high school and middle school students from all fifty states, as well as select members of the media. She's not looking forward to it. In fact, she's dreading it. All she can think is: *What if I have one of my Brain Freezes on live television? What then?* That's one question she knows the answer to—it would be an unmitigated disaster and most likely signal the end of her journey.

"As ready as I'm going to be, I guess," she says, craning her neck to look up at him. "I just wish it could wait until we got settled in at the space station. Like Adesh and Jafari are doing with their students."

"No can do. You're a sitting U.S. senator and the VIP on this expedition. The world demands a bigger piece of you."

That's what I'm afraid of, Gwendy thinks.

Gareth Winston emerges from the lower level, a sour look on his face, and passes within a couple feet of Gwendy's flight chair. He doesn't make eye contact with her or any of the other crew members and doesn't say a word. His lower lip is sticking out. Once he's strapped into his seat, he turns his head and stares silently out the porthole.

Wonder what that's all about, Gwendy thinks. And then it comes to her. Winston must've overheard Stapleton calling her a VIP, and now he's in major pout mode. *What a baby!* She's about to lower her voice and say as much to Stapleton when the comm mic attached to the front of his jumpsuit gives out a loud squawk and Kathy Lundgren's voice inquires: "Bern, are you in the middle of something?"

"Just about to head back to level two. What do you need?"

"Can you accompany Senator Peterson to the flight deck? Immediately."

"Roger that. On our way." He clicks off and looks at Gwendy. "Wonder what that's all about."

Gwendy swallows, her throat suddenly sandpaper dry. "You're not the only one."

It takes them less than a minute to make their way up to the flight deck, but it's long enough for Gwendy to convince herself that the worst is about to happen: Mission Control has somehow discovered her deteriorating condition and they're canceling the scheduled landing at MF-1. There will be no spacewalk. No disposal of the button box. It's over. She's failed.

When they arrive at level one, Operation Commander Kathy Lundgren and two male crew members—Gwendy can't recall their names for the life of her and is too unsettled to try Dr. Ambrose's technique—are buckled into their flight seats surrounded by a U-shaped bank of touchscreen monitors. Directly in front of them is the long, narrow viewing window Kathy had invited Gwendy to look out of a little more than twenty-four hours earlier. Beyond the window lies one of the world's great oceans. Kathy swivels in her chair to face them, her expression unreadable.

"I'm afraid I have some bad news, Gwendy."

Here it comes . . .

"There's been a mishap back in Castle Rock."

"It's not my father, is it?" she asks, all her breath leaving her at once. *Please, he's all I have left.*

Kathy's eyes widen in alarm. "No, no, as far as I know, your father is fine. I'm sorry. I didn't mean to frighten you."

Oh, it's a little too late for that.

"There was a fire at your house, Gwendy. Your

neighbor spotted the smoke and called 911. The fire department was able to catch it early. The majority of the damage was limited to your garage and back porch. There was some additional water damage to the kitchen and family room."

"A fire. At my house." Gwendy feels like she's dreaming again. "Does anyone know how it started?"

"You'll be receiving a number of emails—one from someone at your insurance company, another from a retired policeman named Norris Ridgewick—explaining everything they know." Kathy looks at her with sincere regret. "I'm very sorry, Senator."

Gwendy waves a hand in front of her face. "I'm just glad no one was hurt. The rest are just . . . things. They can be replaced."

"Under the circumstances, we didn't know whether we should tell you right away or wait until we docked at MF-1, or even if we should wait until you were back on the ground. But we were concerned that someone in the media might alert you, so we decided you needed to hear it from us first."

"I appreciate that."

"Gwendy . . . would you like me to reschedule the video conference for another time? I'm sure everyone will understand."

She pauses before answering, purposely giving the impression that she's thinking about it. "I'll be okay," she finally says. "The last thing I want to do is disappoint all those children."

Despite being called "one of public education's fiercest advocates" by a reporter from the *Washington Post* two years earlier, Gwendy's true motivation for going ahead with the video chat has little to do with not wanting to disappoint honor roll students from all fifty states. As desperately as she would like to avoid appearing on live television, she believes that canceling at the last minute would be a very bad idea. It would send the wrong message—one of weakness—to whomever it was searching for the button box. And that's the last thing she wants to do.

It's not a coincidence, she thinks on her way back down to level three. *The fire started in the garage and it spread from there. After all these years, they're getting closer.*

19

As SPRING APPROACHED, GWENDY threw herself into the 2020 Senate campaign with what Wolf Blitzer from CNN described as "fevered abandon." Even with the coronavirus raging across the country—with more than 175,000 and counting confirmed deaths by mid-August—she spent the majority of her days and nights connecting face-to-face with the people of Maine. Masked, she visited hospitals and schools, daycare centers and nursing homes, churches and factories. While the incumbent (and defiantly unmasked) Paul Magowan focused the majority of his attention on big business and corporate incentives and continued to hammer strict borders and the Second Amendment, Gwendy went straight to the people and their day-to-day struggles and concerns. Tip O'Neill once said, "All politics is local," and she believed that. Any place of commerce or education that would have her—as long as masks and social distancing were in place—she went. She even spent a blisteringly hot August afternoon walking door to door in Derry. At one house, a man in a wifebeater tee told her to "get outta my face, you fucking harpy." It made the news, with the obscenity bleeped . . . for all the good that might do.

When she came down with a 102-degree fever and a nasty bout of diarrhea a few days later, most members of her campaign committee were convinced that she'd finally caught the virus and this would mean the end of her run. But, as often was the case, they underestimated her. A negative test and two days of bed rest later, Gwendy was back out on the road and speaking to the men and women stationed at Bath Iron Works. She told a couple of "old Maineah" jokes, which got big laughs. Her favorite was the one about moose-shit pie. In the current version, she changed the name of the lumber crew's cook to Magowan.

Gwendy's father—who'd moved to the first floor of the Castle Rock Meadows Nursing Home earlier in the summer—worried about his daughter, and told her so on more than one occasion. He faithfully watched her appearances on the morning and evening news programs and spoke to her almost every night on the telephone, but he couldn't convince her to slow down. Brigette Desjardin—now taking care of Pippa, Alan Peterson's elderly dachshund—pleaded with her best friend to make time to see a grief counselor, insisting that she was self-medicating with her hectic work schedule, but Gwendy wouldn't hear of it. She had places to go and people to see and undecided voters to win over. Even Pete Riley, the driving force behind Gwendy's Senate run, grew concerned after a while and tried to talk her into easing up. She refused.

"You got me into this. No backing out now."

"But—"

"But nothing. If you don't want me to block your number—which would be bad, with you being my campaign manager and all—let me do my thing."

That was the end of that.

What her family and friends and work colleagues didn't understand was that the engine driving her wasn't grief over Ryan's tragic death. Yes, she was still sad and lonely and maybe even clinically depressed, but if there was one thing Gwendy had learned during her lifetime, it was that you had to move on; honor the dead by serving the living, as her mentor Patsy Follett used to say. Nor was it an inflated sense of political importance. It was the button box, of course, still hidden away on the top shelf in her garage. One day soon she would have to step up and save the world. It was ridiculous, it was absurd, it was surreal . . . and it seemed to be true.

On the last Friday of August, new poll numbers came out showing Gwendy only seven points behind Paul Magowan. This was cause for mighty celebration, according to an ecstatic Pete Riley and the rest of the Maine Democratic Committee. Many members of the media attributed the surge to a wave of sympathy for the recently widowed challenger. Gwendy knew that was some of it but not all of it. She was reaching out to people and a surprising number were reaching back.

By late September, the gap had narrowed to five and Gwendy realized that people weren't just listening—they were starting to believe. As Pete Riley had predicted more than a year before during that first exploratory meeting, the tightening poll numbers soon snagged Paul Magowan's attention and his campaign began to play dirty. Step one was an updated series of television spots highlighting the proliferation of profane language and explicit sex scenes in several of Gwendy's novels. "I guess they're not big on originality," Gwendy snarked to the press after one campaign appearance. "I thought they already ran with the 'Peterson Is a Pervert' angle last August?"

She wasn't nearly as flippant two weeks later when a follow-up commercial aired on prime-time television depicting Gwendy's late husband as a raging anarchist, offering as proof a photograph of Ryan standing next to a burning American flag on a riot-ravaged urban street, as well as his arrest two years earlier at a Chicago protest. What the ad failed to mention was that Ryan had been in Chicago on a work assignment for *Time* magazine, had stopped to take photographs of the burning flag and rioters, and despite having proper press credentials displayed in plain view, had been taken into custody. In the Magowan-campaign photo, the credential hanging around Ryan's neck had been artfully blurred out. Nor did the Magowan ads say anything about any charges being almost immediately dropped.

From there it only got worse. The third wave of TV and radio ads shined a glaring spotlight on Paul Magowan's large and successful family—five children, three boys and two girls, plus sixteen grandchildren, all of whom still called the state of Maine their home—and questioned the fact that Gwendy had never had any children of her own.

"If Gwendy Peterson is such a true believer of the good things in this state and country—as she so often claims—then why hasn't she bothered to bring new life into it? Too busy writing smut and jet-setting around the world?"

As recently as a decade before, such a despicable ad would have torpedoed any chance of Paul Magowan holding on to his Senate seat. But this was a brave new world, populated by a brand-new breed of seemingly shameless GOP candidates.

When Gwendy's father saw the commercial for the first time during Game 3 of the American League Division Series, he became so enraged he climbed out a first-floor window at the nursing home and tried to call a taxi to pick him up. When one of the counselors escorted him back inside a short time later and asked where he had planned to go, Mr. Peterson responded, "To Magowan's campaign headquarters to whup his fat ass."

Gwendy reacted much more diplomatically, at least in public, largely because, at the age of fifty-eight, she'd already had years to come to terms with the reality of the situation. She'd always adored children and wanted kids of her own one day, even before she'd met Ryan and fallen in love. For years after they were married, they tried with no success. It was the fault of neither. They visited the right doctors and took the right tests, and the results always came back the same: Gwendy Peterson and Ryan Brown were two immensely healthy human beings and, according to the rules of medical science, were perfectly capable of producing healthy children. But for some reason, despite all the trying—and they tried a *lot* during those early years—it never happened.

There was a time, not long after the final artificial insemination attempt proved unsuccessful, that Gwendy, alone in the silence of her bedroom, broke down and allowed the tidal wave of grief and anger to crash over her. She'd kicked and screamed and thrown things. Later, after the crying stopped and she'd cleaned up the mess, she called her mother to share the sad news. Mrs. Peterson told her what she always told her: "God works in mysterious ways, Gwendy. I don't understand why this is happening any more than you do, but we have to put our faith in the Lord's hands." And then she added, "I'm so sorry, honey. If anyone in this world deserves to be parents, it's you and Ryan."

Gwendy thanked her mom and hung up the telephone.

She walked to the bedroom window overlooking the front yard and street below, and watched as a young curly-haired boy pedaled a bright yellow bicycle past their house. She watched until he disappeared around the corner.

"I understand why this is happening," she said to the empty house around her. "I think I always have and just didn't want to admit it. It's because of the button box. I was only a stupid kid, but I took and I took and I took. And now it's the box's turn."

In October 2020, with mail-in voting underway and physical voting sites opening their doors in just under three weeks, Gwendy Peterson and Paul Magowan met at the Bangor Civic Center for a long-anticipated tele-vised debate. For ninety minutes, the incumbent senator was rude, arrogant, and condescending, the same behav-ior that had gotten him elected just four years earlier. His challenger was humble, well-spoken, and polite. Except for one fleeting moment in her closing remarks, when she turned to face her opponent and said, "And as for my late husband, you, sir, may try your very best to disparage his good name and reputation, but you know and I know and every person sitting in this auditorium and watching from home on television knows that you, Senator Magowan, are not enough of a man to shine Ryan Brown's shoes or wash the sweat out of his dirty jockstrap."

The majority of the audience in attendance roared their approval and rewarded Gwendy with a standing ova-tion as she walked off the debate stage. When the new poll numbers came out early the next morning, Magowan's lead had shrunk to a paltry three points.

But even with such impressive results, Gwendy knew it would take a miracle to overcome a three-percent deficit in as many weeks. There were no more debates on the docket and, after the public drubbing he'd taken, little chance that Magowan would agree to add one. Word on the street was that he planned to lay low for the rest of the campaign and lick his wounds until election night, when he would resurface and take the stage to accept a surprisingly narrow victory. Gwendy had events planned for every day leading up to the election—sometimes two or three in the same twelve-hour block—but even taken as a whole, she knew it wasn't enough to move the needle three percentage points. They were simply running out of time.

Gwendy believed there was only one surefire way to guarantee a miracle, and it was sitting on a shelf inside her garage at home in Castle Rock. Over the course of the next two weeks—usually while tossing and turning in one hotel bed or another; after a while, they all looked and smelled the same—there were at least half a dozen instances when she convinced herself that pulling out the button box was the right thing to do. Presto! Push the red button and make Paul Magowan disappear like a rabbit in a magician's hat! But each time, her conscience and Richard Farris's words of warning stopped her: *You must resist. Don't touch the button box or even take it out of the canvas bag unless absolutely necessary. Every time you do, it will get more of a hold on you.*

And then, on the Thursday night before Election Day, Gwendy got her miracle.

Like most of his longtime GOP counterparts, Paul Magowan's bread-and-butter constituency was made up of Pro-Life, Pro-Religion, Pro-Build-the-Wall loud and proud NRA members. As a proclaimed Christian and father of five, he spoke often and passionately of his abhorrence of the ungodly and downright evil practice of abortion. He called the doctors that performed such procedures "soulless butchers" and "devils in blood-smeared white coats."

On that Thursday evening, word leaked to the national press that a front-page article in the next morning's edition of the *Portland Press Herald* would be outlining in great detail and providing written documentation that proved Paul Magowan had not only had a year-long dalliance with a young woman from his local church but that he'd also paid—using illegal campaign funds, no less—for her to abort their unborn child.

Magowan's campaign immediately scheduled a late-night news conference to try to get ahead of the story. But it was too late. The ball had already dropped—right on top of Magowan's arrogant and hypocritical bald head—and started rolling downhill. Fast.

When the final votes were tallied a few days later, *New York Times* bestselling author Gwendy Peterson became senator-elect of the great state of Maine. She won by a margin of four points, which meant that thousands of full-time residents had still punched their ticket for Paul Magowan.

Life in America, Gwendy thought when she contemplated all those Magowan votes. *Life in pandemic America.*

20

GWENDY SWIPES TO THE CONTROL screen on her iPad, taps VIDEO LINK, and a blank picture-in-picture display opens in the upper right-hand corner. She hits the REVERSE IMAGE icon and the top of her head appears in the small window. Adjusting the angle, she gives one final tap, and her smiling face fills the entire screen.

"Got it," she says with no small measure of pride.

Gwendy's long gray hair is pulled back into a neat ponytail and there are circles of bright color in her cheeks. Her blue eyes are clear and alert. She looks much younger than her sixty-four years and feels it, too.

"There you are." Kathy Lundgren floats down into view. "Ready for your close-up, Ms. Peterson?"

Gwendy extends her hand. "Of course I am, darling," she says in a haughty tone. Kathy laughs and feigns kissing the senator's hand.

Kathy was worried about Gwendy earlier—when she first told her the news about the fire, the senator had appeared lost, almost in a daze—but now that she's down here face-to-face, she finds that she can't stop staring at her. "My goodness, a couple hours of rest did wonders for you. You look and sound terrific."

"That and a strategic touch or two of makeup." Only Gwendy didn't bring much on this trip. Why would she? She's about as low-maintenance as they come.

"Well, whatever it is, send some my way, why don't you." Adesh Patel glides past Kathy on his way to his flight chair. She gives him a friendly nod and looks back at Gwendy. "A little less than five minutes til go."

Gwendy adjusts the straps on her flight seat and wiggles her hips until she's comfortable. She glances up at the overhead monitors and then down at her iPad. Licking her lips, she tastes a hint of chocolate on the back of her tongue. She instantly feels the *thump-thump-thump* of her heart beginning to race beneath her jumpsuit.

The tiny piece of chocolate had been in the shape of an ostrich. When she'd pulled open the drawstring of the canvas bag and slid out the button box, she'd been amazed at how heavy it felt in her hands despite their weightless environment. Much heavier than she remembered, and somehow significantly heavier than when she was carrying it around inside the reinforced steel case. She knew that made little sense—no sense at all, in fact—but didn't spend much time thinking about it. All things were possible when it came to the button box.

Her decision had already been made by the time she'd punched in the seven-digit code and opened the small white case marked **CLASSIFIED MATERIAL**, so there was little hesitation once the moment came. She lifted the box onto her lap, reached down, and pulled the lever on the left side, the one closest to the red button. And then she'd thought: *If you're monitoring this, Farris, you can kiss my bony white ass.*

The narrow wooden shelf slid soundlessly open from the center of the box. She picked up the chocolate ostrich and popped it into her mouth, barely taking the time to appreciate its fine detail. Closing her eyes, she allowed it to melt on her tongue, savoring the familiar burst of exotic flavor. Once the chocolate was gone, she immediately thought about pulling the lever a second time but fought back the temptation. She knew she was already pressing her luck.

After leaving the control room earlier and assuring a concerned Bern Stapleton that she was okay and just needed to rest, Gwendy retired to her cabin. When she stretched out atop the cramped bunk and buckled herself in, she hadn't even been thinking about the button box and its magic treats. All she wanted was to close her eyes and make the world go away for a short time. She was physically and mentally exhausted—and she was scared. Despite what Kathy Lundgren and Bern Stapleton believed, it wasn't the fire in Castle Rock that had Gwendy so distraught, although that certainly didn't help matters. It was a combination of *everything*. The video conference worried her greatly. One untimely misstep and she knew she was finished. Her heart ached fiercely. Despite the friendships she'd made, she hadn't realized how alone she'd feel on this trip. It had been almost seven years now, but not having Ryan waiting for her back at home left Gwendy feeling forlorn and adrift. And then there were the Brain Freezes. Ever since quarantine—and especially ever since they'd boarded Eagle-19 Heavy—they were coming with an increasing frequency that terrified her. Initially, she'd believed it was stress worsening her symptoms. But in her heart, she knew that wasn't the case. The button box had somehow discovered her plan and was trying to stop her before they reached MF-1.

Reaching down and touching the notebook tucked safely inside the pocket of her jumpsuit, she thought: *How* long until the only things I remember are the words inside this notebook? And what about when I no longer remember how to read . . . ?

Just the thought of that happening made Gwendy want to pull her hair out, or scream, or do both. Lying there, head spinning, staring up at the curved ceiling of her cabin, she'd eventually dozed. And dreamed . . .

Gareth Winston sits cross-legged on the floor beneath his porthole. No other crew members are in sight and the ship is eerily silent. Winston is naked except for a saggy pair of soiled tighty-whities. His man-boobs and bright pink nipples are ringed by unruly snatches of curly dark hair. The button box rests atop his pale chubby legs and at first glance it appears to be smeared in blood. But then Gwendy sees that Winston's sausage-like fingers are dripping with globs of melting chocolate. So are his mouth and all three of his chins. It's everywhere. He reaches down and pulls the lever on the right side of the box. Out slides the wooden tray with a tiny chocolate donkey centered atop it. Winston grabs the chocolate and crams it into his mouth, slurping noisily. "Sooo good," he exclaims, and lifting his arm high above his head, he points a single finger in the air and—never one to pass up on an expansive gesture—twirls it around and around before lowering it in agonizing slow motion until it rests directly atop the red button. He giggles, drooling a rope of chocolate saliva onto his lap—and presses the button. Once. Twice. He looks up then, grinning with stained teeth, and bellows, "There! Now I'm number one in the world!"

Strapped onto her bunk, Gwendy jerked awake with a scream of terror lodged in her throat—and knew exactly what she needed to do.

"Thirty seconds," Kathy Lundgren says.

Gwendy steals a sidelong glance at Winston, who is

buckled into his seat and facing the opposite direction. She checks her teeth in the iPad screen—all clean; *no chocolate!*—and releases a deep, steadying breath. "Here goes nothing, folks." She places her finger over the LIVE VIDEO icon and listens to the Operation Commander count down.

"Five . . . four . . . three . . . two . . . one . . . and you're a go!"

Gwendy puts a big smile on her face and taps the icon. "Greetings, earthlings, from my home away from home, Eagle-19 Heavy. My name is Senator Gwendy Peterson from the great state of Maine and I will be serving as your tour guide today. Before I unbuckle and give you a look at the amazing view just outside this porthole, I want to introduce you to our esteemed flight commander, Miss Kathy Lundgren. Say hi to everybody, Kathy! The three handsome gentlemen sitting to my immediate left are . . ."

21

IN JANUARY 2020—AFTER SERVING in a number of high-profile intelligence positions including Deputy Group Chief of Counterterrorism, as well as CIA Station Chief in London, Munich, and New York—sixty-three-year-old Charlotte Morgan became the eighth appointee (and only the third woman) to be named as Deputy Director of the Central Intelligence Agency.

She was also one of Gwendy Peterson's closest and most trusted friends. They'd first met at a budget meeting during the summer of 2003 when Gwendy was serving her second term in the House of Representatives. Charlotte Morgan was temporarily living in D.C., spearheading a six-month training program for overseas operatives. After running into each other at a number of social functions, including a handful of Orioles games, they became fast friends, bonding over their mutual affection for jogging, junk food, and violent crime novels, especially those penned by the dashing John Sandford.

Charlotte returned abroad when the training program ended, but the two women stayed in touch via telephone and email, and visited often during Charlotte's thrice-yearly trips home. When Charlotte got married to her second husband on a private Delaware beach in 2005, Gwendy served as one of four bridesmaids. The following winter, when Charlotte gave birth to a healthy baby girl—on her forty-ninth birthday!—she and her husband chose Gwendy to be the child's godmother. Years later, when Gwendy's mom passed away on a cold October afternoon, Charlotte hopped on the next available flight from New York and was holding her friend's hand later that same evening. In many ways, Charlotte Morgan became the older sister Gwendy had always wished for.

As Gwendy parked her car by the Lake Fairfax boat ramp in Reston, Virginia, on the morning of December 9, 2023, and spotted her old friend sitting alone on a bench near the water's edge, she prayed that their long history would be enough . . . or at least a start. Charlotte glanced up from the book she was reading, flipped Gwendy a wave, then lifted her hands to her shoulders in a *What's going on?* gesture. Gwendy got out of the car and slowly made her way over to the bench, carrying the canvas bag in her right hand.

"No security?" Charlotte asked, only half-joking.

"I'm driving a rental Kia. That's security enough." *Not to mention the button box*, Gwendy thought.

"You're killing me, dear one," Charlotte said, closing the thick hardcover on her lap. "It's got to be ten degrees out here. Spill it. Why all the secrecy?"

Gwendy took a seat next to her friend, placing the canvas bag by her feet. "Have you ever considered me anything other than completely sane, reasonable, and honest?"

Charlotte's smile faded. She looked closely at Gwendy. "Are you in some kind of trouble?"

"You could say that," Gwendy agreed. "Please answer the question."

"Other than your bullheaded allegiance to the Red Sox, you've proven to be one of the most sane and trustworthy people I know. Top two or three, for sure. You know that."

"Then I need you to listen to me very carefully. Can you do that?"

Charlotte didn't answer right away—she was still too stunned by the turn the meeting had taken. She'd come expecting Gwendy to tell her that she was finally dating someone after the last four years of living like a nun, but this sounded much more serious. She didn't care for the drawn look on Gwendy's face.

"I can do that."

"Be sure, because I'm going to tell you something that will be very difficult to believe. Then I'm going to show you what's inside this bag and give you a demonstration of how it works."

Charlotte leaned forward and gave the drawstring bag a closer look. She opened her mouth to respond, but Gwendy cut her off again. "If you start to interrupt, I'm going to walk back to my car and drive away and pretend this meeting never happened."

"You're scaring me, Gwen. Are you sure we shouldn't call it quits on this conversation right now while we're ahead?"

"Only if you don't want the world to stick around long enough for Jenny to graduate from high school and go to an Ivy League college and have babies of her own one day."

"You're serious?"

"Unfortunately, yes."

The deputy director, never once breaking eye contact, was silent then. It was her job to know when people were telling the truth. "Okay. Tell me."

Gwendy told her.

When she was finished, almost forty minutes later, Gwendy picked up the canvas bag from the grass by her feet, pulled out the button box, and placed it on her lap. It was the first time she'd laid eyes on it in almost twenty-five years. She could hear Richard Farris's voice whisper inside her head: *Don't touch the button box or even take it out of the canvas bag unless absolutely necessary.*

Was a thing absolutely necessary when it was absolutely the only way? Of course it was.

"Do you remember the part of my story about Jonestown?"

Charlotte nodded. "You believe you caused it. Or rather that strange box did. May I . . . ?" She reached for it.

Gwendy pulled it away, clutching it to her chest. Because it would be dangerous for Charlotte to touch it, yes, but that wasn't the only reason. There was jealousy, as well. She thought of Gollum in *The Lord of the Rings*: *"It's mine, precious, my birthday present."* Gwendy didn't want to feel that way about the box, but she did.

It was terrible, but there was no denying it.

"I guess I may not," Charlotte said. She was giving Gwendy a measuring look, and Gwendy knew, old friend or not, she was only a few steps from deciding Senator Peterson was barking mad.

"It would be dangerous for you to even touch it," Gwendy said. "I know how that sounds and what you're thinking, because I'd be thinking it, too. Just give me a little more rope, okay?"

"Okay."

"I thought the part of Guyana I was concentrating on when I conducted my experiment back then was deserted.

I didn't know about Jonestown. Hardly anyone did before it hit the news worldwide. It's not like there was any Internet to check back then. And remember, I was just a kid. This time I did my research and I'm still not sure no one will be hurt. Or killed." Gwendy swallowed. Her throat was bone-dry. "The red button is the least dangerous by far, but it's still a loaded gun. As I found out when all those people drank the Kool-Aid back in 1978."

"Gwendy, you don't really believe that *you*—"

"Hush. No interruptions. You promised."

Charlotte sat back, but Gwendy could still see the worry in Charl's eyes. And the disbelief. There might be a way to fix that.

"I think you should have a piece of chocolate. That might help to open your mind a little."

Curling her pinky, Gwendy pulled one of the levers on the side of the box. Out came a tiny chocolate animal.

"Oh my God!" Charlotte cried, picking it up. "Is it an aardvark?"

"Not sure, but I believe it's an anteater. No two are ever the same, which is quite a trick in itself. Go ahead, try it. I think you'll like it."

"I'm allergic to chocolate, Gwen. It makes me break out in hives."

"You won't be allergic to this. I promise."

Charlotte lifted it to her nose for a sniff, and that sealed the deal. She popped it into her mouth. Her eyes widened. "Oh my *God*! It's so *good*!"

"Yes. And how do I look to you?"

"How . . . ?" Charlotte really looked. "Clear. It's like I can see every strand of hair on your head, every pore on your cheeks . . . you've never been so clear. And lovely.

461

You always were, but now . . . *wow.*" Charlotte gave a small giggly laugh. Not the sort of sound you expected to hear from a CIA topsider, but Gwendy wasn't surprised.

She took Charlotte's hands in both of hers. "What am I thinking? Want to hazard a guess?"

"How could I . . ." Charlotte began, then: "A pyramid. The *Great* Pyramid. The one in Giza."

Gwendy let go of her friend's hands, satisfied.

"How could I know that?" Charlotte whispered.

"It was the chocolate. But not *just* the chocolate. You've trained your mind to read other people. You could say that telepathy is part of your job. The chocolates just give you a head start. My mother ate some, and they made her feel good, but she never had any mind-reading ability." *They just cured her cancer,* Gwendy thought. "It will fade, but you'll feel good for the rest of the day. Maybe tomorrow, as well."

"Look at the water," Charlotte whispered. "The sun fills it with stars. I never saw that before."

Gwendy reached out and turned Charlotte's face back to hers. "Never mind that now. Do you know what's going on in Egypt as of this week? Probably for the rest of the spring?"

Charlotte did. Of course she did; it would have been part of her daily briefings. "A bad outbreak of coronavirus. It's killing a lot of people and the government ordered a lockdown that will last at least until the middle of May. And they are not fucking around. Show up on the street and you're apt to get arrested."

"Yes," Gwendy said. "And that big old pyramid, the oldest of the world's Seven Wonders, is deserted. No tourists snapping pictures. No workmen. It's as close to perfect for demonstration purposes as I can get."

Gwendy squeezed her eyes closed and thought about the Great Pyramid of Giza, aka the Great Pyramid of Khufu, aka the Pyramid of Cheops. She hated the idea of vandalizing it, but it would be a small price to pay for convincing Charlotte.

She told her old friend what was going to happen and then pressed the red button, really putting her arm into it. Five minutes later she was back in her car, speeding north on I-95, trying to make it in time to a lunch meeting in downtown D.C.

Before leaving, Charlotte asked for another chocolate. Gwendy refused, but invited Charl to pull the lever on the other side of the box. Gwendy wasn't sure a Morgan silver dollar would slide out—they didn't always—but this time one did. Charlotte gasped with delight.

"Take it," Gwendy said. "A little thank-you for listening to me and not calling for the men in the white coats."

Later that night, when her cell phone rang, Gwendy was sitting in bed, watching CNN. It was showing drone footage of a monstrous pile of rubble where the Great Pyramid had once stood. NO EARTHQUAKE, the chyron read. SCIENTISTS MYSTIFIED. After a brief search, she found her phone tangled up in a blanket. She picked up after the third ring, knowing who it was on the other end this time despite the UNKNOWN CALLER tag in the phone's ID window.

Charlotte Morgan didn't bother with a hello or any other pleasantries. All she said was "Holy jumping Jesus."

"Yes," Gwendy said. "That about covers it."

"I'll get you on a space trip, Gwen, if it's what you want. That's a promise. It may take awhile, so hang tough. We'll talk."

"But not about this."

"No. Not about this."

"Okay. Make it as soon as possible. Using it today gave me a very creepy feeling. And some very creepy ideas." Some of them had been violent, and strangely sexual.

"I understand." Charlotte paused. "The Great Pyramid. Holy fuck." Then she was gone, saying good-bye no more than she'd said hello.

Gwendy tossed her phone aside and returned her gaze to the screen. Now the chyron read 6 KILLED IN COLLAPSE. They had been young adventurers from Sweden who had broken out of lockdown to explore the pyramid on their own and had been crushed under tons of limestone blocks. To Gwendy it was relearning an old lesson. No matter how careful you were, no matter how good your intentions, the button box always extracted its due.

In blood.

22

THE VIDEO CONFERENCE IS a big hit, a real smasheroo. No slip-ups, no Brain Freezes, and Gwendy actually manages to have fun. In fact, the entire flight crew has a good time, culminating in a rowdy, impromptu toast—vacuum-sealed pouches of orange juice, apple juice, and lemonade raised high in the air—saluting Senator Peterson for a job well done. Even Gareth Winston, who is grasping a fruit juice pouch in each of his meaty palms, looks almost happy for her. *Or maybe*, Gwendy thinks with a certain mean enjoyment, *he finally managed to move his bowels.*

"Okay, everyone," Kathy Lundgren calls out. "Time to get back to work. We have less than twelve hours until we join our Chinese friends at MF-1."

"May we never see them," David Graves grumbles, and Kathy swats him playfully on the shoulder as he floats by.

Gwendy watches as the others begin to stroke their way back to their flight chairs. "Thank you all again! That was an unexpected and much appreciated surprise!"

Gwendy still feels pretty terrific, but the buzz is starting to fade. If her memory is correct—and that's obviously a big *if* nowadays—the chocolate high used to last much longer. Days instead of hours. But then again, it's been more than twenty-five years since she last ate one, so how much does she really remember? Added to that, she's sixty-four now. Not quite a geezer, but getting there.

Or do only men get to be geezers? Maybe she's almost a geezerette.

Either way, she's not complaining. She's thrilled, in fact. Not to mention relieved. The first video conference is behind her. It will only get easier from here on out, now that she knows what to do. And perhaps best of all? Gwendy remembered their names—every last one of the other nine crew members. Plus she remembered their job titles and onboard duties and any other number of details she'd long ago misplaced.

She grabs the iPad from beneath her seat and swipes her way into her secure email account. Scanning the dozens of notices in her mailbox, she stops on an email from Progressive Insurance. It's time-coded from earlier in the day. She opens it.

The email is two pages long and is signed (electronically, of course) by a Progressive representative by the name of Frederick Lynn. She skims its contents. The insurance company is currently working on an estimate of the damage to her house. It has been secured with heavy plastic sheeting and wooden framework where necessary. The power has been turned off and the remaining items in the refrigerator and freezer removed. The Castle Rock Sheriff's Department as well as the Maine State Police will be keeping an eye on it, in case of thieves or ordinary garden-variety souvenir hunters. Also, her neighbors—Ed and Lorraine Henderson—promise to keep a close watch.

The insurance company doesn't expect to hear back from Ms. Peterson until her return from outer space (Mr. Freddy Lynn actually uses those exact words, which brings another smile to Gwendy's face), but they need to ask one important question: Does Ms. Peterson have any pets that may have gotten loose during the fire? They found no food or water dishes, but it's standard procedure to ask. After that, there's a lot of technical policy information she has little interest in reading.

Gwendy thanks God that Brigette has Pippa the sausage dog and hits the REPLY button. She types, "No pets. Thanks for all you're doing." And hits SEND.

I've just sent my first email from outer space, she thinks incredulously.

She refreshes the mailbox screen and scrolls until she finds an email from Norris Ridgewick. It's shorter than the insurance letter, but just barely.

April 17, 2026

Dear Gwendy,

I'm very sorry about the fire. I've spoken with Brian Gardener at the CR Sheriff's Department and he's going to make sure no one gets within shouting distance of your house. I also rode out and talked to your father, so he wouldn't have to hear about the fire on the news. He was pretty down, but I told him the insurance folks would fix it up as good as new. (Although they never do, which we both know.) He asked me to give you all his love.

Now to the real reason I'm writing. I hope you won't be mad, but the last few years I've been doing a little digging of my own about Ryan and his mysterious trip to Derry. A man can only fish so much, you know! You never asked me to get involved, but I figured it was worth a shot. Worst I could do was burn up some gas money and waste a little time. I guess I would've made a pretty crummy detective, because for the longest time I wasn't able to find out much of anything, and I sure didn't get any help from the local constabulary. They basically told me to buzz off. I decided to take one more shot at it last week. No luck. Until, that is, I was getting ready to come on back to the Rock. I stopped to gas up at one of those no-name extra-barrel stations, the kind where a fellow actually pumps your gas and washes your windshield. This guy was named Gerald "Gerry" Keele, an old-timer who was sort of refreshing because he didn't have any of that (excuse the language) "fuck you and the horse you rode in on" Derry attitude. I asked my questions, showed him Ryan's picture, and right away he said yeah. He especially remembered the GWENDY FOR SENATE stickers, because there were three of them plastered across his back bumper.

That makes Gwendy wipe away a tear.

He said Ryan asked directions to Bassey Park because he had to meet a man there, by the big Paul Bunyan statue. Keele laughed and said, "I can give you directions, but you won't find Big Paul because he's long gone." Ryan jotted down the turns and drove off. I thought that was all I was going to get, but then Keele said something else. I was recording on my phone, so I can give it to you exactly. He said, "There's an abandoned warehouse past the gas station, on the corner of Neibolt and Pond. Soon as your boy paid and left, an old Chrysler pulled out from behind that warehouse. Big as a boat it was, and an ugly green color that almost hurt your eyes to look at. I could be wrong, but I almost thought it was following the man you're asking about."

Now I bet I know what you're thinking, Senator Gwendy, because I'm thinking the same: it's a great big damn bust-out-crying shame that there was no surveillance footage of that accident . . . if it was an accident. I would just about love to know if the car that mowed down your husband and left him dead in the street was an old green Chrysler, big as a boat.

Only that doesn't seem right. Didn't someone call her and say her husband had been hit by some other kind of car? And of a different color? Gwendy thinks so, but she can no longer trust her memory. She isn't even sure there *was* a call. At least she can still read, so she finishes Norris's email.

That's all I have, and I think it's all I'm going to get. That's a strange town, and I could live just as long and die just as happy if I never set foot inside the Derry city limits again. I'll keep digging if you want me to, but I honestly don't think there's more to find out. I hope you're not upset I started in the first place. I meant well. In the meantime, safe travels up there. I respect your courage, but all I can say otherwise is better you than me.

Your friend,
Norris

Gwendy can hear Norris's voice—surprisingly deep for a man of his slender build—as she reads the email for a second time. When she's finished, she just sits there staring at the iPad screen, her eyes gradually losing focus. The good feelings she's been reveling in for the past couple of hours have vanished and been replaced by . . . she doesn't exactly know what. *Shock? Confusion? Fear?* Yes, all of those things. Confusion she's used to since her mind started to go. The others, less so.

"Save my seat," she says to no one in particular. "I'm off to use the ladies'." She unbuckles her safety harness and swims her way down to the common area on level four. *What in the world were you up to, Ryan?*

The shiny white lavatory door is closed, and once again Gwendy is reminded of the sterile morgue lockers she's seen so often on television. The panel above the latch reads AVAILABLE. Unsure if she really needs to pee or if she's simply going through the motions, Gwendy reaches for the door. Before she can open it, someone grasps her shoulder from behind.

She lets out a squeak and spins around, arms flailing. Gareth Winston is floating a foot or so off the ground, a startled look on his face.

"Jumping Jesus, Winston! Don't ever sneak up on me like that again!"

"Sorry," he says, drifting backward. He doesn't look particularly sorry. "I didn't mean to scare you. I usually make a lot of noise when I come into a room. I'm kinda clumsy that way." He shrugs his ample shoulders. "But I'm as light as a feather up here. It takes some getting used to."

"It certainly does," Gwendy says.

"Anyway, I just wanted to apologize for giving you a hard time before. It's none of my business what's in that case of yours and I shouldn't have said what I said."

471

Gwendy can't believe her ears. Not that long ago she'd questioned whether the phrase *thank you* existed in Gareth Winston's vocabulary. She would have bet her last dollar that the words *I apologize* did not. She's pleasantly surprised to find that she's mistaken. "Apology accepted."

"When you have as much money as I do, you sometimes fall into bad habits, like always thinking you should get your way. I'm working on it."

"I know quite a few people in Washington, D.C., who could use some help with that. And they don't have a fraction of your bank account."

Winston laughs. "Well, thanks for accepting my apology. I'll let you get on with your . . ." He gestures at the lavatory door. ". . . you know."

Gwendy offers him a genuine smile—she could get used to this new and improved Gareth Winston—and extends her hand. "Thank you for being so gracious."

Winston reaches out and takes it.

Suddenly Winston appears very clear to her, very *bright* and in focus, almost as if he's somehow lit from within, and everything else around him falls away. Thinking about it later, she'll be reminded of a moment from the second time she had the button box in her possession, when she stepped inside the mind of a madman the Castle Rock newspaper called The Tooth Fairy. And, of course, when her old friend Charlotte Morgan knew she was thinking of the Great Pyramid.

Although Gareth Winston is still smiling, he's not smiling inside. He's never smiling inside. But he is *in love. The man he's in love with is sitting behind the wheel of a car. Gareth is in the passenger seat, looking at him. It may be impolite to stare, but*

Gareth can't tear his eyes away from that face. Gareth thinks it's the face of a blond angel. He thinks he would give away everything he owns if the blond angel allowed him just one kiss.

Only in this flash—it lasts maybe two seconds, four at most—Gwendy sees the driver as he really is. His real face is old, haggard, and rotting from the inside out. His eyes are milky with cataracts. His lower lip has lost all its tension and sags away from blackening teeth. She has a terrible premonition that Richard Farris will look this way before too long.

The car is big. And old. The acre of hood is a weirdly vibrant green that hurts her eyes to look at. The word on the oversized steering wheel—

Winston jerks back, breaking their grip. His eyes are wide in their pockets of fat. "Jesus, woman!" No humble I'm-sorry in that voice now. He sounds pissed off. And scared. "What was *that*?"

"I don't know," Gwendy says. The vision is already fading. If she can't get to her little notebook soon, it will be entirely gone, like a dream ten minutes after waking. "Static electricity, I guess."

Dr. Dale Glen goes floating by, peering at something on his iPad. "Very likely. It's common up here." He says it without looking up from whatever he's reading.

"Whew, it was strong, whatever it was," Winston says, and manages a fake comic-book laugh: *Ha! Ha!* "You'll have to excuse me, Senator. I have some emails I need to answer."

Off he goes, leaving Gwendy by the lavatory door. She has to try twice to unlatch it. Adesh floats by and asks if she's okay. She doesn't say anything—isn't sure she can—but nods, her hair floating above her head like seaweed. She finally opens the door and pulls herself inside. She fumbles for the button that will light the IN USE panel on the outside (there are no locks in the common area, a safety precaution in case someone has a medical emergency) and tries to raise the lid on the toilet. It won't come. A red panel lights up, saying PRESSURIZE.

Right, almost forgot (now she forgets so much). She thumbs the button to the right of the toilet and the red light goes out. There's a low humming as the toilet does whatever it's supposed to do so she can lift the lid without yanking all of the air in the tiny capsule first into the bowl and then into space. It occurs to her that if Kathy is up front in the control area, she will have seen the warning light blink on and then off. And if she's not there, Sam Drinkwater or Dave Graves probably is. She hopes they'll just shrug it off. Probably they will, but it's not good. Forgetting such elementary things from their training sessions is definitely NG.

Gwendy lowers her coverall, sits, and turns the proper dial to its lowest setting. She feels a gentle sucking sensation that means her pee will go down instead of just floating around under her butt in globules. She lowers her face into her hands as she urinates. Something just happened when she took Gareth Winston's hand. Something important. Something about a car. Or two cars, of different colors? Possibly something about Ryan as well, but probably not; probably she's mixing up Norris's communique with what just happened when she took Gareth Winston's hand.

Whatever it was, it's gone.

Goddamn what's happening to me, Gwendy thinks. *Goddamn it to hell.*

She might be able to get it back if she eats one of the chocolates, and it's a tempting idea, but she must not. Even one was dangerous, and it probably doesn't matter.

Does it?

23

THE CREW AND PASSENGERS of Eagle Heavy have seen the MF space station on each of their last six orbits. Because each of these orbits varies slightly, making a fan shape on the computer screens, Many Flags sometimes looks "above" and sometimes "below," but it's always on the starboard side and it's always amazing.

"Looks like the space station in *2001*," Reggie Black comments as they pass on their last non-docking orbit. MF is less than 25 miles away on this one. "Only MF has one ring instead of two."

"And more spokes," Jafari says. The two of them are shoulder to shoulder in front of the porthole, with Gwendy floating above and between them. "I believe that in the movie there were only four spokes."

From the control area Sam Drinkwater says, "MF is very similar to Kubrick's version. You have to remember it's not always art imitating life. Sometimes it's the other way around."

"No idea what that means," Gareth says. He's also looking at the MF station, but since the porthole on the right is taken, he's stuck with his iPad and sounds irritated about it.

"It means that the people who designed the station saw the movie," Sam says. "Maybe as children. To them, this is how space stations are supposed to look."

"Ridiculous," Gareth snaps. "It was built as it was simply because form always follows function. Not because some space architect saw a movie when he was five."

Sam doesn't argue the point, maybe because Gareth is the paying passenger (in certain confidential preflight files, Gwendy has seen Gareth—and herself—referred to as "the geese," an old airline term for passengers). Or maybe Sam's just bored with the subject. Either way, Gwendy thinks he's right. When looking at her Apple Watch, she often thinks that some gearhead designer was enchanted by Dick Tracy's wrist radio when he or she was a kid.

In any case, the MF station is huge. The actual specs have left her mind, but she does remember that the end-lessly curving outer corridor circling its rim is two and a half miles in length. *Even with the Great Pyramid gone*, she thinks, *there are still seven wonders in the world.* Except the new seventh is actually *above* the world. And for the next nineteen days, it's going to be their home. Assuming the next couple of hours go well, that is; docking is the most delicate and dangerous part of the entire mission, even more dangerous than their eventual landing on a floating pad off Malta.

Kathy Lundgren comes on the general comm and tells them to don their pressure suits. For a moment Gwendy is bewildered. She knows what the suit is, of course she does; the question is where did she put it?

She sees Adesh and Jafari pulling their storage cases from beneath their seats and almost slaps her forehead. *Duh. Get it together, Gwendy.* Is her memory worse since the last chocolate wore off? She thinks it probably is. The box always exacts a price.

She gets her suit out and slips into it. For a moment

she's distracted by the portside porthole. Did a bird just fly by out there? On the way to the feeder by the picnic table in their—

"Zip up, Senator Gwendy," Dale Glen says, pointing at her open suit.

"Yes. I was just thinking about . . ." Is she going to tell him she thought a bird just flew past, 260 miles above the earth? Or that for just a moment she lost her place in time? "It doesn't matter."

She zips her suit and gets her helmet on and locked, putting her increasingly unreliable mind on hold and letting muscle memory take over. *Click, click, snap,* and done. *Easy as pie,* she tells herself, and connects to her iPad and the screens ahead of her seat. At first there's nothing to see in the forward view, and then that huge and improbable wheel comes over the rim of the earth. It's a majestic, almost heart-stopping sight, revolving slowly and revealing the flags of the sixty-one nations that took part and have the right—theoretically, at least—to use it. *All it needs,* she thinks, *is the soundtrack music from* 2001. *Thus Spake . . . somebody. Can't remember, just that it starts with a Z.*

In the center is a white bubble containing the telescopic equipment Jafari Bankole probably can't wait to get his hands on. Above the bubble is something that looks like a stainless-steel masthead topped with a gray cup lined with glittering gold mesh. It is sending messages to the stars . . . and hoping for a response.

Kathy Lundgren: "Mission Control, are we go for docking?"

Eileen Braddock: "Go for dock, Eagle Heavy, we are green across the board."

David Graves: "Visors down, campers. We've got . . ."

"Seventeen minutes," Kathy finishes. "Crew, roger your visors."

They do.

"Give it to Becky," Eileen says.

"Giving it to Becky, roger," Kathy replies. "No commands, all computer. What do you say, Becky?"

"That I have the bus," the voice of Becky the computer replies.

Dave says, "And what kind of bus is it, Becky?"

"It is a magic bus," Becky says, and actually plays a few bars of the Who song.

"This hardly seems the time for stupid computer tricks," Gareth says. He sounds wound up and pissed off, that amiable tone of voice from earlier outside of the lavatory a distant memory. "Next you'll be asking it to tell knock-knock jokes while our lives are at risk!"

"No one's life is at risk," Kathy says. "This is a walk in the park."

If only, Gwendy thinks.

Now there's a touch of gravity again as Becky fires the aiming rockets in small, feathery bursts.

"Ops, do you want to go around another couple of times?" Eileen asks. "Sunset in twenty minutes, your location."

"Negative, Ground, all good with us, and Becky can see in the dark."

But Kathy and Sam can't, Gwendy thinks, *and computer-directed docking only works if Becky's programming is flawless, and if there's no dreaded holy-shit moment.*

"Roger, Eagle Heavy." This time it's a male voice, Eileen's superior, not a rocket jockey but some political appointee. Gwendy should be able to remember his name—she was the one who appointed him, for Christ's sake—but she can't. She tries some of Dr. Ambrose's tricks, but none of them work.

A sudden brilliant thought strokes across her mind, as scary as a stroke of lightning hitting just feet away: *Where is the button box?* Is it in her tiny capsule of a cabin, or the storage compartment beneath her seat? Oh God, is it sitting home on the high shelf in the garage? What if she forgot to bring it?

She has enough wit to change her comm to private and then select the Bug Man's setting on her iPad. "Adesh, do you know what I did with the steel case I brought on board? The one with—"

"Yes, the one with CLASSIFIED stamped on it." He points down. She looks and sees it's beneath her leg, just as it was on lift-off.

"Thank you," she says. "Forgive the flightiness. I'm a little nervous about the docking."

"Totally understood." He smiles at her through his visor, but there's no smile in his eyes. What she sees there is consideration. Maybe evaluation. She doesn't like it. *They must not know what's wrong with me until the mission is accomplished. After that it won't matter* what *they know.*

There's a thud from above them as Eagle Heavy's docking hatch slides open on its servomotors.

"IDA is in place and green across the board," Becky says. Gwendy has no trouble with that. IDA is the International Docking Adapter, so called because every nation that can send rockets to MF uses the same system. She can remember that, but for the time being her own middle name escapes her.

"Locking hinges in place," Becky says.

491

The cabin rocks port; rocks starboard; comes steady. Little jerks accompany each movement, as if an inexperienced driver is goosing the gas pedal, releasing it, then goosing it again. A metaphor Gwendy could have done without.

"Ten meters," Becky says.

All at once a huge shadow darkens the cabin, causing the interior lights to come on. Gwendy cranes her neck and sees they are passing under one of the MF station's huge spokes, clearing it by what looks like only feet. She can make out every seal and rivet.

"Jesus, too close!" Gareth cries. "Too fucking cl—"

Then his voice is gone. Someone—probably Dave Graves—has cut him out of the general comm. *Which is a good thing*, Gwendy thinks. *No one needs to listen to him bellow.* Nevertheless, she braces herself for a collision that seems almost inevitable. A gloved hand takes hers. It's Jaff. She turns to him and winks. He looks scared to death, but he manages to wink back.

"Five meters," Becky says.

Seconds later there's a bump—not hard but plenty solid. Gwendy has a moment of vertigo and realizes her body hasn't been fully aware of Eagle Heavy's constant motion until it stopped.

"Soft capture complete," Becky says.

Kathy relays that to the ground, and Gwendy hears applause. Beside *his* porthole, Gareth looks bewildered. He can't hear what's happening.

Gwendy selects OPS 1 on her iPad and says, "Kathy, loop Gareth in. I think he'll be okay now, and he should hear everyone in the down-below is happy."

"Roger that."

Becky tells them to stand by for final docking. There are more thuds, harder this time, as the twelve latches engage, two by two.

"Docking sequence is complete," Becky says.

"Good job, Beckster," Dave says.

"Always glad to help," Becky says. "Shall I handle the hatch opening?"

"I'll do that," Kathy says. "Stand down, Becky."

"Standing down."

Sam Drinkwater says, "The hard line is connected. You're go for hatch opening, Kath."

Kathy turns in her seat. "Everyone pressurized? Let me hear your roger."

They give it. Gwendy thinks the rich guy—name momentarily escapes her—looks grumpy but relieved.

Kathy says, "Mission Control, all valves are closed and I'm opening the hatch."

"Roger, Eagle Heavy. You guys have a great time and don't do anything I wouldn't do."

"That gives us a lot of latitude," Kathy says. "We'll talk to you once we're on board Many Flags. Thanks to everyone in the down-below. This is Eagle, over and out."

24

ONE BY ONE THEY float through the hatch, then up the hard line with its blue foam sides, and finally into Many Flags. Kathy Lundgren is first, Gareth Winston last. Gwendy's between Reggie Black, the physicist, and Adesh, aka Bug Man.

Gwendy feels a slight tug of gravity as she enters. Her mind is currently as clear as a bell, and she remembers that the station's slow spin has returned a fraction of her weight. She and the other newbies look around, bouncing slowly up and down: touch and go, touch and go.

Her first thought is that USA Control would look almost like a hotel lobby if the walls weren't lined with equipment, monitors, and a nightmare spaghetti of cords and wires. And if the walls weren't padded, of course. Her second thought is that it's *big*. After two days in Eagle Heavy, the room looks enormous. The ceiling is at least four feet over her head, and one of the walls isn't a wall at all but a long, gracefully curving window that gives a view of pure black punched through with stars.

"Okay to ditch the outerwear, guys," Sam says. "Stow 'em there."

He points to lockers along one wall. There are at least two dozen. Ten have lighted panels with the names of the Eagle Heavy crew. Gwendy bounce-floats to hers and opens it. There's a hook for her suit and a magnetized shelf for her helmet. She's carrying the steel box with **CLASSIFIED MATERIAL** stamped on it, and it would stick to the shelf, but she doesn't want to leave it there. Not with Gareth's locker right next to hers. She sees him watching her, and she doubts it's with admiration for her butt in the red Eagle coverall she's wearing.

"Crew to me for a minute," Kathy says. "Gather 'round."

Gwendy closes her locker and joins the others, holding the steel box by its handle. It makes her think of the lunch box she carried to Castle Rock Elementary long, long ago.

"Air smells better, don't you think?" Bern Stapleton asks her.

"God, yes. Sweeter and fresher."

Also, there's instrumental music drifting down from the overhead speakers. Maybe Seals and Crofts, maybe Simon and Garfunkel. *Like in a mall or a supermarket*, Gwendy thinks. She's aware of something else, too. Below the humming of the monitors and equipment, there's a faint *creaking* sound, almost like an old wooden ship in a moderate wind.

That's a little creepy, she thinks. Then: *Check that, it's a lot creepy. Like a haunted house in a movie. Or a haunted hotel.* Maybe that feeling is stupid, but maybe it's valid. The MF station is huge, and except for them and half a dozen Chinese doing God knows what, it's deserted.

They circle Kathy, rising and falling, touching and going.

"You know most of this from preflight orientation, but protocol demands I give you a quick refresher upon entry to the station. First, accommodations."

She points at the doors marked SPOKE 1, SPOKE 2, and SPOKE 3.

485

"Spoke 1 is flight crew: me, Sam, Dave. Spoke 2 is science crew: Reggie, Jafari, Bern, and Adesh. Spoke 3 belongs to our passengers, Gwendy and Gareth, plus Dr. Glen. I think you newbies are going to be delighted by what you find. Someday not far in the future, TetCorp hopes those rooms and many others like them will be occupied by paying guests. Gwendy and Gareth, you have actual suites. Only a bedroom, sitting room, and a small bathroom, but quite luxy."

"Don't tell the taxpayers," Gwendy stage-whispers. Most of them laugh. Gareth Winston does not, perhaps because the current administration has landed him in the forty-five percent tax bracket. Or maybe he's just impatient with the repetition.

"You'll have to bring your own gear up from the Eagle; all the bellmen up here are on strike."

There's more laughter, and once again Gareth doesn't join in. Gwendy wonders when he last had to carry his own luggage. Maybe when he moved into a college dorm. Maybe never.

"I'll cut the rest of the lecture short, if you promise not to tell Mission Control, but I urge you to review the orientation video on your tablet again. It will guide you around the parts of the station available to us . . . which in this extraordinary circumstance is almost all of it. Jaff, you'll want to visit the observatory and power up what needs to be powered up so you can start sending photos back to Earth. I believe your main interest will be Mars."

"Correctamundo," Jafari says.

"Gwendy, you'll want to check out the weather deck. It's small, but it has tons of equipment and its own telescope. Bern, your lab is next to Adesh's bug suite in Spoke 5."

Gareth interrupts. "What happened to cutting this short? I'd like to get settled in."

Kathy registers momentary irritation at this rudeness, but a moment later it's gone. Gareth is important to TetCorp's plans for tourist travel above the earth and therefore must be cosseted. *Up to a point*, Gwendy thinks. *If he has to be busted on his behavior, I think I can be the bad guy.* She certainly busted the man she replaced in the Senate on *his* behavior, and on statewide TV. She just can't remember his name at present. She's never known such feelings of helplessness.

"I suggest we all settle in," Kathy says. "After one more thing."

Gareth gives a long-suffering sigh. But really, what does he have to do? It's not like he has a job up here, and Gwendy certainly doesn't intend to ask for his help on the weather deck.

"You all have the run of the place, except for Spoke 9. That one is currently Chinese territory." She points to an info panel below the big window, where there are eight green lights and one red one. "Should they unlock—which they do sometimes, to use the exercise room and the International Room, where they play video games and use the canteen machines—you will still stay clear. They are not particularly hospitable. But all spokes lead to the outer rim and that's common territory. I always enjoy a run there. In this gravity, which we call lo-no, I can do a mile in just over two minutes."

"*Please?*" Gareth says, and Gwendy knows what he

487

sounds like: a rich type A passenger at the end of a long flight, dismissing the flight crew the minute the plane touches down. Sometimes Gareth can be friendly, even charming, but she thinks that's just thin paint over a man who expects to be obeyed and kowtowed to. "How about it, Kathy?"

"Big Zoom meeting to get to?" Bern asks mildly.

"None of your affair, Plant Man," Gareth says.

"Go," Kathy says, making an amiable shooing gesture. "Get settled. My advice: take today to explore the station before starting whatever job you came here to do."

Most of them head back down into the Eagle, Gareth Winston in the lead. Gwendy lingers, then makes her slow way to Kathy, who is talking with Dr. Glen. "Got time for a question?" Gwendy asks.

"Of course. How can I help?"

Dale Glen bounces his way over to the window and stands looking out into the infinite blackness, hands clasped behind his back. The others have gone.

"My room," Gwendy says. She can't bring herself to call it a suite. "Does the door lock?"

"None of them do, but your accommodation comes with a security safe, very much like the kind they have in hotel rooms. It *is* sort of a hotel room, actually." She looks meaningfully at the steel box Gwendy's carrying. "You punch in a four-digit combo. Your special cargo should fit quite nicely, Senator."

She's speaking officially because this is official business, Gwendy thinks. "Thank you. That's something of a relief." She glances toward Dr. Glen. He's at a safe distance, but she still lowers her voice. "Mr. Winston—Gareth—has shown . . . um . . . an interest."

"Perhaps he was interested in this, as well." She reaches into the elasticized waist pocket of her jumper. What she brings out, to Gwendy's horror, is her red notebook. The one where she keeps all the things she doesn't want to forget, including the code that opens the CLASSIFIED box.

"He said your cabin door was ajar and he found it floating in the corridor. That must have been the case, because he wouldn't have any reason to be snooping in your cabin, would he?"

"Of course not," Gwendy says, taking the notebook and stowing it in her own pocket. She feels cold all over. "Thank you."

Kathy takes Gwendy by the shoulder. "*Do* you think he was snooping? Because I'd have to take that rather seriously, Mr. Moneybags or not."

The hell of it is, Gwendy doesn't know. She doesn't *think* she left the notebook unsecured, she doesn't *think* she left the door of her cabin unlatched, so it could have floated out in the constant circulation of the air purifiers . . . but she can't be sure.

"No," she says. "Probably not. Kathy . . . you have the Pocket Rocket, correct? It's on board?"

"Yes. Although what it's for is apparently above my pay grade."

"And I'm go for a spacewalk on Day 7?"

Kathy doesn't reply at first. She looks uncomfortable. "That's the plan, but plans sometimes change. Several people have been talking to me, including—"

"Including me," Dr. Glen says. He has rejoined them without Gwendy noticing, and now he asks the very question she's been dreading. "Senator, is there anything you want to tell us?"

25

GWENDY GAVE UP TRYING to believe there was nothing wrong with her on a spring day in 2024, about four months after her meeting with Charlotte Morgan. It was a piddling seven-hundred-word essay that did it. The kind of thing she should have been able to bang out in an hour, nothing but fluff and puff, but it brought down her wall of denial as surely as the magic box's red button had brought down the Great Pyramid of Giza.

The *Washington Post* ran an occasional feature called My Five, in which various famous people wrote about five great (or simply overlooked) things in their home states. John Cusack wrote about stuff in his native Illinois. The mystery writer Laura Lippman wrote about Miss Shirley's Cafe in Baltimore and the swimming hole at Kilgore Falls. Gwendy, of course, was asked to write a My Five about Maine. She was actually looking forward to the assignment when she sat down in the small office of her Washington, D.C., townhouse. Going back to her home state was always a pleasure, even if the trip was only mental.

She wrote about Thunder Hole in Bar Harbor, the Maine Discovery Museum in Bangor, the lighthouse on Pemaquid Point, and the Farnsworth Art Museum. She paused then, thinking she wanted to finish with something that was just plain fun. She sat tapping her nose with the eraser of a pencil from her jar—a habit that went back to childhood—until it came to her. Simones', of course.

She tossed the pencil back in its jar and typed: *My fifth choice is in Lewiston, about 20 miles up the road from my hometown of Castle Rock. Turn right off Lisbon Street onto Chestnut, find a parking space (good luck!), and step into Simones'. It's just a little storefront restaurant, but the smell is heaven. The specialty of the house is crankshafts.*

Here she stopped, staring at the screen. Crankshafts? In a restaurant? What was she thinking?

I wasn't thinking. I was on autopilot and had a senior moment, that's all.

Only it wasn't a senior moment, it was a Brain Freeze, and she'd been having a lot of them lately—walking around looking for her car keys while she had them in her hand, deciding to throw a frozen dinner in the microwave for lunch and finding herself looking for the fridge in the living room, more than once getting up from a nap when she didn't remember lying down. And after missing a couple of committee meetings and one roll-call vote (not important, thank God), she was depending more and more on her assistant, Annmarie Briggs, to keep her apprised of her schedule, a thing she had always taken care of herself. *Forget a roll-call?* the old Gwendy would have said. *Never in this life!*

And now this, staring back at her from the screen of her Mac: *The specialty of the house is crankshafts.*

She deleted the sentence and wrote, *You'll never have a better burgomeister.*

Gwendy looked at this and put a hand to her forehead. She felt hot to herself. Hot and strange. A month before, back home in Castle Rock for the weekend, she had gotten into the car with some specific destination in mind and had found herself at the Rumford Rock 'N Bowl instead, with no idea of what she had set out to do. She'd told herself what the hell, a beautiful day for a drive, and laughed it off.

She wasn't laughing now.

What *was* the specialty of the house at Simones'? A frightening spiral of words cascaded through her mind: catgut, dollface, candlewax, mortarboard.

Mortarboard, that's it! She typed it, but it didn't look quite right.

Annmarie poked her head in. "Going to Starbucks, Senator—want anything?"

"No, but I'm stuck here. What are those things you eat?"

Annmarie frowned. "Have to be a bit more specific, boss."

"They come in bread thingies." Gwendy gestured with her hands. "Red and tasty. You eat them with mutchup at picnics and such. I can't think of the word."

The corners of Annmarie's mouth turned up, forming dimples. The expression of someone waiting for the punchline of a joke. "Uh . . . hotdogs?"

"*Hotdogs!*" Gwendy exclaimed, and actually pumped a fist in the air. "Right, right, of cross it is, of cross!"

Annmarie's incipient smile was gone. "Boss? Gwendy? Are you feeling okay?"

"Yes," Gwendy said, but she wasn't. "I meant of cross, not of cross. Bring me a regular black, will you?"

"Sure," Annmarie said, and left . . . but not before giving Gwendy a final puzzled glance over her shoulder.

Alone again, Gwendy stared at the screen. The word

Annmarie had given her was gone, sliding through her fingers like a small slippery fish. She no longer wanted to write the goddamn essay. And she hadn't meant to say "of cross" but "of course."

"Of cross, of course, of course, of cross," she murmured. She began to cry. "Dear God, what's wrong with me?"

Only she knew, of cross she did. She even knew when it had started: after pushing the red button to give Charlotte Morgan a demonstration of how dangerous the button box was, and how important it was for the two of them to keep it a dead secret between them until it could be disposed of in the ultimate dumping ground.

But Charlotte couldn't know about this.

No one could.

26

Day 2 on Many Flags.

The crew members have started doing their various jobs, with the exception of Gareth Winston, who has no assigned job. There are many wonders to explore in Many Flags, but so far as Gwendy can tell, the billionaire has spent most of the day in his suite. *Like Achilles, brooding in his tent*, Gwendy thinks. She can relate, because she has spent a certain amount of brooding-time herself since Dr. Glen asked his question. Or rather detonated it in her face.

Unlike Gareth, Gwendy has been plenty occupied. She made a brief trip to the weather deck, checking out the various equipment there, and gaping at the earth below her, watching as darkness moved smoothly over North and South America (blue and violet buttons on the button box). She participated in a Health and Human Services Committee meeting via Zoom. She talked about the importance of space exploration to a class of fifth graders in Boise who had won the videoconference with her in some kind of competition (or maybe it was a lottery). She thinks all those things went okay, but the pure hell of it is she can no longer be sure. She swallowed two Tylenol for a stress headache, but she knows it will take more than Tylenol to get her through what comes next.

They all knew or suspected, it seemed. Everyone on board.

Knew what? Suspected what? Why, that Senator Gwendolyn Peterson had slipped a cog or maybe even two. Was a pack of fries short of a Happy Meal. A beer short of a six-pack. That the ever-lovin' *cheese* had started to slip off her ever-lovin' *cracker*. And because they were 260 miles above the earth, with a U.S. senator in charge of some secret mission of A1A importance, Kathy and Dr. Glen had confronted her. They didn't know what was in her steel box, but they *did* know that Gwendy was slated for a spacewalk on Day 7, and when she went out she would be in possession of a small rocket, six feet long and four feet in diameter. No more than a drone, really, only it was pow-ered by a tiny nuclear engine that could keep it driving onward and outward for perhaps as long as two hundred years. After that it would continue forever on pure inertia.

That nuclear power plant, although no bigger than a model train engine, was powerful. If the operator—Gwendy—fucked up the initiation sequence while she was floating around out there, it could either blow a hole in the MF station or possibly destabilize it, sending it either into deep space or plunging into Earth's atmosphere, where it would burn up. Not that Gwendy would know; she'd be incinerated in the first two seconds.

Kathy had been as delicate as she could be. "I wouldn't feel comfortable sending you out there, even with a buddy, if I felt you were suffering some mental debility."

Dr. Glen was blunter, and she had to respect him for that. "Senator, do you suspect you might be suffering from early-onset Alzheimer's Disease? I hate to ask the question, but under the circumstances I feel I have to."

Gwendy had known it might come to this, and had worked out her story with Dr. Ambrose, who had agreed

495

to help her with only the greatest reluctance. They both understood that the best story was one that incorporated as much of the truth as possible. In accordance with that, she told Kathy and Doc Glen that because she had been entrusted with something of gravest importance to the entire world, she'd been under severe stress for *two freaking years*, she hadn't been sleeping well, and that was why she sometimes forgot things. Kathy readily admitted that ninety-five percent of the time Gwendy had handled herself up to or above the accepted standard.

"But we're in space. Things can go wrong. We don't talk about it when we do our PR stuff, but everyone knows it. Even Gareth knows it, which is why he's prepared to perform certain tasks in an emergency situation. Ninety-five percent isn't good enough. It's got to be one hundred."

"I'm fine," Gwendy protested. "Good to go."

"Then you won't mind taking a test, will you?" Doc Glen said. "Just to ease our minds before we send you into space with an important something we don't know about and a powerful nuclear device that we do."

"All right, fine," Gwendy said. Because really, what else *could* she say? Ever since Richard Farris had shown up for the third time, she had felt like a rat in an ever-narrowing corridor, one that had no exit. *It's a suicide mission*, she'd told Farris that night on the back porch, *and you know it.*

The test had been set for 1700 hours, and at this moment it was 1640. Time to get ready.

Which meant it was time to take the button box out of the safe.

27

WHILE SERVING IN THE U.S. House of Representatives, Gwendy had had good connections. As a member of the Senate, she had even better ones, and she never needed one more than after her latest Brain Freeze. *The specialty of the house is crankshafts, for Christ's sake.* She thought of calling Charlotte Morgan, then rejected the idea out of hand. Charlotte was a spook, after all. She might decide that letting Gwendy hold on to the button box was too great a risk. Gwendy knew that letting anyone else hold on to it would be an even greater one.

After some thought she called one of her new friends: Mike DeWine at the NSA. She told him she needed to make an appointment with a psychiatrist who was completely trustworthy. She asked if Mike knew such a person, knowing he would; the NSA kept a close watch on any developing mental problems in its staff. Secrets must be kept.

"Losing your grip, Senator?" Mike asked amiably.

Gwendy laughed cheerily, as if that wasn't exactly what she was afraid of. "Nope, my marbles are all present and accounted for. I'm involved in a review of the NDS—that's for your ears only, Mike—and I have some very delicate questions."

NDS stood for National Defense System, and that was

enough for Mike. No one likes the idea of mentally unstable people in charge of the nuclear arsenal.

"Is there a problem I should know about?"

"Not at present. I'm being proactive."

"Good to know. There's a guy . . . hold on a sec, the name escapes me . . ."

Join the club, Gwendy thought, and couldn't help smiling. Losing one's shit really did have its funny side, she supposed. Or would, if a box that could destroy the world wasn't involved.

"Okay, here it is. Norman Ambrose is our top go-to shrink. He's on Michigan Avenue." Gwendy wrote down the address, plus Ambrose's office number and personal cell. *Thank God for NSA info*, Gwendy thought. "He's probably booked into the twenty-third century, but I think you'll be able to jump the line. Being a United States senator and all."

Gwendy was able to jump it and was sitting in Dr. Ambrose's office the following afternoon. After listening to him reiterate his promise of absolute confidentiality, she took a deep breath and told him she was afraid she was suffering from early-onset Alzheimer's or dementia. She told him that if it was true, no one could know until she completed a certain high-priority task.

"How high?" Ambrose asked.

"The highest, but that's all I can say. It may be a year before I can do the job I need to do. More likely two. It might even be three, but God, I hope not."

"May I assume that if certain people discovered your condition—if it indeed exists—this job would be taken from you?"

Gwendy gave him a bleak smile. "That can't happen. If anyone tried, it would be a disaster."

"Senator—"

"Gwendy. Please. In here I'm Gwendy."

"All right, Gwendy. Is there a history of Alzheimer's or dementia in your family?"

"Not really. My Aunt Felicia went gaga, but she was in her late nineties."

"Uh-huh, good. And you lost your husband fairly recently?"

"Yes."

"I'm very sorry for your loss. Added to that you have all the responsibilities of a new senator to deal with. You may be suffering from simple stress."

"There's no blood test for Alzheimer's, is there?"

"Unfortunately, no. The only way we can confirm the diagnosis—other than by observing the constant deterioration of the patient's mental faculties—is by autopsy after death. There's a written test that is a good marker, however."

"I should take it."

"I think that's a good idea. In the meantime, can I suggest a practical way of dealing with these Brain Freezes, as you call them?"

"God, yes! I'd do enemas three times a day if I thought it would help!"

Dr. Ambrose smiled. "No enemas, just a process of association, and you may have almost come to it on your own." He had a yellow legal pad on his lap. Now he turned back a page and studied the notes he'd made during her story. "When writing about this little restaurant, Simones',

PARK
FUN
AMUSEMENT PARK
RIDES
FERRIS
FARRIS!

you found you were unable to remember a certain word. Do you remember it now?"

"Sure. Hotdogs."

"But you wrote—?"

"Crankshafts," Gwendy said, and felt herself blush.

"You knew it was wrong, so you tried again. Do you recall your second stab at it?"

Gwendy was having a clear day, not even a trace of mental fog, and she remembered at once. "Burgomeister." Her blush deepened. "I wrote 'You'll never have a better burgomeister.' Stupid, right?"

"I don't think so." Ambrose leaned forward. "What usually goes with hotdogs at a picnic or a barbecue, Gwendy?"

She understood at once. "Hamburgers!"

"I think your mind was trying to form a chain of connections that would lead you back to the word you were looking for. Crankshafts are straight cylinders. So are hotdogs. Burgomeisters are a step closer. I believe if you'd taken your eyes from the screen with your essay on it, and relaxed your mind, you would have found the word."

"Can I train myself to do that?"

"Yes." He said it without hesitation. "This is a trainable skill. Tell me, do you have a pet?"

"No. My father does. A troublesome old dachshund."

"What is the troublesome dachshund's name?"

Gwendy opened her mouth, came up blank, and closed it again.

"Fucked if I can remember. Sorry, that just slipped out. This thing . . . it's infuriating."

Ambrose smiled. "Quite all right. Can you associate your way to it? Look up at the ceiling. Let your mind run

501

in neutral. This is a process we teach to patients in the early stages of Alzheimer's, but also to recovering stroke victims. Don't push. Don't *hunt*. Your mind knows what you want, but it needs to take a detour, and detours take time."

Gwendy looked up at the ceiling. She thought about her father's smile, so warm and welcoming . . . she thought about the maroon sweater he always wore when the weather turned cold . . . watching musicals with him and Mom on TV because they loved them and would sing along . . . Gwendy watching and singing along with them . . . *West Side Story* was her favorite, but her father's was that one with Ben Vereen. That one was—

"His dachshund is Pippa. My dad named her after his favorite musical. *Pippin*."

Ambrose nodded. "You see how it works?"

Gwendy began to cry, which didn't discommode Ambrose in the slightest. He just handed her a box of Kleenex. She supposed tears in this office were pretty common.

"Will it always work?"

Ambrose grinned, making him look boyish. "Does anything?"

Gwendy laughed shakily. "I suppose not."

"Depending on how your test comes out, Gwendy— we'll do that today, as your situation is clearly difficult—I may prescribe drugs that might slow the progression of your illness. Which, I want to emphasize, is not yet proven. At this point simple stress seems more likely to me."

You may be a great headshrinker, but I don't think you're much of a liar, Gwendy thought. *You've seen all these symptoms before. It's not, as they say, your first rodeo.*

"What drugs?"

"Aricept is my go-to. Exelon sometimes works well in the early stages. But all that is putting the cart before the horse. We need to see how you do on the mini-cog. Come back at five this afternoon, if your schedule permits."

"It does." Gwendy had cleared the day for Ambrose.

"In the meantime, get something to eat and help yourself to a caffeine drink. Coffee, soda, even a Monster Energy."

"Thank you, Dr. Ambrose."

"You're very welcome, Senator."

"Gwendy, remember?"

"Yes. Gwendy. And I don't suppose you can tell me anything about this job that's so important?"

She gave him a level look—her Senator Peterson look. "You wouldn't want to know, Dr. Ambrose. Believe me."

She donned a headscarf and dark glasses and slipped into a nearby Burger King where she ordered a Whopper with cheese and a large order of fries, and slurped a large Coke until the straw crackled in the bottom of the cup. Her first bite of the Whopper made her realize that she was ravenous. She supposed relief spurred appetite. And sharing the burden, of course. Now she had a strategy to cope with the Brain Freezes, and she could hope that Ambrose was right and it was only stress. The test—what Ambrose had called a mini-cog—might confirm that.

She laughed when Ambrose began asking the questions because they reminded her of the test Donald Trump had boasted about passing. *Easy-peasy*, she thought . . . but by the time she completed it she was no longer laughing. Neither was Ambrose.

She did okay on the season (spring) and the date, but

could not immediately remember what month it was. She was sure she could have used Ambrose's associative method and come up with it if he'd given her time, but he didn't. She was even worse at counting back from a hundred by sevens. She got to ninety-three, then said eighty-five, which was really just a guess. She was able to repeat back *apple-table-penny* five minutes later but found herself completely incapable of spelling *world* backward. There was plenty of stuff she got right—copying a cartoon drawing, folding a sheet of paper in thirds—but there were distressing and inexplicable (to her, at least) failures. When Ambrose asked her to draw a clock face, for instance, she drew an oblong with a curve like a smile beneath it. She showed it to him and said, "I think this might be wrong."

So *much* was wrong.

And the wait for her trip into space stretched out ahead of her, with no firm date set and so many days to struggle through.

But I have to try!

28

AND NOW THE TIME has come to do that.

Gwendy pulls the lever that dispenses the chocolates. Out comes a butterfly with tiny, perfectly scalloped wings. She pops it into her mouth. Warmth spreads throughout her body and lights up her brain. Then, for the first time in her long and complicated history with the button box, she pulls the lever again. For a moment nothing happens and she's afraid the box is refusing her, but then another chocolate comes out. She doesn't bother to examine it, just swallows it down. The world leaps forward into all her senses. The clarity is painful but at the same time wonderful. She can see every grain in the box's mahogany surface. She can hear every creak as the MF station makes its endless journey through space. She can't hear the Chinese in their spoke, but she senses their presence. Some are eating, some are playing a game. Mahjong, perhaps.

She takes a deep breath and can feel it filling her lungs and enriching her blood. The knock at the door sends waves of vibration across the room. *It's a V shape*, Gwendy thinks. *Like birds heading south for the winter.*

"Gwendy?" Kathy asks. "Are you ready?"

"Just a second!" She puts the button box back in its bag and stows it in the closet wall safe, which is hidden behind her spare pressure suit. She thumbs the CLOSE button and hears the lock engage. She checks for her notebook in the pocket of her jumpsuit, then shuts the closet, bounce-walks to the door, and opens it.

"Ready," she says.

29

THERE'S A SMALL CONFERENCE room in Spoke 1, next to the ops room. Present for Gwendy's mental acuity test are Kathy Lundgren, Dr. Glen, and Sam Drinkwater. Sam doesn't know that Gwendy has a special high-priority mission (unless Kathy has told him, that is), but he's going to be her buddy on her Day 7 spacewalk, so Gwendy supposes he has a right to be here. It would be his responsibility, after all, if she became disoriented and freaked out while they were tethered together.

Doc Glen clears his throat. "Gwendy—Senator—I hope you understand that we have to—"

"To take every precaution," she finishes. She knows she sounds impatient. She *is* impatient. No, more than that. She's angry. Not at them, exactly, but at having to be here and having such a terrible responsibility thrust upon her. "I understand. Let's get to it. I have emails to write and weather info to collate."

The others exchange looks. This isn't the smiling, friendly woman they are used to.

"Er . . . fine," Doc Glen says. He powers up his tablet, then takes an envelope from the breast pocket of his coverall. "It won't take long, an hour max. I'll give you a number of questions to answer and certain tasks to perform. Just relax and do the best you can. To begin with . . ."

He opens the envelope. Inside are eight metal squares.

He puts them down in the center of the table on a magnetized rectangle, which he turns to face Gwendy. Words have been printed on the squares in Magic Marker.

go   mother   must   store   the   to   I   for

"Can you arrange these to make a sentence?"

Gwendy moves the words around on the magnetized rectangle with no hesitation. She turns it to face the three crew members—*My judges*, she thinks resentfully—on the other side of the table. "Clever that there's no capital letter," Gwendy says. "Makes it a bit harder. Intentional, I suppose."

They look at how she's arranged the words. "Huh," Sam says. "It's a sentence all right, but not the one I would have made."

"And if there's a handbook that goes with this test," Gwendy says, "it's probably not what the people who made it expected. Which is a bit dumb, if you don't mind me saying. You were expecting 'I must go to the store for mother,' weren't you?"

Sam and Doc nod. Kathy just looks at her with a small smile. Maybe it's admiration, probably it is, but Gwendy doesn't care. They brought her in here like a test animal and expected her to perform—hit the lever and get a piece of kibble. And so she has. Because she has to, and doesn't that just suck?

Gwendy's sentence reads *for mother I must go to the store.*

She says, 'I must go to the store for mother' is the simple way to do it, but simple isn't always best. It's ambiguous. Does it mean 'I have to go there because mother wants pasta and a quart of Ben & Jerry's' or does it mean 'I have to go to the store because mother is there and she

508

needs to be picked up.' Some ambiguity is still there in my sentence, but it's less because 'mother' comes first. My sentence says it's almost certainly an errand." She gives them a hard smile without a shred of good humor in it. "Any questions?"

There are none, and although Doc goes through the rest of his questions and tasks, the test is effectively over with that little lesson in syntax. Gwendy finishes the whole thing in nineteen minutes and stands up, holding the edge of the table to keep her feet from floating off the floor.

"Are you satisfied?"

They look back at her uncomfortably. After a brief silence Kathy says, "You're angry. I get that and I'm sorry, but we're in an environment where there's no room for error. And I think I speak for Sam and Doc when I say you've eased our minds considerably."

"Completely eased mine," Sam says. "I have no hesitation about suiting up with you and going outside."

"I *am* angry," Gwendy says, "but not at you guys. Your jobs are difficult, but so is mine. The difference is that mine is thankless. This damned country is so polarized that forty percent of the electorate in my home state thinks I'm a piece of shit no matter what I do."

She surveys them and yes, she *is* angry at them, at this moment she almost hates them, but it won't do to say so. Still, she has to vent. If she doesn't, she'll explode. Or go back to her room and do something stupid. Something that can't be taken back.

"You haven't lived until you've seen signs saying COMMIE BITCH waving at you from the back of your town hall meetings. On top of that, my husband is dead, half my fucking house burned down, and I had to come in here so you guys could make sure I don't need to be fitted up with Pampers and a drool-cup."

"That's a little heavy," Kathy says mildly.

"Yes, I suppose it is." Gwendy lets out a sigh, thinking, *You want heavy? Try living with what's in my wall safe. That's* really *heavy.* "Can I go now? Got work to do. You guys probably do, too. Sorry about the mouth. It's been building up."

Doc Glen stands up. Floats, actually. He reaches a hand across the table to her. "No need to apologize on my behalf, Gwendy." She's glad he's left her title behind and reverted to her name. "You've got some hard bark on you, and in your job that's a requirement. Get some rest. I can't give you an Ambien, but maybe a glass of warm milk before you turn in will help. Or a melatonin. That I do have."

"Thanks." Gwendy takes his hand. There's no flash, only a sense that he means well. She looks around and forces herself to say it. "Thank you all."

She leaves and returns to her suite in great lolloping leaps, her hands opening and closing. *I could fix this whole problem with the button box*, she's thinking. *And you know what? It would be a pleasure.*

Once inside she opens the closet door, moves the spare pressure suit aside, then makes herself stop. She wants to take the button box out—*it* wants *me to take it out*, she thinks—and in her current state of mind the buttons along the top would look too inviting. She had to eat the chocolates so she could pass their goddamn test, but now she's faced with this *anger*, this *fury*, and it's like a black doorway she dares not go through. What's on the other side is monstrous.

How I hate it, Farris said. *How I* loathe *it.* If she never understood that before, she understands it now. But he said something else, and it resonates in her mind now: *There is simply no one else I trust to do what needs to be done.*

She understands, even in her current state, that if she takes the button box out now, that trust will almost certainly be broken. He gave it to her because she's strong, but there are limits to her strength.

If I have to feel this way, I have to focus it on something other than the box and stay focused until the effect of the chocolates wears off. What?

But with her mind clear, the answer is also clear. She bounces to her desk and powers up her iPad. The emails she sends from her senatorial account are encrypted, and that's a good thing. She writes to Norris Ridgewick.

> *Norris: You said that on your trip to Derry you met with "the local constabulary." The detective in charge of investigating Ryan's death was Ward Mitchell. Did you meet him? And if you did, did you trust him?*

She sends the email to the down-below and walks back and forth through her suite (which doesn't take long), pulling restlessly at her ponytail. She can't seem to sit still, not in her current state. She reaches out for Gareth Winston, like she did for the Chinese in their spoke, and finds him. He is on his computer. Writing an email. She can't see it but she knows that's what it is. There's a word in his mind that she gets clear, although she doesn't know what it means. The word is *sombra.*

Norris may not reply for an hour or more, she thinks, *and Mom used to say a watched pot never boils.*

She decides to walk (maybe even run) the outer rim—anything to burn off this wild and dangerous energy. She puts on shorts and a tee shirt with CASTLE ROCK OLD HOME DAYS on the front, and is just lacing up her sneakers when her laptop chimes with incoming mail. She leaps across the room like Supergirl and settles in front of the screen. The message is brief, to the point, and totally Yankee.

Hey Gwendy,

Met Mitchell, talked to him, wouldn't trust him as far as I could sling a piano. He couldn't wait to get rid of me. Want me to take a trip to Derry and go at him a little harder? Happy to do it. By the way—any idea what got your Ryan haring off to Derry in the first place?

Norris

She wishes she could answer that question, but she can't. Her best guess is that someone told Ryan they had dirt on Magowan, or dirt on her. Either might have gotten him to take a ride north. Did it make any difference? Of course not. No matter what the pretext, Ryan remains dead.

As for sending Norris up to Derry . . . no. Norris isn't the man for that job. She believes the flash she had when she took Gareth's hand was a true insight. She believes that she saw Gareth in one of the two old cars that were in Derry on the day Ryan died. She believes Ryan may have been killed in an effort to derail her senatorial campaign. And she believes that her house was burned after certain men—perhaps driving perfectly maintained old cars—searched it for the button box, came up empty, and reached the logical conclusion: she has it with her in space. Sending Norris to Derry might only succeed in getting him killed.

Without the special chocolates lighting up her brain, she would have doubted this scenario. *No*, she thinks, *I wouldn't have been able to think of it in the first place; I would have been too addled.* With that brain-booster on board, however, she doesn't doubt it. Not one tiny bit. She wonders if Gareth started agitating for a tourist run into space after she didn't drop out of the race against Magowan. No, probably not until after she was elected and got on the Aeronautical and Space Sciences Committee.

"Someone was really thinking ahead," Gwendy mutters to herself. Her hands are clenching and unclenching. Each clench is hard enough to make her short nails dig into the soft meat of her palms. "Someone was really *planning* ahead." Then, for no reason at all, she says, "Sombra sombra sombra." She'll hunt for it on the Net, but she has something else to do first, far more important.

She sits down and sends an email to Deputy CIA Director Charlotte Morgan.

> *Charlotte—I have reason to believe that my husband may have been murdered in an effort to get me to drop out of the Senate race in 2020. I also think it has to do with the item I am carrying. I suspect that Gareth Winston knows about the item, and he may have the code that opens the safety box containing the item. How that happened is a long story for another time. What I want from you is what's known as a "black bag job,"*

and it has to happen <u>immediately</u>. The detective in the Derry PD who supposedly investigated Ryan's death is named Ward Mitchell. I think he knows more than he's telling. My friend Norris Ridgewick (ex-police, sharp as a knife blade) concurs. I want you to send a team to collar Detective Mitchell, sequester him, and persuade him to talk by any means necessary. I believe someone is trying to stop me before I can dispose of the item under my care, and perhaps (likely!) take possession of it. I believe that someone is Gareth Winston, and if he has the code to the safe box, the only thing standing in his way is an electronic Mesa wall safe. It's the kind hotels use, and a third-rate burglar could crack it. You know what the stakes are—remember the pyramid? I understand that my chief suspect is a fabulously wealthy man, but he may not be in charge. Whoever is, they're thinking years ahead, and that scares me. Don't even consider that this is paranoia. It's not. Grab Ward Mitchell and shake him he rattles. Let me hear back from you immediately, Charlotte.

Gwendy

She pauses, then adds a PS: *Does the word "sombra" mean anything to you?*

Gwendy could check that for herself, but now that her two important emails have been sent, she finds herself looking at the closet again, and thinking about the button box. She wonders if she could concentrate on Gareth Winston having a heart attack and make it happen by pressing the red button. *You wonder, Gwendolyn? Is that all?* She voices a humorless bark of laughter. There's no wondering about it; she knows she could. Only there might be collateral damage. What if the station's electrical system shorted out? Or a high-pressure oxy line went blooey?

She comes out of these thoughts to realize she's no longer at her desk. No, she's at the closet. She's opened it, she's pushed aside the spare suit, and she's reaching for the safe's keypad. In fact she's already pushed the first number of its simplistic four-digit combination. Gwendy puts one hand over her mouth. With the other she pushes the CANCEL button and closes the closet door.

She decides she'll go for that run after all.

30

GWENDY BLOWS BY A couple of sweat pants–wearing, AirPods-equipped Chinese women halfway around the rim. They give her a startled look but return her wave. Kathy Lundgren hadn't been exaggerating earlier when she'd boasted about running a two-minute mile. Not by much, anyway. Gwendy hasn't gone for an actual run in over a decade, but it feels as if she's nearly flying. When she gets back to her suite in Spoke 3 her shirt is damp with sweat and she's breathing hard, but she feels more like her old self. She still feels the siren call of the button box when she passes the closet door, but it's not the imperative it was before. More like simple longing. An ache. Sort of like the one she feels for Ryan. It's awful to think of the button box and her dead husband in the same category, but that seems to be the case. Gwendy's glad to feel better again but knows it will come at a cost; she's already starting to lose her crystal clarity of thought. Soon the fog will descend again, and maybe thicker than ever.

The message light is flashing on her laptop. She enters the password that will transform the gibberish of letters and symbols into words (delighted she doesn't have to use the little red notebook to refresh her memory). The message is from Charlotte, and it's entirely satisfying.

Trust you completely. Team on the move to Derry. You will get a video record of Detective Mitchell's interrogation, hopefully tomorrow, your Day 3 on the MF. I understand there were some concerns about your mental abilities up there. Although I will be on pins & needles until your mission is completed, that made me laugh. Can't imagine anyone less likely to "lose the plot," as they say.

How does the Sombra Corporation figure into this? Any idea? You can read a certain amount about it on the Net, but it's mostly speculation. We at the Company know more, but not a hell of a lot. They keep a tight lid. Best guess is that their aggregate worth may be greater than that of China and the U.S. combined. Hard to believe but I'm assured it's almost certainly true. If so, they make WinMark LTD, Winston's company, look small in comparison. Not to mention Amazon. So yes, it's possible Gareth Winston might be working with or even for the Sombra Corp if the reward was great enough. No way to tell. All I can say is <u>**BE CAREFUL**</u>.

C

Gwendy reads this over three times. She has to, because the sense of some lines is getting a bit dim. Her anger is also dimming out. What remains is focused on Detective Mitchell, with his dismissive little smile and empty eyes. *Also the Magowan button on his shirt, don't forget that.* No, she hasn't forgotten it (at least not yet). She wants that video. She wants to see him away from his strangely shitty little city, in a small room with soundproof walls, preferably in a black hood that will be whipped off once he's been wrist- and ankle-chained to the table. Gwendy supposes they don't do it that way anymore; she's sure that the CIA has drug cocktails that will render the likes of Ward Mitchell entirely pliable, but . . .

"But a girl can dream," she says softly.

She showers off her sweat, then goes down to the weather deck. She's scheduled for a video conference with the National Weather Service at 4 p.m. Eastern time. That's hours from now, but she'd had to get out of there. For the time being, at least, being close to the button box isn't safe.

31

DAY 3 ON MANY Flags.

Gwendy is at the desk in the small living room of her suite, going over stacks of appropriation requests. She's thinking that a single look at this untidy pile of paperwork would cause anyone with the idea that the life of a United States senator is glamorous to think again.

What she's really doing, of course, is listening for the chime of her laptop, signaling a message from Charlotte. It's chimed with several incoming messages already, including one from the vice president wishing her well, but nothing from Charlotte. It's probably too early, but that doesn't keep her from hoping.

The other thing she's doing is resisting the call of the button box. It's in the steel CLASSIFIED box, and the steel CLASSIFIED box is in the safe, and the safe is in the closet, but that call still comes through loud and clear. She doesn't want to push the buttons so much as she wants to pull the lever that dispenses the chocolates. She's actually having a pretty good day, memory circuits all firing as they are supposed to, but she misses the weird and wonderful clarity she felt when she was doing the mental acuity test yesterday. A chocolate animal (or two!), and she could fly through this boring paperwork. This is a practical lesson in why drug addicts are addicts.

The knock at her door is a relief. She would welcome

a distraction . . . as long as it isn't Winston, that is. She has no urge to see him today. In fact she would be happy not to see him at all until she's completed her task, although she knows that's probably unlikely. For one thing, they all eat together. There's no room service on the MF station.

It's not Gareth. It's Reggie, the physicist. His last name temporarily eludes her, but she doesn't stress about it, just relaxes and uses Dr. Ambrose's chain-of-association trick. Best concert she ever saw? AC/DC, at TD Garden in Boston. Best song? "Back in Black." And whoomp, there it is.

"Reggie Black, as I live and breathe," she says. "What can I do for you?"

He's fiftyish, with fluffs of white hair that float on either side of his bald pate. And he's grinning. "Adesh just showed me something wild. Do you want to see?" He glances past her at the littered desk and his grin fades. "I guess you're busy."

"I can take a break. All you have to do is tempt me."

"Consider yourself tempted. This is crazy cool."

He takes her to the lab Adesh has set up in Spoke 5, where there's lots of space. Based on the signage, Gwendy deduces it was last used by a French team. On the lab's door there's a sign that reads ADESH "BUG MAN" PATEL. KNOCK BEFORE ENTERING.

Reggie knocks. "Okay to come in?"

"Come, come," Adesh says, and opens the door before Reggie can. He sees Gwendy and smiles. "Ah, the esteemed senator! Welcome to Entomology Wonderland!"

They step in. Gwendy sees a row of plexiglass cases

with beetles and bugs in some of them, spiders in others. Including Olivia the tarantula. *Ugh*, Gwendy thinks. The far end of the room has been sealed off with floor-to-ceiling plexi, creating a larger cage with smaller cages inside it.

"Show her the trick with Boris," Reggie Black says. And to Gwendy, "It's an authentic mind-blower."

Adesh wags his finger at Reggie in a schoolteacherly way. "It is no trick, Reginald. It is *training* and *adaptation*." To Gwendy: "Besides, I find the flies much more interesting. Ordinary houseflies—*Musca domestica*—but their zero-g behavior is fascinating and illuminating."

"Sure, but the scorpion is cool," Reggie says. "Boris is *money*."

Adesh looks perplexed.

"The best," Gwendy translates. "He means the best. Or maybe the flashiest."

"Oh, it's flashy, all right," Reggie says. "The Bugster's probably got it on video, but it's better live. Assuming you have enough *Musca domesticas*, old buddy."

"Plenty of flies," Adesh agrees. "I am saving the cockroaches."

Ugh, Gwendy thinks again.

Adesh takes a remote control from its magnetized disc and points it into the big cage. The door of one of the small cages—the smallest, not much bigger than a woman's makeup case—slides up and several *Musca domesticas* fly out. But not for long. They stop flying and just hang in the air, as if on strings.

"My God!" Gwendy says. "Are they sick?"

"No, they are in what you might call energy-saving

mode," Adesh says. "They used their wings at first, but quickly learned they do not need to. Nor do they need to rest by landing. If houseflies can be said to enjoy anything, they enjoy zero-g."

"Boris, Boris, Boris!" Reggie chants.

Adesh sighs, but Gwendy thinks it's just for show. He's enjoying this, too. She doesn't think it matters if it's men of science or men chopping wood, they all like showing off. Of course, so do women.

Adesh presses another button on his remote control and Boris the scorpion crawls out, claws clicking, his loaded stinger arched over his back. "*Pandinus imperator*," Adesh says. "Emperor scorpion. Its sting is rarely fatal to humans, but for its prey—"

"There he goes!" Reggie cries. "Upsy-daisy, Boris! My *man*!"

Claws still clicking, Boris floats upward and hangs in midair like the flies on the far side of the cage they share.

Adesh raises his voice and calls, "Boris! *Maar!*"

Boris gives his tail a single hard flex, propelling himself across the room like a bullet. Two of the flies escape, but Boris catches the third one in his claws, mashes it, and pops it into his alien maw. Gwendy is repulsed and fascinated in equal measure. The scorpion's forward motion propels it toward the wall, but before it hits, Boris does a forward roll and uses his armored tail to push himself back the other way. He finishes up in almost exactly the same place he started and just hangs there.

"Amazing," Gwendy says. "How do you get him back in his cage?"

"I put him in myself," Adesh says. "I don a glove to

do it. I have no urge to be stung, even if it's no worse than the sting of a bee. Boris is trainable, as you see, but he is far from tame. No, no, no."

"And *maar*? What does that mean?"

Adesh goes to the door of the big containment facility, then turns back and gives her a gentle smile in which one gold tooth twinkles. "Kill," he says.

32

WHEN GWENDY GETS BACK to her quarters, the light on her laptop is flashing. Five fresh emails have come in, but the only one she cares about is Charlotte Morgan's. She pushes aside her paperwork and opens it.

Gwen: I didn't think this story could get any stranger, but boy was I wrong. You were on the money about Detective Mitchell knowing more than he was telling. Take a look at the attached video and get back to me with further instructions. It's pretty lengthy—once we got the guy talking, he wouldn't shut up—but most of what you're looking for can be found starting at around the seven-minute mark.

I've also attached a second, much shorter video that came from the iPhone of an eyewitness to Ryan's accident (which as you surmised wasn't an accident at all). The phone belongs (or belonged) to a man named Vernon Beeson, from Providence, Rhode Island. He was on his way to Presque Isle to see his sister. He never arrived. We can't know for sure, but I wouldn't be surprised if he is now floating around in the Derry sewer system. Mitchell claims a patrolman found the phone in a trash can outside Bassey Park. Mitchell also claims not to know what happened to Mr. Beeson. All we could get out of him on that subject was "Maybe the clown took him." Weird, huh?

Very *weird*, Gwendy thinks, and resists the sudden urge to pull the little chocolate-dispensing lever on the side of the button box. She goes back to Charlotte's communique instead.

It's hard to watch, Gwen, even harder to believe, and I wouldn't blame you one bit if you decided to hit the DELETE button without ever opening it. I might even suggest you do exactly that, but I know it's not my place. We found Mr. Beeson's phone locked away in the gun safe in Mitchell's basement, right where he told us it would be.

Last thing I'm going to say and then I'll let you get to it. I've said it before: please be careful, old friend. I know you must feel as though you're all alone up there, but I promise you're not. Sending love and luck your way. Godspeed.

C

The video attachments located at the bottom of the email are labeled MITCHELL and DERRY. Gwendy knows she should open the Ward Mitchell interrogation first—after all, the fate of the world may rest on its contents—but she can't help herself. Taking slow and steady breaths, like she's learned from years of yoga classes, she slides the cursor over to the DERRY file and clicks on it. A window opens in her laptop's upper right-hand corner. She hits the ENLARGE icon and a surprisingly clear wide-angle view of the intersection of Witcham and Carter Streets fills the screen.

On the right side of the video she can see a couple of run-down houses, window shutters hanging crooked or absent altogether, paint peeling in long, curling strips, brown lawns overgrown even at the tail end of November. An old bicycle with a missing rear tire leans against one of the porch railings.

Across the street, kitty-corner from the house with the bike, is an abandoned Phillips 66 gas station, the pumps out front long ago removed. Weeds grow in wild spurts between the cracks of broken pavement. Someone has spray-painted DERRY SUCKS across the faded brick façade. Just beyond the boarded-up office, Gwendy can make out the gated entrance to Bassey Park.

Whoever is filming—Beeson, presumably—has the sound turned on and she can hear the loud undulating whistle of a cold late-season wind blowing across the rooftops. A discarded piece of trash tumbles across the sidewalk—Gwendy's almost certain it's a McDonald's hamburger wrapper—and disappears down the deserted street. It's half past noon on the day after Thanksgiving, but there's not a single living soul or automobile in sight.

And then there is.

An old Volkswagen Bug, traveling north on Witcham, putters through the intersection. The driver, an older man with a wild tuft of scraggly white hair and round John Lennon eyeglasses, is looking around like he's lost. And maybe he is; he's certainly driving slowly enough. Right behind him, riding the VW's rear bumper, is a black truck with jacked-up snow tires and a full-sized American flag flapping from a metal pole jutting out of the rear of its double-wide bed. She can hear the throaty boom of the truck stereo's bass even with the dark-tinted windows closed up tight.

Gwendy has just enough time to take it all in and wonder *why in the world is the person filming this?* when Ryan appears on-screen. It suddenly feels as if all of the air has been sucked from the room. She bites her lower lip and leans closer to the laptop.

He enters from the bottom right corner of the screen, sauntering along the sidewalk with that long, confident stride she remembers so well. He's wearing his favorite winter coat—a long-ago Christmas gift from Gwendy's parents—and a red-and-white New England Patriots ski cap. Every once in a while he sneaks a glance at the row of nearby houses, but it's clear that the main focus of his attention is the cell phone he's carrying in his right hand. He's studying the display like he's following directions.

Reaching the corner of Witcham and Carter, he stops with the tips of his L.L. Beans dangling over the curb. He looks both ways, like an obedient little boy who's prom-ised his mother to always be careful crossing the street, and then down at his phone again.

And then he starts across.

The Cadillac—a garish shade of purple, obscenely wide and long, with a pair of dime-store fuzzy dice dan-gling from the rearview mirror—slams into him before he reaches the street's center line. Gwendy hears the meaty *thunk* of impact, and then her husband is flying through the air. He hits the pavement and actually bounces, not once but twice, before rolling to an abrupt facedown stop at the opposite side of the intersection. A ragged trail of dark blotches tracks his progress across the roadway.

The Caddy keeps on going without even a flash of its brake lights. It's not until the next day, while showering, that Gwendy realizes she never once heard the sound of the Cadillac's engine. She could hear the sewing machine *putt-putt-putt* of the VW Bug, the angry growl of the black pick-up's V-8, the bass thud of heavy metal from the truck's sound system, but when it came to the purple Caddy . . . nothing. Almost as if it *had* no motor.

What remained of Ryan's shattered body lay halfway on the shoulder of Carter Street, his broken legs splayed at grotesque angles atop a narrow strip of dirt and grass separating the curb from the sidewalk. His ski cap, along with one of the boots and wool socks he was wearing, had been torn away by the force of the crash. The boot and sock are nowhere to be found, but Gwendy can see the pale pink skin of Ryan's left foot resting mere inches away from a FOR SALE BY OWNER sign poking out of the frozen ground. The back of Ryan's head—as caved-in and lopsided as a pumpkin left rotting in a field—no longer resembled that of a human being.

Gwendy jerks away from the screen, a loud sob lodging in her throat. For one panic-stricken moment, she fears she might actually choke to death on her grief. She sits back and once again focuses on her breathing. The suffocating sensation gradually loosens its grip. Eyes filled with tears, she turns back to her laptop. And gasps.

There's a car stopped in the road beside Ryan's lifeless body. It's not quite as wide as the Cadillac, and it's sleeker, built lower to the ground, and painted such a dazzling shade of cartoon green that it almost hurts to look at. *It doesn't look real*, Gwendy thinks with morbid fascination. *It looks like a child's toy come to life.*

She immediately recognizes the car as the same vehicle in which she'd seen Gareth Winston sitting beside the blond man when she touched Winston's hand outside of the lavatory on Eagle Heavy. *He was there*, she thinks, squeezing her fists together so hard the color fades from her fingertips. *Maybe not in Derry, and maybe not on the day they killed my husband, but the son of a bitch was inside that car. And was he making some kind of a deal? Of course he was, because that's what guys like Gareth do: they make deals.*

"He's one of them," she says aloud to the empty sitting room.

As Gwendy watches, the doors of the car (*an old green Chrysler, big as a boat*, she suddenly remembers from her old friend Norris Ridgewick's email) swing open and four men step out onto Carter Street.

"What the—" She never finishes the sentence.

The men are unnaturally tall and thin. And dressed identically—wearing long yellow dusters and bandanas over the lower halves of their faces—like a gang of Old West outlaws. They amble to the front of the car and stand shoulder to shoulder, surrounding the body. Looking down, one of the men places a dark-gloved hand on his chest and bends over, howling with a high, barking laughter that Gwendy is somehow able to hear over the whine of the wind. It's an ugly animal sound, and she quickly lowers the volume on her laptop. The others soon join in, gesturing at the fallen body, hooting and guffawing. One of the men abruptly spins in a tight circle and begins hopping from one foot to the other, performing some kind of lunatic jig, slapping at his thighs with furious delight.

Gwendy abruptly stops the video—and hits REWIND. She doesn't go back very far, maybe ten or twelve seconds. She isn't sure if her eyes are playing tricks on her or if what she thinks she just saw is real.

She hits PLAY and watches as the man launches into his bizarre dance, and then it happens again. The man begins to fade in and out—not in and out of focus, but in and out of *existence*. One second he's whole and solid, the next he's blurry and only partially there.

And then it's all four of the men.

While everything else in the video remains crystal clear—if Gwendy leans close enough to the screen, she can almost make out the phone number printed at the bottom of the FOR SALE BY OWNER sign—the four men in the yellow dusters have begun to shimmer. Looking at them now is a little like staring at a heat mirage rising off the highway in the middle of a summer heat wave. *This isn't what they look like,* Gwendy thinks with calm assurance. *This isn't what they look like at all. It's as if they're wearing costumes and masks to make them appear human, but the disguises are only temporary, and I'm sitting here watching as they fade in and out of reality. Even the goddamn car is wearing one. It's lost its edges. Its shape no longer looks quite solid.*

And apparently she's not the only one who notices. For the first time since he started recording, Vernon Beeson, from Providence, Rhode Island, zooms in for a closer look. The houses and gas station and Bassey Park all fall away. As the front end of the Chrysler, with its acre of shiny green hood, rushes forward and fills the screen, Gwendy

suddenly wishes she were wearing her flight helmet so she could lower the visor. Looking at the four men and their funny green car doesn't just make her eyes want to water, it makes her *brain* want to water. The camera slowly pans away from the Chrysler and once again finds the men at the side of the road. Even up close, they continue to blur in and out, as if they're being seen from behind a dirty pane of rain-streaked glass. One of the men is standing directly in front of Ryan's body, sparing Gwendy an up-close-and-personal look at the gruesome details. She swears if he moves one step to the left or right, she's going to scream, or throw her laptop across the room, or both. There's a sudden burst of ear-piercing static and then the screen goes dark. And remains that way for what feels like a long time. Just when she's convinced the video is over, it sparks back to life again.

In the interim, cameraman Vernon Beeson has given up on the close-up and is pulling back to the original wide-angle view. As the row of houses reappears on the right side of the screen, the abandoned gas station and Bassey Park creep back into view on the left. The four masked men standing across the intersection gradually re-gain their focus, albeit from a distance. The static is gone.

Gwendy glances at the time code in the upper corner of the video screen and is astonished to discover that she's only been watching for three minutes and forty-seven seconds. It feels so much longer than that.

The men in the yellow dusters and bandanas have grown quiet. They shuffle closer to each other, standing with their heads pressed together—*palavering*, Gwendy thinks—and then they break up their impromptu huddle. Three of the men return to the car. Even with the volume turned down, the slamming of the car doors is very loud inside the small sitting room. The fourth man waits on the side of the road until the Chrysler speeds away—with not so much as a whisper of its engine—and then he jaywalks across Carter Street and disappears into the cold afternoon shadows of Bassey Park.

Ryan's body remains silent and still on the shoulder of the road.

Nobody else comes, because in Derry, nobody ever does when things like this happen.

A few seconds later, the video ends.

33

GWENDY'S ANGER IS BACK. Her face feels as hot as a furnace and her jaw aches from grinding her teeth. She wipes away tears with a Kleenex, uses it to noisily blow her nose, and then stuffs it in the zero-g wastecan. While her shell-shocked mind is unable to fully comprehend what she's just witnessed, she knows enough to call it what it is: cold-blooded murder. Someone—the blond stranger from her vision, the odd men in their yellow coats, or maybe even Gareth Winston—lured her husband to Derry and ran him down in the middle of the street like a stray dog. *Were they all working for Sombra?* Gwendy guesses they were. *Are.*

Even from across the room and inside the closet, she can hear the steady hum of the button box calling to her. *Just because you hear it*, she reminds herself, *doesn't mean you have to listen to it.* She already knows what it's saying anyway. Ever since they landed on Many Flags, the button box is like a broken fucking record. *Just one more piece of chocolate, Gwendy girl, that's all. Just one more delicious bite-sized animal and you'll think clearer and you'll sleep better and you'll never forget another goddamn thing. Or, better yet, why not press the red button and make all your troubles disappear? Starting with your billionaire friend. You know you want to . . .*

"You're damn right I want to," she snaps, yanking another Kleenex from the box. "And if he'd actually been there in the video, I don't think I could hold back."

Gwendy shoves the voice into the corner of her broken brain—it's getting more and more difficult to do this as her journey nears its end—and clicks on the MITCHELL file. There are a series of loud beeps and then the video begins.

The interrogation room is small and plain. Three gray walls. A tinted viewing window occupies the upper portion of the fourth. It's impossible to tell who is watching from behind the dark glass, but Gwendy guesses that Charlotte Morgan is one of them. Possibly the only one.

There are four men crammed inside the room. One of them, wearing a dark suit and holstered sidearm, leans against the only door. His face is blurred, and for a fleeting instant, Gwendy thinks he's one of *them*—the men in the yellow coats—but then she quickly realizes the man's face has been purposely obscured to protect his identity. A second agent's face has also been hidden. He's sitting behind a narrow desk, studying an open laptop. To his immediate right is the agent in charge, whose unblurred face instantly reminds Gwendy of her father's youngest brother, Uncle Harvey. With his tortoiseshell glasses and bushy mustache, this guy looks like he could be just about anyone's favorite uncle or maybe even a science teacher from the local high school, the one who gets voted school favorite in the yearbook. Both of the agents sitting behind the desk are dressed in slacks and Oxford shirts. No jackets or ties.

The final man in the room is the guest of honor. Ward Mitchell is wearing a loose-fitting orange jumpsuit with the sleeves rolled up. He's seated in a straight-backed metal chair that has been securely bolted to the floor. Gwendy can see he's struggling to keep his head up and his eyes open. There's a darkening bruise rising beneath one of his eyes and both of his lips appear to be swollen. That dismissive little smile of his is nowhere to be seen. Mitchell's arms are propped up in front of him atop the desk. A small surgical tube runs from the bend of his right arm to a portable IV stand. A bag of clear fluid hangs on the uppermost hook, honey-dripping top-secret contents into Mitchell's bloodstream. There's a pressure cuff wrapped around the detective's left bicep, as well as a tangle of wires leading from just inside the collar of his jumpsuit to the back of the agent's laptop.

"Let's start with your name." The agent's voice is firm but pleasant. He even sounds like a science teacher.

Mitchell blinks and looks around the room as if he's just awakened from a deep sleep. He clears his throat. "Ward Thomas Mitchell."

"Age?"

"Forty-four."

You look older, Gwendy thinks, not without satisfaction.

"Address?"

"1920 Tupelo Road. Derry, Maine."

"And you're from Derry originally?"

"Born and raised there."

Well, that explains a lot, the senator thinks.

"Occupation?"

"Derry PD. Almost thirty years. Detective the last twelve."

"Married?"

"Divorced."

"Kids?"

"One. A boy."

"How ol—"

She knows what they're doing, easing him into it with

easy questions, but this isn't what she came for. Gwendy presses the arrow button on her laptop and fast-forwards the video. She forgets what she's doing for a moment—a mini Brain Freeze, here and gone in a matter of seconds—and advances too far. She quickly hits REWIND and watches as the time code begins to reverse. Finally stopping at the 5:33 mark, she presses PLAY. Her hands are shaking.

". . . referenced strange occurrences in Derry. Can you give us an example?"

Mitchell gives a confidential smile. His eyes are drifting around in their sockets. Gwendy thinks she might have seen people this cataclysmically stoned, but not since college. "I've heard voices."

"Like in your head, Detective?"

"No-ooo . . . from inside the drains at my house."

"Really?" The head guy glances at the tinted window and wiggles his eyebrows. "From the drains, huh?"

"Once . . . I'd just turned off the water after taking a shower . . . someone called out to me from inside the drain. And then they started laughing."

"They?"

"It sounded like kids. A whole bunch of kids laughing."

"And this voice, what did it say to you?"

"My name."

The agent in charge scratches his chin. This time he gives the eyebrow waggle to his partner.

"Another time I was loading the dishwasher and I heard that same voice coming from the kitchen sink. It said, 'We're saving you a seat, Warthog.' No one's called me that since I was a snot-nose kid at Derry Elementary."

"Anything else?"

Ward Thomas Mitchell, aka Warthog, laughs. But there's no laughter in his eyes. "There's the clown."

"Want to see a clown, Ward, look in the mirror," one of the others says. He sounds disgusted.

Mitchell pays no attention. "Back when I was a rookie, I started having bad dreams. They got so horrible I was afraid to go to sleep at night. I was being chased in the sewers by someone dressed as a clown."

Gwendy suddenly thinks of her old friend's story about a clown with big silver eyes chasing her in Derry. She's also thinking about her father and his warnings about the town. So out of character for him. She's almost certain that something happened to her father during his short stay in Derry—something horrible—but he's never admitted as much, and she doubts he even remembers now. Or maybe he does and is just too frightened, even after all these years, to talk about it.

"Later that same year, my rookie year, I caught a 911 for a domestic right around Christmas. Neighbor reported loud crashes and screaming coming from the house next door. When I pulled up, a man was sitting on the front porch, covered in blood. He was crying and holding a butcher knife. He'd just finished slicing and dicing his wife and twin girls, and arranging their bodies around the dining room table. He'd placed salads in front of each of them and laid out napkins on their laps. We found a pan of burnt-to-a-crisp lasagna still baking in the oven. The man gave up without a fight, and when we cuffed him and put him in the back of a squad car, he said clear as day—and I'm not the only one who heard him that night—*"The clown made me do it.*" And then he never spoke a single word again. Ever. He's still up at Juniper Hill as far as I know."

The lead agent yawns and shuffles his notes.

"Moving ahead, Detective. On Friday, November 29, 2019, Mr. Ryan Brown of Castle Rock was killed in a hit-and-run in your jurisdiction. You were the lead detective on scene and in charge of the case, correct?"

"I wasn't first on scene, but yes, I was the detective in charge."

"And the results of your investigation?"

"We were unable to locate or charge any suspects." Mitchell once more flashes the goofball smile.

"Did you actually search for any suspects?"

"Nope."

"Was there, in fact, anything even resembling an official investigation into Ryan Brown's death?"

"Nope." This time the goofball smile is accompanied by a small chuckle.

"And why not, Detective?"

"Because of the money."

"Are you saying you were bribed not to investigate Ryan Brown's death?"

"Yup."

"By whom?"

"I don't know. Never got a name."

"Are there other members of the Derry Police Department involved in this conspiracy?"

"Yup."

"And who might they be?"

"Officers Ronald Freeman and Kevin Malerman." Mitchell raises a fist. "My *bros*!"

"What can you tell us about the man who bribed you?"

"Tall. Thin. White. Wearing a long yellow coat. Old-fashioned, kinda sharp-looking white dress shoes. He talked funny."

"You mean he spoke with an accent?"

"No, like his tongue was too big for his mouth. Or maybe like his voice box was stuffed with crickets."

All the interrogators stir at that.

"Anything else?"

"Yup," Mitchell says agreeably, "he wasn't human."

"Excuse me?"

"His face . . . it kept changing. Slipping."

Gwendy's throat is suddenly desert-dry.

"His face was slipping? Not following you, Mitchell."

"It was like he was wearing a mask, but not the rubber or cheap plastic kind kids wear on Halloween. It kept slipping, giving me glimpses of what was underneath."

"And what was that?"

"A monster."

"Can you describe what you saw under the mask?"

"Dark bristly hair, scaly skin, red lips, black eyes. And some kind of a snout. Like a wolf or a weasel. Maybe a rat."

"How many times did you meet with this wolf-man?"

"Twice. He initially approached me at the crime scene. And then a second time at my home when he brought me the money."

"How much did the man pay you?"

"One hundred thousand dollars."

One of the others says something. It's off-mic, but Gwendy thinks it might have been "Fuck me."

"Did he explain why he wanted the Ryan Brown investigation to go away?"

"Nope."

"Did he say if he was working for someone else?"

"Nope."

"The man was alone both times?"

"Yup." Mitchell pauses and adds, "I thought he might kill me, you know."

"What kind of vehicle did the man drive?"

"Never saw one. He arrived on foot both times. He had a button on his lapel. At first I thought it was some kind of a badge. But it wasn't. It was a big crimson eye and it was watching me the whole time we talked."

The man by the door says, "A tinfoil hat can help with that." There's some laughter, but the chief interrogator doesn't join in and it dies quickly.

"Had you ever met the victim, Ryan Brown, before his death?"

"Nope."

"Did you play any role in luring Ryan Brown to Derry?"

"Nope."

"How about Gwendy Peterson? You knew who she was?"

"Sure. The bitch always polluting my TV before the election. All those damn commercials. I couldn't watch a single Red Sox game that season without having to listen to her libtard drivel."

Gwendy extends her middle finger to the laptop screen.

"Do you know a man named Gareth Winston?"

"No, but I've heard the name."

"Where?"

Mitchell gives his loopy smile. "Not sure."

"Last question for now and then we can take a short break. Have you ever heard of the Sombra Corporation?"

"Nope."

"You're certain of that?"

"Yup."

And that's all there is.

34

GWENDY FIRES OFF A brief note to Charlotte Morgan, thanking her and commending her for a job well done. There's nothing else Charlotte can do for her at the moment, but that could change in a hurry.

Gwendy's anger has diminished, but it's been replaced by a soul-dragging heaviness that makes her head feel as if it weighs about a million pounds. It was just yesterday that she couldn't sit still—did she really go for a run or did she dream that?—but now she can't seem to make herself get up off the tiny sofa. She considers stretching out and taking a nap, but every time she closes her eyes, she sees Ryan's lifeless body and the trail of bloody smear marks across the road, and all she hears in the dark silence of her mind is that awful high, barking laughter.

Finally, after giving herself a pep talk (at age sixty-four, Gwendy's mental pep talks are still delivered in her mother's voice), she closes her laptop and forces herself to get up and get moving. After depositing a handful of balled-up Kleenex in the zero-g wastebasket and closing the lid, she washes her face with cold water. *Four more days*, she reminds herself again, staring at her reflection in the bathroom mirror. She's not happy with what she sees. Her eyes are swollen from crying, and there's a hint of barely contained hysteria in her gaze. *NG*, she thinks. *Better do something about that before you show up at dinner.* The last thing she needs to do is give Kathy and company a reason to start worrying about her again.

But those men weren't men. They were from . . . somewhere else. Probably the same somewhere else the button box came from. Did Mr. Farris steal it to keep it safe? Gwendy doesn't know—probably never will—but she thinks there's a good chance he did.

It occurs to Gwendy there's one thing she does know: she's about to break bread with a man who had a hand in her husband's death. How heavy that hand was she isn't sure, but that doesn't really matter. Does it? There's a brief moment where she struggles to remember the man's name— she thinks it might be Gary or maybe even Gregory—but then it comes back to her in a flash of certainty that is rare for her during these dark times. His name is Gareth Winston. He's a billionaire, but he'll never have enough money or power. He'll always want more. And he knows the combination to the steel case marked **CLASSIFIED MATERIAL**. She's sure of that, too.

35

THERE ARE FOUR OF them at the table when Gareth Winston bounce-walks his way into the cafeteria. Gwendy is sitting next to Adesh Patel. She looks younger and livelier than the reflection she saw in her bathroom mirror minutes ago. She's just finished telling Kathy Lundgren and Bern Stapleton all about Boris the scorpion's impressive display in the Bug Lab. At the conclusion of her story, she jumps to her feet, exclaiming, "*Maar!*" and lunges across the table toward her former training partner. Bern Stapleton nearly screams and spills half a cup of apple juice, which floats in front of his jumpsuit. He's still trying to catch it with a ball of napkins when Gwendy spots Winston.

Please keep going, she thinks. *Please sit somewhere else.*

But of course he doesn't. Squeezing his considerable bulk onto the chair, Winston settles with a grunt. He immediately reaches for his food tray, detaches it from the magnet holding it to the table, and floats it over to him. He peers through the thin mesh, nods approvingly at what he sees, opens the diagonal zip in the center of the mesh with a thumbnail, and begins to eat pasta in greedy gulps. A few drops of red sauce float in front of him. To Gwendy they look like drops of blood.

"Not bad," he says, finally looking up at the others. "It's not Sorrento's in the Bronx, but it'll do in a pinch."

"I'm so glad you're pleased," Kathy says. "Perhaps

TetCorp can hire the head chef from Sorrento's to handle meal preparations for their Mars shuttles."

"Now that's an idea," Winston says, pointing a finger at the flight commander and chewing noisily. He looks over at Adesh. "They even have a vegetarian menu for people like you."

The entomologist leans close to Gwendy and whispers, "People like me, don't you know."

"There's a lovely Italian restaurant in Maine called Giovanni's. You ever heard of it, Mr. Winston?" It's an innocent enough question, but something in Gwendy's tone causes the others at the table to turn and stare at her. Only Winston doesn't seem to notice.

He shakes his head. "Can't say I have. Where is it?"

"It's in a little town called Windham, about forty-five minutes north of Castle Rock. They make a stuffed shrimp *a la Guiseppi* to die for. It's been written up in all the foodie magazines."

"Hmpph." He takes a drink of lemonade and belches into his hand. "I'll have to check it out sometime."

"I've actually been meaning to ask you," Gwendy says. "Have you spent much time in Maine during your travels?"

"Not really. Visited a couple of times. Once to go moose hunting in the Allagash. But the trip was a bust."

"My wife and I went camping at Acadia National Park the summer after we got married," Bern Stapleton says. "Beautiful place. I'm pretty sure we conceived our first child inside that tent."

"TMI," Kathy says. "*Way* too much."

"Adesh," Bern says, "please have the birds-and-bees talk with Commander Lundgren. I think it's time."

Kathy whacks the biologist on the shoulder. Laughing, he gets up from the table and collects his tray. "Off to get some work done. Be good, kids."

"I'm right behind you," Adesh says, standing and clearing his place. "I have a Zoom conference to prepare for."

"Good luck," Kathy calls as the two men walk away.

"I'm surprised you've seen so little of my home state," Gwendy continues, once again staring at the billionaire. "With all that money, I figured you've been everywhere twice."

"Well, excuse me for stating the obvious," he says, "but with all that money, I wouldn't exactly call Maine a desired destination. Paris, Tortola, Turks and Caicos, now those are a different—"

"Have you ever been to Castle Rock?" Gwendy asks, cutting him off. "How about Derry?"

"No and no," he snaps, letting go of his fork. He quickly snatches it out of the air in front of him when it begins to float up toward the ceiling. "I've never been to Castle Rock and I've never been to Derry. Now, can I finish eating my dinner in peace?"

"Of course," Gwendy says, slipping on her Patsy Follett smile. "Just one last thing—I wanted to thank you for returning my notebook. Lucky for me you found it."

"Yeah, well, you ought to be more careful."

She starts away, then stops and turns back. "Maybe you should be, too."

A flush rises in his cheeks. *Gotcha*, Gwendy thinks.

A few minutes later, while scraping their plates into the vacuum receptacle at the other side of the cafeteria, Kathy asks, "What in the hell was that all about?"

"What do you mean?"

"C'mon. You were *poking* at him."

"I was just curious."

"About what?"

"How he'd respond to a poke. Did you see that flush?"

Kathy frowns. "I didn't notice."

Gwendy watches her walk away, thinking: *Test or no test, she still doesn't trust me completely. Well, I've got news for you, lady. The feeling is mutual.*

On the way back to her quarters, Gwendy makes a brief diversion to the weather deck to check on the latest readings. She knows that some staff members back in the down-below—maybe even most of them—don't expect her to perform much more than a lick and a promise when it comes to her climate monitor duties. But that just makes her want to exceed expectations and prove them all wrong; it's how she's always been wired.

Her laptop is back in her room, so she scribbles a couple of notations in a Moleskine ledger and returns it to its place in the top drawer of the desk. When she's finished, she writes a reminder note about tomorrow's video conference with faculty members from the University of Maine and sticks it right in the middle of one of the monitor screens. No way can she forget that. She hopes.

When she gets to her room a short time later, she makes a beeline for the sofa. She's suddenly exhausted and all she wants to do is lie down and rest her brain. *It's strange*, she thinks. She watched a video earlier this afternoon of her husband being murdered—not to mention the four odd creatures in yellow coats and their mile-long ugly green car (*if it even was a car*, she thinks)—but after shoveling a bit of shit in Winston's direction at dinner, she feels a little more in control of things. In fact, she feels surprisingly steadfast. For the first time in days, she's not even thinking about the button box and its magic bag of tricks and treats. Eyes growing heavy, she props a pillow under her head and gets comfortable. Just before she dozes off, she notices her laptop sitting open on the coffee table and thinks: *Wait a minute, didn't I close that before I left? And put it away?*

Probably she didn't. She's gotten so forgetful. Then her eyes slide the rest of the way shut—and she's sleeping the dreamless sleep of the innocent.

36

Day 4 on Many Flags.

Gwendy brushes her teeth, rinses the night cream off her face, and ties her hair back in a ponytail. Then she dresses in blue shorts and an Eagle Heavy tee. She figures a vigorous walk around the outer rim might help to keep her head clear and increase her appetite for breakfast. She never seems to be hungry anymore, and that worries her. Take last night for example. She enjoyed her time at the dinner table—especially poking Gareth Winston, which was the high point—but she barely touched the food on her tray. She will this morning, appetite or no appetite. Only three more days until her spacewalk with the Pocket Rocket, and she can use all the calories she can get.

Gwendy doesn't even consider going for a run. That little act of misguided lunacy—chocolates or no chocolates—could have easily backfired and ended in disaster. She can picture the scene without even trying: *The senator from Maine floating on her back, unresponsive as her misfiring sixty-four-year-old heart sputters. Dale Glen, surrounded by the other crew members, dutifully administering epinephrine and doing CPR. Alas, the sputtering heart quits. After a few more minutes of trying to jump-start it, a grim-faced Dr. Glen calls it. Kathy Lundgren hurries back to Spoke 1 to tearfully notify Eileen Braddock at Mission Control. Before the body of Maine's junior senator has even had time to grow cold in the infirmary (Gwendy* assumes that's where she'd be taken), *Gareth Winston slips into her suite and steals away with the button box. End of story. Maybe the end of everything.*

Pure crap, of course—her heart checked out fine after half a dozen treadmill stress tests. Plus, paranoid fantasies sometimes accompany Alzheimer's. That was just one of the fun facts about the illness she discovered (and now wishes she hadn't) on the Internet. There's even a name for it: sundowning. And since sundown up here happens roughly every ninety minutes, that leaves plenty of opportunity for weird thoughts.

I am not *sundowning!*

Maybe not, but still, no running. Best to be safe.

A brisk walk will do me fine, she thinks, sitting down on the edge of the sofa cushion. Bending over, she slips on her sneakers, first the right, then the left. Then she reaches down, picks up the laces—and stops. She has no idea what to do with them.

"Oh, come on," she admonishes herself. "Of course you know how." What was that shoe-tying rhyme she learned in preschool? Something about bunny ears, wasn't it? The bunny ears being the loops you made in the laces? She can't remember, only that it ended *beautiful and bold.* Right now Gwendy doesn't feel beautiful *or* bold. Just scared. She tries—at least a half-dozen times—but doesn't even come close.

Finally, after a brief bout of crying and a thoroughly unsatisfying temper tantrum in which she kicks off both sneakers and sends them floating across the sitting room, Gwendy pulls up a YouTube tutorial on her laptop. The girl in the video is five years old. Her name is Mallory and she's from Atlanta, Georgia. The senator watches the ninety-second video three times from start to finish, murmuring the words to the accompanying song, which she now remembers perfectly: *Bunny ears, bunny ears, playing by a tree. Crisscrossed the tree, trying to catch me. Bunny ears, bunny ears, jumped into the hole, popped out the other side beautiful and bold.*

She finally manages to tie her Reeboks. Even then, they're a little loose.

By the time she heads out the door, half an hour later than planned, Gwendy Peterson is daydreaming about the button box again. And singing about bunny ears.

37

SHE'S HALFWAY AROUND THE outer corridor when Adesh Patel catches up with her.

"Good morning, Senator. Mind some company?"

"Not at all," Gwendy says.

But she *does* mind. The last thing she wants on this horrible morning is company. She's cranky and frightened and filled with doubt. *What if I have another Brain Fart? See, that's not even right! What if I have another Brain* Freeze, *and he runs back and blabbermouths to Kathy? What then?*

As if reading her mind, Adesh gently touches her on the shoulder and asks, "Can we stop for a minute? I wanted to tell you something at dinner last night, but we were never alone long enough and I didn't want to say it in front of the others."

Gwendy stops walking and turns to face him. "Is something wrong, Adesh?"

He lowers his eyes and shrugs. "Yes . . . no . . . I mean, I don't really know, I guess."

"Well, spit it out and let's figure it out together."

"I'll try." He takes a deep, wavering breath. "When Doc Glen and Commander Lundgren first came to me asking questions about you, I had no idea what their specific concerns were or what they were thinking. I figured it was because you're . . . well . . ."

"Because I'm *old*? It's okay, it's true. And not a dirty word."

Adesh shakes his head. "No, ma'am. You might be older than the rest of us, but you're not old. Now my Grandma Aanya, she's old."

"Point taken," Gwendy says. "Say on, O revered Bug Man."

"Well, it was only later, when I found out about the cognitive assessment test they made you take, that I went back to them and spoke my true mind."

"They didn't make me do anything, Adesh. I agreed."

Adesh nods, then shakes his head. "Nevertheless, I was very angry when I heard what they did. And I told them so."

Gwendy is genuinely touched. "You're a good friend. Thank you."

"And when I heard that you passed the test with flying colors, I marched right back in there and said, 'I told you so.' A brilliant woman like you could never fail such a basic assessment."

If only you knew, she thinks sadly.

"Anyway, I needed to get that off my chest. In case people tell you, 'That Bug Man, he spoke out of turn.' It's the correct phrase, isn't it? Out of turn?"

"Yes."

"I just wanted you to know I had to speak my mind."

She floats up a few inches to give his shoulder an affectionate squeeze—and that's when she sees it. Maybe thirty yards behind them, where the inner wall of the corridor curves out of sight, someone is standing in the shadow of the big overhead air purifier, watching them. Before

Gwendy can call out or get a better look, the figure disappears. *Winston?* she wonders.

"... say the word."

She turns back to Adesh. "I'm sorry ... I missed that. What did you say?"

"I said if there's anything I can do to help you, anything at all, please just say the word."

Gwendy's mind—suddenly very clear, and what a gift that is—flashes to her laptop. Probably she forgot to put it away, just as she forgot her notebook on Eagle Heavy. But if she *did* put it away ... and then it was not only back on the coffee table but *open* ...

"As a matter of fact, there might be something." Because of all the people she rode the rocket with, Adesh Patel is the one she trusts the most.

"Tell me," he says.

38

THE ZOOM MEETING WITH the University of Maine faculty and staff goes well. Gwendy experiences one minor hiccup—when speaking with the director of Athletics, she accidentally refers to the Black Bears men's basketball team as the Blueberries—but she catches herself right away and makes a joke of it. Everyone enjoys a laugh and she quickly moves on to other topics.

The rest of her afternoon is spent writing a blog entry for the National Geographic Society (complete with a couple of Dave Graves's photos) and video conferencing with the vice president about climate control issues. She has always found the man well-meaning but stupid . . . which pretty well describes Gwendy herself these days, unfortunately. In between these chores, she catches up on emails and practices tying her shoes (murmuring the bunny song as she does). At some point, she closes her eyes and tries reaching out to Gareth Winston, but nothing comes back to her. Not even the subtlest vibrations confirming his presence on the space station. Another chocolate animal might help, but it also might be a very bad idea.

At one point, Gwendy finds herself looking out the big main window with no idea how she got there. Or when.

NG, she thinks.

At dinner, Winston sits about as far away from Gwendy as is possible. *Wonder why*, she thinks with a satisfied smirk.

For dessert, Sam Drinkwater surprises the crew with a pan of homemade chocolate brownies, still warm from the oven. Gwendy eats two, including a crunchy corner piece, her favorite ever since she was a young girl. They're certainly not the button box's special chocolates—for starters, they taste nothing alike, and for finishers, they possess not even a hint of magic—but the brownies are delicious just the same. A cozy and much-needed reminder of home and simpler times.

After dinner, Gwendy stops by the weather deck. Her work is done for the day, but she's not quite tired enough to call it a night. She also doesn't want to return to her room just yet. Ever since the upsetting incident involving her running shoes, the button box's voice has grown louder and more insistent and more difficult to push away. She's hoping that staring into the enormous telescope for ten or fifteen minutes will be just the ticket for her beleaguered brain. But that's not the only reason she likes coming here.

In some ways the Many Flags weather deck—with its own gigantic window like a hanging glass ornament, and its softly humming monitors—reminds Gwendy of Our Lady of Serene Waters Catholic Church back in Castle Rock. She finds the atmosphere calming for both the body and the soul, and it provides her a sort of celestial cathedral in which to reflect. And the view is—no pun, just truth—downright heavenly.

All of this is a miracle, she thinks, staring out at the dark expanse of . . . everything. *How many other worlds exist in this endless sea of stars and planets and galaxies? How many other life forms might be staring back at me right at this very moment?*

She remembers a warm July night when she was

eleven—the summer before the button box first entered her life. A month earlier, just before the end of the school year, Gwendy's fifth-grade science teacher, Mr. Loggins—who more often than not taught his daily lessons with a big green crusty booger visible in one or both nostrils—had taken the class on a field trip to the planetarium. Most of the kids, already snared in summer vacation's web of promise, spent those ninety minutes in the dark throwing jelly beans at their friends, gossiping about who was and who wasn't invited to Katy Sharrett's end-of-year pool party, and making fart sounds by stuffing their hands into their armpits.

Not Gwendy. She had been fascinated. When she got home from school later that afternoon, she'd immediately begged her parents to buy her a telescope. After intense negotiations involving her weekend chore duties, Mr. and Mrs. Peterson agreed to share the cost with their daughter (seventy-five percent mom and dad, twenty-five percent Gwendy). On the first Saturday afternoon of summer break, Gwendy and her father drove out to the Sears store on Route 119 in Lewiston and picked up a Galaxy 313 StarFinder at thirty percent off the ticketed price. Gwendy was ecstatic.

On the July night she's thinking about, the telescope was set up in the corner of the backyard, just a few paces away from the picnic table and grill. Her father, who had come outside earlier, was snoring in a lawn chair, a couple of empty cans of Black Label lying beside him in the freshly cut grass. After a while, her mother appeared and tucked the fuzzy red blanket from the den sofa over him. Then she joined her daughter by the telescope.

"Take a look, Mom," Gwendy said, stepping aside.

559

Mrs. Peterson peered into the eyepiece. What she saw—a twisting band of shimmering stars as brilliant and bright as rare diamonds—stole her breath.

"It's the constellation Scorpius," Gwendy explained. "Made up of four different star clusters."

"It's beautiful, Gwendy."

"Some nights, when it's clear enough, you can see a huge red star right there in the middle. It's called Antares."

Fireflies danced in the darkness around them. Somewhere down the street a dog began barking.

"It's like looking through a window at heaven," Mrs. Peterson said.

"Do you . . ." All of a sudden Gwendy's tone was unsure. "Do you really think there's . . ."

Mrs. Peterson stepped away from the telescope and looked at her daughter, who was no longer staring up at the night sky. "Do I think what, honey?"

"Do you really think there's a heaven?"

Mrs. Peterson was instantly struck with such an overpowering swell of love for her daughter that it made her heart ache. "Are you thinking about Grandma Helen right now?" Mrs. Peterson's mother had passed away earlier in the spring as a result of complications from early-onset diabetes. She was only sixty-one. The entire family had taken it hard, especially Gwendy. It had been her first intimate experience with death.

Gwendy didn't answer.

"You want to know what I believe?"

She slowly raised her eyes. "Yes."

Mrs. Peterson glanced over at her husband. He had rolled onto his side with his back to them and was no longer snoring. The blanket had fallen onto the grass. When she looked back at her daughter standing there in the dark, Mrs. Peterson was shocked at how small and fragile the eleven-year-old looked.

"First of all, I want you to pay special attention to exactly what I just said. I asked if you wanted to know what I *believed*, right? I didn't ask if you wanted to know what I *thought*. There's a difference between the two. Does that make sense?"

"I think so."

"*Thinking* something is more often than not about logical or intellectual deduction. And that's a good thing. Like the things they teach you about at school. Proper thinking leads to learning and learning leads to knowledge. That's why you know so much about so many interesting things like the scorpion constellation."

"Scorpius."

"Exactly," Mrs. Peterson said, ruffling Gwendy's hair. "But *believing* . . . now that's something different. Something much more . . . . personal."

"You mean like Olive Kepnes believing in the Loch Ness monster and aliens? Those are personal choices for her?"

"That's one way to look at it. But I was thinking of God. The Bible tells us that He's real, there are hundreds of stories about Him, but we've never seen Him with our own eyes, right? And no one we know—no one who's even alive right now—has ever seen Him either. Right?"

"Right."

"But many of us still choose to believe that He exists. And that kind of belief, the kind that comes from deep within your heart and soul, the kind that may at times even appear to defy common logic, is *faith*."

"We learned about faith a long time ago in Sunday school."

"Well, there you go. I have faith that there's a God watching over all He's created, and I have faith that there's a wonderful place waiting for all those who choose to live a good life. I don't know what heaven looks like or where it is or even if it's an actual physical place. In fact, I kind of have my doubts about the whole 'angels wearing white robes floating around on clouds playing harps' scenario."

Gwendy giggled, and Mrs. Peterson felt that ache in her heart again. It wasn't a bad ache.

"But yes, I believe heaven exists and Grandma Helen is there right now."

"But *why* do you believe those things?"

"Look around us, Gwendy. Tell me what you see."

She looked to her left and then her right, and then up at the sky. "I see houses and trees and stars and the moon."

"And what do you hear?"

She cocked her head to the side. "A train whistle . . . the Robinsons' German shepherd barking . . . a car with a bad muffler."

"What else? Listen closely this time."

She cocked her head again, to the opposite side this time, and Mrs. Peterson lifted a hand to her face to cover a smile. "I hear the wind blowing through the treetops. And an owl hoot-hooting!"

Mrs. Peterson laughed. "Now tell me quick, what's your favorite memory of Grandma Helen?"

"Her Christmas cookies," Gwendy answered right away. "And her stories! I loved her bedtime stories when I was little!"

"Me too," Mrs. Peterson said. "Now take a look through your telescope again."

She did.

"All of those things you just answered—and so much more; my gosh, *so* much more, dear girl; think of your Grandpa Charlie and your best friend, Olive; think of those amazing star clusters of yours; and before you go to sleep tonight, take a good long look at yourself in the mirror—*those* are the reasons why I believe. Do you think all those miracles could exist without a God? I don't. And do you think—"

Before she could finish, a shooting star raced across the night sky. They stared at it with breathless wonder until it eventually flared out and disappeared. Mrs. Peterson wrapped her arms around her daughter and pulled her close. When she spoke again it was barely a whisper, and Gwendy realized that her mother was either crying or close.

"And do you think God would've bothered to create all those miracles and not have created a heaven to go right along with them?" She shook her head. "Not me."

"Guess I don't, either," Gwendy says now, standing in front of the weather deck's floor-to-ceiling window. And for perhaps the first time in her adult life, she truly believes it. Gwendy has an unobstructed bird's-eye view of Earth below, but she doesn't even give it a glance. Instead, she gazes far off into the mysteries of the up-above and forever-onward, and whispers, "For me, you were the biggest miracle of all, Mom."

39

Day 5 on Many Flags.

Gwendy is almost to the cafeteria—close enough to smell freeze-dried scrambled eggs and sausage in the pleasantly filtered air of Spoke 4—when she realizes she left her red notebook back in the suite. Earlier this morning she put it down on the coffee table next to her laptop so she could type out a quick email and told herself not to forget it. But, like so many other things these days, she *did* forget. *NG*, she scolds herself, and pivots in mid-bounce like a ninja in one of the ridiculous chop-socky movies Ryan used to love so much.

Despite this little speed bump, today has been a good day. Maybe even a great day. For the first time since saying goodbye to Earth's atmosphere—*Who am I kidding?* she thinks; *for the first time in probably five or six years!*—Gwendy Peterson enjoyed an uninterrupted night of sleep. She'd dreamt she was camping out with Olive Kepnes in her backyard in Castle Rock. They'd toasted marshmallows, flipped through a new issue of *Teen Beat* magazine (Shaun Cassidy oh God such a hunk!), and giggled about cute boys until the sun came up.

When she'd awakened, fifteen minutes before her alarm was set to go off, she felt like a brand-new woman—brimming with energy and determination and, most importantly, clarity. *Don't forget hope*, she'd told her reflection in the steamed-up mirror after a long, relaxing shower. *Two more days and all of this madness will be over.*

Gwendy is humming the theme song to *The Sopranos* and practically skipping down the main corridor in Spoke 1 when she runs into Dr. Glen heading in the opposite direction. When Dale looks up and sees the senator, he flashes a grin. "Someone got up on the right side of the bed this morning."

"Absolutely, Doc. I'm a free woman. No Zoom meetings, no conference calls, no weather girl duties. Not a single thing on the schedule today. I just might crawl back into bed after breakfast and stay there for the rest of the day! So I ask you, who's got it better than me?"

He raises his eyebrows as he glides past her on the tips of his toes. "I guess that would be no one, at least not up here."

"See you at breakfast in a few," she says, cheerfully waving a hand over her shoulder. "Just need to grab something from my room."

"Want me to wait?"

"Nope, go on ahead. I'll be right behind you."

Gwendy is still smiling when she opens the door to her suite. She takes a couple of steps inside—and freezes.

Gareth Winston is down on one knee in front of her sitting room closet. The door is open and Gwendy's extra pressure suit has been pushed out of the way. She can see some kind of gadget— shiny black metal, not much larger than an iPhone—attached to the keypad on the safe. Several dark wires run from the base of the gadget to what looks like a small calculator with a digital readout screen. Winston is holding the calculator thingamajig in his hands. When Gwendy bursts into the room, he drops it and scrambles to his feet, leaving the gadget to float.

565

"What are you doing here?" She's pretty sure she already knows the answer. Her brain may be broken, but she's not stupid. "Do you have any idea how much trouble you're in? Tampering with classified material is a federal offense."

"I don't believe I'm in any kind of trouble at all, Senator." Winston's eyes look nervous, but his voice never wavers.

"I guess we'll see what Commander Lundgren has to say about that." She turns to leave.

Rattlesnake quick (*and twice as mean*, she has just enough time to think), Winston lunges across the sitting room and grabs her arm. If Gwendy hadn't just seen it with her own eyes, she never would've believed the man was capable of moving that quickly. *Of course*, she thinks, *that's zero-g for you.* His fingers dig into her flesh as he drags her toward the center of the room and shoves her down onto the sofa. "Even if you somehow managed to get away, it would be too late by the time you got back with the others."

"What do you mean, *too late*?"

"You see that little black box over there?" He gestures to the gadget affixed to the safe's keypad. "That marvel of technology is called a LockMaster 3000. It's available to the public for not much more than the cost of a decent laptop. It usually takes no more than ten minutes to reset a four-digit combination and provide a new entry code. These Many Flags safes are a little trickier, probably because Tet is expecting some high-powered people to eventually be using the quarters up here, but in the end it'll do the job. May take twenty minutes or even half an hour, but oh yes, it'll get there."

"I'd be back here a lot quicker than half an hour—and with plenty of help, too."

He scratches his chin thoughtfully. "That's assuming I let you go anywhere. It's a fair assumption on your part, I suppose—as a U.S. senator, you're used to going wherever you want, whenever you want—but this time the assumption would be wrong. I don't want to go all Snidely Whiplash on you, dear, but why would I set you free to roam before I get my hands on the button box? And once I do . . . goodness! Who knows what might happen?"

When she hears the words *button box* come out of Gareth Winston's mouth, for a dizzying moment Gwendy thinks she may pass out. *That would be a very bad idea*, she thinks. *That would be the end of everything.*

"What do you know about the button box?"

"Some, but not enough. I'm counting on you to fill me in on the rest."

"Never," she says.

He smiles. "Spoken like a true movie heroine, but I think you will."

"Let's cut to the chase, Winston, okay? We sit and wait for your little gadget to do its thing, you take possession of the box, and then what?"

"Then you have an unfortunate accident. If the box can't provide it, I have something that can."

She bares her teeth in a humorless grin. "They'll all know, Winston. My God, you have to see that. And you'll go to prison—federal prison, not some state dump—for the rest of your life."

"I don't think so," he says, shaking his head so rapidly the flesh on his cheeks jiggles back and forth like Jell-O.

567

STEPHEN KING

"Several on board suspect you're . . . how shall I say this? Mentally challenged."

"The cognitive test—"

"Sam Drinkwater and Dave Graves think you cheated somehow—that nobody could score as high as you did."

"I'm losing my mind, but I'm still smart enough to cheat?"

Gareth snickers. "I believe you just described most of your colleagues in the House and Senate, not to mention the president himself: just smart enough to cheat. But let's not talk politics. Let's get back to you instead. A fatal accident would be mourned, of course—you'd be a national hero, maybe get your face on a postage stamp, not to mention a million tee-shirts—but no one would be that surprised. Not really. Cognitive issues so blatant you were forced to take a test? I wouldn't even be surprised if some of the bigwigs at TetCorp lose their jobs as a result of it. The media will say your unsound mind should have shown up sooner, that somebody missed it. Doctor Glen will undoubtedly come in for his share of the blame."

"I've sent emails," Gwendy says, gesturing to her laptop on the coffee table. "Friends in high places back in the States know all about you, Winnie. They know you stole the combination to the security case, for one thing."

The lizard smile disappears from Winston's face. It's a possibility he hasn't considered. "Suspicion is one thing, but providing proof is quite another. And that would be nearly impossible without any witnesses."

He pulls a small object from his pocket and holds it up for her to see. It looks like a tube of lipstick, and it's the same weirdly vibrant green as the Chrysler from the

Derry video. A cartoon green. It hurts Gwendy's eyes to look at it.

"A good friend of mine gave this to me. No idea what it's made of but I can tell you this: it's virtually undetectable by modern security systems. And it's lethal. All you have to do is point, then twist the little metal loop in the base. One spray and it turns your insides into jelly. There's plenty of juice inside this canister to take care of the entire crew if necessary."

"How would you get back? You gonna fly the ship home yourself?" And then before she can stop herself: "Your little blond friend teach you how to do that, too?"

Before Gwendy can react, Winston has her pinned against the back of the sofa, his meaty forearm pressing down on her throat. There's a thunderstorm in Winston's eyes, and for a terrifying moment Gwendy is certain he's going to kill her right now. "How do you know about Bobby?"

"I . . . saw it in a dream," she manages to get out. "You were sitting inside a car with him. A green car."

For the first time, Winston looks unsure. And scared—that, too. "Then you know enough not to fuck around with these people." He removes his arm from her throat. "I don't think Bobby's his real name and I don't think he's human. He and his friends mean business, and so do I." He pauses. "He's beautiful, though. Like an angel. Except sometimes it looks like there's something inside him, his real self, and that's not so beautiful." He lowers his voice. "His real self has *fur*."

Sudden tears spill from Gwendy's eyes, and she silently scolds herself for showing weakness. She lifts a trembling hand to her neck and rubs the already sore muscles. It feels like something inside of her is broken.

"If you were to kill me and the rest of the crew, you'd be stranded here. You'd *die* here, Winston."

The ugly grin resurfaces on Winston's overfed face. "Let's just say I could hitch a ride back with my Chinese friends."

"They would never allow . . ." She stops as the reality of his words hit home. "They . . . you . . . you son of a bitch, you bribed them."

"I wouldn't necessarily call it a bribe." He chuckles into his fist. "Bribes are for pikers, dear. This was an investment in their future."

"Why are you doing this? Is it money?" *Keep him talking, keep him talking.*

"Don't be foolish. I have more money than I could spend in a thousand lifetimes."

"Then why?" Almost pleading now. "Why do you want it so badly?"

"That's quite a story." He glances over at the closet where the LockMaster 3000 is busy doing its thing. "But since we have time, why not?" He props his feet up on the coffee table and crosses his arms behind his head, like he's back home in his MetLife Stadium skybox watching the Giants and the Eagles square off on a Sunday afternoon. "In October of 2024 I was in St. Louis for my father's funeral . . ."

40

THE NAME OF THE *funeral home is Broadview & Sons, and once he signs off on the bill, Gareth Winston beats feet out of there. Winston hates funeral homes. Almost as much as he hated his father.*

It was the oldest story in the book—nothing the devoted son accomplished was ever enough to please the overly critical father with the razor-sharp tongue, so at some point, the son simply stopped trying.

Lawrence Winston III, also known as dear old Dad, made his piddling fortune selling commercial real estate and collecting rent checks on almost five hundred two- and three-bedroom apartments in a string of downtown high-rises. In the late '80s, a reporter from the St. Louis Post-Dispatch *referred to the senior Winston as "a part-time slumlord and full-time scumbag." When Gareth banked his first billion at age thirty-three, the first thing he did was FedEx his father a photocopy of that newspaper article and a handwritten note on company stationery:*

> **I still can't hit a curve ball or a 2 iron. I still don't have an Ivy League diploma. I'm overweight. And I'm still not married to a beautiful Catholic virgin from across the river. But I'm filthy-ass rich and you're not. Have a miserable fucking life.**
> **Gareth**

And then he never spoke to the man again.

Not even when his father called to make amends from his deathbed.

The hard truth of the matter is if it weren't for his mother—whom Winston still adores and makes a point of calling every Sunday night no matter where he is in the world, a tradition that first began after Winston left home for college—he wouldn't have even come home for the funeral, much less footed the bill. But she begged him over the telephone, and if there is one person in this world Winston can't refuse, it's his mother. Corny but true.

After the obligatory reception, there's a car waiting to take Winston back to his hotel suite, but he decides to walk instead. He needs the fresh air, plus he'd skipped breakfast this morning and is starving. Walking at a rapid pace, he cuts across McKinley Avenue, picks up South Euclid, and then takes a left onto Parkview. From there, he stops to buy three hot dogs and a bottle of Diet Pepsi from a street vendor and settles his considerable bulk on an empty bench overlooking the northeastern corner of Forest Park. From where he's sitting he can spot the pale oval of the skating rink—still six weeks out from opening weekend—as well as the seventh fairway of the Highlands Golf Course, which he wouldn't be caught dead playing. It's strictly for small-timers.

He's wiping a dribble of mustard off his shirt when a fluorescent green Chrysler swings up to the curb beside him. It looks to be roughly two miles long. Winston gives the car a once-over but is unable to determine what year it rolled off the assembly line. All he knows is that it looks very old and in cherry condition, and he's never seen another car like it. I wonder if it's for sale, *he thinks idly.*

The driver's-side window glides down. A man with short blond hair and striking emerald eyes, the bottom half of his face

hidden behind a red bandana, leans his head out of the car and says, "Hop in. Let's go for a ride."

Winston grins. He's always liked a cheeky bastard, having been one himself all his life. "Nice ride, mister, but that's not gonna happen." He starts to ask the stranger why he's wearing a mask—few people wear masks anymore, not since the arrival of the vaccines a couple years ago—but he never gets that far.

"I don't have much time, Mr. Winston. Get in."

Winston's eyes narrow. "How do you know my name?" The answer to that is obvious: he's seen it in the papers or on one of the business channels, where Gareth Winston is a fixture. "Who are you?"

"A friend. And I know lots of things about you, Mr. Winston."

Because of the red bandana, Winston is unable to see the stranger's mouth, but he's nonetheless certain that the man is smiling. "I don't know who the hell you think you're talking to, but—"

"When you were twelve, you broke into your neighbors' house while they were away on vacation. Frank and Betsy Rhineman. Nice people. It's a shame their son died so young."

"How do you know the—"

"You stripped out of the swim trunks you were wearing and slipped on a pair of Mrs. Rhineman's panties—pale yellow with a black lace border, not too frilly—ate an ice cream sandwich you found in their freezer, and shot some billiards in the game room. Then, before you changed back into your trunks and scooted home for dinner, you returned upstairs and masturbated on the bedspread in the Rhinemans' guest bedroom."

"You're lying!" Winston bellows, startling a young mother walking by pushing a baby stroller. She quickly crosses the street to put some distance between them. "Stop it right now!" The billionaire's face has gone beet-red and his eyes are bulging.

"You still have the yellow panties to this day. They're tucked away in a safety-deposit box at your bank in Newark. Along with a few other equally distasteful treasures."

"Fake fucking news! None of what you're saying is true!"

"Would you like to hear some more?"

Winston is quiet for a moment, his broad chest rising and falling in great heaves. Then he asks in a quiet voice, "What do you want?"

"To make you an offer. The most generous offer you've ever been presented with. Get in the car, Mr. Winston. Let's chat."

"Sounds too good to be true, and what sounds that way never is." But he's already getting up from the park bench, leaving behind his lunch trash and walking toward the car.

"Could be," the stranger says, and removes the bandana from his face.

Winston takes a good look at the stranger and does a double take, then a triple take. And suddenly there's no longer any question in his mind about getting inside the car. He isn't gay—has never found the male form even remotely attractive, especially his own—but the blond man is so breathtakingly beautiful Winston wants to hold the man's face in his hands and kiss him. He wants to feel those lips and taste that breath. He looks like an angel, Winston thinks, opening the passenger door and sliding into the seat. As soon as he closes the door, a loud buzzing rises in the basement of his brain, like thousands of flies crawling over a rotting corpse. He turns to the man as the car pulls away from the curb. "Where are we going?"

"Just up the street and around the corner. For a little privacy."

A chill dances along Winston's spine at the mention of the word privacy. He feels an instant tightening in his groin. The man cruises two blocks east and pulls into the parking lot of an abandoned warehouse. He drives around back and stops in front of an empty loading dock. Winston can see shards of broken glass, several rusty needles, and a scattering of used condoms lying on the asphalt outside of the car. But he doesn't care. Just like he doesn't care about the insistent buzzing deep in his brain. All that matters now is the blond angel sitting next to him.

The man switches off the engine and turns to him. "Allow me to properly introduce myself." He extends his right hand. "You can call me Bobby."

Winston reaches over and takes his hand. The man's skin feels smooth and pleasant, like warm butter. The tightening in the crotch of Winston's slacks deepens to a dull throbbing.

"What I have to say to you, what I have to offer you, won't take long," the stranger says. "But I need you to listen very carefully."

Winston, adrift in a haze, slowly nods his head.

"My associates and I are well aware of your great wealth, Mr. Winston. But, as you know, there are other standards by which to measure one's legacy." He leans across the seat, close enough for Winston to feel the man's breath wash over him. Winston's already wide eyes widen some more. "Power. Control. Territory.

"There are other worlds than these. Many. You can rule one of them. Not just a company, not just a continent, but an entire world. And you can do it for an eternity."

The buzzing sound inside of Winston's head has diminished. Now he hears something else: the sound of distant waves crashing on a rocky shore. He likes the idea of ruling a world; who wouldn't? It's bullshit, of course, but it would be very nice. Excellent, in fact. He could see himself in a castle by the sea . . . listening to those crashing waves . . . a thousand people bowing down as he stands above them . . . hell, ten thousand! As the Beach Boys' song says, wouldn't it be nice.

"All we need from you is a particular item. It is in possession of a woman named Gwendolyn Peterson—"

"The senator?"

"The very same. We can try to take it ourselves—in fact, we have tried—but the Tower is strong."

"What tower?" Winston asks in a voice that sounds nothing like his own.

"The only one that matters." The blond man reaches over and places a hand on Winston's knee. Winston shudders in plea- sure. He might be gay after all—at least in this man's presence. "Gwendolyn Peterson has what we need to destroy the Tower. You must find it and bring it to us. Because of your enormous wealth and political connections, you are uniquely fitted for this task."

"You're insane." The roar of the ocean swells inside Winston's head.

"Close your eyes," Bobby commands.

Winston is helpless not to obey. It's like being hypnotized. He feels the kiss of a cool breeze upon his face and smells a tinge of salt in the air as soon as his eyes are shut. And then he can taste it on his tongue—the ocean! The sound of crashing waves grows louder, only now it's not just inside his head; it's everywhere. A bird cries out somewhere above him—a gull of some kind—and a chorus of birds answers it.

"Now open them."

Gareth Winston opens his eyes and he's no longer sitting in the green Chrysler behind an abandoned St. Louis ware- house. Instead, he's sitting beside the blond man in a meadow of windswept grass. He stands up and looks down at a churning sea of emerald water. Hundreds of feet below, white-tipped waves crash upon an endless shoreline of jagged rock and sand. The sky above them is streaked with purple and yellow, and there are *birds—hundreds of them!—floating on the wind. The sun rising over the watery horizon is a deep crimson.*

This is real, *he thinks.* My God, this is real.

"What have you done to me?"

"Turn around, Mr. Winston."

He does. Slowly. Like moving in a dream, but this is no dream.

The man points off to the west at a distant city that stretches as far as Winston's eyes can see. The early-morning sunlight glints off the windows of scores of tall buildings. A complex spiderweb of roadways and bridges weaves its way through the shimmering metropolis. It's too far away for Winston to determine the type of vehicles that are currently traveling those roads, but there are many of them. In the sky above the city, there's nary a hint of smog or pollution.

"How big is it?" *Winston asks in dazed awe.*

"Bigger than New York City, Chicago, and Los Angeles combined. And still growing. Surrounded by nearly fifty thousand acres of virgin woodland."

Winston whistles appreciatively.

"There are another two dozen cities just like it scattered throughout the world I'm offering you."

Winston points a finger at a long, dark scar of barren land a few miles directly in front of them. Tiny black figures, like busy ants in a child's ant farm, scurry back and forth in staggered lines. "What's that over there?"

"That," *the man says, a satisfied smile creeping across his face,* "is your diamond mine."

"Really?"

"Really." *For the first time since he stood up from the park bench, there's a glimmer of the old Gareth Winston. His eyes look greedy—and hungry.*

578

"And over there," his new friend continues, pointing to a sprawling castle sitting atop a hilltop overlooking the ocean, "is your home. One of many, I might add. For this residence alone, you employ—a rather kind way of wording it considering you tender none of them a salary—more than two hundred men and women from a nearby village. In exchange for their loyalty and labor, you might allow them to grow their own food tax-free."

"Of course," Winston mutters. In spite of his amazement, his businessman's brain is ticking over. "And possibly medical care. People who think loyalty can't be bought are idiots. There'd have to be some sort of retirement benefits . . . at least for those close to me . . ."

Bobby laughs. The teeth that are momentarily exposed are not those of an angel; yellow and crooked, they are the teeth of a rat. "See? You've already begun to plan. Given your extraordinary mind, you should be quite the successful ruler. And as the years, the decades . . . the centuries! . . . roll by, you will become not a man but a god to those you rule over."

"And there are women?" Winston asks, looking and sounding more and more like his old self with each passing minute. "Not that I've ever had much luck with that."

"Luck plays no role here. Not when you're the king. Not when you're young and handsome and strong."

Winston laughs. "Not so young and strong anymore. And never very handsome, I'm afraid."

"I respectfully disagree, Mr. Winston." He gestures behind them. "Take a look."

When Winston turns and sees the tall, ornate mirror—with its glittering gold trim and polished, hand-carved oak legs—positioned in the long grass, his mouth drops open. When he sees his reflection in the mirror, he gasps.

He appears as young and slim as the morning he drove away to college.

"Here, in your world, you'll look this way forever. And as for being handsome, although you never truly believed it thanks to your father's constant disparagements, you were, at one time— and remain so here, as you can see for yourself—a young man of considerable physical appeal. Your father stole from you the most important gift a young man can possess: self-confidence." The blond man grins. This time his teeth are very straight and white. "But your father is no longer with us, now is he?"

"No, he is not." Winston looks around. "This is real?"

"Yes."

"Could I come here again?"

"To visit, yes. To live and rule . . . not until you bring us what we want. The button box."

Winston finds himself remembering a class he had in college, and a particular line from that class. He didn't understand it then, but now he does. "If it's real, and if I can, I will. I promise."

The man—Bobby—turns Winston away from the mirror. Bobby wants his undivided attention. "Gwendolyn Peterson has been tasked with getting rid of this rather special box once and for all, and there is only one place in her world—or any of the others—where this can happen."

"Where?" Winston asks.

The blond man stops walking. "How would you feel about taking a trip to outer space, Mr. Winston?"

41

"DON'T TELL ME YOU actually believed that cock-and-bull story about ruling your own private world," Gwendy says. "You're one of the most successful businessmen in history. I can't believe you'd take a few moments of . . . I don't know . . . hypnosis as reality."

Winston gives her an odd, knowing smile. "Do *you* believe it?"

Gwendy actually does. She can believe in other worlds because she cannot believe the button box came from hers. Before she can open her mouth to tell a lie that might not sound very convincing, there's a *beeeep* sound.

"Ah!" Gareth says. "I believe the safe has a new code and can now be opened. So why don't we—"

Before he can finish, both of their phones give off the distinctive double tone that means an incoming text from the station rather than a message from the down-below. They both take out their phones, Gwendy from the center pocket of her coverall, Winston from the back pocket of his chinos. Gwendy thinks, and not without sour amusement, *We're like Pavlov's dogs when it comes to these things. The fate of the earth may be at stake, but when the bell rings we salivate. Or in this case, read the text.*

The identical messages are from Sam Drinkwater: **Joining us for breakfast?**

"Text him back," Winston says. "Say we're in a serious

conversation . . . no, *negotiation* . . . about the future of the space program, and they should eat without us."

Gwendy is on the verge of telling Mr. Billionaire Businessman Gareth Winston to stuff it . . . but doesn't.

This has to end, here and now.

That thought sounds like Mr. Farris. Whether it is or isn't doesn't matter. Either way it's true.

She moves closer to Winston (*ugh*) so he can read the text she's preparing to send. It's exactly what he told her to say, with one addition: **Important we not be disturbed until 1100 hours**.

"Excellent. I'm going to open the safe. I can't wait to see what Bobby was so excited about. You, my dear, should sit right where you are like a good little Gwendy." He shows her the green lipstick tube. "Unless, that is, you want to find out what it feels like to die with your guts melting inside you."

He starts to rise, but she takes his arm and pulls him back down. In zero-g, it's easy. "Help me get my head around this. One hypnotic trance and you just fall into line? I don't believe it. You're not that stupid. In fact, you're not stupid at all."

Winston probably knows she's just trying to buy time, but he preens at the compliment anyway. Gwendy gives him her best wide-eyed tell-me-more look. It usually works in Senate committees (at least with men), and it works now.

"I have been back to Genesis many times," he says. "That's what I call my world. Nice, eh?"

"Very," Gwendy says, doing the wide-eyed thing for all she's worth.

"It's real enough. Bobby—he says I'd never be able to pronounce his real name—has given me certain instructions for going there. I could go there now, if I liked. My visits are necessarily short, but once I give him—and his controllers—this box of yours, I'll go there for good." He gives her a goony smile that makes her doubt his sanity. "It's going to be *great*."

"A hallucination," Gwendy persists. "Had to've been. This Bobby sold you a grander version of the Brooklyn Bridge." She shakes her head. "I still can't believe you fell for it."

He smiles indulgently and reaches inside his shirt. He brings out a pendant on a silver chain. In the gold setting is a huge diamond. "From my mine," he says. "I have others at my home in the Bahamas, some even bigger. This one is forty carat. I had one of similar size appraised, first to make sure it was real and second to determine its worth. The Swiss jeweler who looked at it almost had a heart attack on the spot. He offered me a hundred and ninety thousand dollars, which means it's probably worth twice or three times as much."

He drops the pendant back inside his shirt. "Genesis is real enough, and when I'm there I'm young and virile. The women . . ." He wets his fat lips.

"No more panty stealing, I take it," Gwendy says.

He gives her a glowering look, then actually laughs. "I suppose I deserve that. Don't know why I told you. No— no more panty stealing." He looks away from Gwendy, and she thinks that while he's distracted she might be able to grab something and whack him on the head. Except everything is fastened down, and the idea of clonking someone hard enough to knock them out in zero-g conditions is ridiculous.

When he looks back at her, he's wearing a rueful smile that's almost likable . . . or would be if he were not threatening her life and planning to steal the button box she's been charged with guarding and ultimately disposing of.

"When Bobby took me that first time, I remembered something a teacher said in an Ancient History class I took in college. I didn't want to take the damn thing, cut most of the classes and hired some grind to do my final paper, but that one thing stuck in my head. It was from an old Greek—I think he was a Greek—named Plutarch. Or maybe he was a Roman."

"Greek," Gwendy says. "Although he *became* a Roman."

Winston looks annoyed at the interruption. "Whatever. This Plutarch wrote something about a conqueror named Alexander. I can't remember the exact wording, but—"

Gwendy interrupts again. She likes interrupting him, and why not? He has not only interrupted her task, he's threatening to permanently interrupt her life. "'When Alexander saw the breadth of his domain, he wept for there were no more worlds to conquer.'"

Instead of looking pissed off, Winston smiles so widely that the bottom half of his face almost disappears, and Gwendy thinks again that he's insane. *The prospect of having his own world, one where he can rule forever, has driven him over the edge. Maybe it would anybody.*

"That's it! Exactly! And I was like Alexander, Senator Peterson! I had no more worlds to conquer! I had reached my limit! And what did I have to look forward to? Growing older? Watching helplessly as I grew fatter, as my face began to wrinkle, as my body began to deteriorate?

And my mind!" The smile becomes a nasty grin. "You'd know about that, wouldn't you?"

Gwendy doesn't take the bait. "For the sake of argument, let's say that world exists, Gareth. Even if it does, you won't get it. Not if you give them the button box."

Winston's grin fades. What replaces it is a look of narrow distrust. "What do you mean?"

"What I say. Give it to them and the world ends. If this Tower is as powerful as you say it is, *all* worlds end. Including yours, diamonds and all."

He gives a scornful laugh. "Why would these people— Bobby's people—do that? They'd die along with everyone and everything else."

"I think . . . because Bobby's people, those who pull his strings like he pulled yours, are the lords of chaos." And then, in a voice she doesn't recognize as her own, Gwendy cries, "Let the Tower fall! Rule, Discordia!"

Winston recoils as if that voice were a hand that had struck him. "Are you insane?"

It was Farris's voice, Gwendy thinks. *I don't know how or why—he must be dead by now—but it was.* Then she remembers the last time she saw him, on her porch in Castle Rock. *I'll help if I can*, he said that night.

"Think about what you're doing, Winston. For God's sake, *think*."

"I have. And I know when someone is trying to fuck with my head. Let's get a look at this fabled button box. Sit where you are, Senator. You won't get a second warning."

Of course not, Gwendy thinks. *The only reason I'm still alive is because he needs to make sure he has it. Once he does, he'll point that tube at me and—*

"Ah," Winston says. He's peering at the safe, which

puts him between Gwendy and the door. "The reset combo is 1111. I believe even someone who's losing her mind could remember that one."

He removes the LockMaster and pushes the combo—*beep-beep-beep-beep*. She hopes the gadget didn't work, that the safe will remain shut, but the door swings open when Winston pulls the handle. Out comes the steel case with **CLASSIFIED MATERIAL** stamped on it. "I don't need to consult your little notebook again for the code to this one," Winston says. "One look was enough. Unlike yours, my memory is in perfect working order. People are amazed at my recall."

"Don't sprain your shoulder patting yourself on the back," Gwendy says coldly.

Winston laughs. Now that he has the case Gwendy swore to protect with her life, he seems quite cheerful. Perhaps he's thinking of his diamond mine. Or having a ménage à trois with two beautiful young women. Or a ticker tape parade in one of his fine new cities with thousands of people shouting his name. Gwendy could tell him about the black button—the Cancer Button that supposedly ends everything—but would he listen? No. He is Alexander, with a new world to conquer.

"1512253 . . . and presto!" He opens the steel box. He looks inside. His eager smile dissolves. "What . . . the *fuck* . . . is *this*?"

He takes out a white feather. When he lets it go, it floats in front of his face. Winston bats it away. He turns the security case so she can see inside. With the feather now out of it, the case is completely empty.

"Surprise, Mr. Winston," Gwendy says, and the

slack-jawed shock on his face makes her laugh. But then shock is replaced by a look of fury Gwendy hasn't seen before. Suddenly she can see the Gareth Winston who lives inside, and he's no laughing matter.

I'm looking at a human wolf, she thinks.

Then he grins, which is even worse.

He lets go of the CLASSIFIED case, leaving it to float near the longtime talisman she calls her magic feather. He glides across to her. She shrinks back involuntarily and raises her hands to protect her throat.

"Oh, I'm not going to choke you," he says, still smiling. "I might kill you"—he raises the green cylinder—"but it won't be a hands-on affair. And it will be *very* unpleasant."

Gwendy thinks, *The black button is the Cancer Button and that green thing is the Tube of Death. I've wandered into a fucking comic book.*

He shows her the ring on the bottom of the tube. "If I twist this all the way while it's pointed at you, the disintegration of your organs will be instantaneous. I know, because I've tried it."

"On one of your subjects," Gwendy says. Her voice sounds far away. "In Genesis."

"You *are* a bright one, at least when you're in your right mind. Too bright for your own good. The point is, my dear, that if I twist the ring slowly . . . a teeny-tiny bit at a time . . . you'll die in excruciating agony. You may actually feel your heart come loose from its moorings and drop into your stomach *while it's still beating.* Wouldn't *that* be something to experience!"

Yes, it's a comic book, all right, she thinks. *Too bad I can't just shut it and toss it in the UV waste disposal. Too bad it's actually happening.*

"You see," he says, as if speaking to a child, "I've come too far to turn back now, Senator. I have burned my bridges. Which is all right because, unlike you, I have an escape hatch. One that will take me to another world. A world I've already come to love. Let me tell you what's going to happen if you don't get with the program, you smartass bitch. You die—miserably, screaming through your disintegrating vocal cords— and then the rest of our Eagle Heavy compatriots die. Once the killing's done I will call in my Chinese allies and we will search this place until I find what I came for. When I do, I will exit my current abode in a kind of space taxi provided by a corporation you may have heard of—"

"Sombra."

"Yes! Good for you! I'll turn over the box to those who want it so badly, and exit this reality for a much more pleasant one. Do you understand?"

"I believe the smartass bitch is following you," Gwendy says.

"None of that has to happen, Gwendy. You can live. The rest of the crew can live, which will please me. You might not believe it, but I've come to like them. I will take the button box and go."

Given a choice between believing that and believing in the tooth fairy, I'd opt for the fairy, Gwendy thinks, but she nods as if she believes him. He's pointing the tube at her and fiddling with the ring on the bottom in a way that makes her very nervous. Only *nervous* is too mild a word for it. She's scared to death.

"Now we come to the Final Jeopardy question," Winston says. He's still grinning, but Gwendy can see beads of perspiration on his forehead. He's scared, too. That gives her at least some comfort. "Where is it?"

She opens her mouth, closes it, then opens it again.

"You're not going to believe this, Gareth, and I know you won't like it, but it's true. I can't remember."

42

HE STARES AT HER, eyes slitted. "You're right. I don't believe it. You aced the cognitive test they gave you. Dr. Glen was very impressed."

"I had the chocolates then."

"If you don't start making sense, dear, you are going to be very sorry."

Note to self, Gwendy thinks. *Having a panty thief call you* dear *is extremely repulsive.*

"The button box dispenses chocolates. They're brain boosts." They do much more, some of it not good, but this is no time for lengthy explanations. "I took a couple before the test. As you see, I can't do that now because the box isn't h—"

"I don't believe you. It's hogwash."

"Says the man who believes he's going to rule an entire planet, complete with pulp novel slave women and a handy nearby diamond mi—"

He slaps her. In zero-g it's not hard, like a slap underwater, but it shocks her. She has been hit before, but not since childhood. The one who hit her lived to regret it . . . but not for long. Her eyes flash wide, and he sees something in them that makes him dance-float backward, leveling the tube at her.

She thinks, *I'm not a proponent of the death penalty, but if I get a chance,* dear, *I'm going to kill you. If you'd been involved in Ryan's death, I'd try to kill you twice. Luckily for you, that happened before you got involved in this business. At least if I can believe your story.* And she does. According to Winston, he met Bobby four years later, and what reason would he have to lie? All their cards are pretty much on the table now.

"You don't want to make fun of me, Senator. That's one thing you absolutely don't want to do."

"I'm not. *I can't remember where I put it.*"

"In that case I have no use for you, do I? I'll have to find it on my own, with the help of my Chinese associates. After I negate the rest of the crew, that is." He raises the tube, and she sees in his eyes that he means to do it.

"Give me a minute to think. Please."

"I'll give you thirty seconds." He lifts his watch to his face. "Starting right now."

Gwendy knows Winston thinks she's faking; Gwendy knows she isn't. She needs to use Dr. Ambrose's trick, find a chain of association and follow it to the location of the button box. Only her time is fleeting and she can't find a starting link. Her mind is whirling.

Yes, Richard Farris says, *this isn't good. You are in dire straits.*

That lights her up, and when Winston aims the tube, she raises a hand. "Wait! Wait! I can get it!"

Dire Straits. Not Ryan's favorite band, but one of them . . . and he loved that song about how sometimes you're the windshield and sometimes you're—

"The bug! Sometimes you're the windshield and sometimes you're the bug!"

"What in Christ's name are you talking about, woman?"

"About the Bug Man. The only person in the crew I

trust one hundred percent. The only one who believes in me completely. Adesh. I gave him the button box. I told him to put it in his lab."

"Really?"

"Yes."

"Do you know *where* in the lab?"

Gwendy doesn't have a clue. "Yes. I'll show you."

"I should kill you and find it myself," he says. He raises the green tube . . . then lowers it again. And smiles. "But you've been troublesome, dear. *So* troublesome. I think I want you to watch me take possession of your precious box. I might even let you live. Who knows?"

You know, Gwendy thinks. *And I know.*

"Let's go, while they're still all at breakfast." He gestures with the tube. "After you, Senator."

43

SPOKE 5.

They float-walk down the corridor past signs in French: LAVEZ-VOUS LES MAINS and RAMASSE TA POUBELLE and even NE PASSE FUMER, which Gwendy would have thought a no-brainer. But with the French and their Gauloises, who could tell?

There's that steady low creaking. Gwendy has gotten used to it, but Winston, it seems, has not.

"I hate that sound. It's like the whole place is coming apart."

"No," Gwendy says, "you'll be the one tearing it apart. Tearing *everything* apart."

It doesn't even touch him. *Classic narcissist*, she thinks. Maybe it's true to some degree of all mega-successful businessmen and women. God, she hopes not.

"Why did you give it to the brownie? And what did you tell him?"

The brownie, Gwendy thinks. *Jesus. And he probably thinks of Jafari as the blackie.*

"Because I trusted him, I told you that. As for what I told him . . ." She shook her head. "Can't remember."

This is a lie. Now she remembers everything. How hard it was to actually hand it over, for one thing. She remembers Adesh's look of curiosity, and most of all she remembers telling him he must not touch the buttons. *You*

603

may feel an urge to do just that, but you must resist it. Can you? Adesh had said yes—yes, he was quite sure he could— and because Gwendy had to trust someone, she gave him the box. Then had to resist her own almost insurmountable urge to snatch it back, cradling it to her breasts and shouting, *Mine! Mine!* She even remembers thinking about Gollum again, and how he called the One Ring his precious.

But she had given it over.

"Well, here we are," Winston says. He examines the sign on the door: ADESH "BUG MAN" PATEL. KNOCK BEFORE ENTERING. "Maybe we'll skip the knocking part."

Gwendy wishes, not for the first time, that the doors of the rooms, suites, and labs on the MF station had locks. But they don't.

"You first, dear. I'm not expecting a surprise, but always safe, never sorry."

She depresses the latch and steps inside. Soft sitar music is playing from a boombox, which is strapped to the center worktable to keep it from floating away. Some small gadget is tucked under the strap.

The second thing she sees is the last thing she expected. She told Adesh to put the button box in one of the drawers, there are at least fifty of them, but it's right out in the open, lying on the floor of the large cage where Adesh does his insect flight experiments. She can clearly see the tiny levers on the sides, and the colored buttons lining the top. The door to the cage is standing open.

"What's with the flies?" Winston asks. There are six or seven of them hanging motionless above the button box. "Are they dead?"

"Resting," Gwendy says. "According to Adesh, they've adapted quite well to zero-g conditions." She's looking at the boombox and the thing on top of it. Now she understands. How Adesh could have foreseen this situation is beyond her, but yes, she understands and knows what she must do.

If she can.

"Go in there, Senator. Get the box and give it to me."

She says, very slowly and clearly: "The fuck I will. I protected it as long as I could and as well as I could and I'm not handing it over to you or anyone. Get it yourself."

"Very well. But I think you'll come with me." He grabs her by her shoulder, fingernails digging into her flesh. "*Dear*."

She pretends to struggle, backing up just far enough so her butt is against the worktable with its microscope, monitors, and centrifuge. She puts a hand behind her, hoping she looks like she's trying to hold on to the table but actually grabbing for the gadget on top of the boombox. *Please God, don't let him see and don't let me drop it*, she thinks. Not that it will drop; it will float.

She almost does lose her grip, but then the controller is in her hand and pressed against the small of her back. Winston snarls and points the green tube at her. "Enough! Get in there!"

"All right. I'll go. Just stop hurting me."

"I'll do more than hurt you. *Get in there*. You're not running for the door, if that was in your mind."

If he looked down he'd see she's hiding something, a flat eight-inch rectangle that looks like a TV remote. It's pretty obvious. But Gareth Winston's attention is mostly focused on the thing he's come so far to obtain. His prize. *His precious*.

They float into the large cage, Gwendy first. She manages to get the controller into the center pocket of her coverall while pretending to rub her hurt shoulder. Winston has slipped behind her, shoving her along.

"Over there. Against the wall."

He gives her a hard push. Gwendy floats backward. *Please let this work. Oh God, please.*

He bends down and picks up the button box. A soft sigh escapes him. To Gwendy it sounds almost sexual.

"I feel it," he says. "It's powerful, isn't it?"

"Very powerful," Gwendy agrees. The controller Adesh has left for her is just another button box, only with four buttons instead of eight. She doesn't know which of them opens Boris's cage, so she lays her index finger across all four and pushes them.

Winston doesn't notice. He's running his own finger over the buttons: light green and dark green for Asia and Africa, blue and violet for North and South America, orange for Europe, and yellow for Australia. Plus the two at the ends: red for wishes that turn dark no matter how well-meant, and the black one. The Cancer Button.

Meanwhile, the buttons on the controller have opened four cages. The doors rise soundlessly. Black ants float up from one, red ants from another, cockroaches from a third. From the fourth comes Boris. *Pandinus imperator.* He rises, tail cocked.

"What do they do, these buttons?" Winston asks. He has forgotten Gwendy completely in his absorption. "What happens when you press them?"

"Bad things," Gwendy says.

"And the levers on the sides? What do *they* d—"

"Turn around," Gwendy says. And then, with great pleasure: "Look at me, you fat psychotic piece of shit."

His mouth drops open in surprise. His eyes widen in their pockets of puffy flesh. He turns. Gwendy suddenly realizes that Boris may not respond to her voice, so different from Adesh Patel's, but it's too late to worry about that now.

She screams, *"MAAR!"*

She need not have worried. Boris lashes his poison-laden tail and speeds across the room, ignoring the flies in favor of a much bigger target. Winston cries out and raises a blocking hand, but in zero-g he's far too slow. Gwendy is savagely delighted to see Boris's stinger bury itself dead center between Winston's eyes.

He shrieks in pain and horror as he flails at the scorpion with both hands. There's a hole the size of a pencil point where the stinger went in. It's dribbling blood and the flesh around it is already beginning to swell.

"Get it off me! Jesus fucking Christ GET IT OFF ME!"

Winston is batting at it with both hands. Boris disengages and avoids him easily, flicking his armored tail and zipping away. The button box floats in front of Winston, forgotten. His weapon—*the Green Tube of Death*, Gwendy thinks—is also floating, but the rapid batting of Winston's hands, which continues even when Boris has cruised out of slapping range, sends it in Gwendy's direction, lazily turning end over end.

She reaches for it.

Winston also reaches for it, but the eddy set up by Winston's hands is in Gwendy's favor. She snatches the tube. Winston tries to grab her ponytail and she sends it flying away from him with a shake of her head. She risks a glance down at the tube, wanting to make sure the ring end is pointed at herself. *If it was the wrong way around and I blew my own guts to soup, I probably wouldn't even have time to appreciate the irony*, she thinks, at the same time ducking in slow motion to avoid Winston's equally slo-mo round-house punch.

"Say goodbye to the smartass bitch, Winston." Gwendy points the tube and twists the ring in the base.

There's no sound. There's no comic-book death ray. Gwendy has a moment to think it was all a bluff, and then the front of Gareth Winston's white shirt blooms with red flowers. His eyes melt and roll down his cheeks in thick blue tears. Gray stuff begins to pour out of the empty sockets and from his nostrils. Gwendy realizes she's looking at his liquified brains and begins to scream.

Adesh has also left his phone, powered up, on the central worktable, and set his smart watch to monitor it. The crew is sitting around the mess room table, shooting the shit and drinking post-breakfast coffee, when his watch lights up. Adesh pushes the stem and they all hear Gwendy's screams.

The screams have stopped by the time they get to the Spoke 5 entomology lab. Gwendy is backed up against a wall as far from the big enclosure as she can get, with her fisted hands pressed to her mouth and the button box in her lap. There's a babble of exclamations.

Kathy: "What in the hell—"

Adesh, shaking his fists in the air: "You got him! He said you would!"

Jafari: "Got who?"

Dr. Glen: "Oh my dear God in heaven."

Doc has followed Gwendy's frozen gaze to the big cage, where the late Gareth Winston's clothes are floating in a pool of blood and decomposing organs. His throat has been blasted open. What remains of his face looks like a wrinkled and deflated rubber mask. It's crawling with red and black ants.

Even at this moment, Adesh is the scientific observer rather than the horrified witness. "The ants, they swam down to him! Adaptive behavior! Remarkable!"

Reggie Black leans over and loses his breakfast. Which floats around him in wet chunks. Sam Drinkwater and Dave Graves do the same. Sam manages to catch most of his ejecta, but soon it's oozing through his cupped hands.

"Get out of here!" Kathy snaps. "Everyone out! We're sealing this room! If he's got some kind of Andromeda Strain–type disease—"

"He doesn't," Gwendy says. "His only disease was greed. And he died of it."

44

AN HOUR LATER THE nine remaining Eagle Heavy crew members are sitting in the conference room. At Gwendy's strong suggestion, which has been seconded from the down-below by CIA Chief Charlotte Morgan, the Chinese have been locked off. They will still be able to access the outer rim, but they won't be able to enter any spokes but their own. Neither Charlotte nor Gwendy thinks the Chinese will be a problem, but Gwendy is a believer in the late Gareth Winston's mantra: always safe, never sorry. *Of course*, she thinks, *he never expected Boris.*

The button box sits in the middle of the table beside an open (but highly protected) downlink to Charlotte's office in D.C. Kathy reaches for the box, and Gwendy has to restrain herself from pushing the commander's hand away.

After one touch, Kathy pulls her hand back on her own, and fast. Her eyes are wide. "What *is* that thing?" And without waiting for a reply: "I want a complete report, Gwendy. You may be a United States senator, but up here I'm in charge, and I'm ordering you to tell me everything." She sweeps a hand around the table. "*All* of us."

Gwendy has no problem with that, and not just because they deserve to know. She will also need their cooperation to complete her final task. Charlotte is silent, but Gwendy knows she's listening.

"I will, but I need to know something first." She turns to Adesh. "You set a trap for him, didn't you?"

Adesh nods.

"How did you know to do that? Did you see a man? About your height, wears a black derby hat?" The idea that Farris—sick or well—can be here is ridiculous. At the same time it seems perfectly reasonable to Gwendy. In her experience, Farris can appear anywhere, and disappear just as quickly. It makes her think of an old song by Heart, the one about the magic man.

"I saw no one," Adesh says, "but I heard a voice. In my head. You see . . . I'm sorry, this is embarrassing."

"No need to be embarrassed," Gwendy says, and takes his hand. "I believe you just played a very large part in saving the Earth and everyone on it."

Sam Drinkwater makes a scoffing sound. Kathy, who has touched the button box and felt its power, makes no sound at all. Her attention is riveted on Gwendy and Adesh "Bug Man" Patel.

"You said not to push the buttons, not to even touch them, and I kept that promise. You must believe me, Gwendy."

Gwendy nods. Of course she does.

"But . . . you said nothing about the tiny levers on the sides."

Now Gwendy gets it. She smiles.

Adesh unbuttons his pocket and brings out a Morgan silver dollar. He floats it across to her, heads and tails spinning lazily above the table. She doesn't have to look at the date to know it's 1891.

"The first lever I pulled produced that. I was always

going to give it to you, Gwendy—I hope you believe that, too."

"Yes," she says, and floats it back with a flick of her finger. "But I want you to keep it. As a souvenir. Then you pulled the other one, yes? And got a chocolate."

"It was a thing of beauty," Adesh says, almost reverently. "A little chocolate scorpion, just like Boris."

"*Pandinus imperator.*"

He smiles and nods. "Who could say anything is wrong with your memory? It was too perfect to eat, but . . ."

"You ate it anyway."

"Yes. Something told me to. The desire was too strong to resist. And that is when I heard the voice. It sounded very old . . . very tired and rather far away . . . but completely sure of itself. It said you would see . . . and know what to do . . . when the time came."

Gwendy's eyes fill with tears. It was Farris, all right, her private deus ex machina. Old and tired, perhaps even dead, but still *somewhere.* And if anyone deserved a deus ex machina, it was she. And didn't her personal god from the machine have to be the man who'd gotten her into this in the first place?

"Maybe we could go back to the beginning?" Bern Stapleton suggests. "I for one would like to hear how one of the richest men on Earth ended up a puddle of goo with ants crawling on what remains of his face."

"A very good idea," Kathy says. "Let's hear it, Senator. From the beginning."

While I still can, Gwendy thinks, because Adesh is mistaken—there's *plenty* wrong with her memory. It has begun to fog over again. She knows where she is, she knows these people are the crew she came up here with . . . but she can't remember any of their names except for Adesh Patel and Kathy London. *Is* it London? No matter. She leans across the table, pulls the lever on the right side of the button box, and pops a chocolate koala bear into her mouth. The fog rolls away. But of course it will be back, and soon the chocolates will disappear into deep space.

"The beginning was when I was twelve," she says. "That's when I saw the button box for the first time and took possession of it . . ."

She talks for forty-five minutes, pausing for sips of water. No one interrupts, including Charlotte Morgan, who is hearing the whole story for the first time.

45

WHEN SHE'S FINISHED, THERE'S thirty seconds of silence while the eight of them digest what she's told them. Then Reggie Black clears his throat and says, "Let me be sure I understand you. You claim to be responsible for Jonestown, where nine hundred people died. This woman in Canada was responsible for the coronavirus, which killed four million and counting—"

"Her name was Patricia Vachon," Gwendy says. Nothing wrong with her memory now. "And it wasn't her fault. In the end, she just couldn't resist the pull of the box. Which is exactly what makes it so dangerous."

Reggie makes a seesawing gesture with his hand— maybe *si*, maybe *no*. "And you also destroyed the Great Pyramid in an earthquake, killing six more."

Charlotte speaks up for the first time. The speaker is so good she could almost have been in the room with them. "Not an earthquake, sir. No cause has been attributed."

"I didn't want anyone to die," Gwendy says. She can't keep the tremble out of her voice. She is thinking about her old friend Olive Kepnes, who died on the Suicide Stairs between Castle Rock and Castle View. "Not ever. I thought the part of Guyana I was concentrating on was deserted. The Pyramid was supposed to be locked down, totally empty, because of a fresh COVID outbreak." She leans forward, scanning them with her eyes. "But those young people were there, on a lark. This is what makes the button box so dangerous, don't you see? Even the red button is dangerous. It does what you're thinking of . . . but it does more, and my experience has been that the more is never good. I don't think the button box could be destroyed even in a nuclear furnace, and it works on the possessors' minds. Which is why Farris kept passing it on to new owners."

"But always coming back to you," Jafari said.

"Tell me," Reggie says, smiling. "Was the box also responsible for 9/11?"

Gwendy suddenly feels very tired. "I don't know. Probably not. People don't need a button box to do horrible things. There's plenty of evil fuckery in the human spirit."

Sam Drinkwater says flatly: "I'm sorry, but I can't believe this. It's a fairy tale."

From the speaker, Charlotte says, "Is that Ops Drink-water?"

"Yes, ma'am."

"All right, Mr. Drinkwater, listen up. I have seen the interrogation with Detective Mitchell. Everything Gwendy has told you about the death of her husband is true. The cell phone footage is very disturbing, but our techs tell us none of it has been rigged or spiced up with special effects. As for the Great Pyramid, I was there when Gwendy named it and pushed that red button hours before it fell to pieces for reasons the science guys still can't figure out. I'm lifetime CIA, I don't believe anything unless I can prove it, and I believe this. I don't think the man who bribed the detective was human . . . or not precisely human. And I believe that box you're looking at is more dangerous than all the nuclear weapons on Earth put together."

"But—"

"No buts," Charlotte says briskly. "Unless you think a hardheaded businessman like Gareth Winston died for a fantasy." She pauses. "Which reminds me, we have to come up with a cover story to explain his death. Whatever it is, it's going to shock the markets."

"Need to think about it carefully," Kathy says. "Maybe . . . Gwendy? Are you all right?"

"Fine," Gwendy says. "Little bit of a headache." Actually, an idea.

Doc Glen says gloomily, "We'll have to shovel him up, you know. And that gadget he had is enough to convince me that something beyond our understanding is at work here. That gadget goes with him."

"Absolutely," Kathy says.

Reggie Black—who, Gwendy believes, would have sided with Doubting Thomas in the Bible—shakes his head. "I'm willing to accept that it's all very strange. I'm not willing to accept that pushing that black button could destroy the whole world." Gwendy almost expects him to add, *Let's try it and see, shall we?* But he doesn't. Which is good. If he even made a move toward the button box, Gwendy would have leaped across the table to stop him.

"It doesn't matter," Adesh says. "Surely you all see that?"

They turn puzzled looks on him, Gwendy included.

"We send the box away in the device we call the Pocket Rocket. Whether it's a thing of supernatural evil or just a box that gives out chocolates and silver dollars . . ."

He shrugs and smiles. It's a very sweet smile. "Either way, it's gone. The Pocket Rocket won't even be orbiting the earth with the rest of the space junk we have been charting." The smile becomes dreamy. "It will be off to the stars, never to come back."

This logic is irrefutable.

Kathy Lundgren turns to Gwendy. "We'll do it tomorrow. You and me. My ninth spacewalk, your first. The one that's televised back home to your constituents will be your second, but no one has to know that, do they?"

"No," Gwendy says.

Kathy nods. "We'll watch the Pocket Rocket heading out toward the moon, and Mars, and the great beyond. With its cargo on board."

"It sounds fine. What about Winston?"

"For the time being, until we can decide how he died, Mr. Winston is okay. Just suffering a touch of zero-g space sickness and holed up in his cabin. Not feeling well enough to communicate with the down-below. Or do you disagree?"

"No," Gwendy says. "That's fine for now."

She's still sorry about what happened in Jonestown, even though she guesses much of it was the fault of the Reverend Jim Jones. She's sorry about the destruction of the Great Pyramid, and sorrier about the lives lost when it disassembled. But she's not sorry about Gareth Winston.

"Which one of the levers dispenses the chocolates?" Reggie Black asks.

"That one." Gwendy points.

"May I?"

Gwendy doesn't want him to touch the box, but she nods.

607

Reggie pulls the lever. The slot opens and the shelf comes out. It's empty.

Gwendy turns to Adesh. "You try."

The tiny shelf has gone back in. Adesh hooks his pinky around the lever and pulls gently. Out comes the shelf, this time bearing a small chocolate weasel. He looks at it, but gives it to Bern. The biologist examines it, then puts it in his mouth, fingers ready to take it out if it's nasty. Instead, his eyes half-close in an expression of ecstasy.

"Oh my God! Delicious!"

Reggie Black looks put out. "Why didn't it work for me?"

"Maybe," Gwendy says, "the box doesn't like physicists."

46

THAT NIGHT.

Gwendy is walking the outer rim of the Many Flags space station. It makes its usual creaks and groans, haunted house sounds that the other man, the bad man, didn't like, but Gwendy doesn't mind them. She can't remember the bad man's name, although she's sure she could come up with it using Dr. Ambrose's chain of association. *I'd just start with cigar,* she thinks.

The man walking beside her doesn't seem to mind the creaking sounds, either. His face is serene and he's very beautiful. Except his beauty is a mask. Sometimes his features waver like water in a pond blown by a strong breeze and she can see his real face and head. He's some sort of weasel, like the chocolate treat the biologist got. Gwendy can't remember his name, either. That's all right. She can remember the name of the man-who-isn't-a-man, though: it's Bobby. That's what the bad man called him. She thinks: *Cigar.* She thinks, *Who smoked cigars?* Winston Churchill did. And there it is.

"The bad man's name was Garin Winston," she says.

"Close enough," Bobby says. "It doesn't matter, he's dead."

"Melted," Gwendy says. "Like the Wicked Witch in *The Wizard of Ooze.*"

"Close enough," Bobby says again. "What matters is this: there are other worlds than these."

"I know," Gwendy says. "Someone told me, but I don't remember who. Maybe Mr. Farris."

"That meddler," Bobby says.

They walk. The space station creaks. They see no one, because this is sleep time on MF. Except for the Chinese, holed up in their spoke, they are alone in the haunted house.

"There are twelve worlds," Bobby says. "Six beams, twelve worlds, one at each end of each beam. And in the center is the Tower. We call it Black Thirteen."

"Who is we?"

"The taheen."

This means nothing to Gwendy.

"The beams hold the worlds and the Tower powers the beams," Bobby says in a lecturely tone. "Only one thing can destroy it, now that the Crimson King is dead."

"The button box," Gwendy says, but Bobby smiles and shakes his head. He makes a come-on gesture with hands that sometimes blur into paws with sharp claws at the ends. The gesture says *you can do better*. Gwendy starts to protest that she really can't, she's suffering from early-onset Alzheimer's (probably caused by the box, but who knows for sure), then realizes she can. "The black button *on* the button box. The Cancer Button."

"Yes!" Bobby says, and pats her shoulder. Gwendy shrinks away. She doesn't want him to touch her. It makes her feel the way the station's creaks and groans made the late Garin Winship feel. "You must not send the box away, Gwendy. What you need to do is push the black button. Destroy the Tower, destroy the beams, destroy the worlds."

"Rule Discordia?"

"That's right, rule Discordia. End the universe. Bring the darkness."

"Like in Jonestown? Only everyone and everything?"

"Yes."

"But *why*?"

"Because chaos is the only answer."

He looks down. Gwendy follows his gaze and sees she's holding the button box.

"Push it, Gwendy. Push it now. You must, because—"

47

GWENDY WAKES AND IS horrified to discover she really is holding the button box, and her thumb is actually resting on the black button. She's standing in front of the open safe in her closet, the spare pressure suit crumpled at her feet.

"Chaos is the only answer," she whispers. "Existence is a dead equation."

The urge to push the button, if only to end her own misery and confusion, is strong. She would like Farris to step in as he did for Adesh and rescue her, but there is no voice in her head and no sense of him. She groans, and somehow that sound breaks the spell.

She puts the button box back in the safe, starts to swing the door shut, then decides she's not done with it quite yet. She doesn't want to touch it for fear that horrible compulsion might come back, but she has to. She pulls one of the levers and a chocolate comes out. She pops it into her mouth and the world instantly clarifies.

She pulls the lever again, afraid the little platform will slide out empty this time, but another chocolate appears. It's a dachshund that looks exactly like her father's long-time companion, Pippa. She goes to put it in her pocket—it's for later—but then realizes she *has* no pockets. She's in her sleep shorts and a University of Maine tee. But that's not all. She's got a sneaker on one foot, a sock on the other, and she's wearing a pair of the insulated work gloves each member of the crew has been issued. There's probably a reason for the gloves—on Eagle Heavy and the MF station there's a reason for every bit of clothing and equipment—but she can't remember what it is. Sudden temperature drop, maybe? Her deteriorating condition keeps manifesting itself in different ways, and she sees now that she has written LEFT and RIGHT on the gloves.

But how long before I forget what those words mean? How long before I can't read at all?

These thoughts make her feel like crying, but she can't waste any time on tears. She doesn't know how long the chocolate will keep her in the clear, and the spare is for tomorrow, right before she and Kathy Lundgren suit up for their spacewalk at 0800 hours.

Kathy.

With her mind right, she realizes what she should have known much earlier.

Gwendy goes to her phone, selects Kathy's name from the MF directory, and makes the call. As the officer in charge of the mission, First Ops, Kathy always keeps her phone on. She'll hear the beep and respond. She *must* respond, because what Gwendy has realized is that she can't do this on her own. If she tries, Kathy will stop her. Unless, that is, she has reasons not to.

The phone only rings once, and when Kathy answers, her voice is clear and crisp. Maybe not sleeping at all, no matter how late the hour. "Gwendy. Is there a problem?"

"A solution, I think. I need to talk to you."

"All right." No hesitation. "Come to my quarters."

48

KATHY LUNDGREN'S QUARTERS ARE smaller and more austere than Gwendy's, but she has cocoa packets squirreled away and makes them each a cup. The sweetness reminds Gwendy of her early childhood—cocoa with her dad on early summer mornings with a mist still on the lawn.

After one sip, she puts her cup on the little table beside Kathy's narrow bed (no sitting room here) and tells Eagle Heavy's First Ops what she's been trying to hide. "You were right. Doc was right. Even Winston knew. I do have early-onset Alzheimer's, and it's now progressing very rapidly."

"But the test we gave you proved—"

"It proved nothing. I aced it because of the chocolates, but the effects don't last. A few minutes ago I woke up wearing gloves and one sneaker. The sneaker wasn't tied, because I can't remember how to tie my shoes anymore."

Kathy looks at her in silent horror, which Gwendy understands, and sympathy, which she hates.

"For awhile I still could, because I found a jingle on the Net that I learned when I was in primary school—"

"Something about bunny ears?"

As anxious and afraid as she is, that makes Gwendy laugh. "You too, huh? Only now I can't remember the jingle. Unless I've eaten a chocolate, that is."

"You ate one before coming here, I assume."

Gwendy nods. "But they're dangerous, like everything to do with the button box. And the box is getting stronger while I get weaker. When I woke up, just before I called you, I had it in my hands and I was getting ready to push the black button. My thumb was actually on it."

"Thank God you're getting rid of it!"

"*We're* getting rid of it. And that's not all." Gwendy takes a deep breath. "I want to go with it."

Kathy has been bringing her cup to her mouth. Now she sets it down hard. "Are you *crazy*?"

"Well, yes. That's sort of what Alzheimer's *is*, Kath. But at this moment I've never been saner. Or more present." She leans forward, pinning Kathy's eyes with her own. "When the button box goes, the chocolates go. If I'm still here, my decline will be very rapid. By the time we get back to Earth, I might not even know my own name."

Kathy opens her mouth to protest, but Gwendy overrides her.

"Even if I do, the time will come when I don't. I'll be wearing diapers. Sitting in my own piss and shit until someone comes to change me. Staring out the window of some expensive rest home in D.C. or Virginia, not knowing what I'm staring *at*. Having just enough brainpower left to know that I'm lost and can never find my way back to myself." *Rule Discordia*, she thinks.

She's crying now, but her voice remains steady.

"I could tell you that I'd find a discreet way of committing suicide when we get back to the down-below, but I don't think I could be discreet, and I don't think I'd know how to do it. I might *forget* to do it. And Kathy, I'm only sixty-four, and physically healthy. I could go on like that for ten years before pneumonia or a mutated form of COVID took me. Maybe fifteen or twenty."

"Gwendy, I understand, but—"

"Please don't condemn me to that, Kathy. Listen. When I was a little girl, my folks bought me a telescope. I spent hours looking at the planets and stars through it, often with my father, but once with my mom. We looked at Scorpius and talked about God. I want to go with the box, Kathy. I want to point the Pocket Rocket toward Scorpius and know that someday millions of years from now, I might actually get there." She smiles. "If there's life after death—my mother believed that—I might be there in spirit. To greet my perfectly preserved body."

"I do understand," Kathy says, "and I would if I could. But you have to think of me a little bit, okay? Think about what would happen to me afterward. Losing my commission and my job—which I love—wouldn't be all. I'd probably go to jail."

"No," Gwendy says. "Not if everyone else goes along with what I have in mind. Sam, Jaff, Reggie, Adesh, Bern, Dave, and Doc. And they will, because it will stop an investigation that would shut down TetCorp's plans for space exploration and tourist travel for a year. Maybe two or even five. Tet's in a race with SpaceX and Blue Origin now. That guy Branson, too. Do you think our guys want to get years behind?"

Kathy is frowning. "I don't know what you're . . ." She stops. "Winston. You're talking about Winston."

"Yes. Because any story you cobble together to explain his death will be suspicious."

"Explosive decompression—"

"Even if Dave Graves could rig the onboard computers

to show there had been such a decompression—and I have my doubts—a story like that would shut down the MF," Gwendy says. "All those tourist plans—Tet's *and* SpaceX's—would be frozen. That's in addition to the investigation into you and the whole crew." Gwendy pauses, then plays her trump card. She has saved it for last, as she always did in contentious committee meetings. "Plus there's me. I'd be questioned, and with my ability to think rapidly bleeding away, who knows what I might say?"

"Jesus Christ," Kathy mutters, and runs her hands through her short hair.

"But there's a solution." This is also the way she played it in committee hearings, learned from Patsy Follett. *First hit 'em with the sledgehammer*, Patsy used to say, *then offer them the painkillers.*

"What solution?" Kathy is looking at her mistrustfully.

"Our spacewalk tomorrow is unauthorized, right? No one knows about it but Charlotte Morgan and our Eagle Heavy crew mates."

"Right . . ."

Gwendy sips her cocoa. So good, with its memories of Castle Rock on summer mornings with her father. She puts it down and leans forward, arms on her thighs, hands clasped between her knees.

"We're not going to take that spacewalk."

"We're not?"

"No. *Gareth* and I will take it, unbeknownst to you or anyone else in the crew. We decided to do it on our own, and because we're inexperienced, we didn't use tethers or a buddy cable. Something went wrong and we just floated away into the void."

"Why would you do a crazy thing like that?"

617

"Why did the *Mary Celeste* show up deserted, but seaworthy and under full sail? What happened to the crew of the *Carroll A. Deering*?" There's nothing wrong with Gwendy's recall for the time being; she hasn't thought about the *Carroll Deering* since a book report she did in the eighth grade. "No one knows. And if you eight can keep a secret, no one will ever know why Winston and I decided to go for a little stroll in space."

"Hmm," Kathy says. "To be cold-blooded about it—"

"I want you to be."

"It would solve two problems. We wouldn't have to explain the gooey death of Gareth Winston, and we wouldn't have to worry about you saying certain things as your . . . umm . . . *condition* worsens."

"Charlotte Morgan will help you," Gwendy says. "She'll make sure she's in charge of debriefing the crew, and she'll apply a coat of whitewash, for obvious reasons. Also, she'll want to get her hands on that disintegrator thingie."

"I suppose she would. I need to think about this."

Gwendy takes her hands and squeezes them lightly. "No," she says. "You don't."

49

BACK IN HER QUARTERS, Gwendy sits down at her desk, opens the RECORD app on her phone, and begins talking immediately. There's no time to waste—the chocolate may start wearing off anytime—but it doesn't take long to say what she has to say. When she's finished, she scribbles a quick note. She rubber-bands it to her phone and puts the phone in a manila envelope. She begins to close it, then thinks again and adds something else. She seals it and writes ADESH on the front in big capital letters.

Then she goes back to bed. She falls asleep with two hopes: no more dreams of the monster that calls itself Bobby, and that when she wakes up, her mind will wake up with her.

50

THE CREW MEETING IN the conference room takes place at 0600. Kathy lays the situation out with a crisp conciseness Gwendy couldn't possibly have matched now that the effects of her late-night chocolate treat are almost gone. They are bright men and they understand. They also understand the solution Gwendy has proposed will save a great deal of trouble, expense, and possible Senate hearings where they will be mercilessly grilled on nationwide TV.

There is only one substantive question and it comes from Reggie Black. "What happens to Winston? Or what remains of him?"

"Vaporized with the rest of the trash before we leave the station," Sam Drinkwater says, and makes a sucking sound. "Poof. Gone."

No one has anything to say to that.

When the meeting ends, the crew stands in a kind of receiving line. Each of them hugs Gwendy. Adesh is last. "I'm sorry," he says as he hugs her. "You've been so brave. You don't deserve this and I am so, so sorry."

She hugs him back. "I have an envelope for you. My phone is inside, with a message for my father. Would you take it to him?"

"It will be an honor."

He wipes his eyes, but his tears—emblems of his grief and regard—float in front of his face.

"And I'm going where no woman has gone before, so don't cry for me, Margentina." She frowns. "Is that right? Margentina?"

"Absolutely," Adesh says. "Absolutely right."

51

0730.

There are airlocks on the MF, one in the outer rim beyond each of the even-numbered spokes, but Gwendy and Kathy will egress from Eagle Heavy, where the air tastes stale and the three crew station levels feel abandoned. Before suiting up, Gwendy pops the chocolate she saved into her mouth.

"Don't suppose you have another one of those, do you?" Kathy asks.

Gwendy considers, shrugs, and then loosens the drawstring top of the aluminum-quilted bag on the bench beside her. She brings out the button box. It feels dull now, powerless, as if resigned to its fate, but Gwendy doesn't trust that. She pulls the lever that delivers the chocolates. The cunning little platform slides out, but there's nothing on it.

"Sorry, Kath. The button box giveth and sometimes it don't giveth."

"Roger that. Would have liked to try one, though. Are you good, Gwendy?"

Gwendy nods. She's very good. With the chocolate on board, she's clear as a bell. The woman who had to print RIGHT and LEFT on her gloves is gone, but she'll be back.

Or maybe not.

"What's funny?" Kathy asks. "You're smiling."

"Nothing." But because something more seems re-quired, she adds, "Just excited about my first spacewalk."

Kathy makes no reply, but Gwendy can read her thought: *First and last.*

"Are you sure the computers in Mission Control won't register us opening the airlock down here?"

"Positive. These computers are all off until the return. To conserve power."

They float their way into the airlock, helmets under their arms, and sit on the two benches. The space is tight—all spaces are tight on Heavy—and their knees touch. Gwendy starts to put her helmet on, but Kathy shakes her head. "Not yet. Sixty inhales and exhales first. Prebreathing, remember?"

Gwendy nods. "To purge the nitrogen."

"Right. Gwendy . . . are you sure?"

"Yes." She answers with no hesitation. Everything is in place, the story they will tell later set and agreed to by all hands. Gwendy and Winston weren't at breakfast, but no one thought that was unusual because they are passen-gers, supercargo, and have the luxury of sleeping in. No one will start to worry until at least 1000 hours, and by then Kathy will be back on board the MF. There will be a search. It will be at least 1400 before Sam Drinkwater calls the down-below to tell them the VIPs are missing and may have drifted away while attempting a spacewalk. Terrible accident, God knows why they would have done something so foolish, blah-blah-blah.

Gwendy gets a little woozy from the fast respiration. Kathy tells her that's normal and will pass by the time they egress Eagle Heavy. After two minutes of breathing,

Kathy tells Gwendy it's time to put on her bucket. "And remember, helmet-to-helmet comm *only*. No one hears but just us girls. Let me hear your roger."

"Roger that," Gwendy says, and dons her bucket. Kathy moves to help her secure it, but Gwendy waves her off, does it herself, and looks for the green light on the little control panel at mouth level. When she sees it, she dons her gloves, secures them, and waits for a second green light. She makes a thumb-and-finger circle to Kathy, who returns the gesture.

Kathy closes the door to Eagle Heavy and the two of them sit waiting for the airlock to depressurize.

"Reading me, Gwendy?"

"Loud and clear."

"Set your suit temp to maximum hot, then adjust it down."

"How long will the heat last?"

"In theory, as long as your breathable air, just shy of six hours. The heat may actually last longer, but . . ." Her shrug says the rest: *But you won't feel it.*

There's a belt around Gwendy's waist with two or-dinary high-altitude carabiners attached. She knots the drawstring bag with the button box around one of them. Kathy attaches the buddy cable to the other. They are now tethered together like scuba divers: the instructor and the pupil.

"Ready to EVA?" Kathy asks.

Gwendy makes another thumb-and-forefinger circle. She thinks, *Oh yes, very ready. Been waiting for this ever since I first looked through my telescope, over fifty years ago. I just didn't know it.*

"Don't wait too long to lower your outer visor. Night pass ends in just about seven minutes."

"Roger."

Kathy turns the red lever in the center of the airlock's outer door, then pulls it.

0748.

The airlock opens on the stars.

52

THEY FLOAT INTO SPACE, tethered. Gwendy can hear her own breathing and, through the helmet-to-helmet comm, Kathy's. Beside them is Eagle Heavy, and she can see where someone from the ground crew has printed GOOD LUCK YOU GUYS on the fuselage in Sharpie. Below them is Earth, blue and cloud-streaked, with a golden nimbus growing on one gorgeous shoulder. *Here comes the sun*, Gwendy thinks.

Kathy leads them slowly downward, using indented handholds on Heavy's flank. Near the bottom, these handholds are smudged from the blast of the last rocket bursts, as Kathy lined them up for docking.

On the way down they pass hatches labeled A through E. The last one, Hatch F, is just above the rocket boosters. It's the only one with a keypad; the others can be opened with a simple socket wrench. Kathy has to duck under a solar panel to get at it. She raises the little plexi shield over the pad and punches the combination Gwendy has given her. It's the same one that opened the CLASSIFIED case.

The thing Kathy floats out makes Gwendy smile. The Pocket Rocket is four feet long, or maybe a bit less. To Gwendy it looks almost exactly like the craft that brought Kal-El, aka Superbaby, to Earth. Her father gave away most of his old comic books (or lost them), but Gwendy found a box of *Superman*s in the attic and read them eagerly, again and again.

Kathy floats the Pocket Rocket up between them. There's a hatch on top, held by simple latches that look about as high-tech as the ones on the Scooby-Doo lunch box Gwendy carried to elementary school. Kathy flips them, reaches inside, and brings out a controller that looks like the one Gwendy used to release Boris in Adesh's lab. Except this one is smaller, and there are only two buttons.

Another button box, Gwendy thinks. *Those damn things are my destiny.*

Kathy points to the drawstring bag floating around Gwendy's waist, then points at the open hatch on top of the Pocket Rocket. Her meaning is clear, *put it inside*, but all at once Gwendy doesn't want to.

Mine, it's mine. This one really is my destiny.

Kathy raises her outer visor and Gwendy can see she's frightened. Even though Kathy has never seen the button box in action, she's scared to death. That expression is enough for Gwendy to free the bag from the carabiner holding it. She can feel the corners of the button box inside.

No, the thing called Bobby whispers in her head. *Don't do this. The Tower must not stand. Rule Discordia!*

Then she thinks of Richard Farris's weary face when he said, *How I loathe it.*

"Rule my ass," she says. She doesn't just place the button box in the Pocket Rocket's belly; she rams it in.

"Say again?" Kathy asks.

"I wasn't talking to you," Gwendy says, and flips the latches closed.

Meanwhile, the controller is floating away. Gwendy reaches for it, but at that moment the sun comes over the curve of the earth's horizon, blinding her. She forgot something after all—to lower her outer visor. She slams it down, panicked. If the controller is lost . . .

But Kathy has snatched it just before it can drift out of reach. She hands it to Gwendy.

"Last chance, hon. You don't have to go with it."

"No," Gwendy agrees, "but I'm going to. I *choose* to. Give me a hug, Kathy. Probably ridiculous, but I need it."

The two of them hug clumsily in their bulky suits while the newly risen sun turns their visors into curved oblongs of amber fire. Then Kathy lets go, unclips the buddy cable from her waist, and reattaches her end to a D ring on the Pocket Rocket's rounded nose. Gwendy supposes that handy ring allowed some crane operator to lift the Pocket Rocket up to the F hatch.

Kathy says, "The engine is nuclear powered—"

"I know—"

Kathy ignores her. "And no bigger than a cigarette pack. Marvel of technology. Push the top button to power it up. You'll start moving immediately, but very slowly— like a car in low gear. You understand?"

"Yes."

"Tap the lower button and you'll speed up. Each time you tap it, you'll speed up more. Following me?"

"Yes." And she is, but she's looking at the stars. Oh, they are gorgeous, and how can anyone look at that spill of light and believe life is anything but a hall of mysteries?

"There's no guidance system. No joystick. Once you start you just *go*, and you can't come back. *You can't come back, Gwendy.* Do you understand?"

"Yes."

"All right, then." Kathy reaches behind herself and

grasps one of the handholds. Soon she will follow them back up, kicking her feet like a diver seeking the surface. Back to warmth and light and the companionship of her crew mates. "If you meet any ETs, tell them Kathy Lundgren says hello."

"Roger that," Gwendy says, and gives a salute. *Six hours*, she thinks. *I have six hours to live.*

"God bless you, Gwendy."

"And you."

There's nothing left to say, so Gwendy pushes the top button on her last button box. A dull red ring glows in the Pocket Rocket's base, a paltry light that's no match for the sun's splendor. Is it giving off harmful radiation? Possibly, but does it matter?

The slack runs out of the buddy cable, it pulls taut, and then Gwendy is moving away from Eagle Heavy and beneath the outer ring of the Many Flags station. She knows no one is watching, but she gives it a wave anyway. Then it's behind her. She taps the speed control button twice, lightly, and begins to move faster, flying horizontally behind the Pocket Rocket with her legs splayed. It's a little like surfing, but it's really like nothing she has ever experienced. *Like no one has ever experienced*, she thinks, and laughs.

"Gwendy?" Kathy's voice is growing faint. Soon it will be gone. Already the MF is receding, glowing in the sunlight like a jewel in the navel of the earth. "Are you okay?"

"Brilliant," Gwendy says, and she is.

She is.

53

Now there's just the red ring of the Pocket Rocket's nuclear drive ahead of her as it tugs her steadily onward into the black. It reminds Gwendy of the dashboard cigarette lighter in her father's old Chevrolet. There's a temperature gauge among the dozen or so digital readouts inside her helmet and it registers the outside temperature as −435 Fahrenheit, but her suit is a toasty-warm seventy-two degrees. Her remaining oxygen is down to seventeen percent. It won't be long now. Of course there's no speed gauge among the readouts, so Gwendy has no idea how fast she's going. There's little or no sensation of movement at all. When she peers over her shoulder (not easy in the suit, but possible), Earth looks exactly the same—big, blue, and beautiful—but the MF station is lost to view.

Gwendy looks ahead again, at the Milky Way. She wishes the brightest of its stars was Scorpius, but she's pretty sure it's Sirius, also known as the Dog Star because it's part of the Canis Major constellation. That makes her think of her father's sausage dog, Pippin. Only that's not right, is it?

"Pippa," she whispers. "Pippa the dachshund."

She's losing it again. The fog is closing in.

Gwendy fixes her eyes on Sirius, which is roughly at ten o'clock in her field of vision. *Second star on the right and straight on till morning*, she thinks. *What's that from?* Hansel and Gretel, *isn't it?* But that's not right. She trawls her dimming mind for the correct story or fairy tale, and finally comes up with it: *Peter Pan.*

Fifteen percent oxygen now, and it will be a race between the end of her breathable air and the end of her ability to think. Only she doesn't want to go out that way, not knowing where she is . . . or if she does know that (outer space is kind of hard to mistake for the bus station in Castle Rock, after all), why she's out here. She'd like to go out knowing all this happened for a *reason.* That in the end, she completed the task set before her. That she saved the world.

"*All* the worlds," she whispers. "Because there are more worlds than ours."

She doesn't *have* to go out puzzled and confused, nor does she have to go out cold and shivering if her heat quits before her breathable air. (She seems to remember Carol— if that's her name—saying the heat would last longer, but her suit's temp has begun to drop a degree at a time.) She has another option.

She has only one disappointment. In 1984, ten years after Richard Farris gave her the button box, he came to take it back. He sat in her small kitchen with her. They had coffee cake and milk, like old friends (which they sort of were), and Mr. Farris had told her future. He said she was going to be accepted at the Iowa Writers' Workshop, and she was. He told her she was going to win an award (*Wear your prettiest dress when you pick it up*), and she did. Not the Nobel, but the Los Angeles Times Book Prize was not to be sneezed at. He told her she had many things to tell the world, and that the world would listen, and that had been true prophecy.

But the mysterious derby-wearing Mr. Farris had certainly never told her she would end a mostly warm and loving life in the deep cold of outer space. He'd told her she'd live a *long* life. Sixty-four wasn't young, but she didn't consider it old, either (although in 1984 she probably would have considered it ancient). He told her she would die surrounded by friends, not alone in the universe and being tugged ever deeper into the void behind a tiny rocket that would continue running on power for seventy years or more and then continue in an endless inertial glide.

You will die in a pretty nightgown with blue flowers on the hem, Farris had told her. *There will be sun shining in your window and before you pass you will look out and see a squadron of birds flying south. A final image of the world's beauty. There will be a little pain. Not much.*

No friends here—the last ones she made were far behind her.

A spacesuit instead of a pretty nightgown.

And certainly no birds.

Even the sun was gone for the time being, temporarily eclipsed by the earth, and was she crying? Dammit, she was. The tears didn't even float because she was under constant acceleration. But the tears were fogging up her visor. The star she'd been watching—Rigel? Deneb?—was blurring.

"Mr. Farris, you lied," she said. "Maybe you didn't see the truth. Or maybe you did and didn't want me to have to live with it."

No lie, Gwendy.

His voice, as clear as it had been as they sat in her kitchen forty-two years ago, eating coffee cake and drinking milk.

You know what to do, and there's still enough of that last chocolate in your brain to give you time to do it.

Gwendy uses the valve on the left side of her helmet to begin bleeding the remaining air from her suit. It disappears behind her in a frozen cloud. Her visor clears and she can see that star again: not Rigel, not Scorpius, but Sirius. Second star on the right.

A kind of rapture steals into her as she breathes the last of her thinning air.

I am in bed now, and I am old—much older than sixty-four. Yet the people who surround me are young and beautiful. Even Patsy Follett is young again. Brigette Desjardin is here . . . Sheila Brigham . . . Norris Ridgewick . . . Olive Kepnes is here, and . . .

"*Mom? You hardly look twenty years old!*"

"*I was, you know,*" Alicia Peterson says, laughing. "*Hard as that might be for you to believe. I love you, hon.*"

And now she sees—

"*Ryan? Is it really you?*"

He takes her hand. "*It is.*"

"*You're back!*"

"*I never left.*" *He leans down to kiss her.* "*Someone wants to say goodbye.*"

He stands aside to let Mr. Farris come forward. His sickness is gone. He looks like the man Gwendy first saw sitting on a bench near the Castle View playground when she was twelve. He's holding his hat in his hand. "*Gwendy,*" *he says, and touches her cheek.* "*Well done, Gwendy. Very well done.*"

She's not in space, not anymore. She's an old woman lying in her childhood bed. She's wearing a pretty nightgown with blue flowers on the hem. She has done her duty and now she can rest. She can let go.

"Look out the window!" Mr. Farris says, and points.

She looks out. She sees a squadron of birds. Then they are gone and she sees a single shining star. It's Scorpius, and heaven lies beyond it. All of heaven.

"Second star to the right," Gwendy says with her final breath. "And straight on . . . straight on til . . ."

Her eyes close. The Pocket Rocket with the button box in its belly drives onward into the cosmos, as it will for the next ten thousand years, towing its spacesuited figure behind.

"Straight on til morning."

EPILOGUE

ONE NIGHT SOME TIME after all these things, Gwendy Peterson's father sits at his window in the nursing home where he lives—frailer, more unsteady, but, as he often says, *not too bad for an old fella*. He's looking out at the stars and thinking that somewhere out there in their endless multitude, his daughter continues her pilgrimage. Her phone, brought to him by a nice Indian man named Adesh Patel, is in his lap.

Patsy Follett, Gwendy's mentor, might not have had as many witty sayings as Oscar Wilde, but she'd had her share. One of them was *A scandal lasts six months. A scandal that's also a mystery lasts six years.* It's only been three years since Senator Peterson and the billionaire businessman disappeared into space, but the march of current events has driven it from the forefront of people's minds. Not from Mr. Peterson's, however. It's hell to outlive your only child, and the fierceness of his loss is mitigated by only two things: the knowledge that he can't have much longer himself, and that he has her voice to comfort him. Her last recorded message. The world doesn't need to know she died a hero; it's enough for Mr. Peterson that he knows.

A week after Adesh Patel's surprise appearance, Gwendy's dad had another visitor. A woman this time. The day manager of the Castle View Nursing Home—a haughty little fellow with a pencil-thin mustache who insisted the residents address him as Mr. Winchester—sauntered into the sun-room where Alan was playing hearts with Ralph Mirarchi, Mick Meredith, and Homer Baliko. He introduced the tall blond lady towering over his shoulder as Deputy Director Charlotte Morgan of the Central Intelligence Agency. He quickly shooed the other men out of the room, and after offering their guest a ridiculous half-bow, left them alone.

The woman flashed Mr. Peterson a bemused look—a look that said *I'm sorry you're stuck here with such a first-class tool*—and sat down across from him. "Please call me Charlotte, Mr. Peterson. I'm an old and dear friend of your daughter's."

"In that case, you better call me Alan." He rubbed the gray whiskers on his chin, wishing he'd shaved this morning. *This lady is a looker.* "And I don't figure you came all this way to talk about spies and foreign policy."

"No, sir, not today." She smiled and reached over to touch his hand. "But I do have something important to tell you. Something highly confidential that you must promise to never repeat to anyone else."

He raised his right hand in the air. "So help me God."

"That's good enough for me." She took a quick glance over her shoulder to make sure they were still alone in the sun-room. Mr. Peterson, suddenly feeling as if he were playing a bit role in a James Bond spy film, did the same. When he looked back at his daughter's old friend, he was surprised to see that there were tears shimmering in her eyes.

"I could lose my job and end up in Leavenworth for what I'm about to tell you, but I don't care. I loved Gwendy. She was family."

"Whatever it is, it'll go to my grave with me." *And probably sooner than later*, he thought.

"Your daughter didn't sneak out for an illicit space-walk. Anyone who truly knew her knows that part of the story is bullshit." She took a deep breath—the kind that says *you're past the point of no return now*—and continued. "Gareth Winston was a bad man, Mr. Peterson. And he'd gotten a very bad idea into his head—a *dangerous* one. Gwendy found out and put a stop to it before it was too late. She sacrificed her life so that others—*millions* of others—could live. I suppose that sounds awfully dramatic, but I swear to you it's true."

Alan nodded. "That sounds like our Gwendy."

"I can't even begin to imagine the courage it took for her to do what she did. But she completed the task willingly, and I believe with only one regret: that she would never return home to see you again. She talked about you and your wife all the time. She adored you, Mr. Peterson."

"The feeling was mutual," he said in a choked and tired voice.

With the memory of her visit fading, he stares down at the iPhone resting in his lap. And as he has done on so many other occasions, he presses the PLAY button and closes his eyes.

Hi Dad. I don't have much time, but I wanted to tell you I'm sorry. Please don't be too sad, and whatever you do, don't waste a precious minute on being angry or bitter. And no matter what you hear or see on the news, just remember this: I had a job to do, an important one, and I did it the best way I knew how. A long time ago, back when I was a little girl in pigtails running around the playground at Castle View Park, you told me something I've never forgotten: when faced with the choice of doing the right thing or nothing at all, you do what's right. Every single time. I am so proud to be your daughter. There isn't a better father anywhere in the world. Please smile when you think of me. Please remember the good times. How lucky we were—you and me and Mom! The Three Musketeers, she used to call us! Okay, I better get going. You know how I hate to be late. Goodbye for now, Pa. I love you with all of my heart, and I will see you again. Mom and I both will. I left you a surprise inside the envelope. It's yours now. Take good care of it. It's very special. You might even say it's . . .

"Magic," he whispers in the silence of his dark room.

Alan Peterson pulls out the small white feather from the pocket of his robe. It's never far from him these days. He stares at it, remembering, and then places the feather upon the windowsill beside him. It's immediately bathed in moonlight. His eyes are once again drawn to the night sky outside the window. There are so many stars tonight. Even with the oak tree blocking much of his view, he can spot the Milky Way and Taurus the Bull. High above its tallest branches, Orion the Hunter peers down at him. The words suddenly slip into his head unbidden. Mr. Peterson has no idea where they came from or what they mean, but he likes the sound of them so much he says them out loud: *There are other worlds than these.* Sitting there, staring up at the infinite darkness, he thinks they are easy words to believe.

ACKNOWLEDGMENT

IT'S USUALLY PLURAL, AS in *acknowledgments*, but we decided not to do the whole Academy Awards shtick, since there's no music to play us offstage. Lots of people helped, including our families, who give us the time and space to do this crazy job, and all those helpers know who they are. But Robin Furth, who aided Steve on the last three volumes of the *Dark Tower* books, deserves special mention. All that stuff about prepping for takeoff, the takeoff itself, the docking with our (decidedly fictional) space station? That's all Robin. She sent us fact sheets, she sent us videos, and when we got things wrong she corrected us (gently, lovingly). If it feels real, that's because most of it really is. *Gwendy's Final Task*—and her final adventure—isn't dedicated to Robin, but it could have been; her help was enormous.

Oh, and before we let you close the book (assuming you haven't already), we want to thank *you*, Constant Reader. We're so happy you invested your time, money, and imagination in our little story.

—Stephen King & Richard Chizmar

ABOUT THE AUTHORS

STEPHEN KING IS THE author of more than sixty books, all of them worldwide bestsellers. His recent work includes the short story collection *You Like It Darker, Holly* (a *New York Times* Notable Book of 2023), *Fairy Tale, Billy Summers, If It Bleeds, The Institute, Elevation, The Outsider, Sleeping Beauties* (cowritten with his son Owen King), and the Bill Hodges trilogy: *End of Watch, Finders Keepers,* and *Mr. Mercedes* (an Edgar Award winner for Best Novel and a television series streaming on Peacock). His novel *11/22/63* was named a top ten book of 2011 by the *New York Times Book Review* and won the Los Angeles Times Book Prize for Mystery/ Thriller. His epic works *The Dark Tower, It, Pet Sematary, Doctor Sleep,* and *Firestarter* are the basis for major motion pictures, with *It* now the highest-grossing horror film of all time. He is the recipient of the 2020 Audio Publishers Association Lifetime Achievement Award, the 2018 PEN America Literary Service Award, the 2014 National Medal of Arts, and the 2003 National Book Foundation Medal for Distinguished Contribution to American Letters. He lives in Bangor, Maine, with his wife, novelist Tabitha King.

RICHARD CHIZMAR IS THE coauthor (with Stephen King) of the *New York Times* bestselling novella *Gwendy's Button Box* and *Gwendy's Final Task,* and the solo novella *Gwendy's Magic Feather.* Recent books include *Memorials,* the *New York Times* bestsellers *Becoming the Boogeyman* and *Chasing the Boogeyman*, *The Girl on the Porch*, *The Long Way Home*, his fourth short story collection, and *Widow's Point*, a chilling tale about a haunted lighthouse cowritten with his son Billy Chizmar, which was recently made into a feature film. His short fiction has appeared in dozens of publications, including *Ellery Queen Mystery Magazine* and *The Year's 25 Finest Crime and Mystery Stories*. He has won two World Fantasy awards, four International Horror Guild awards, and the HWA's Board of Trustees award. Chizmar's work has been translated into more than fifteen languages throughout the world, and he has appeared at numerous conferences as a writing instructor, speaker, panelist, and guest of honor. Follow him on X: @RichardChizmar, or visit his website at RichardChizmar.com.

ABOUT THE ARTIST

Keith Minnion made his first professional story sale to *Asimov's SF Adventure Magazine* in 1979. His third story collection, published in 2020, is *Read Me & Other Ghost Stories*. Also published in 2020 is his second novel, *Dog Star*. Keith is a former book designer and illustrator and only gets pulled out of retirement—kicking and screaming—for worthy book projects like this one. He is a former schoolteacher, DOD project manager, GPO printing contract specialist, and officer in the U.S. Navy. He currently lives in the Shenandoah Valley of Virginia, pursuing oil painting and woodworking, and is well into his third novel, tentatively titled *The Demon of Bushwick*.